TWO MEN, TWO WORLDS—

AND ONE NAME

There should have been no connection between them.

Morg Brannock, building a Western empire dollar by dollar, possession by possession.

Lon Brannock, making his living on the turn of a card, and staking his life on the speed of his gun.

But now Lon Brannock was lying bleeding on a saloon floor, with a dead man at his feet and a lynch mob already starting to form.

And the only man who could stem the flow of blood and stop the flood of vengeance was Morg Brannock . . . if he wanted to risk all he had and was to save his kin . . . and if he dared risk his life on his Brannock nerve and Brannock luck. . . .

A DISTANT LAND

"MATT BRAUN HAS A GENIUS FOR TAKING CHARACTERS OUT OF THE OLD WEST AND GIVING THEM FLESH-AND-BLOOD IMMEDIACY."
—Dee Brown, author of
Bury My Heart at Wounded Knee

A DISTANT LAND

Matt Braun

A SIGNET BOOK

NEW AMERICAN LIBRARY

PUBLISHER'S NOTE

This book is a work of fiction. Names, characters, places, and
incidents either are the product of the author's imagination or are
used fictitiously, and any resemblance to actual persons, living or
dead, events, or locales is entirely coincidental.

SIGNET TRADEMARK REG. U.S. PAT. OFF. AND FOREIGN COUNTRIES
REGISTERED TRADEMARK—MARCA REGISTRADA
HECHO EN CHICAGO, U.S.A.

SIGNET, SIGNET CLASSIC, MENTOR, ONYX, PLUME, MERIDIAN
and NAL BOOKS are published by NAL PENGUIN INC.,
1633 Broadway, New York, New York 10019

First Printing, March, 1988

1 2 3 4 5 6 7 8 9

PRINTED IN THE UNITED STATES OF AMERICA

To
Betty
and
all the Moores

1

The sky was overcast, threatening rain. A blustery wind whistled across the river and slammed into the ferry landing. The passengers stood huddled at the foot of the gangway.

Clint Brannock waited off to one side. The badge of a deputy U.S. marshal was pinned to his mackinaw and he was leading two horses. With him was a gaunt-faced man whose hands were secured by wrist manacles. The prisoner's name was Abner Hoxletter.

On the opposite shore stood Fort Smith. The river roughly paralleled the boundary separating Arkansas and Indian Territory. There was no bridge spanning the broad stream and ferryboats were the sole means of conveying freight and passengers from one side to the other. Travelers in either direction had no choice but to await the next ferry.

West of the landing was the Nations. Homeland of the Five Civilized Tribes—Cherokee, Chickasaw, Choctaw, Creek, and Seminole—it was so named because they had chosen to follow the white man's path. Bounded by Texas, Kansas, and Arkansas, the Nations was still a long way from civilized. Deputy marshals operating out of Fort Smith were responsible for enforcing the law west of the river.

Three days past, Clint had taken Hoxletter into custody. A horse thief by trade, Hoxletter was one of many white men who sought refuge in the Nations. The chase had lasted the better part of two weeks, ending in the land of the Cherokees. Wiser than he looked, Hoxletter had prudently offered no resistance. The alternative to arrest and prison was an unmarked grave somewhere in Indian Territory. Dead men were seldom transported back to Fort Smith.

By custom, lawmen and their prisoners were boarded first. After leading their horses up the wide gangway, Clint and Hoxletter moved to the foredeck of the ferry. The other passengers were a mix of tribesmen with business in Fort Smith and white traders returning from the Nations. Once loaded, the gangway was raised and the ferry pulled away from the landing. The crossing was made by a system of towropes working in concert with the swift-running current.

Standing at the bow, Clint watched the approach to Fort Smith. Originally an army post, the town was situated on a sandstone bluff overlooking the juncture of the Arkansas and Poteau rivers. With time, it had become a center of commerce, serving much of Western Arkansas and a good part of Indian Territory. The largest settlement bordering the Nations, it boasted four newspapers, three banks, and thirty saloons. The saloons, in particular, enjoyed a captive trade from transients bound for the great Southwest. By federal law, the sale of firewater was banned throughout the red man's domain.

From the wharf, Clint and Hoxletter followed Garrison Avenue. The street ran through the center of town, which had all the earmarks of a prosperous frontier community. On the far side of the business district, they approached the garrison of the old army post. Abandoned some years before by the military, the compound was now headquarters for the Federal District Court of Western Arkansas. And the indisputable realm of Judge Isaac Charles Parker—the Hanging Judge.

Clint had served under Judge Parker for the past six years. Unlike many federal marshals, he had chosen not to put away his gun with advancing age. He was now in his late forties, but nonetheless an imposing figure of a man. Tall and sledge-shouldered, he was still lean and tough, with the look of vigorous good health. His sandy hair and his mustache were peppered with gray; yet the force of his pale blue gaze was undiminished by time. Nor had age dimmed his zest for the challenge of the chase. He still hunted men.

Not as sudden as he'd once been, Clint was nevertheless widely feared. Time had slowed his gun hand, but he had learned that speed was a marginal factor in a shootout. What counted most was awareness, that blend of instinct and experience that forewarned violence. A man alerted to danger was able to act rather than react, and therefore gained an edge. At that point it became a matter of deliberation, an instant of cool nerve required for an accurate shot.

Over the last twenty-two years Clint had served as a cavalry scout, an army investigator, and a lawman in various guises. In all that time, he'd been wounded twice by men who valued speed over accuracy. Neither wound was serious and neither stopped him from finishing the job. He was reputed to have killed seventeen men by adhering to a simple but deadly credo. His first shot was the last shot of the fight.

The old military garrison was a grim setting for the work carried out by Judge Parker and the marshals. A bleak two-story building housed the courtroom and offices for the federal prosecutors. As many as ten cases a day were tried, and few men were acquitted. The majority were given stiff sentences—all the law would allow—and quickly transported to federal prisons. Convicted murderers were allowed one last visit with immediate family. Then they were hanged.

Another stone building, formerly the post commissary, was situated across the old parade ground. A low, one-story affair, it was headquarters for the U.S. marshal and his complement of deputies. In the center of the compound, within clear view of both buildings, stood the gallows. Constructed of heavy timbers, it had four trapdoors, each three feet wide and twenty feet long. There was adequate space for twelve men to stand side by side and plunge to oblivion on the instant. The structure was roofed and walled, so that executions could be performed even in bad weather.

Crossing the compound, Clint left the horses hitched outside the main building. He marched Hoxletter down a short flight of steps and halted before a stout door. The prison lockup was located in a dungeonous cellar large enough to accommodate almost a hundred inmates. He lifted a heavy door-knocker and gave it three sharp raps.

A judas hole slid open, then slammed shut. Jack Frazer, the prison warden, unlatched the door. He was brutish in appearance and talked like a man with a bad cold. His nose had been broken several times and a gold tooth gleamed from the center of his mouth. He nodded to Clint.

"Who you got there?"

"Abner Hoxletter," Clint said. "Charged with horse stealing."

Frazer grunted coarsely. "Horse thieves always welcome. We got 'em packed eight to a cell."

While Clint unlocked the manacles, Frazer entered the prisoner's name in a ledger. Hoxletter was turned over to a guard and they disappeared down a dim corridor. After closing the ledger, Frazer looked up from his desk. His mouth curled in a wolfish grin.

"You're just in time for the party."

"How so?" Clint asked.

"Hangin' day," Frazer said, chuckling. "We're fixin' to lose some of our steady boarders."

"Anybody I know?"

Frazer ticked off four names. One of them was a man Clint had captured only last month. All were convicted murderers, and their appeals to Judge Parker had been routinely denied. Justice was swift and certain in the Fort Smith court.

"Got the word yesterday," Frazer said. "The judge ordered the four of 'em to take the drop at once. Guess he figures the more the merrier."

Clint shrugged. "Sounds like another one of his object lessons. Ought to make a big splash in the newspapers."

"What the hell!" Frazer crowed. "They don't call him the Hanging Judge for nothin'."

From the prison lockup, Clint walked back across the compound. A crowd was gathering before the gallows and he was reminded that most Westerners approved of Judge Parker's harsh methods. The Eastern press, on the other hand, never missed a chance to slander the jurist. His attitude toward the death sentence was variously termed "barbarous" and "a thing of infamy."

Appointed to the bench in 1875, Isaac Parker had jurisdiction over Western Arkansas and all of the Nations. A wilderness area which encompassed some 74,000 square miles, it was a haven for cutthroats of every description. To enforce his orders, the judge was assigned two hundred U.S. deputy marshals, and the almost impossible task of policing a land virtually devoid of law. Four months after taking office, he had sentenced six convicted murderers to be hanged simultaneously.

The thud of the gallows trap that day called the attention of all America to Judge Parker. Newspapermen poured into Fort Smith, and a crowd of more than five thousand gathered to witness the executions. The press immediately tagged him the Hanging Judge, and decried the brutality of his methods. In the furor, the purpose of his object lesson was completely lost. Yet the reason he'd hanged six men that day—and went on to hang forty-three more in the next twelve years—lay just across the river.

Gangs of white outlaws made forays into Kansas, Missouri, and Texas, and then retreated into Indian Territory. There they found perhaps the oddest sanctuary in the history of crime. Though each tribe had its own courts and Light Horse Police, their authority extended only to Indian citizens. White men were exempt from all prosecution except that of a federal court. Yet there were no extradition laws governing the Nations; federal marshals had to pursue and capture the wanted men. Curiously enough, the problem was compounded by the Indians themselves.

The red man had little use for the white man's laws. All too often the Indians connived with the outlaws, offering them asylum. The marshals were looked upon as intruders in the Nations, and the chore of ferreting out fugitives became a murderous task. It was no job for the faint of heart, as evidenced by the toll in lawmen. Over the past twelve years nearly forty federal marshals had been gunned down in Indian Territory.

Once across the compound, Clint entered the old commissary building. Inside the main office, he found John Carroll, the U.S. marshal, seated at a battered rolltop desk. Carroll was a stocky bulldog of a man, with ruddy features and a brushy ginger mustache. He was a political appointee, rather than a veteran lawman, and reported directly to Judge Parker. His principal job was assignment of cases to the deputy marshals.

"Hello there, Clint," he said, looking up from a stack of papers. "We'd about given you up for lost."

"Took me longer than I expected. Hoxletter was always one jump ahead."

"Any trouble?"

"Nothin' to speak of," Clint said amiably. "Once I caught him, he came along peaceable. I just dropped him off at the lockup."

"Good work," Carroll observed. "All in the nick of time, too."

"How's that?"

"The judge wants to see you."

Clint pulled out the makings. He creased a rolling paper and sprinkled tobacco into the fold. Stores now carried the new tailor-made cigarettes, but he found them too mild for his tastes. He stuck with the roll-your-owns.

Watching him, Carroll marked again that his eyes were never still. The slightest movement or sound attracted Clint's attention. His glance was quick but sharp, and even in the midst of rolling a cigarette, he seemed aware of all about him. Carroll often thought it was why he'd survived six years in the Nations. Nothing took him by surprise.

Clint sealed the rolling paper and popped a sulfurhead on his thumbnail. He looked at Carroll over the flare of the match. "The judge say what he wants?"

"Yes and no," Carroll said with an odd smile. "I suggest you ask him yourself."

"Sounds mysterious."

"Let's just say it's out of the ordinary. Judge Parker prefers to tell you personally."

A commotion from the courtyard interrupted them. Clint turned and moved to the window, followed by Carroll. Outside a growing crowd of spectators was gathered before a roped-off area fronting the gallows.

A holiday atmosphere seemed to prevail, and an excited murmur swept through the onlookers as the four condemned murderers were marched across the compound. George Maledon, the official executioner, led them up the gallows steps.

Hushed, the spectators watched as he positioned the prisoners on the center trap. Maledon was a slim, stoop-shouldered man with a full beard and close-set eyes. All business, he went about his work with an air of professional detachment. As the death warrants were read, he moved from man to man, slipping a hangman's noose over their heads. A craftsman of sorts, he prided himself on breaking necks rather than strangling men to death. He was careful to center the knot directly behind the left ear.

A minister began intoning a final prayer. The condemned men stood with their arms strapped to their sides and their ankles tightly bound. Their expressions were strangely resigned and they appeared to be listening intently to the preacher. Maledon once more moved down the line, fitting black hoods over their heads. Then, as the prayer ended, he walked to a wooden lever behind the prisoners. The crowd, morbidly curious, edged closer to the scaffold.

A loud *whump* suddenly echoed across the courtyard. The four men dropped through the trapdoor and hit the end of the ropes with an abrupt jolt. Their necks snapped in unison, and their heads, crooked at a grotesque angle, flopped over their right shoulders. The spectators, staring bug-eyed at the gallows, seemed to hold their breath. An oppressive silence settled over the compound.

Hanging limp, the dead men swayed gently, the scratchy creak of taut rope somehow deafening in the stillness. One eye on his pocket watch, Maledon finally nodded to the prison physician. Working quickly, the doctor moved from body to body, testing for a heart-beat with his stethoscope. A moment later he pro-nounced the four men officially dead.

The crowd began drifting away. Clint walked back to the desk and snuffed his cigarette in an ashtray. When he turned around, Carroll was still staring out the window. There was a look of ghoulish fascination on the marshal's face.

"Anything else?" Clint asked.

"No," Carroll said quietly. "Nothing else."

"Guess I'll go see what the judge wants."

Carroll merely nodded. Clint stepped into the hall-way and moved toward the main door. As he emerged from the building, the bodies were being lowered from the scaffold. Four wooden coffins were positioned be-neath the structure and several guards were attending to the dead men. Glancing at them as he went past, he retraced his path across the compound.

Clint marked the date as Marsh 2, 1887. Since sign-ing on as a deputy, it was the third time he'd seen four men hanged at once. In that same six-year period, he had killed seven men by his own hand. Lately he'd come to the conclusion that the threat of death was no deterrent to hardcases and outlaws. Still, there was something to be said for the finality of hanging, and law enforced by the gun. Dead men never again com-mitted murder.

There were times when Clint considered quitting. Elizabeth Brannock, the widow of his eldest brother, still operated the family ranch in New Mexico. In 1881, after his brother had been murdered, he'd taken it upon himself to square the account. Charged with manslaughter, he'd been released on condition that he exile himself for a period of one year. A month later, his reputation untarnished by the incident, he had gone to work for Judge Parker. Had he wished, he could have returned to New Mexico anytime within the past five years.

What kept him from leaving was still another branch of the family. While he was unmarried, Clint nonetheless had a strong sense of duty. His second brother, dead since 1874, had left a widow and two boys. The woman was a full-blood Comanche and continued to live on the reservation in western Indian Territory. Her welfare was of concern to Clint, and he looked upon the boys as his own sons. His work as a marshal allowed him to visit them with some frequency, and the bond had grown closer over the years. For that reason, he had never seriously considered returning to New Mexico.

Earlier today he'd thought to ask for a week off. His last visit to the reservation had been at Christmastime, fully two months past. But now, crossing the compound, his mind turned to other matters. A personal summons from Judge Parker was unusual under any circumstances. All the more so when the reason was shrouded in mystery.

A clerk ushered him into the judge's chambers. Isaac Parker was in his early fifties, a stout six-footer with a well-trimmed mustache and goatee. He was as demanding of himself as he was the officers of the court and the deputy marshals. He observed no holidays except Christmas and Sundays, and he seldom recessed court before early evening. His docket was restricted almost exclusively to criminal cases.

No jurist had ever been invested with such unlimited power. There was no appeal from his pronouncements, and more men had died on the Fort Smith gallows than anywhere else in America. In a newspaper interview, he had once outlined his views on the death sentence. "People have said that I am a cruel and heartless man. But no one has ever pointed to a single case of undue severity. On the bench, I have ever had but a single aim: Permit no innocent man to be punished; let no guilty man escape."

Attired in a black cutaway coat and high starched collar, Parker greeted Clint with genuine warmth. Over the years he'd come to admire Clint's cool judgment and nervy quickness in a tight situation. Of all the deputy marshals, he believed Clint to be the one officer who was more dangerous than the outlaws they hunted. What he had in mind today would require nothing less.

After they were seated, Parker went straight to the point. "I issued orders that no one was to mention it until I'd told you myself. Ernie Wilson was killed last week."

Clint's face took on a sudden hard cast. Ernie Wilson was a fellow marshal and perhaps his closest friend. His voice betrayed nothing of what he felt. "Where'd it happen?"

"Cherokee Nation," Parker said. "Outside the town of Whiteoak."

"Who killed him?"

"Rafe Dixon."

The name required no elaboration. Rafe Dixon was a white man, the leader of a band of outlaws. Within the last few months, the gang had robbed a bank in Arkansas, another bank in Kansas, and a railroad express car in southern Missouri. After each holdup, the robbers scattered to the winds and took sanctuary in the Nations. Ernie Wilson had been assigned the job of bringing Dixon to justice.

"Ernie was no greenhorn," Clint said at length. "Dixon must've taken him unawares."

Parker nodded dourly. "From what I gather, Dixon ambushed him. Wilson was apparently shot in the chest and fell off his horse. Then he was deliberately shot in the head. There were powder burns on his temple."

"Dirty sonovabitch," Clint said in a flat monotone. "He executed Ernie, didn't he?"

"I'm afraid so."

There was a long beat of silence. Clint seemed turned to stone, his eyes cold and remote. "Ernie deserved better," he said finally. "That's no way to die."

Parker's expression darkened. When he spoke, there was an undercurrent of rage in his voice. "I intend to make an example of Rafe Dixon. No man murders one of my marshals with impunity."

"Are you assigning me to the case?"

"Yes," Parker said without inflection. "However long it takes, I want you to find Dixon."

"And after I find him—?"

Parker paused as though weighing his words. He looked curiously like a philosopher contemplating some complex abstraction. "Given my choice," he said, "I would prefer to hang Dixon. On the other hand, if his death were reported in the Nations, justice would be served equally well. Do you take my meaning, Mr. Brannock?"

"Yessir, I do."

"In that event, I wish you good hunting."

Clint heaved himself to his feet. He nodded once, then turned and walked to the door. With his hand on the knob, he looked back. "Judge, would you like me to wire you the news?"

"I'd like that very much, Mr. Brannock."

"Consider it done."

The door opened and closed. Isaac Parker tilted back in his chair, put his fingertips together. A slight smile played at the corner of his mouth.

He thought Rafe Dixon was as good as dead.

2

A wind mourned through the leaves of the cotton-woods. Hazy sunlight rippled across the waters of the Rio Hondo, warming the valley. Umber grasslands, like a wave crashing against a wall of stone, swelled toward the distant mountains.

Elizabeth stood at the parlor window. She was lost in reflection, and her mind wandered down odd little byways of memory. She remembered the day Virgil had brought her to the Hondo, how proud he'd been. Working together, partners as well as man and wife, they had put down their roots here. Those were the golden years, when they'd transformed the valley into a great ranch and called it Spur. And now, strangely, it seemed so long ago. Another life.

A striking woman, Elizabeth was tall and statuesque. Her features were exquisite, and though she was forty-two, she looked ten years younger. Her eyes were hazel, alert and inquisitive, and she wore her hair in the upswept fashion. Yet, for all her beauty, there was something in her manner that commanded attention. Her force of character ensured that people were rarely unaware of her presence. The *mexicanos* had aptly nicknamed her *La Mariposa de Hierro*—the Iron Butterfly.

The name was now known throughout New Mexico Territory. In 1881, following her husband's death, she had assumed the reins of Spur. While she shared the inheritance with her daughter Jennifer and her son Morgan, there was little doubt as to whose will prevailed. Nor was there any question that she'd become a persuasive force in territorial politics. Her coalition of Anglos and *mexicanos* controlled almost half the seats in the legislature. Still, quite apart from her political power, the ranch remained her touchstone. She drew strength from the land, the Rio Hondo and the valley.

Headquarters for all of Spur was a large compound in the center of the valley. Along the north bank of the Rio Hondo, the buildings were formed in an irregular crescent beyond the main house. Situated opposite a central commissary were the bunkhouse and a combination kitchen and dining hall. Nearby were the corrals and various outbuildings for blacksmithing, carpentry, and general storage.

The main house overlooked the river. Shaded by cottonwoods, it was a vast sprawl of adobe, built along the lines of a *hacienda*. The walls were three feet thick, with deep-set windows and hewn rafters protruding from a flat roof. A galleried veranda, with rockers and a porch swing, ran the length of the front wall. Comfortable winter and summer, the house was sheltered by foothills to the south.

Some thirteen years past, the Brannocks had purchased a Spanish land grant totaling 100,000 acres. The holdings were located in the center of the valley and surrounded on all sides by public-domain lands. With the death of John Chisum in 1884, the vast Jinglebob spread on the Pecos had been sold off piecemeal. Spur then became the largest outfit in Lincoln County, breeding both cattle and horses. Fifty cowhands worked the livestock herds that wore the ⛤ brand.

Hondo Valley was situated in the foothills of the Capitan Mountains. The river meandered through a lush grazeland roughly twenty miles long and some three miles wide. To the west lay the town of Lincoln, and eastward the Rio Hondo eventually converged with the Pecos River. Surrounded by craggy slopes, the valley was sheltered from the harsh blast of winter and watered by spring melt-off from the mountains. A natural basin, hidden away from the world, it seemed fashioned for raising livestock.

Staring out the window, Elizabeth looked toward the snowcapped mountains. She was waiting for Morg and his cousin, Brad Dawson, who was the ranch foreman. A vagrant thought surfaced, prompted by her daydreaming about family. Her last letter to Clint had gone unanswered and she wondered why he hadn't replied. That was unlike him and it left her vaguely troubled.

When time permitted, she and Clint managed to visit one another. She considered him her dearest and oldest friend, a brother rather than a brother-in-law. Yet they hadn't seen each other in nearly a year, and she missed him terribly. All too often she found herself wishing he would return to New Mexico, join her in operating Spur. But then, upon reflection, she knew it would never happen. He was wedded to the law and would likely die wearing a badge. She nonetheless dreamt of having him near and refused to abandon hope.

Morg and Brad rode up to the house. As they dismounted, she was reminded that the Brannock blood always showed. They were both tall and rangy, strapping six-footers, larded with muscle. Morg was clean-shaven, with wavy blond hair and his father's blue eyes. While Brad's mother had married a Dawson, his Brannock heritage was nonetheless apparent. His eyes were the color of carpenter's chalk and his wheat-colored hair was matched by a bristly mustache. He was a second cousin to Morg and Jennifer, and his looks pegged him as family. He might well have been their brother.

For all the similarity, Morg and Brad were a study in contrasts. At twenty-five, Brad was more mature and somewhat serious by nature. He was a slow, thoughtful talker, with an easy smile and a wry, offhand humor. Morg, who had just turned twenty, exuded the vitality and vigor of youth. Yet his brash self-assurance and cocky manner was deceptive. He had inherited his father's head for business, and beneath the sportive manner there was a shrewd mind at work. Older men quickly learned to respect his opinion.

Today's meeting was to review the business affairs of Spur. Late that afternoon, Elizabeth was departing for Santa Fe, where political matters demanded her attention. She wanted a report from Brad, who was in the midst of preparing for spring roundup. As for Morg, she had recently entrusted him with additional responsibility. An offshoot of the family holdings was a ranch located in the Cherokee Outlet, at the northern boundary of Indian Territory. Though the foreman was reliable enough, Elizabeth generally made three trips a year to inspect the operation. Tomorrow, for the first time, Morg was scheduled to go in her place.

A room off the central hallway had been converted into an office. There, seated around a large desk, Elizabeth and the boys reviewed their business interests. To a great extent, Brad's report was the reason for the meeting. Not quite seven years ago, he had come west from Missouri, the original home of the Brannock clan. After starting as a cowhand, he had worked his way up to *segundo* and then to trail boss.

He displayed a natural savvy of cattle and possessed all the qualities of leadership. Three years past, he had been promoted to foreman of Spur.

Under Brad's guidance, the longhorn herds were gradually phased out. The ranch had switched instead to breeding shorthorn Durhams, relying on blooded stock. A chunky animal, far beefier than the old longhorns, the Durhams had proved to be a profitable venture. Horses were no less a mainstay of the Spur operation. Several breeding pastures were maintained for cowponies, draft horses, and general work animals. Across the West, cattlemen and farmers, as well as livestock traders, provided a steady market. The proceeds from horse sales rivaled those generated by the Durhams.

Elizabeth was an astute businesswoman. Following Brad's report, she paused, weighing all she'd heard. Then she lifted an eyebrow in question. "When can you start roundup?"

"Depends on the weather," Brad explained. "So far, it looks to be an early spring. I'd judge we'll get under way about mid-April."

"And the first trail drive?"

Spur was roughly a hundred miles from the nearest railhead. Brad scratched his jaw, reflective a moment. "Give or take a week," he said at length, "I'd calculate the middle of May. What with the gather and branding, it'll take nearabout a month."

"How large an increase do you expect?"

A flicker of humor showed in Brad's eyes. "Well, our bulls are mighty dependable critters. I'd say we'll equal last year's calf crop. Maybe even better it."

Elizabeth nodded with an approving smile. She then turned her attention to another matter. Unlike the old days, Spur no longer laid claim to public-domain lands within the Hondo Valley. Times had changed, and she considered it morally reprehensible to hold grazeland by right of force. Nor was she an advocate of stringing barbed wire; the only fences on Spur were those enclosing the breeding pastures. Still, a large ranch always needed more graze, and she'd undertaken a program of acquiring privately held land.

To that end, she had placed Morg in charge of the project. One group of landowners was the homesteaders, who began moving into the valley the summer of 1882. Five years were required to prove their claim and many would shortly receive valid title. The other group was composed of *mexicano* farmers who held title by virtue of ancient Spanish land grants. Morg was a personable negotiator and he spoke fluent Spanish. His days were spent cajoling landowners and haggling over price.

Elizabeth looked at him now. "Have you made any progress with the Horrells?"

"The Horrells," Morg said with a sudden grin, "and the Tuckers. They've both got an itch to pull up stakes."

"Are they agreeable to our offer?"

"It's in the bag." Morg's grin broadened. "Got 'em to sign the papers just this morning. Counting all the relatives, we'll come out with another full section."

Elizabeth appeared pleased at the prospect. "Aren't you the sly one?" she said. "That's almost a thousand acres in the past month."

"Nothin' to it," Morg said bluffly. "All you need's a gift for gab and a wad of greenbacks. Works every time."

Elizabeth smiled. "If that's true, why haven't you convinced the Pérez family? Aren't they susceptible to your charm?"

"Don't worry," Morg assured her. "Nobody holds out forever. I'll get 'em yet."

"Listen to him," Brad joked. "Sounds like a drummer selling corsets. Pure hokum."

"Says you!" Morg countered. "How'd you like to make a small wager?"

"Another time," Elizabeth cut in. "I have to leave in a few minutes. Have we anything more to discuss?"

"Guess not," Morg said. "Unless you want to talk about the Outlet."

"I've already told you what you need to know. Go there and learn the operation for yourself. We'll talk when you return."

The meeting ended on that note. Elizabeth shooed them out of the office and went to pack her bag. Brad declined Morg's invitation for a cup of coffee. He was expected at one of the breeding pastures and already running late. He rode off toward the northern foothills.

Morg wandered back to his bedroom. He found his wife seated in a rocker, staring listlessly out the window. Scarcely six months past, they had been married at the Methodist Church in Lincoln. She'd gotten pregnant on their wedding night, and in his view, she hadn't been the same since.

Formerly Louise Stockton, she was the daughter of a rancher on the Rio Felix. At nineteen, she was a blond tawny cat of a girl with bold eyes and a delicate oval face. Her features, not to mention the swell of her abdomen, had filled out as her term progressed. She was thrilled by the prospect of motherhood, but disconsolate over her condition. She felt ugly and unwanted, and desperately unloved.

Entering the bedroom, Morg tried to divine her mood. These days she was either warmly affectionate or irritable and waspish, with no middle ground. She was particularly bitter about his forthcoming trip to Indian Territory. As though walking on eggshells, he crossed to the rocker and bussed her on the cheek. She sniffed, averting her face.

"Well?" she demanded tartly. "Have you got your marching orders?"

Morg stared at her in mild astonishment. "What are you talking about?"

Her chin tilted. "Wasn't that what your mother was doing just now—issuing final instructions?"

"For Chrissake," Morg said, rolling his eyes. "Just leave her out of it, will you? I'm going because I have to go."

"No, you're not." She sulked. "You're going because you *want* to go. To get away from me."

Louise felt somehow like a castaway. Before she'd become large with child, Morg had been tender and unstintingly passionate. She remembered him as an ardent lover, infinitely wise in the ways of a man and woman. By breathtaking stages, he had never failed to bring her to complete and wondrous satisfaction. She cherished those intimate moments and still ached for him with an imperishable desire. All of which merely underscored her melancholy moods. He hadn't touched her in almost a month.

"Won't you change your mind?" She entreated him with her eyes. "Wait till after the baby's born—please."

"I can't," Morg said with an aimless shrug. "That's three months off, and we've got a business to run. I don't have any choice."

"What about me?" she stormed. "You're leaving and your mother's leaving. And I'll be here all alone!"

A shadow of irritation crossed Morg's features. He saw tears well up in her eyes and he tried to fathom why she was being so unreasonable. Words failed him and he suddenly turned away. She burst out crying as he went through the door.

He wondered why the hell he'd ever gotten married.

*   *   *

A short while later Elizabeth emerged from the house. John Taylor was waiting with a buckboard and team, and he assisted her into the front seat. Her leather carryall was already stowed in back with his warbag.

Taylor was a retired gunman. Years ago, when Elizabeth and her husband were threatened by political assassins, Taylor had been hired as her bodyguard. After her husband was killed, the political climate in New Mexico had calmed somewhat. But Taylor had elected to stay on at Spur and Elizabeth welcomed the decision. By then, she'd come to think of him as a companion and a loyal friend.

Elizabeth seldom entertained the notion of marrying again. Her time was devoted instead to the ranch and a whirlwind of political activities. Yet she was not unaware of the gossip surrounding herself and John Taylor. He was a man of saturnine good looks, on the sundown side of forty, with a tough, rather sinister visage. Wherever she went, he accompanied her, for a woman could hardly travel the backcountry alone. Still, in all their travels, she'd never once considered him anything more than a friend. She was comfortable with his company.

For his part, Taylor treated her with understated reverence. He was beguiled by her elegance and thought her the most desirable woman he'd ever known. But he had long since parted with the idea that the feeling was mutual. Nor was he blind to the chasm separating them on a social level. She was a lady of prominence and wealth, and a political activist of enormous prestige. At best, he was a retired "shootist" who had killed more men than he cared to remember. He contented himself with being her companion and her trusted

confidant. So far as he knew, there were no secrets
between them.

Glancing at her now, he kept his tone light. "How
long we stayin' in Santa Fe?"

"Only a day or so," Elizabeth said. "I've arranged a
meeting with Salazar and Martínez."

"In the same room?" Taylor smiled lazily. "That
oughta be a regular cat-and-dog fight."

Lorenzo Salazar was an influential *rico*, one of the
old-line political aristocracy. His rival, Antonio Martínez, was a young *jefe político*, idealistic and ambitious. One sought to maintain the time-honored
hierarchy and the other sought widespread political
reform. Their antagonism threatened to split Elizabeth's coalition along factional lines. She had arranged
the meeting in the hope of negotiating a compromise.

"I'm afraid you're right," Elizabeth said, almost to
herself. "Neither of them has any respect for the other.
It's a touchy situation."

Taylor chuckled softly. "Just lemme know if you
need a referee. I'm a old hand at settlin' disputes."

"Let's hope it doesn't come to that."

Elizabeth fell silent. She remained thoughtful and
somewhat distracted during the drive to town. They
arrived late that afternoon, with the sun dropping
lower toward the mountains. From Lincoln they would
take the overnight stage to Socorro, the nearest railhead with passenger service. Tomorrow, by train, they
would travel on to Santa Fe.

Lincoln was the county seat, a center of trade for
outlying farms and ranches. Taylor dropped her off at
a house on the north side of the town's main street.
He then drove on to the livery stable, where the
horses would be stalled until their return. Elizabeth
proceeded up the walkway to a small frame house

painted white with green shutters. A simple hand-lettered sign was mounted beside the door.

JENNIFER BRANNOCK, M.D.
Clinic Hours Tuesday & Friday

Twelve years ago Elizabeth had organized a free clinic for poor *mexicanos*. The local physician, Dr. Chester Wood, had been her strongest supporter. Jennifer, who was only a girl at the time, had become fascinated with the world of medicine. Dr. Wood encouraged her interest, and was largely responsible for her decision to enter medical school. At age twenty, she had graduated from Tufts University, located in Boston. She was the first woman doctor to establish practice in New Mexico.

A year had passed since her return to Lincoln. In that period, with Chester Wood's public support, Jennifer had overcome the pervasive distrust of lady doctors. Four months ago, when Wood died of a stroke, she'd bought the house and continued to operate the clinic. She practiced general medicine, and though barely twenty-one, she had already developed a reputation as a skilled surgeon. She was now the only physician within a forty-mile radius of Lincoln.

The last patient was leaving as Elizabeth entered the clinic. Jennifer greeted her with a warm hug and a look of pleasant surprise. Apart from the normal affection of a mother and daughter, there was a sense of mutual respect between them. In their own way, each of them had made her mark in what was essentially a man's world. Elizabeth was particularly proud that her daughter had stormed the barriers excluding women from the medical profession.

"I've only a minute," she said quickly. "John and I are catching the evening stage."

"Oh?" Jennifer said, smiling. "What's the burning issue this time?"

"Nothing too exciting," Elizabeth confessed. "Another squabble between the old guard and one of the young *jefes*. Sometimes I wonder why I bother."

"You wouldn't have it any other way. I think you enjoy all the backbiting and intrigue."

Jennifer looked amused. She wore a pleated skirt and a ruffled blouse with a high collar. Tall and willowy, she had a stemlike waist and long, lissome legs. Her eyes were hazel and her auburn hair was drawn back and pinned, accentuating her expressive features. She was compellingly attractive, a mirror image of her mother.

"Well, anyway," Elizabeth said, changing the subject. "How are things with you? Any news yet?"

"News—?"

"Don't be coy, Jen. You know very well I'm talking about Blake. Has he asked you or not?"

"Honestly, Mother," Jennifer groaned. "You really are incorrigible. Anyone would think you're in a rush to marry me off."

"I am," Elizabeth said with mock seriousness. "I won't have a daughter of mine end up a spinster."

Jennifer had been keeping company with Blake Hazlett, a local attorney. Elizabeth approved of the match and never failed to voice her opinion. Their bantering was by now something of a ritual.

"Spinster indeed!" Jennifer said indignantly. "I'll marry when I'm ready to marry, thank you very much."

Elizabeth laughed happily. "I suggest you not wait too long. Good men are hard to find."

"Oh, what a terrible thing to say! And you one of the original suffragists."

"Women's rights have nothing to do with a warm

bed. Your father and I reconciled that point very nicely."

The west-bound stage clattered past. Through the window, Elizabeth saw it roll to a halt in front of the express office. She kissed Jennifer on the cheek, waving gaily, and hurried out the door. On the street, she set off at a brisk pace uptown.

Jennifer watched from the doorway. She thought how proud her mother looked, almost stately. There was a strength about the matriarch of the Brannock family that touched something in others. People were instinctively drawn to her, infused with her energy and determination. She was, in a word, indomitable.

A small irony flashed through Jennifer's mind. Her mother was forever coaxing her toward the wedding altar. Yet, though she was still a stunning woman, Elizabeth ignored the overtures of her many male admirers. In that respect, she seemed perfectly content with memories, a time of unexpired emotions. A bright remembrance of days past.

The memory of her father was no less real to Jennifer. And the thought occurred that her mother had used a shopworn phrase to express a deeper truth. Perhaps, after all, good men were hard to find.

3

Younger's Bend was located in the Cherokee Nation. There one of the frontier's most notorious bandits maintained a stronghold. Her name was Belle Starr.

Clint was looking for a lead. Like many lawmen, he relied heavily on informants when tracking a fugitive. Belle Starr was a convicted horse thief and reportedly involved in a string of penny-ante holdups. She also swapped information when it was to her advantage. Clint planned to ask her about Rafe Dixon.

Three days had passed since his meeting with Judge Parker. Clint was mounted on a sorrel gelding and traveling light. Late yesterday he'd camped at the juncture of the Arkansas and Canadian rivers. From there, he had followed the Canadian in a southwesterly direction. He was now some forty miles upstream.

Farther west lay the Creek Nation and a short distance south lay the Choctaw Nation. Younger's Bend, which was on the fringe of the Cherokee Nation, was ideally situated to the boundary lines of all three tribes. Belle Starr's place was hacked out of the wilderness, well off the beaten path. She lived there with a Creek half-breed who called himself Jim July.

Clint considered the Nations as hostile territory. Law enforcement among the tribes was conducted under the strangest circumstances ever faced by men who wore a badge. With the advance of civilization, a new pattern of lawlessness began to emerge on the western plains. The era of the lone bandit gradually faded into obscurity, evolving into something far worse. Outlaws began to run in packs.

Local peace officers found themselves unable to cope with the vast distances involved. Gangs made lightning strikes into surrounding border states, and then retreated into Indian Territory. In time, due to the limits of state jurisdiction, the war became a grisly contest between the gangs and the federal marshals. Yet it was hide-and-seek with a unique advantage falling to the outlaws.

A wanted man could easily lose himself in the mountains or along wooded river bottoms. The favorable terrain and general atmosphere of sanctuary were improved by too few lawmen chasing too many desperadoes. The Nations swarmed with killers and robbers and dozens of small gangs like the one led by Rafe Dixon. Outnumbered and outgunned, the marshals were seldom afforded the luxury of conducting a manhunt in force. They generally rode alone into Indian Territory.

Adding to their burden was the trade in whiskey. By federal law spirits in any form were illegal in Indian Territory. For selling or bartering, there was a five-hundred-dollar fine. Smuggling or attempting to transport alcohol into the Nations brought a three-hundred-dollar fine. Operating a still for the manufacture of spirits carried a fine of one thousand dollars. Popskull and rotgut were nonetheless staple commodities of trade throughout the tribes. From the marshals' standpoint, the problem was compounded by the attitude toward lawmen. Whiskey traders, whether white or red, were willing to kill to avoid arrest.

To survive, a marshal had no choice but to play by the same rules. Yet a fast gun and the willingness to

kill were not enough. Operating alone, a lawman first
had to outwit his prey, somehow gain an edge. That
required developing sources of intelligence, unsavory
alliances with informants who were themselves windward of the law. Over his years in the Nations, Clint
had cultivated many such contacts. But the one he
valued the most was the Bandit Queen, Belle Starr.
Her one allegiance in life was to herself.

Myra Belle Shirley was a native of Jasper County,
Missouri. In 1865, her family resettled in Texas on a
hardscrabble farm. There, at the age of nineteen, she
married a young horse thief named Jim Reed. Several
years were spent on the run, with the law always one
step behind. At last, with no place to turn, Reed
sought refuge in Indian Territory. Belle shortly joined
him, and her career as a lady bandit began in earnest.

The Reeds were given sanctuary by Tom Starr, a
full-blood Cherokee. Starr and his eight sons were
considered the principal hell-raisers of the Cherokee
Nation. Belle, the only white woman present, was
accorded royal treatment by the Starrs. Then, in the
summer of 1874, she abruptly became a widow. Jim
Reed was trapped following a stagecoach robbery and
slain by lawmen. Never daunted, Belle soon shed her
widow's weeds and married Sam Starr.

The eldest son of Old Tom Starr, Sam owned a
parcel of land on Younger's Bend. From there, he and
his gang of misfits rustled livestock and occasionally
ran illegal whiskey. Belle, who was a dominant woman,
shortly became the brains of the outfit. She planned
their jobs and shrewdly brought the men together only
when a raid was imminent. Afterward, the gang members scattered to Gibson and other railroad towns to
squander their loot.

For years, Belle and Sam were virtually immune to
arrest. Younger's Bend was surrounded by wilderness

and mountains, and the only known approach was along a canyon trail rising steeply from the river. So inaccessible was the stronghold that lawmen—both Light Horse Police and federal marshals—gave it a wide berth. Myra Belle Starr gloried in her notoriety and flaunted her reputation as a lady bandit. She believed herself beyond the law.

In 1883, Clint proved her wrong. He lured Belle and Sam out of Younger's Bend and arrested them for horse theft. Convicted in Judge Parker's court, the Starrs served five months in federal prison at Detroit. After being released, they returned to the Nations and once more attempted to form a gang. But Sam gradually lost his battle with alcohol, and in 1886, he was killed in a gunfight. Belle, who believed in short mourning periods, wasted no time in finding another man. She took Jim July as her common-law husband.

These days Belle and her Creek paramour dabbled in stolen horses. Still, almost four years had passed since she'd last been arrested. Some attributed her good fortune to the remote location of Younger's Bend. Others assumed she had grown smarter with age. A few men, all of them deputy marshals, knew that she was protected by Clint Brannock. He allowed her to steal horses, and thereby maintain her coveted reputation as the Bandit Queen. She, in turn, acted as his personal informant.

In the lowering dusk, Clint emerged from the canyon trail. He visited Younger's Bend only at night, and in secret. Before him, surrounded by dense woods, lay a stretch of level ground. Not fifty yards away, a log house stood like a wilderness fort where the trail ended. A flock of crows cawed and took wing as he rode forward. From the house a pack of dogs joined in the chorus.

One window was lighted by a lamp. The door of the

house opened and a woman stepped onto the porch.
She hushed the dogs with a sharp command and stood
waiting with her hands on her hips. Clint reined to a
halt in the yard, mindful of their agreement. She would
abide no lawman in her house, and on his nocturnal
visits, he never dismounted. He nodded pleasantly.

" 'Evenin', Belle."

" 'Evening, marshal."

From the corner of the house a man materialized
out of the shadows. He moved forward, holding a
double-barrel shotgun cradled in his arms. As he crossed
the porch, Clint recognized him as the half-breed Creek,
Jim July. He was lithely built, with bark-dark skin and
muddy eyes. His face was pinched in an oxlike
expression.

"How's tricks, Jim?"

Clint's question drew a sour grunt. July moved
through the doorway and disappeared inside the cabin.
He detested any lawman, and in particular, he disliked
Clint. His resentment stemmed from the fact that his
woman was forced to play songbird for a *tibo* marshal.
Still, for all his rough ways, he'd never once voiced an
objection. He was allowed to stay on at Younger's
Bend only so long as he behaved himself.

Belle waited until he was out of earshot. In the spill
of lamplight, she was revealed as a singularly unattractive
woman. She was horse-faced, with a lantern jaw and
bloodless lips and beady close-set eyes. Her figure was
somehow mannish, with wide hips and shoulders, and
almost no breasts beneath her drab woolen dress. Her
hold over men was all the more puzzling in broad
daylight. She looked vaguely like a prune wearing a
wig.

"Lemme guess," she said at last. "You stopped by
for supper."

"Not tonight," Clint said in a neutral voice. "I'm looking for somebody."

Belle gave him the fisheye. "Who you after now?"

"Rafe Dixon."

"Figures the Judge would've sent you. Word's around that Dixon killed a marshal."

Clint's stare revealed nothing. "What else do you hear?"

"Just talk," Belle said hesitantly. "Dixon's stayin' out of sight."

"Any idea where he went to ground?"

"No, not just exactly."

"Like hell," Clint said with a measured smile. "C'mon, stop dancing me around. What've you heard?"

Belle opened her hands, shrugged. "There's talk he crossed paths with a Light Horse patrol. Way I got the story, they turned stone-blind. Just kept on riding."

"Whereabouts did they cross paths?"

"Nobody's sayin'."

"Then how'd you hear about it?"

"From a friend in Tahlequah."

Clint looked at her with narrow suspicion. "Are you telling me it's common knowledge?"

"Yeah, I suppose," Belle said cautiously. "Leastways, it's no secret."

A moment elapsed while Clint weighed her statement. Tahlequah was the capital of the Cherokee Nation. Major D. W. Lipe, head of the Light Horse Police, was headquartered there. Yet no word of sighting Dixon had been forwarded to Fort Smith.

"Hard to believe," he said finally. "Why would the Light Horse protect Dixon? He's a white man."

"So what?" Belle said with a lopsided smile. "Just because he killed a marshal doesn't change anything. The Light Horse figure it's one *tibo* against another."

"You might have a point there."

Belle laughed without humor. "No maybe about it. The Light Horse aren't no different than the rest of the Cherokees. They all hate your guts."

"I reckon they do at that. Anyway, thanks for the tip, Belle."

"Keep it in mind the next time me and Jim steal some horses."

Belle watched him ride out of the yard. Unlike other lawmen she'd known, she harbored a grudging admiration for Clint. He was hard as nails, but he always stuck to his word. For the past four years, he had kept her out of Judge Parker's courtroom. And that in itself gave her the best of the bargain.

She silently wished him luck with Rafe Dixon.

Late the next afternoon Clint rode into Tahlequah. While he'd been there many times before, he always felt himself the foreigner. White men were tolerated but never welcomed in the Cherokee capital. Federal marshals were viewed with even greater distrust.

However unwelcome, Clint was nonetheless impressed by the Cherokee people. In the old tribal language, the word for Cherokee was *Tsalagi*. The ancient emblem of bravery was the color red, and courage was believed to originate from the east, where the sun rose. Freely translated, *Tsalagi* meant "Red Fire Men" or "Brave Men." While most Cherokees had been converted to the Christian faith, tribal lore had not disappeared entirely from everyday life. Even today, the people still thought of themselves as the *Tsalagi*.

The Cherokees' ancestral homeland originally encompassed Alabama, Georgia, and Tennessee. In 1830, under pressure from white frontiersmen, Congress passed the Indian Removal Bill. Enacted despite the Cherokees' protests, the legislation granted Western

lands to the Five Civilized Tribes in exchange for their
ancestral birthright. A total of eighteen thousand Cherokees was herded westward over what became known
as the Trail of Tears. Of that number, more than four
thousand perished before reaching Indian Territory.
The Cherokees still honored their memory by resisting
white domination.

For all that, Clint thought it ironic that they had
adopted the white man's form of government. The
Cherokee Nation was virtually an independent republic, with a tribal chief who acted as head of state. The
tribal council, similar in structure to Congress, comprised two houses, and there were two political par-
ties. Yet, unlike the Western Plains tribes, the Cherokees accepted no annuities or financial assistance from
Washington. Nor were white men allowed to own
property except through intermarriage.

The Cherokee economy was founded on an agrarian
base. As with the white world, some people were
farmers, and others, clearly, were gentleman farmers.
Outside Tahlequah there were baronial estates, with
colonnaded homes and sweeping lawns. The setting
was one of antebellum plantations transplanted from a
more gracious era; before the Civil War many Cherokees were slave owners as large as any in the South.
Still, the lavish estates were outnumbered manyfold by
log cabins and unpretentious frame houses. Wealthy
Cherokees, like wealthy whites, simply lived on a scale
befitting their position.

Tahlequah itself was considered the hub of progress
in Indian Territory. The capitol building, which was a
two-story brick structure, dominated the town square.
Nearby was the supreme court building, and around
the square were several prosperous business establish-
ments. One of these was the *Cherokee Advocate*, a
newspaper printed in both Cherokee and English. Of

all Indians, the Cherokees were the only ones with an alphabet, and therefore a written language. No other tribe was able to preserve its culture so completely in the ancient tongue.

Clint dismounted in front of the capitol building. All government offices, as well as the tribal council chambers, were housed there. The building was only slightly less stately than the capitol in Arkansas, and there was an air of bustling efficiency about the place. As he went through the broad entryway, Clint marked again that the men who governed here wore swallowtail coats and conducted themselves like seasoned diplomats. It occurred to him that they were no less dignified than their counterparts in other frontier capitals.

On the second floor, Clint was ushered into the office of Major D. W. Lipe. As a deputy marshal, he'd had previous dealings with the Light Horse Police. He knew that Lipe, who was an astute politician, wielded considerable power within the Cherokee Nation. He reminded himself to watch his mouth, and his temper. Nothing would be gained by accusations and harsh words. His purpose was to gather information.

Lipe was swarthy, somewhat darker than the usual Cherokee, with marblelike eyes. He made no attempt to shake hands, greeting Clint instead with a curt nod. Nor did he extend the courtesy of offering Clint a chair. His mouth was razored in a faint smile.

"Marshal Brannock," he said civilly. "What brings you to Tahlequah?"

"Rafe Dixon," Clint told him.

"Of course," Lipe said matter-of-factly. "I understand he killed one of your marshals."

"We have reason to believe he's holed up somewhere in the Cherokee Nation."

"Do you, indeed?"

"For a fact," Clint said, no timbre in his voice. "I've

been told your Light Horse know the location of Dixon's hideout."

Lipe sat perfectly still for a moment. "Are you accusing me of harboring a fugitive?"

"Not yet," Clint said equably. "I'm requesting your assistance in a criminal matter."

"And if I choose to decline the request?"

"Judge Parker would likely get his bowels in an uproar. Knowin' him, he'd probably file a formal protest with Washington."

For an instant their eyes locked. Then, as though unperturbed, Lipe made an offhand gesture. "One good turn deserves another," he said. "Are you open to a trade?"

Clint held his gaze. "Try me."

"A federal warrant has been issued on a young Cherokee. He's charged with operating a whiskey still."

"And—"

Lipe smiled. "His father is an influential member of the tribal council."

"Dixon for the boy," Clint said stolidly. "Is that the deal?"

"Exactly."

Clint nodded. "I'll arrange to have the charges dropped."

"In that event," Lipe said, "I suggest you confine your search to White Oak Creek. Perhaps three or four miles west of Vinita."

Vinita was a small settlement northwest of Tahlequah. Clint considered a moment, thoughtful. "When I get there," he asked, "what will I find?"

"Dixon and two of his men. At last report, they were living in an old cabin."

"What happened to the rest of his gang?"

"I presume they're scattered until the next job."

"Your turn now," Clint said, apparently satisfied. "What's the boy's name—the whiskey peddler?"

"Bluejacket," Lipe replied. "Joe Bluejacket."

"I'll attend to it when I get back to Fort Smith."

Clint turned away from the desk. He went out the door without a parting word or a backward glance. On his way down the stairs, he silently cursed Lipe for demanding a trade-off. But then, on second thought, he figured he'd come out ahead on the deal. A whiskey peddler for a killer.

Judge Parker would have approved.

A crude but stoutly built log cabin stood in the center of the clearing. Smoke drifted skyward from the mud chimney, silty against an early-morning sun. There was no other sign of activity.

Clint was seated in a stand of trees on the opposite side of the creek. Shortly before dawn, he'd hidden his horse farther downstream. Then, ghosting through the woods, he had taken a position across from the cabin door. He waited now for the door to open.

Across his knees was a Colt rifle chambered for .50-95 caliber. A pump-action repeater, it was a shade faster than a Winchester carbine. Spent shells were ejected by a backward stroke of the foregrip, and a fresh round was chambered on the forward stroke. Beneath the octagon barrel was a cartridge magazine that held ten rounds. The massive fifty-caliber slug would down man or beast with a single shot.

The rifle typified Clint's approach to his work. A seasoned manhunter always sought any advantage possible. One way to gain an edge was to be better armed, assured of a knock-down shot every time the trigger was pulled. Another way was to get the drop on a man and permit him only an instant's warning. Anyone fool enough to ignore the warning was then

shot without hesitation. By adhering to such precepts
a bold lawman often lived to be an old lawman.

Today, Clint had all those factors working in his
favor. His position gave him a wide field of fire, allowing him to cover the cabin and the clearing. He knew
Rafe Dixon on sight and he intended to wait until the
element of surprise gave him a decided edge. The
speed of the pump-action repeater whittled the odds
down even further, and thus he had no qualms about
tangling with three men. Nor was he concerned with
taking prisoners. A coldblooded murderer deserved
nothing. . . .

The door opened. Clint got to his feet, still concealed behind a tree. He thumbed the hammer on the
rifle, watching as a man emerged from the cabin.
Three horses were penned in a corral out back and the
man walked in that direction. Clint lost sight of him
but heard him talking to the horses. Through the open
door the interior of the cabin was black as a cave.

Several minutes passed in silence. Abruptly, leading
a saddled horse, the man reappeared around the corner of the cabin. Halting, he stepped into the saddle as
a second man moved through the doorway. A moment
elapsed before a third man emerged from the cabin.
He was lean and stringy, with dark matted hair and a
handlebar mustache. His face decorated wanted dodg-
ers throughout the territory. His name was Rafe Dixon.

Clint barked a sharp command. "Don't move! You're
covered!"

The mounted man spurred his horse. Dixon clawed
at a holstered pistol and the other man was only a beat
behind. Still framed in the doorway, Dixon cleared
leather and looked toward the treeline. Clint shot him
in the chest.

The impact of the slug dropped Dixon in his tracks.
As he went down, the other man got off a hurried

snapshot and whirled toward the corner of the cabin. The bullet whanged through the trees directly over Clint's head. He drew a bead and fired.

Stumbling forward, the man slowed, then suddenly buckled at the knees. His eyes rolled back in his head and the pistol fell from his hand. He slumped at the waist and toppled facedown in the dirt. His right leg twitched in a spasm of afterdeath.

Clint pumped another round into the chamber and turned upstream. He got a last glimpse of the man on horseback disappearing around a bend in the shoreline. His finger eased off the trigger and he looked back toward the cabin. Neither of the men had moved.

Quitting the treeline, Clint waded across the creek. He approached the fallen men with the rifle held at hip level. Dixon was sprawled in the doorway, his shirtfront splattered with blood. The other man lay puddled in gore, half his rib cage blown away. A quick check revealed that the cabin was empty.

Clint felt neither elation nor remorse. He'd done his job, killing swiftly and cleanly when his warning was ignored. He thought Ernie Wilson would rest easier knowing that Dixon was dead. Still, he regretted having allowed the third man to escape. He disliked unfinished business.

No job was done until all accounts were settled.

4

On March 10 Morg arrived in Kansas. He stepped off
the train in Caldwell, a town three miles north of
Indian Territory. Directly across the line was the Cherokee Outlet.

From New Mexico, Morg had traveled north to
Colorado and then eastward across the Kansas plains.
It was his first extended trip away from Spur and the
Hondo Valley. He tended to think of it as a pilgrim-
age, one meant to broaden his horizons. He was being
exposed to a world beyond the sphere of his youth.

Morg never questioned the purpose of the trip. His
mother was grooming him to assume the reins of Spur.
While she was a shrewd businesswoman, her principal
interest lay in politics. She foresaw a time when she
would relinquish control of the family enterprises to
her son. The first step in that long-range plan was his
inspection of the Outlet ranch.

One day he would be expected to fill his father's
boots. The idea was at once a stimulus and a matter of
some trepidation. His father was a figure of mythical
proportions, larger than life. People still spoke of Virgil Brannock's vision and his almost godlike force of
character. Dead six years, he even now haunted the
minds of those who had known him.

To a degree, Morg walked in his father's shadow.
He'd been there the day his father was killed, and the

39

memory was still sharp, still painful. Yet the experience had aged him, thrust him abruptly into manhood.
Overnight his outlook had changed, and he'd stopped
thinking like a fourteen-year-old. His formative years
became instead a time of early maturity.

During those years, Morg had discovered something
about himself. He was a quick learner, mentally sharp,
and often given to insights beyond his experience. He
found himself comfortable in the company of older
men, unfazed by the difference in age. He felt himself
their equal and he'd seldom been proved wrong. What
they saw in him was what he had finally seen in himself. He was, in many respects, the very incarnation of
his father.

Floyd Dunn saw it too. As foreman and general
manager of the Outlet ranch, he was a man of some
position. Until Morg stepped off the train they had
never met, and he might well have viewed the youngster as an upstart. But from the moment they shook
hands, they got along famously. Dunn was immediately impressed by Morg's physical similarity to his
father. Even more, he was impressed by the young
man's knowledge of cows.

At twenty, Morg was already a veteran cattleman.
He'd begun working roundup as a boy, and by age
sixteen he was considered a top hand. He was a skilled
roper, a passable broncbuster, and no stranger to the
rigors of a trail drive. All the more important, he
understood bloodlines and herd management and possessed a keen eye for horseflesh. Far from a wealthy
young tyro, he was a product of the bunkhouse. Whipcord tough, and savvy to the ways of cowhands, he
knew his business.

Dunn was a graduate of the same school. A whisk-
ery Texican, he was bowlegged from a lifetime spent
in the saddle. In 1876, after ramrodding a trail herd to

Kansas, he'd been hired to run the Outlet spread. He had no family, and at the age of fifty, he considered the ranch his only home. He revered the memory of Virgil Brannock and looked upon Elizabeth as a natural phenomenon. He took their son to be one of his own.

The ranch was located on the Cimarron River, some forty miles inside Indian Territory. Aside from Dunn's ramshackle log cabin, there were a bunkhouse and corral and several outbuildings. The outfit carried ten full-time hands on the payroll and hired a dozen more during roundup. Every fall, upwards of four thousand shorthorn beeves were trailed to railhead at Caldwell. There the cows were sold to Eastern cattle buyers.

Morg moved into the cabin with Dunn. For the next few days, the old Texican showed him around the spread. The land was lush with graze, and tributaries branching off the river provided abundant water. The operation was tightly run and the books indicated that Dunn was a stickler for details. Every year for the past eleven years he had managed to turn a profit that any cattleman would envy. His word was law with the hands and he brooked no nonsense from anyone. He ran the ranch like a hardnosed drill sergeant.

The inspection left Morg suitably impressed. He saw nothing out of order and found little that might be improved. What intrigued him most was the Texican's garrulous recollections of days past. At night, seated at the cabin table, Dunn invariably turned talkative. Unlike other old-timers, he spoke not of trail drives and stampedes and fabled cowtowns. His ruminations were about the man who had hired him long ago, Virgil Brannock. And a dream centered on the Cherokee Outlet.

Virgil Brannock first saw the Outlet in the summer of 1876. By then Spur was already one of the largest spreads in New Mexico. What he sought was a similar operation, closer to the Kansas railheads. His goal was expansion, and like any true visionary, he saw potential often overlooked by lesser men. His search that summer ended on a dogleg bend in the Cimarron. Within the space of a year, he founded the ranch and formed an alliance with the Cherokee tribe. A short while later he took on the federal government.

The Outlet was a bizarre creation spawned earlier in the century. When the Five Civilized Tribes were re-settled in Indian Territory, the Cherokees were granted seven million acres bordering southern Kansas. As a further concession, they were granted a corridor ex-tending westward, which comprised another six mil-lion acres. Designated the Cherokee Outlet, the legal status of this strip was forever in question. By treaty, the tribe was forbidden to dispose of it in any manner.

For nearly a half-century, the Outlet remained un-occupied and forgotten. The Cherokees rarely ven-tured into the western grant, for their lands to the east were sufficient for the entire tribe. Then, in the early 1870s, the Chisholm Trail was blazed through the heart of Indian Territory. Texas cattlemen were quick to discover the rolling plains watered by the Canadian and the Cimarron. A perfect holding ground for trail-weary longhorns, the Outlet was within a short dis-tance of the Kansas border. Herds were halted and allowed to fatten out before the final drive to a railhead.

By late spring of 1881 some twenty ranchers had staked out permanent cowcamps in the Outlet. Among them was Virgil Brannock, and he possessed a fore-sight the others lacked. Envisioning problems from the federal government, he organized the Cherokee Cat-tlemen's Association. The ranchers elected him presi-dent and he promptly negotiated a ten-year lease with the Cherokee tribal council. The lease covered more than a million acres and enriched the tribal treasury by $100,000 a year. Everyone involved benefited by the arrangement.

From time to time, the bureaucrats in Washington attempted to overturn the lease agreement. But Virgil Brannock had formed a lasting alliance with the Cherokee Nation. After his death, other men stepped forward to head the Cattlemen's Association. The Cherokees proved to be tolerant landlords and staunch allies, working to preserve their annual lease payment. For the past six years, every effort by the government to create discord had been turned aside. Harmony still prevailed between the Cherokees and the ranchers.

"Folks don't forget," Dunn remarked late one night. "Your pa wrote his own epitaph when he formed the Association. He was a helluva man."

"Yeah, he was," Morg said with a note of pride. "When I was a kid, he used to talk to me about the future. He opened my eyes plenty."

"Know what you mean," Dunn said breezily. "Gawdalmighty, he was a regular bearcat when it come to plannin' ahead. Always saw that rainbow out there in the distance."

Morg nodded vigorously. "And the rainbow was just as important as the pot of gold. I remember him saying the money's only a yardstick. It's what you build that counts."

"By jiggers!" Dunn hooted. "You sound just like him. Damn me if you don't."

A sudden grin cracked Morg's face. "I've got a ways to go, but I figure to make my mark. He taught me to aim high."

Dunn looked at him thoughtfully. "Your ma ain't no slouch either. Got a real head on her shoulders."

"Tell me about it," Morg said, laughing. "Back

home they call her the Iron Butterfly. Nobody's got the best of her yet."

"Speakin' of which," Dunn observed. "The government's nippin' at our heels again. Looks to be a lulu of a fight."

"What's the problem?"

"Boomers," Dunn said angrily. "Gawddamn sodbusters lookin' to gobble up Injun land."

"You sound like it's serious."

"Liable to be the ruination of us all!"

Morg looked puzzled. "Are you saying they've got their eye on the Outlet?"

"Not just exactly," Dunn grumped. "You'll hear all about it tomorrow night. We're set to attend an Association meeting."

"Why not tell me now?"

" 'Cause it's got more twists than a barrel of snakes. Ain't no way I could explain it."

On that somber note the conversation ended. Dunn snuffed the lamp and peeled down to his longjohns. Morg undressed in the dark, then crawled into his own bunk. His last waking thought was a word he'd never before heard.

He wondered what "Boomers" were.

Caldwell was the last of the cowtowns. With the railroads spreading throughout Texas, even Dodge City was slowly withering away. The era of the great trail drives was gradually fading into history.

Herds from the Outlet ranchers were now the mainstay of Caldwell's continued prosperity. The Cherokee Cattlemen's Association maintained offices on Chisholm Street, and the members regularly met there once a month. Tonight's meeting had been convened on short notice and the ranchers were in a sober mood. There was talk of trouble emanating out of Washington.

Joe Pardee was the current president of the Association. His beard was dappled with gray and his hair was thinning above a craggy forehead. He was a plain-spoken man who gave the impression of wisdom garnered through age. Like most of the other members, he was a Texan who had invested heavily in the Outlet. The only spread not owned by a Texan was Spur's operation on the Cimarron. Nobody held it against Floyd Dunn that he worked for a New Mexican outfit.

Upon arriving, Dunn introduced Morg to the various members. He was readily accepted, for the men there remembered his father with great admiration. Joe Pardee wrung his hand with genuine warmth, welcoming him to the gathering. Then, as the ranchers got themselves seated, Pardee called the meeting to order. He stood at the front of the room, staring them into silence.

"Glad you could make it," he said, nodding around the group. "We've got a pisspot full of things to discuss and none of it good news. So bear with me while I bring you up-to-date."

For all his rough edges, Pardee was an articulate speaker. He began by sketching a broad outline of the situation and the origin of the problem. At root was the fact that so many people coveted Indian lands. A flood of immigrants and settlers had already claimed the choice homesteads. The clamor to open all public lands to settlement intensified as the westward migration gained strength. In the forefront of the movement were the Boomers, an army of some ten thousand settlers. Too late to claim homesteads in Kansas, they were encamped along the border of Indian Territory.

One of the prime targets of the Boomers was the Unassigned Lands. Ceded by the Creeks and the Seminoles as a home for tribes yet to be resettled, the Unassigned Lands embraced some two million acres of well-watered, fertile plains. White settlers were also eyeing the Cherokee Outlet, a vast landmass roughly 150 miles in length. Word of this grassy paradise had drawn the attention of the Boomers as well as vengeful politicians. Washington had never forgiven the cattlemen, or the Cherokees, for circumventing the edict against leasing agreements.

In short order, a public outcry arose over both the Unassigned Lands and the Outlet. The Boomers were backed by several influential factions, all of which had a vested interest in the western expansion. Politicians and merchant princes and railroads, all looking to feather their own nests, rallied to the cause. Alone in their opposition to settlement were the Five Civilized Tribes. Their dealings with the government formed a chain of broken pledges and unfulfilled treaties. They saw settlement as a device for the enrichment of white businessmen and greedy politicians.

In Washington these same politicians were holding out a wide array of enticements. Efforts were under way to convince the Five Civilized Tribes that their best interests would be served by abolishing tribal government. They were told that full citizenship within the Republic would afford them voting rights and equality before the law. Still, based on their experiences with *tibo*'s promises, they had good reason to doubt the faith of the government. Indian leaders, as well as the lowliest tribesmen, were unwilling to exchange independence for the dubious privilege of citizenship.

For all their resistance, however, the Indians were weighed down by a sense of fatalism. Thoughtful men knew that the Nations were in the process of slow but certain absorption into the white culture. The Five Civilized Tribes numbered less than fifty thousand peo-

ple, and much of their land lay untilled. The movement to gain control of the Nations—23,000,000
acres—would ultimately put the tribes in an untenable
position. For no one seriously doubted that the true
goal was the dissolution of all of Indian Territory.

Over the past two years the pressure to open Indian
lands to settlement had steadily mounted. Legislation
enacted by Congress in 1885 paved the way for purchase of all unused land from the Five Civilized Tribes.
Only a month ago the Severalty Act was passed, which
made settlement of Indian Territory a virtual certainty.
Negotiations were even now under way to bring about
the allotment of lands in the Nations, forcing each
tribesman to accept the same 160 acres awarded to
white settlers under the Homestead Act. Worse, there
was talk in Congress of creating from Indian lands
what would be called Oklahoma Territory. The future
was there for all to see.

"No doubt about it," Joe Pardee concluded. "We're
between a rock and a hard place. Unless something
happens fast, we're gonna lose the Outlet."

"So what'd we do?" one of the ranchers asked.
"Damned if I'll give up without a fight."

"There's more'n one way to fight," Pardee noted
slyly. "What we've gotta do is take a trick out of their
own book—outfox the bastards."

"How you plan to pull that off?"

Pardee launched into an explanation. His scheme
was to purchase their Outlet holdings directly from the
Cherokee Nation. Now was the time to act, while they
still had the leverage of a lease agreement, and before
Indian lands were opened to white settlement. Once
ownership was in private hands, the Outlet would be
immune to the threat from Washington. Yet the price
had to be right, so generous that the government
couldn't claim they were hoodwinking the Cherokees.

He proposed that the Association offer three dollars an acre for title to the Outlet lands under lease.

"Jesus Crucified Christ!" another Texan yelped. "You're talkin' about three million dollars. Where're we gonna get that kind of money?"

"We'll borrow it," Pardee informed him. "We'll mortgage our herds and throw in the land as extra collateral. There's plenty of bankers that would cotton to the idea."

"And foreclose muy damn pronto if we couldn't meet the payments. Where'd we be then?"

"Where we are now," Pardee countered. "Up shit creek without a paddle. What choice do we have?"

The Association members bitched and grumbled. When it became clear that no one had a better idea, they finally put it to a vote. There were a few dissenters, but the majority agreed it was worth a try. Joe Pardee was authorized to approach bankers in Caldwell and Wichita.

Morg was unsettled by what he'd heard. Some vague premonition told him that it would never work. The federal government was clearly determined to do away with all of Indian Territory, including the Nations. And Washington would view a ragtag bunch of ranchers as an obstacle to that goal. He thought the Association members were living on borrowed time, a year or two at best. In the end, they would all be ousted from the Outlet.

The meeting adjourned a short time later. Morg and Floyd Dunn, along with the other members, trooped upstreet to a saloon. Standing at the bar, they were approached by a sturdy, thick-set man with a badge on his chest. Dunn introduced him as Jack Selman, Caldwell's town marshal.

"Brannock," Selman repeated, staring at Morg. "You any relation to Clint Brannock?"

"Sure am," Morg said. "He's my uncle."

"Small world," Selman said, pulling an envelope from his pocket. "A wire come in for Clint tonight. Figured I'd pass it along to Floyd."

Morg studied the telegraph envelope. The message was from the U.S. marshal in Fort Smith. Addressed to Clint, it had been sent in care of the Spur Ranch, Cherokee Outlet. He looked up at Selman. "Any idea what it's about?"

"Only a hunch," Selman said. "Week or so ago your uncle killed a couple of wanted men down in the Nations. A third one got away."

"And they think he's headed toward the Outlet?"

"That'd be my guess," Selman allowed. "More'n likely they figured Clint would stop by the ranch. So they sent the wire here."

Morg invited the lawman to join them for a drink. The barkeep brought another glass and poured. Selman and Dunn began talking, but Morg listened with only half an ear. His mind was on other matters.

He tried to remember how many men his uncle had killed.

Late the next afternoon Clint forded the Cimarron. Sundown was only an hour away and he hoped to make the ranch by nightfall. A warm bed and a hot meal sounded inviting. For the past week, he'd been tracking the third gang member. While the trail zigzagged and backtracked, the general direction was northwest. The man clearly believed he was being pursued and had resorted to evasive tactics. So far none of his dodges had worked.

Unconcerned, Clint doggedly stuck to the trail. His years as a cavalry scout enabled him to follow sign over the roughest ground. His one concern was that the man would quit the wilderness and head for a

town. Where people congregated, a trail could be lost
in an instant. Wooded terrain, even the open plains,
was far more suitable to a manhunt.

With onrushing darkness the hoofprints began drifting off to the north. Clint studied them a moment,
aware that he might lose the trail if he tracked any
farther. He calculated he was no more than a mile
from the ranch and a hot meal. Whether or not the
man made a run for Caldwell was something he could
better determine at first light. He turned west along
the river.

Stars dotted the sky by the time he sighted the
ranch. When he stepped down from the saddle, the
cabin door opened. Framed in a shaft of lamplight, he
saw Morg standing behind Floyd Dunn. His surprised
look was replaced by a wide grin as the youngster
hurried forward and pumped his hand. They hadn't
seen each other in almost a year and he'd hardly
expected to find Morg in the Outlet. His detour suddenly took on the overtones of a reunion.

Oddly enough, Morg evidenced no surprise that their
paths had crossed. The reason became apparent when
they entered the cabin and he produced the telegram.
He explained how he'd come by it the night before,
while in Caldwell. In passing, he mentioned that Jack
Selman, the town marshal, thought it had to do with
law business. His instructions were to hand it over at
the first opportunity.

Clint tore open the envelope. There were two message slips inside, one from John Carroll, the U.S.
marshal. He stated that he was forwarding a wire from
the Indian agent at the Comanche reservation. The
second slip was a duplicate of the agent's message. It
was dated March 14, two days past.

The message was short. Clint's eyes narrowed as he
scanned it quickly, then read it again. His mouth went

tight and his expression turned curiously stoic. He silently handed the message slip to Morg.

    CLINT BRANNOCK
    U.S. MARSHAL'S OFFICE
    FT. SMITH, ARKANSAS
        YOUR SISTER-IN-LAW GRAVELY ILL.
        URGENT YOU COME AT ONCE.
                GEORGE HAZEN
                AGENT, FORT SILL
                INDIAN TERRITORY

"Sounds bad," Morg said, glancing up. "Are you going?"

"Wouldn't think of doing otherwise."

"What about the man you're after?"

"To hell with him," Clint said shortly. His gaze shifted to Dunn. "Floyd, will you loan me a fresh horse?"

"Shore will," Dunn replied. "But gawddamn, Clint, you ain't plannin' on leaving tonight, are you?"

"Yeah, I am," Clint said. "Just as soon as you rustle up some hot grub. I travel better on a full belly."

Ten minutes later Clint swung aboard a roan gelding. His hat was pulled low and the collar of his mackinaw was turned high against the chill night air. A short distance from the cabin he again forded the Cimarron.

He rode south under pale starlight.

5

A routine day at the clinic began early. The first patients started arriving shortly after breakfast. By midmorning the waiting room was usually crowded, with more gathered on the walkway outside. Seldom was the last patient attended until sometime after sundown.

Unlike most frontier doctors, Jennifer never traveled the backcountry circuit. The distances involved would have required her to be out of the office at least two days a week. She responded only to emergency calls, driving her own buggy and team. The balance of the time she kept regular office hours.

The system proved to be immensely practical. Her practice covered hundreds of square miles and Lincoln was centrally located. The patients came into town for treatment rather than relying on infrequent medical visits to their homes. The end result was that she saw more people and cured far more illnesses.

Some problems required a departure from her routine. There was no hospital in Lincoln and therefore no facilities for extended medical care. A childbirth, or any condition that left a patient bedridden, was attended in the home. Friends and family were depended upon to provide nursing care for prolonged illnesses. Hardly the perfect situation, it was nonetheless accepted by people accustomed to fending for themselves.

Jennifer's staff consisted of two *mexicano* women. Rosa, the nurse and surgical assistant, had been inherited from Dr. Chester Wood. She was capable and levelheaded, with an accumulated storehouse of practical medical knowledge. The other woman, Lupe, was younger and still somewhat inexperienced. Her duties revolved around sterilizing instruments and dressings, and maintaining the clinic in a state of cleanliness. Winter and summer, she kept caldrons of water boiling on an old woodburner stove.

The patients today were a representative lot. Jennifer had lanced an inflamed boil, treated a woman for blinding headaches, and examined an elderly man suffering from cystitis. The latter condition was a bladder infection, resulting in a burning sensation during urination. A sample of the man's urine was cloudy in color and showed traces of blood. He was running a slight fever.

By necessity, Jennifer was her own pharmacist. From supply houses back East, she ordered roots, herbs, and other natural materials. Using these base elements, she then mashed and pounded with mortar and pestle until the desired prescription was formulated. Once mixed, the compounded powders were packaged in squares of heavy paper. For all the advances in science, pharmacology offered few miracles. Some illnesses were still treated with rudimentary medicine.

The woman with a headache was ordered to take an enema with strong black coffee, cooled and undiluted. Afterward, she was to rest in a darkened room and avoid spicy foods for twenty-four hours. For the man with cystitis, Jennifer prescribed a potion of baking soda and water every two hours for three days. To flush out the bladder, he was required to drink five quarts of water daily. Should the symptoms persist, he was to return on the fourth day.

The elderly man typified one of Jennifer's major problems. All too many men were reluctant to consult a woman physician about personal ailments. Anything that required an examination of their private parts brought on an attack of male modesty. She chided them, remarking that she'd been raised on a ranch where bulls displayed no modesty whatever. Despite her casual attitude, the situation had improved only by degree. Some men still traveled fifty miles to see a male doctor.

Jennifer was keenly aware of the underlying prejudice. However enlightened the times, a female physician was severely stigmatized because of her sex. Following the Civil War, in the face of public disapproval, women began to invade the medical profession. At first they tended to specialize in the treatment of women and children, practicing gynecology and obstetrics. Even so, male physicians attempted to exclude them from all educational institutions. Johns Hopkins and Harvard, the two most prestigious medical schools, routinely denied entrance to women.

Harvard medical students protested with a resolution that stated: "No woman of true delicacy would be willing in the presence of men to listen to the discussions of subjects that necessarily come under consideration." Boston was nonetheless a hotbed of feminist activity, and the location of the first medical college for women. A unique institution, the New England Hospital for Women and Children was owned and operated exclusively by women. There the internship training denied by other hospitals was provided to aspiring lady physicians.

By 1884, when Jennifer entered medical school, less than three percent of all doctors were women. She chose one of the few coeducational institutions in the country, Tufts College. Her courses included anatomy, pathology, physiology, and pharmacology. She attended advanced lectures at City Hospital, where female students were allowed to observe operations in the hospital amphitheater. She interned there as well, working the charity wards with both male and female patients.

Female students were also allowed to witness autopsies conducted by the county coroner. The experience proved invaluable when students were later required to dissect cadavers. The old days, when "resurrectionists" raided cemeteries for bodies, were long since passed. Jennifer worked on cadavers excavated from potter's field for use in medical colleges. There again she was fortunate, for the dissections were performed on both men and women. She graduated with a knowledge of anatomy essential to the practice of general surgery.

After returning to Lincoln, she gained even wider experience. Dr. Chester Wood permitted her to assist in operations and quickly came to trust her ability. On occasion, she managed to enlighten him on new techniques developed in Boston and in European medical centers. By the time he died, Wood looked upon her as a colleague, a worthy successor. Her skill at the operating table was no less persuasive with the townspeople. Anglos and *mexicanos* alike accepted her despite the fact that she was a woman. Only some of the stodgier men still resented her because she wore skirts.

Late that afternoon her surgical skills were put to the test. A wagon rolled to a halt in front of the clinic. The driver owned a ranch on the Rio Bonito, west of Lincoln. One of his cowhands was stretched out on a pallet of blankets in the wagonbed. Several townsmen were summoned from upstreet and they assisted in unloading the cowhand. While the rancher supported his head, they carried him into the clinic.

The rancher told a familiar story. Working a bunch of cattle, the cowhand's horse had spooked and thrown him from the saddle. Cowhands were dumped all the time and generally managed to walk away. But this time the man had tumbled backward out of the saddle, arms and legs akimbo. As he fell, the horse lashed out with its hind hooves and kicked him in the head. His skull was crushed.

Jennifer had him placed on the operating table. Rosa brusquely waved the men out of the inner office and closed the door. The cowhand was unconscious, the crown of his head matted with blood. A quick examination revealed an ugly wound approximately two inches in diameter. Underneath the tangled hair and bone fragments, a section of the brain was exposed. His breathing was shallow and his features were ashen.

Unfastening his shirt, Jennifer checked his heartbeat with a stethoscope. His pulse was feeble and his skin was cold to the touch. She then checked the pupils of his eyes, noting that they reacted to the overhead reflective lamp. With a needle, she pricked his finger and watched his hand retract. Finally, she inspected the crotch of his trousers and found he'd passed a small amount of urine.

The signs were better than Jennifer had dared expect. While the injury was serious, there was no indication of compression of the brain. The absence of paralysis, combined with the other favorable symptoms, gave her hope. Yet there was still the matter of the gaping hole and the exposed brain tissue. Staring down at the man, she suddenly recalled a lecture from medical school. Her professor had spoken of an ancient surgical procedure, reportedly traced to Egyptian times. No physician outside Boston was known to have attempted the operation.

Jennifer moved through the door to the waiting room. She ordered the rancher to take a silver dollar and hurry downstreet to the town blacksmith. She wanted the coin placed on an anvil and hammered into a thin disk, at least three inches in diameter. Lupe was then instructed to await his return and sterilize the disk. Time was the enemy and she told the rancher to run all the way. His eyes clouded with a question, but her stern look dampened his curiosity. He rushed out the door.

Lupe brought hot water and soap and Jennifer scrubbed for the operation. With a straight razor, she then shaved the cowhand's head, leaving the crown bald. Rosa fetched a bottle of carbolic solution and used the antiseptic to cleanse the bare spot. When she finished, Rosa moved to the side of the operating table. She waited with a sponge and a vial of ether, should the injured man regain consciousness.

Working with a probe and forceps, Jennifer gently removed splinters of bone from the wound. Several minutes passed before she satisfied herself that no foreign matter endangered the brain. As she straightened up, Lupe entered the room holding a wad of sterile dressing. She commented that the blacksmith had obligingly dropped everything else and rushed the job along. Within the folds of the cloth lay a shiny wafer of silver, slightly convex in shape. It was still warm from being sterilized.

Scalpel in hand, Jennifer quickly incised four lines radiating outward from the wound. She next peeled the flaps aside and gingerly implanted the silver disk over the exposed brain tissue. From the instrument tray she took a surgical needle and threaded it with catgut. A stitch at a time, she sutured the scalp closed with meticulous care. When she tied off the last suture, a spot of silver the size of a quarter was all that remained visible. She stepped back to admire her handiwork.

The cowhand groaned. His eyes fluttered open and he stared up at the overhead lamp with a groggy expression. He licked his lips and blinked into the harsh light. His voice sounded parched. "What happened?"

"You're fine," Jennifer said, moving to the side of the table. "You'll be up and around in no time."

"I don't—" His eyes focused and he stared at her. "That you, Doc?"

"Yes, it's me."

Jennifer smiled and took his hand. So far as she could recall, she had never seen him before. Which made the operation a milestone in more ways than one.

Today was the first time anybody had called her Doc.

Jennifer's living quarters were at the rear of the clinic. The furnishings were an eclectic blend of chintz and patterned slipcovers and dark hardwood. A broad window looked westward toward the mountains.

Early that evening Blake Hazlett found her seated in the parlor. After supper, he usually stopped by for an hour or so. Over a brandy, they shared the day's experiences and remarked on the state of things in Lincoln. He was as intrigued by her clinic as he was by his own law practice.

Blake was a stocky, amiable man with an even disposition and a contagious laugh. His hair was dark and curly and his mustache was the color of lampblack. Three years ago he'd opened an office in Lincoln and he now handled most of the legal work for Spur.

Through Elizabeth, he had met Jennifer upon her return from medical school. They had been keeping steady company for the past nine months.

Tonight Jennifer was in a pensive mood. Her face appeared drained and her eyes were oddly vacant. She stared off into some thoughtful distance. Blake settled into an overstuffed chair and pulled out a tobacco pouch. He loaded his pipe, then fired up in a cloud of smoke. He looked at her inquisitively.

"Thought you'd be ready to celebrate," he said. "The whole town's talking about your operation. They say you brought that cowhand back from the dead."

"Hardly." Jennifer's voice was troubled. "We can't even provide him with proper medical care. He's been moved to a room in the hotel."

"I recall we've had this discussion before. You're talking about a hospital, aren't you?"

"Yes," Jennifer said quietly. "It's like practicing medicine in the Dark Ages. Any civilized town would have built a hospital years ago."

Blake laughed good-humoredly. "People around here pride themselves on being tough. A hospital sounds like some sissified Eastern notion."

Jennifer gave him a tired smile. "Perhaps we need an asylum more than a hospital. Anyone who thinks like that should be committed."

"What we need is a drink."

Blake got to his feet. He moved to an ornately carved cabinet and poured from a brandy decanter. When he returned with her glass, he stooped down and brushed her lips with a kiss. She looked at him strangely.

Their relationship was curiously unemotional. Jennifer was comfortable with him and she preferred his company to that of other men she'd met. Still, her feelings about him veered wildly, and she often re-

flected on the absence of passion between them. She
sometimes wished he would sweep her off her feet.

Blake lifted his glass. "To the lady Doc," he said
with a waggish grin. "The toast of Lincolntown."

Jennifer laughed deep in her throat. His sunny nature was irresistible and he never failed to lighten her
mood. She wondered now whether her mother was
right, after all. Perhaps there was more between a
man and woman than fervid passion.

Perhaps, in the end, simple affection was enough.

Hondo Valley was bordered on the south by a low
line of foothills. Some ten miles beyond the hogback
ridges lay the Rio Felix, with its headwaters in the
westward mountains. The river snaked through a land
of broken plains and sparse graze.

Brad rode there once a week. He had homesteaded
a quarter-section on the Rio Felix and built a crude
log cabin. Farther downstream was the ranch of Homer Stockton, Morg's father-in-law. Upstream were
the *jacales* and patchy farmlands of several *mexicano*
families.

North of the river, a good part of the land was
public domain. Over the last year, Brad had put together a herd of some fifty cows. Crossbred stock,
longhorn cows topped by shorthorn bulls, they were
able to forage for themselves and required little care.
He generally rode over late on Saturday and stayed
through Sunday.

The operation was financed on a shoestring. Apart
from his wages as Spur's foreman, Brad had no money
of his own. Nor was he willing to approach Elizabeth
for a loan, even though she considered him family.
While she never spoke of it, she looked upon his
outside venture as a threat. She feared the small spread
might grow into something larger, and lure him away

from Spur. Her concern was justified, for his attitude had undergone a gradual turnaround. He was tired of working for someone else.

Elizabeth had returned from Santa Fe earlier in the week. A letter was waiting for her from Morg, who was still at the Cherokee Outlet ranch. When she read it aloud at the supper table, her pride was all too evident. Brad sensed she was grooming the youngster for greater things, and rightfully so. But the fact that Morg would one day take over Spur did nothing to improve his lot in life. He would still be a hired hand.

Cottonwoods and willows bordered the Rio Felix. Brad reined to a halt beneath the trees and sat staring at his cabin. Hardly more than a shanty, it was a one-room affair with furnishings as Spartan as a monk's cell. Off in the distance he saw the cattle cropping bunch-grass and spotted several new calves. He grunted sharply, reminded that roundup time was fast approaching. For him, it would be a one-man roundup.

A vague unease settled over Brad. He was no longer content with his job at Spur, where he often felt like the poor relation. Nor was he wildly enthused by the idea of his own pinch-penny spread, merely grubbing out an existence. Late at night, he sometimes wondered why the hell he'd staked the land and built the cabin. He seemed to itch with something that couldn't be scratched. He felt restless and bored and oddly trapped. His life was dull as dirt.

Glum as a sore-tailed bear, he turned his horse west along the river. Some three miles upstream he rode into the yard of Alfredo Ramírez. One of the many *mexicano* farmers on the upper Rio Felix, Ramírez worked a harsh plot of ground and ran a few head of sheep.

He was a small man, with seamed leathery features and a wizened expression. His wife was a happy dump-

ling of a woman who had given him a brood of seven
children. The oldest, scarcely nineteen, was a girl named
Juanita.

Ramírez welcomed Brad into his humble adobe. A
peaceful man by nature, he held no particular animosity toward *gringos*. He was honored that the foreman
of Spur showed such an interest in his eldest daughter.
Every Saturday night Brad took supper with the family, and by now it had assumed the aspects of a court-
ing ritual. Even the younger children were aware that
Juanita had her eye set on marriage. They waited
expectantly for her to spring the snare.

Señora Ramírez was also favorably inclined toward
the match. While the men sipped *tequila*, she and
Juanita bustled around setting the table. Supper consisted of roast kid, *frijoles* and *tortillas*, and coffee
laced with goat's milk. The children stuffed their
mouths, one eye on the wealthy Anglo, and maintained a respectful silence. Alfredo Ramírez, as the
man of the house, set the tone of the conversation. He
spoke with Brad of sheep and cows and the prospects
of a long, dry summer. The women listened with rapt
attentiveness.

After supper, Juanita threw a *rebozo* over her shoulders. As though on signal, the children began helping
their mother clear the table. Ramírez rolled himself a
cornhusk cigarette and settled into a chair before the
fireplace. No one seemed particularly interested when
Juanita opened the door and stepped outside. Brad
collected his hat, all too aware that he was the subject
of intense, carefully concealed scrutiny. He mumbled
a hurried good night as he went through the door.

Juanita strolled off toward the river. She moved
with sinuous grace, lithe and youthful, her breasts
jutting from beneath the shawl. Her features were
delicate, with high cheekbones and an olive complex-

ion. There was a smoldering sensuality about her, some combination of innocence and earthiness that Brad found strangely beguiling. He thought she had the most provocative eyes he'd ever seen in a woman.

On the riverbank, she paused beneath a tall cottonwood. Starlight filtered through the leaves overhead and bathed her face in a shimmering glow. She turned and looked at him with a catlike smile. He met her gaze, found something merry lurking there.

"What is it, *querido*?" she said lightly. "You seem so thoughtful tonight."

"*Nada*," Brad replied. "I've just got things on my mind, that's all. Not long now till roundup."

"*Madre mía!*" she said in a wounded voice. "We have only one night a week together. You should be thinking of me—not your cows!"

Brad smiled broadly. "When I'm with you nothing else occupies my mind for long. I would be a *manso* otherwise."

"No, not you," she said with an indrawn breath. "I have reason to know you are not a tame bull. *Verdad*?"

"You are a small, wicked *bruja*. You try to put a spell on me with such talk."

Her eyes gleamed with mischief. "And do I succeed?"

"Sometimes," Brad said, deadpan.

"Sometimes!" she repeated with mock outrage. "You sound like a man who has had his way too often."

Brad beamed at her with genuine affection. "However often would never be often enough."

She laughed and tossed her head. Brad held out his arms and she stepped eagerly into his embrace. Her hands went behind his neck, pulling his mouth down, and she kissed him with a fierce, passionate urgency. The taste of her lips was a honeyed sweetness, at once intoxicating and warm. His arms tightened, strong and demanding, holding her closer still. When at last they separated, her voice was breathless, soft and husky.

"Oh, *caro mío*, how I've missed you."

The *rebozo* fell from her shoulders. They stood for a moment, words forgotten, entwined together like wisps of smoke. Then her mouth opened and she kissed him feverishly. Her nails taloned his back.

He slowly lowered her to the ground.

6

Fort Sill was located deep in Indian Territory. The cavalry regiment stationed there had not fought an engagement in almost twelve years. The army was now reduced to the role of benign watchdog.

Three miles south of the fort was the agency headquarters for the Comanche and the Kiowa. Once the scourge of the Southern Plains, the horseback tribes were now wards of the government. Hounded into submission in 1875, the last of the warlike bands had been driven onto the reservation. There they undertook a hard journey along the white man's road.

The reservation spread westward toward the Texas Panhandle, bounded on the north by the Washita River and on the south by the Red. West and north of the agency, the Wichita Mountains jutted skyward, the red granite slopes wrapped in a smoky haze. Sweeping eastward from the foothills were rolling prairies crisscrossed by lowland streams.

By treaty, some three million acres had been ceded to the hostile tribes. The Bureau of Indian Affairs, though somewhat misguided in its efforts, sought to transform horseback warriors into farmers. Over the past decade many of the younger men had adapted and begun to till the soil. Others took jobs in the sawmill and the blacksmith shop operated by the agency. A smaller number, fluent in English, hauled freight bound for the reservation from distant railheads.

Few of the older men were willing to labor in the fields. Hunters and warriors, still tied to the ancient ways, they were unimpressed by the wonders of modern agriculture. With their families, they congregated along Cache Creek, west of the agency. Their existence revolved around annuity goods, food and clothing doled out by the government. Yet they refused the offer of lumber and nails, unwilling to live in the white man's boarded structures. They clung to the hide lodges of their ancestors.

One lodge along the wooded stream was the home of Little Raven and her sons. Long ago she had married a white Comanchero, a renegade who traded with the warlike tribes. A widower, previously married to a white woman, his name was Earl Brannock. To their wedding lodge he brought a son by that marriage, a boy called Lon. She had adopted the youngster as her own, and in time she gave birth to another son. In the Comanche tongue he was known as Bull Calf. His Christian name was Hank.

Late in 1874, Earl Brannock had been killed at the Battle of Palo Duro Canyon. Little Raven, with Lon and Hank, fled onto the Staked Plains with the Comanche survivors. Some months later, pressed relentlessly by cavalry units, the band surrendered at Fort Sill. While Little Raven converted to the white man's religion, she followed the old ways in all other things. Her home for the past twelve winters had been the lodge on Cache Creek.

Grievously ill, Little Raven was now confined to her bedrobes. A persistent cough had worsened over the last few months, steadily sapping her energy. Her features grew wan and her breathing gradually deteriorated into a hoarse rasp. Finally, when she began coughing blood, the post surgeon was summoned from Fort Sill. By then, the disease had spread throughout her lungs, and there was nothing to be done. Her condition was diagnosed as consumption, and the surgeon's prognosis was grim. He gave her less than two weeks.

Today, as he had for the past ten days, Major Perry Traber stopped by to check on his patient. He was a short, bespectacled man, with metal-framed glasses perched on the bridge of his nose. His compassion toward the Indians was widely known, and yet he bitterly resented those who clung to the ancient ways. While there was no cure for consumption of the lungs, he felt Little Raven should have sent for him earlier. He was now able to do scarcely more than relieve her agony. He kept her dosed with laudanum, an opiate sedative.

Lon and Hank waited outside the lodge. The elder, Lon, was twenty-one and bore an uncanny resemblance to his father. He was a strapping six-footer, full-spanned through the shoulders, his hair bleached copper by the sun. His eyes were striking, yet cold, a peculiar shade of blue. There was a quiet confidence about him, and his manner was deceptive. Other men crossed him at their own peril.

By contrast, Hank had inherited his mother's broad features and dark hair. Yet like his half-brother, his eyes were blue, and his light-bronze skin immediately pegged him as a half-breed. He was almost fifteen, tall for his age, with the lithe, muscular build of his father. A prankster of sorts, he smiled easily and viewed life with sportive good humor. He was a steady, carefree youngster, slow to anger.

Neither of them was talkative today. They stood locked in glum silence, their features wooden. Overnight their mother had taken a turn for the worse, lapsing into periods of delirium. The end was near, and though it was unspoken, they both wished her suffering would quickly cease. Waiting now for the doctor, they stared morosely toward the spires of the distant mountains. There was nothing either of them could say that would console the other.

Major Traber emerged from the lodge. He gave them a hopeless shrug and a dark empty look. "She's holding on," he said dolefully. "God knows what's keeping her alive. I certainly don't."

"She's not ready," Hank said half-aloud. "Not yet."

Traber squinted at him. "What do you mean—not ready?"

"I told her our uncle was on the way. She's waiting until he gets here."

"Hardly likely." Traber's headshake was slow and emphatic. "In her condition, the next breath might be the last. Willpower alone wouldn't keep her alive."

"So you say," Lon muttered roughly. "Why else would she hang on?"

Traber avoided a direct reply. He knew Lon to be a hardcase and a troublemaker, and he saw no reason to provoke an argument. He nodded tersely. "Let me know if there's any change. Otherwise, I'll come by again tomorrow."

When Traber drove off in his buckboard, Hank went back inside the lodge. Lon walked down to the creek and seated himself at the base of a tree. A short-barreled Colt, carried in a crossdraw holster, protruded from beneath his coat. He adjusted the pistol to a more comfortable position, then lit a slim black cheroot. He exhaled smoke, staring vacantly out across the stream. Unbidden, his mind drifted backward in time.

A good part of his life had been spent on the reservation. Though white by birth, he had chosen to live among his adopted people, the Comanche. He had taken their ways and become a disciple of their last great war chief, Quanah Parker. He'd practiced the peyote religion and acquired a reputation as a rebellious hell-raiser. For a time, seeking independence, he had retreated to the fastness of the Wichita Mountains. On his own, answerable to no one, he had lived the simple life of a woodsman and hunter.

In the summer of 1881, all that had changed. With Quanah Parker, he'd traveled to Doan's Crossing, a waystation for trail herds on the Red River. There, after goading a surly Texan into drawing, he had killed his first man. The following summer, the cowhand's four brothers had come looking for him. Alerted by Comanche friends, Lon had ambushed the brothers on the trail to his wilderness cabin. When the shooting ended, two brothers lay dead and the other two retreated to Texas. At seventeen, Lon had already gunned down three men.

The Fort Sill commander ordered him off the reservation. Stubborn proud, he'd refused to join his lawman uncle in Fort Smith. Instead, he had turned to his father's original trade, that of a professional gambler. Enduring the lean times, he had slowly learned the craft, developing into a skilled poker player. For the last four years he'd worked the gambling circuit throughout Texas, following a wide swing that took him as far south as the Rio Grande. Wiser now, and warier, he kept a sharp lookout wherever he traveled. Word was out that he was still being hunted by the last two Jarrott brothers.

Every six months or so Lon returned to the reservation. These days he was generally in the chips, for he had acquired the knack of reading men across a poker table. He always brought presents for his mother and Hank, and the visits were something of a homecoming. Even now, he continued to think of himself as a Comanche rather than a *tahboy-boh*. On this trip, however, the presents had gone unopened. He'd arrived to find his mother frail and wasted, near death. Another week and he would have been too late.

Lon was seldom given to emotion. As a boy, he had been inducted into the Comanche ways, where stoicism to pain was expected of men. Later, approaching manhood, he'd killed the three Texicans with no lingering aftereffects. Four years on the gambling circuit, where death was every man's companion, had further hardened him. In large degree, the life he'd led had brutalized him, turned him dispassionate and cold. Other men read that in his flat stare and his cool display of nerve. He would not hesitate to kill when provoked. Nor would he lose any sleep after the fact.

Yet now, staring across the creek, he felt his eyes mist. A lump formed in his throat and his vision blurred as he blinked back the tears. The woman who had been like his mother lay dying, one quick step from the grave. She was the only thing he revered in all the world, and her passing seemed to him beyond comprehension. He felt helpless, somehow broken by the prospect of having her taken from his life. Death suddenly seemed all too personal, a thing of dread and unleashed emotions. He grieved for her, and with her, the loss of something inside himself. When she died, the best part of his life would go with her.

The sound of hoofbeats broke his spell. He turned and saw a horseman rein to a halt before the lodge. He blinked again, clearing his vision, and abruptly recognized the rider. Tossing his cheroot into the stream, he climbed to his feet and walked forward. His features were once more a mask, revealing nothing.

Clint stepped down from the saddle. His eyes were bloodshot and his jawline was covered with stubble. He hadn't slept in nearly three days and he felt tired to the bone. His horse was spent and he took a moment to loosen the cinch. As he straightened up, he heard a footstep to his rear. He looked around.

"Hullo," Lon said, stopping a pace away. "Where'd you come from?"

"The Outlet," Clint said without elaboration. "How's your mother?"

"Tomorrow would've been too late. She won't last out the night."

Clint's features went stony. He looked down, studying the ground for a long moment. When he glanced up, his mouth was set in a tight line. "What's wrong with her?"

"Consumption," Lon told him. "The doc says her lungs are plumb shot. She can't hardly draw a decent breath."

"No way to pull her through?"

"No," Lon said, averting his eyes. "No way."

The flap on the doorhole swung open. Hank stepped outside and stopped, momentarily taken aback. Then he crossed to where they stood, gamely trying for a smile, and nodded to Clint. He extended his hand.

Handshaking was a solemn affair among the Plains tribes. Though a white custom, the Indians had adopted it as a universal sign of peaceful intent. The Comanche, once the most feared warriors on the Southern Plains, placed great importance on gestures of friendship. Between blood relatives, the ritual assumed even more significance.

Clint clasped the boy's hand in both his own. He saw pain and sadness in the youngster's eyes, a deep inner sorrow. "Lon told me everything," he said. "Your mother was always a brave woman and she would want you to be brave. Knowing her, she has no fear of the shadow land."

"She goes gladly," Hank said in a hushed voice. "She believes she will join my father in the *tahboy-boh*'s heaven."

A mental image flashed before Clint's eyes. He saw his long-dead brother, grinning and proud, as though frozen in a moment of time. He cleared his throat. "We must be happy for her, then. She and your father were always of one spirit."

Lon put his hand on the boy's shoulder. There was a prolonged silence while the three of them stood searching for words. At last, as though by unspoken agreement, they walked toward the lodge. The youngsters moved aside at the doorhole, and Hank pulled back the flap. Clint ducked through the opening.

Little Raven lay motionless on her bedrobes. A trade blanket covered her, folded neatly beneath her chin. Her hair, cropped short according to Comanche custom, was streaked with gray. Her features were ravaged, taut and emaciated, blanched by a deadly pallor. She labored for breath, the sound ragged and harsh.

Clint knelt down beside her. Their relationship was warm and close, and he was genuinely fond of her. He thought of her as a good woman and a good mother, and he'd always admired her sense of family. Her life had been devoted to the boys, and he knew her to be a woman of fierce loyalty. He gently brushed a stray lock of hair off her forehead.

The touch of his hand was like a curative. Little Raven shuddered and her eyes slowly rolled open. She struggled back through the threshold of consciousness, fighting the hold of the laudanum. The haze lifted and her eyes focused on him. A faint smile softened her features.

"I've waited for you," she whispered. "I knew you would not fail me."

"No, little sister," Clint said, his voice clogged. "I would never fail you."

"Then you must do something for me . . . a vow."

"Whatever you ask," Clint said. "You have my oath on it."

Her hand appeared from beneath the blanket. She took hold of his arm and squeezed it with all her strength. "I give you my sons. They are in your lodge now . . . your blood . . ."

"Our blood," Clint said hollowly. "From the time you cross over, they will be as my own."

Little Raven nodded, her features serene and without pain. Her gaze went past him, settling on Lon and Hank. She stared at them, still smiling, as though burning their faces into memory for all time. Then, like a falling leaf, her hand dropped from Clint's arm.

A long sigh claimed her last breath. The light went out in her eyes and she slumped back on her bedrobes. Her features relaxed in a restful, faraway look, a look of final peace. Her mouth was still etched with a faint smile.

She crossed over to the shadow land.

A drenching, windswept downpour had fallen throughout the night. By morning, the wind dropped off and the rain squall drifted southward. The sky remained metallic and cold, suffused with dark clouds.

The cemetery was located on a grassy knoll beyond the agency buildings. A picket fence enclosed the burial ground, and wooden crosses stood stark and solitary under the overcast skies. It was the final resting place for Comanches who had followed the Jesus Road. Converts to the Christian faith were interred there with appropriate ceremony.

Late that afternoon family and mourners gathered for the services. The coffin bearing Little Raven rested on boards laid across the open grave. Clint, with Lon and Hank at his side, stood before the coffin. Quanah

Parker, surrounded by his wives and children, was immediately behind them. Of the other mourners, almost a hundred in number, at least half of them still practiced the old tribal religion. They congregated nonetheless out of respect for a woman who had befriended them all.

The rites of burial were performed by a Methodist minister. He was a shambling, unkempt man attired in a black broadcloth coat and rumpled trousers. His mission was to convert the heathens into God-fearing Christians and every Sunday he preached hellfire and brimstone. Today he delivered a stirring eulogy to Little Raven Brannock, praising her as a mother and a woman of Christian charity. That she had been summoned in the flower of life he could only attribute to the will of the Lord God Jehovah. The mourners bowed their heads as he concluded with the Twenty-third Psalm.

After the services, Quanah Parker approached Clint. There was mutual respect between them, even though neither considered the other a friend. Clint had served as a civilian scout for the Fourth Cavalry Regiment, the unit that had driven the Comanche onto the reservation. Quanah held no grudges about the past, but his memory was sharp for those long-ago battles. He still thought of Clint as a scout.

"*Hao*," he said, shaking hands with a hard up-and-down pump. "Death brings us together again. But then, we are not strangers to such things, are we, scout?"

"No," Clint agreed. "We've both seen our share."

Quanah nodded owlishly. "What will become of Bull Calf? Will you leave him with his people?"

"I am his people," Clint said. "We are of the same blood."

"Think on it," Quanah replied formally. "Among

the *tahboy-boh*, blood does not count. He will be a half-breed, still a Comanche."

Quanah was a half-breed himself. His mother, a white girl named Cynthia Ann Parker, had been taken captive during a Comanche raid on Texas. Shortly after being forced onto the reservation, he had assumed the family name as his own. He told his people it was a gesture of his willingness to follow the white man's road. Still, as all would attest, it made him no less a Comanche.

Before Clint could reply, the minister stopped to offer his condolences. Quanah's seven wives, not to mention a rowdy pack of children, were the preacher's great embarrassment in life. All the more so since the Comanche chief had been baptized into the Christian faith. The three of them chatted for a few minutes, then Quanah and the minister wandered off.

Clint turned back to join the boys. They were standing by themselves, just outside the gate to the graveyard. As he approached, they exchanged a glance and suddenly fell silent. Their look was oddly conspiratorial, and he caught an undercurrent of tension. Some visceral instinct warned him that trouble was afoot. His gaze fixed on Lon.

"What's the problem?"

"We've talked it out," Lon said with a half-smile. "Hank figures Fort Smith doesn't suit his style. He'd prefer to ride with me."

"With you?" Clint looked surprised, then suddenly irritated. "Hell, you follow the gambler's circuit. That's no life for a boy."

"It beats Fort Smith," Lon countered. "You're always off in the Nations somewhere. That'd leave him to fend for himself."

"Not by a damnsight," Clint said gruffly. "I room in a boardinghouse and the landlady's like an old mother hen. She'll see to it he goes to school and does his lessons."

"Yeah, I'll bet," Lon scoffed. "And he'll wind up the town 'breed. What sort of life is that?"

"The subject's closed," Clint said with strained patience. "Hank goes with me and that's final."

"Maybe you ought to ask him what he thinks."

Clint turned to the boy. "What do you say, son? Wouldn't you like to give Fort Smith a try?"

Hank fidgeted uncomfortably. "Tell you the truth, I'd sooner stay here. Either I go with Lon or I don't go nowhere."

Clint's tone was severe. "Lon runs with a rough crowd. You're a little young for that, aren't you?"

"I'm near fifteen," Hank said stoutly. "I can take care of myself just fine. Besides, brothers ought to stick together."

Before Clint could reply, he was distracted by an approaching horseman. A trooper from the garrison reined to a halt and saluted smartly. "Got a wire for you, marshal," he said, extending an envelope. "The colonel told me to find you lickety-split."

"Tell him I'm obliged."

The trooper touched his cap and rode off. Clint tore open envelope and scanned the telegraph message. The dateline was Fort Smith and it was signed by John Carroll, the U.S. marshal. His face registered blank astonishment.

> GOVERNOR OF NEW MEXICO REQUESTS YOUR IM-
> MEDIATE TRANSFER. YOU ARE FORTHWITH ASSIGNED
> TO U.S. MARSHAL'S OFFICE, SANTA FE. TRANSFER AP-
> PROVED BY PRESIDENT GROVER CLEVELAND. REPORT
> SANTA FE SOONEST.

Clint wagged his head back and forth. He looked up with a wry smile. "How'd you boys like to see New Mexico?"

Lon eyed him with narrow suspicion. "What are you talkin' about?"

"I've just been reassigned," Clint said. "I'm ordered to report to Santa Fe pronto."

"So?"

"So there's lots of mining camps in New Mexico. And I hear it's hog-heaven for gamblers. Feel like a change of luck?"

Lon examined the notion. "What about Hank?"

"We'll all go together," Clint said, spreading his hands. "Until I get settled, Hank can stick with you. How's that sound?"

A moment elapsed while they stared at one another. At length, Lon glanced at the boy. "What d'you say, sport? Got a yen to see New Mexico?"

Hank shrugged. "I'm game if you are."

"Hell, why not?" Lon said. "I've worn out my welcome in Texas anyway."

"It's settled then," Clint said, nodding at them. "We'll leave tomorrow."

On the way back to the lodge, the boys were curiously silent. Clint looked like a cat spitting feathers, and tried to hide it. By a stroke of luck, he'd been granted what seemed a timely reprieve. For New Mexico represented a whole new game where Hank was concerned.

One way or another he meant to see the youngster wind up where he belonged. On the Rio Hondo, with the Brannocks. The sound of it gave his spirits a sudden boost.

He'd been away too long himself.

7

The train chuffed to a halt before the Santa Fe depot. Hooked onto a long string of boxcars was a lone passenger coach. The conductor opened the door and stepped outside.

Elizabeth emerged from the coach, followed by John Taylor. He walked ahead, her leather carryall in one hand and his warbag in the other. At the end of the stationhouse, he signaled one of the horse-drawn cabs waiting on the street. The driver hopped down to assist with the luggage.

All the other passengers were men. They rushed past Elizabeth, hurrying toward the line of cabs. By the time she crossed the platform, Taylor was waiting beside the open door. He assisted her inside and ordered the driver to take them to the Exchange Hotel. They settled back for the short ride uptown.

Santa Fe lay in the shadow of the Sangre de Cristos. At an altitude of seven thousand feet, the town was surrounded by mountain ranges. Across the river from the train station was a broad plaza dominated by the governor's palace. The architecture was mostly adobe and the plaza was crowded with shops and businesses.

The date was April Fool's Day. Approaching the plaza, Elizabeth thought there would be few practical jokes exchanged today. An urgent wire from Ira Hecht had summoned her to Santa Fe. Though somewhat cryptic in nature, the message hinted at a political emergency. Hecht was the coordinator and chief strategist of her reform coalition.

Elizabeth's association with Hecht went back to 1881. As a stepping-stone into politics, she had organized a legal-assistance service for poor *mexicanos*. Her purpose was to combat widespread land frauds by Anglo speculators. Hecht, an idealistic young attorney, had been selected as head of the operation. Working together, they had assembled a network of lawyers throughout the territory. Their efforts in the courts had brought about judgments favoring small landowners.

Opposition to reform was centered around the Santa Fe Ring, an unsavory alliance. The Ring members were principally influential Republicans who controlled the economic lifeblood of the territory. At the time, the mastermind behind the Ring was a man named Stephen Benton. He commonly resorted to violence and assassination as a means of enforcing his will. Finally he'd gone too far by ordering the murder of Virgil Brannock. A week later, Clint had killed him in a shootout on the plaza.

With Benton's death, the Santa Fe Ring had fallen into temporary disarray. Elizabeth and Hecht, working swiftly, had created a coalition of *mexicanos* and progressive Anglos. Since then, they had managed to elect roughly half the members of the territorial legislature. But the Ring still controlled the other half, and a new leader had emerged in the person of Thomas Canby. Wiser than his predecessor, Canby refrained from violence and relied instead on racial animosity. He masterfully pitted the Anglos against the native New Mexicans.

Unlike other border regions, New Mexico was never a melting pot of cultures. An influx of Anglos into Texas and Arizona had swamped the *mexicano* population. But the descendants of the colonial Spaniards still constituted a majority in New Mexico Territory. Stubbornly resistant to change, they held to their language and their traditional way of life. In effect, they refused to adapt, even in their attitude toward politics. They clung to the customs of another time, their Old World values.

The problem was a constant source of friction within Elizabeth's coalition. At the top of the social order were the *ricos*, men with large holdings in livestock and land. By tradition, they provided the leadership at the local level, and their wealth enabled them to exert a great deal of influence. For the most part, the native political bosses—the *jefes políticos*—were the tools of the *ricos*.

The *mexicanos*, by and large, tended to support the system. Their principal concern was sufficient land to farm and adequate pasture for their stock. Tradition dictated that the common man had no interest in politics beyond the local level. By custom, the larger affairs of government were left to men of position and wealth, the *ricos*. So it was that a small group of men determined the results of any election. County offices, as well as seats in the territorial legislature, were controlled by an old and established order.

Elizabeth's goal was to forge a coalition of Anglos and *mexicanos* that would work to everyone's benefit. Yet the *ricos* were jealous of their power and evidenced little interest in social change. The *jefes políticos*, who were ambitious and interested in feathering their own nests, were often more susceptible to the idea of a coalition. Still another group, known as the young *políticos*, was opposed to both the *ricos* and the old-line *jefes*. A new order of *mexicano* politicians, they were pragmatic and not bound by ancient customs.

Any alliance, even with an Anglo, was worthy of consideration.

All the factional bickering weakened the coalition. Elizabeth urged unity for the common good, and spent half her time refereeing disputes. A running climate of intrigue kept the *ricos*, the *jefes*, and the young *políticos* jockeying for position. Added to all that was the attitude of many progressive Anglos who supported her efforts. They saw the *mexicanos* as politically naive, unable to grasp the larger concept of solidarity. The coalition, in no small measure, survived in spite of itself.

On the ride uptown, Elizabeth wondered what new emergency awaited her. After checking into the hotel, she took a few minutes to freshen up and change her dress. Then she met Taylor in the lobby and they walked to the corner, skirting the plaza on the north side. West of the business area, they proceeded along a sidestreet and turned into a storefront office. The interior was sparsely furnished with a rolltop desk, several wooden armchairs, and a row of file cabinets. A faded picture of Abraham Lincoln hung over the desk.

Hecht greeted them with obvious relief. He was small and slightly built, his eyes magnified by thick-lensed glasses. His mild, unobtrusive appearance belied both his zealousness and a brilliant legal mind. He fought oppression as though ordained for the task.

"Glad you're here," he said, motioning them to chairs. "Sorry if my wire sounded a bit vague. I couldn't afford to put the information over the telegraph."

"What information?" Elizabeth asked. "I hope it's nothing to do with the coalition."

"Yes and no," Hecht said, his eyes grave. "You'll recall I've developed various sources of intelligence.

One of them is a *mexicano* servant in the governor's palace."

"And?"

"There's a strong rumor circulating among the governor's staff. So far, it hasn't gone past that stage. It's all very hush-hush."

Elizabeth looked at him seriously. "What sort of rumor?"

"From what I gather," Hecht said hastily, "Governor Ross has gone off the deep end. He intends to declare war on *Las Gorras Blancas*."

"That's insane," Elizabeth said, clearly alarmed. "Any official move against the White Caps would merely enhance their cause. He'll make martyrs of them."

"It gets worse," Hecht said, his voice low and troubled. "I understand the governor plans to issue a dead-or-alive warrant on Miguel Ortega."

"Oh, my God!"

Elizabeth appeared stunned. Miguel Ortega was the leader of a secret organization known as *Las Gorras Blancas*, or White Caps. The name stemmed from the fact that they wore masks to conceal their identity. Ortega and his night riders, all *mexicanos*, employed organized violence as a means of intimidation. Their avowed enemies were large Anglo landholders.

The animosity was an outgrowth of disputes over the land. Anglo cattlemen were drawn to New Mexico by the lure of old Spanish land grants. The grants were mired in a tangled body of law and imprecise boundaries, which provided loopholes for the stockgrowers. Their purpose was to acquire title to grazeland by right of possession. The instrument of their landgrabbing scheme was barbed wire.

The *mexicanos* were bitterly opposed. Under Spanish rule, and later under the Mexican government, land grants were awarded to groups of settlers. By tradition, as well as official decree, ownership of the land was communal. House plots and patches of farmland were considered the personal property of individuals. But pasturelands and watering holes, the bulk of any grant, were shared by all. Grant boundaries were vague and unimportant, for use of the land was determined by ancient custom.

Nothing in the *mexicanos'* culture prepared them for the concept of "owning" water. Nor were they able to accept the idea of communal pastureland being deeded to a single individual. Anglo cattlemen, on the other hand, were insistent on private ownership. Their method was to acquire title to land along streams and rivers, filing claim under the Homestead Act. By agreement among themselves, cattlemen declared that a rancher's range covered all grazeland served by his water rights. *Mexicano* farmers were effectively displaced from their ancient Spanish grants.

Still another dodge was employed by large cattlemen. They obtained ownership to land within a grant by purchasing title from the original holder. Afterward, they argued that title to house lots and cultivated fields also included an interest in the communal lands. The *mexicanos* contended that common lands could never pass into absolute ownership. Without the consent of all grant holders, they asserted, the land could not be divided into parcels.

The stockgrowers' response was barbed wire. After purchasing a tract, they would often string fences across vast sections of the communal land. Along streams and rivers, where homesteads had been filed, they would fence in all land bordering the waterways. Further, without the shadow of a title, the cattlemen proceeded to erect fences on great stretches of public domain. Their attitude was that possession represented nine points of the law. Barbed wire made it a reality.

To Elizabeth, it was like a recurrent nightmare. During the early 1880s, she had battled land fraud throughout the territory. With Ira Hecht, and the lawyers of the legal-assistance service, she had won the fight in the courts. Land speculators, who relied on phony surveys and political bribes, were effectively routed. Legal precedents were established which protected *mexicanos'* rights under the old Spanish grants. Wholesale land fraud became a thing of the past.

Then, not quite two years ago, barbed wire found its way to New Mexico. Promptly dubbed "the devil's hatband," its prickly spikes enabled a rancher to contain vast herds of cattle. No less significant, it made anyone who crossed the fenceline a trespasser on private property. Streams and rivers were fenced off, and *mexicano* shepherds were denied access to traditional grazelands. Barbed wire, in large degree, replaced the shady land speculators of years past. The Spanish grants were once again under siege.

As before, Elizabeth championed the cause of the common man. Her reform movement was composed of small ranchers and hardscrabble Anglo farmers as well as *mexicanos*. Yet these were poor people, and apart from the sums she contributed, the coalition was always strapped for funds. Her opposition, headed by Thomas Canby, suffered under no such limitations. The Santa Fe Ring, and its political apparatus, was generously funded by large cattlemen. Their donations ensured the ranchers a strong voice in the legislature.

The embittered *mexicanos* saw their way of life being destroyed. For them, a return to the traditional use of common land represented survival itself. By custom, however, they had never sought redress of wrongs through legislative assemblies or the vote. Nor were they willing to trust *gringo* courts for an equitable settlement of their grievances. Their choice was sullen acceptance or direct action, and they were a people who placed great honor on a man's defense of his rights. Barbed wire finally pushed them over the edge.

Miguel Ortega was a phantom. Little was known about him before he formed the original cadre of *Las Gorras Blancas*. But the movement spread rapidly, gaining strength and members, operating under a tight code of silence. Their targets were the landgrabbers, the complex of bankers, ranchers, and railroads, those who profited at the expense of the people. They stampeded cattle herds, ripped out railroad tracks, and burned Anglo businesses to the ground. The unifying symbol of their hatred was barbed wire.

Within the past year the White Caps had destroyed untold miles of fenceline. Tangled bales of wire were heaped atop a pile of fenceposts and turned into a bonfire. Anglo ranchers found threatening notes tacked to their doors, ordering them off the land. In several instances, when cattlemen fought back, their barns and outbuildings had been razed. Earlier in the year, the home of the Surveyor General had been torched within sight of the territorial capitol. No one had yet been killed, but the level of violence steadily increased.

"There's more bad news," Hecht said now. "Thomas Canby and his cronies have submitted a petition to Congress. They want a special court established to settle the land disputes."

Elizabeth regarded him thoughtfully. "I assume their own judges would be appointed to the court. And rule against the *mexicanos*."

"Exactly," Hecht said, then shrugged. "It's larceny on a grand scale. Millions upon millions of acres."

"What position has the governor taken?"

"Complete cooperation," Hecht replied. "He added his official endorsement to the request."

"Well—" Elizabeth said after a long pause. "It appears the governor no longer represents the people. He's joined forces with Canby and the Santa Fe Ring."

Hecht nodded solemnly. "That's how I assess it."

"I daresay two can play at the game. Contact our friends in Washington and let them know we oppose the plan. Ask them to lobby against its passage."

"I can try," Hecht said with no inward conviction. "Frankly, I think it's a waste of time and energy. Canby has the resources to bribe every politician in Washington."

"In that event," Elizabeth remarked, "perhaps I should have a talk with the governor. If nothing else, I might persuade him to change his mind about Miguel Ortega."

Hecht shook his head wonderingly. "I could sell tickets to that little dust-up. He hates outside interference worse than the devil hates holy water."

"Then he shouldn't have sold his soul to the Santa Fe Ring."

The meeting ended on that note. Taylor, who hadn't said a word throughout the conversation, exchanged a knowing smile with Hecht. Neither of them doubted that Elizabeth would beard the governor in his own den. Around Santa Fe, she was spoken of as "a woman with starch in her corset." She never took no for an answer.

The governor's palace occupied the entire west side of the plaza. A vast sprawl of adobe, it had been built in 1609 by the first Spanish viceroy. At various times it had flown the flags of Spain, Mexico, and the Confederacy. Following the Mexican War, it became the official capitol of New Mexico Territory. The governor's offices and living quarters occupied the central portion of the building.

Outside the main entrance, Elizabeth stumbled onto Thomas Canby. He was emerging as she and Taylor approached, and he quickly tipped his hat. A man of intellect and charm, he was of medium stature with agatelike eyes and tufts of snowy hair. He exuded the bearing and presence that comes with power.

"Mrs. Brannock," he said, scrupulously polite. "I heard you were in town."

Elizabeth forced a smile. "I must say you're well-informed, Mr. Canby. I've only just arrived."

"And here you are," Canby said genially. "I hope you have an appointment with the governor. He's somewhat pressed for time today."

"I presume you would know better than most. I understand you have his ear these days."

"Shifting tides," Canby said with a dry, scornful chuckle. "The ebb and flow of politics, Mrs. Brannock."

"No doubt," Elizabeth replied with perfect civility. "Although I would have thought 'strange bedfellows' the more appropriate axiom."

Canby laughed and again tipped his hat. Elizabeth moved past him into a central hallway, trailed closely by Taylor. She entered an anteroom and announced herself to the governor's appointments secretary. The man asked her to wait, then slipped through the door of an inner office. Taylor took a seat on a wide leather sofa.

A few moments later Elizabeth was ushered through the door. Governor Edmund Ross greeted her with feigned good humor. He was a huge man, with muttonchop sideburns and sweeping mustaches. As a political appointee, he owed allegiance to no one except the president. Still, he'd learned to respect Elizabeth's pragmatic approach to a man's game. He motioned her to a chair.

"Good of you to drop by," he said expansively. "Compared to my usual visitors, you're like a breath of fresh air."

"I know," Elizabeth said, smiling sweetly. "I just ran into Tom Canby on his way out."

Ross chose to ignore the gibe. "Well, now," he said pleasantly, "what brings you to see me, Mrs. Brannock? Nothing serious, I trust."

"I believe 'crisis' would be the better word."

"What seems to be the problem?"

Elizabeth looked at him without expression. "I understand you've endorsed Canby's scheme. The petition requesting a land-claims court."

Ross nodded sagely. "It's hardly a scheme, Mrs. Brannock. Such a court will resolve one of the most critical issues of our time."

"On the contrary," Elizabeth corrected him. "Canby and his crowd will handpick the judges. Every decision rendered will favor Anglo business interests and large ranchers."

"Aren't you being a tad too cynical?"

"Aren't you supposed to be the governor of *all* the people? You've endorsed a scheme that will deliberately discriminate against *mexicano* landowners."

"Don't presume to lecture me," Ross said with a flare of annoyance. "Until you have a better idea, I suggest you reserve judgment."

"By tomorrow, a bill will be introduced on the floor of the legislature. And it will be far more equitable for everyone concerned."

Elizabeth went on to explain. She proposed an act that would allow landholders within a grant to file for incorporation. An elected board of trustees would then determine the legitimate landowners and the extent of their holdings. All communal lands would be administered by the trustees.

"In effect," she concluded, "it would allow the people to resolve their own differences—with no outsiders involved."

Ross angled his head critically. "What it would do is guarantee a *mexicano* board of trustees. And those trustees would in turn rule against the cattlemen. I could never sign such a bill."

Elizabeth returned his gaze steadily. "Your veto would have grave political consequences, Governor. It would publicly brand you a tool of the Santa Fe Ring."

"Pure tripe," Ross said, his voice tight. "I do my duty as I see it, Mrs. Brannock. I'm certainly not accountable to you."

"Just between us . . ." Elizabeth paused, looked him directly in the eyes. "If you were an elected official—accountable to all the people—that *would* change your mind. Don't you agree?"

"No, I do not," Ross said curtly. "Now, unless you have something further to discuss . . ."

"One more thing," Elizabeth informed him. "I hear you're planning some sort of action against *Las Gorras Blancas*. Is that true?"

Ross's tone turned cold. "I will not allow a gang of thugs to terrorize the countryside. I intend to stop them."

"Governor, I've never for a moment condoned their methods. However, they have widespread support within the *mexicano* community. Any aggressive act on your part might very well incite more violence."

"I accept the risk," Ross retorted. "New Mexico will not be held hostage to a ragtag band of revolutionaries."

Elizabeth forced herself to stay calm. "I also heard you plan to issue a warrant for Miguel Ortega—dead or alive."

Ross strummed the tip of his nose. "You'll be interested to know I've arranged the transfer of your brother-in-law. He's en route to Santa Fe at this very moment."

"Clint?" Elizabeth looked at him, astounded. "You're assigning Clint to catch Ortega?"

"I can think of no one better qualified for the job. He's the most respected manhunter of our day. I suspect he'll make short work of Señor Ortega."

"Then it's true," Elizabeth said, openly concerned. "You want Ortega dead."

"I want law restored," Ross said with chilling simplicity. "Whatever measures I take are meant for the common good."

"Don't be absurd! You and Tom Canby have already rendered a verdict. And you've selected Clint as your executioner."

"Your words, Mrs. Brannock, not mine."

Elizabeth stormed out of the office. Taylor jumped to his feet and fell in beside her as she swept through the hallway. On the street, she abruptly stopped, staring blankly across the plaza. She seemed overwhelmed by the irony of the situation.

For years she'd wanted nothing more than to have Clint home again. And now, for all the wrong reasons, he was returning to New Mexico. She thought God had a warped sense of humor.

8

A midday sun stood fixed in the sky. Lincoln's three saloons were serving the noontime crowd and several loafers were congregated on the courthouse porch. Horses lined the hitch racks along the street.

Morg dismounted outside the clinic. He was riding a blood-red bay with a blaze face and four white stockings. He left the gelding at the hitch post and turned toward the walkway. He was whistling softly to himself.

Scarcely ten days past, Morg had returned from the Cherokee Outlet. His head was buzzing with ideas, some good and some not so good. Foremost among them was the conviction that the Outlet ranch was operating on borrowed time. He remained convinced that all of Indian Territory would be opened to settlement. Pressure from homesteaders would merely speed the federal government's agenda.

Upon arriving at Spur, Morg hadn't paused to catch his breath. Louise had greeted him with teary-eyed happiness, demanding attention. But his thoughts were elsewhere, and he'd put her off with the press of other matters. Shortly after walking into the house, he had drawn his mother into her office and closed the door. Their discussion lasted until long past midnight.

The gist of Morg's argument centered on the Outlet. Like a swami, he'd peered into a crystal ball and seen the future. Sooner or later, it was inevitable that they would lose the ranch on Cherokee lands. The subsequent loss in revenue would represent a severe blow to their overall operation. He was convinced that they should diversify now, expanding into areas unrelated to cattle. He suggested a move into the timber business.

Elizabeth was taken aback. She'd never before considered a venture outside ranching. Yet Morg's assessment of the Outlet was grounded in solid logic, a blunt truth. Then too, he was his father's son and possessed that rare gift of foresight. While she knew nothing of the timber business, she saw the wisdom of spreading their interests into other fields. She asked for details.

The idea was no overnight bombshell. Morg was a keen observer of people and events. When it suited his purpose, he was also a good listener. Nor was his vision limited to the Hondo Valley and Spur. There was a questing quality about him, and it fed what amounted to an innate curiosity. The whys and wherefores were more interesting to him than the happening itself. He always looked for the reason.

Developments of the last few years intrigued him. One lay to the west of Lincoln, in the high-country mining camps. There, principally in the towns of Nogal and White Oaks, new discoveries had brought about a resurgence of boom times. Old mines were being reopened and new shafts were being sunk to previously unimagined depths. Quartz mining, conducted far underground, required substantial tunnels. And every tunnel required loads of stout timbers.

To the east lay the Pecos Valley. Formerly the domain of John "Jinglebob" Chisum, it was now populated by swarms of homesteaders and small farmers. Until the early 1880s, the land was thought to be unsuitable for anything except grazing cattle. But the area was riddled with artesian springs as well as tributaries branching off the Pecos River. Some men thought it might be transformed into bountiful farmland, with long growing seasons. The climate was temperate and the soil was rich with minerals.

On a ranch northeast of Roswell, Pat Garrett installed the first irrigation project. The former sheriff of Lincoln County, Garrett was better known as the man who had shot Billy the Kid. But his irrigation ditches, drawing on the Berrendo River, brought him newfound celebrity. Other farmers began irrigating from exposed artesian springs and there was talk of drilling wells to tap the underground reservoirs. By 1886, the Pecos Valley was dotted with farms, and land values had soared. Irrigation was proceeding at a feverish pace.

Field crops of wheat, corn, and oats thrived in the moderate climate. Alfalfa grew like wildweed and provided six cuttings over the season. Apple trees held the promise of vast orchards, and some farmers were experimenting with cotton. The town of Roswell expanded by leaps and bounds, with new businesses opening their doors every day. A building boom had been under way for the past year, and the population had swelled beyond all expectations. The Pecos Valley was reveling in a time of prosperity.

The growth of Roswell, added to the resurgence of the mining camps, produced a steady demand for lumber. The source of that timber lay in the Capitan Mountains, roughly north and west of Lincoln. At the lower elevations, below six thousand feet, the most common trees were cedar, piñon, and juniper. Far above, on the windswept slopes, were firs and aspen and spruces. In between, there was a vast forest of ponderosa pine, the prime source of commercial lumber. These stately giants were there for the taking.

Oddly enough, the demand for lumber far outstripped the supply. And that inconsistency, uncovered by Morg in his travels, had caused him to investigate further. He found several sawmills scattered throughout the mountains; but there was only one timber operator of any size. His name was Ralph McQuade and he carried less than twenty lumberjacks on his payroll. In effect, McQuade had a captive market and no competition. The door was wide open.

Morg proposed the organization of a timber company. He explained how it could be financed, using only a portion of the profits from the Outlet ranch. In his opinion, that made more sense than plowing money back into a cattle spread they would eventually lose. Lumberjacks could be found, and he estimated the initial investment at something less than $50,000. He believed the operation could turn a profit in six months, certainly no more than a year. From there on, the potential appeared to him virtually unlimited.

Elizabeth agreed. As with the ranch, the timber project would be a family enterprise. She arranged for funds to be shifted into a new bank account designated the Brannock Timber Company. The project was Morg's creation and she wisely gave him a free hand. Her one condition was that he not ignore his duties at Spur, which would remain the foundation of all they might achieve in the future. Other than that, she asked nothing more than to be kept abreast of events.

For the next week, Morg was like a perpetual-motion machine. West of Lincoln, he leased a thousand acres of mountainous timberland. He then journeyed north, touring logging camps in the Sangre de Cristos range. Higher wages, abetted by a case of whiskey, enabled him to pirate a crew of lumberjacks, complete with foreman. On his way home, he stopped off in Albuquerque, ordering various pieces of equipment. All the basic supplies for a camp were ordered at the general store in Lincoln.

By the end of the week, his personal life was a
wreck. Louise hardly spoke to him when he returned
home, greeting him with cool indifference. She walked
around in a snit, as though punishing him with her
silence. While the tactic got his attention, his mind
was still diverted by the timber project. For the first
time in his life, he had complete control of a business
enterprise, absolute authority. The prospect proved to
be heady stuff, and his energy was boundless.

Today marked an end to the planning phase of the
operation. His new foreman, along with five lumberjacks and the camp cook, were due to arrive on the
east-bound stage. Tomorrow, the balance of the crew,
another half-dozen lumberjacks, was scheduled to arrive. Four wagonloads of equipment and supplies were
parked behind the store, and teams of draft horses
were stalled in the livery stable. He'd left nothing
undone on a checklist that ran to several pages. The
Brannock Timber Company was ready to commence
operations.

Entering the clinic, he found Jennifer taking lunch
with her assistants. He accepted a cup of coffee, but
excitement stilled his appetite. When he refused anything to eat, Jennifer walked him from the kitchen to
the privacy of her office. She thought he looked like a
man who had discovered the secret of winged flight.
His nervous energy was disconcerting to watch, and
she wondered when he'd last slept. He kept pacing to
the window, darting glances upstreet.

"Calm down," Jennifer admonished. "You know
the stage never runs on time. It's always late."

"Helluva note," Morg grumped. "Today of all days."

Jennifer tried to distract him. "How's Louise? Any
change in her condition?"

"Not that you'd notice. She's her usual self—snippy
and out of sorts."

"That's not uncommon with pregnant women. They feel bloated and unattractive, particularly with their first child. Quite often their personalities undergo a pronounced change."

"Tell me about it," Morg said peevishly. "She acts like I got her in a family way out of spite. Hell, she's the one that wanted a baby!"

Jennifer sniffed. "I suppose you never gave it a thought. Or don't you know how babies are made?"

"C'mon, sis," Morg groaned. "I've got enough worries without that. If you have to lecture somebody, lecture Louise."

"Well, you might try paying more attention to her. I mean, after all, she's only nineteen! She needs reassurance."

"Yeah, and I've been busier than a one-legged man in a kicking contest. I could use a little appreciation myself."

"Fiddlesticks," Jennifer chided him. "You've never needed reassurance in your entire life. I wonder that you haven't gotten chapped lips from kissing cold mirrors."

"Think I'm sold on myself, do you?"

"You're cocky as a barnyard rooster. You always have been."

Morg mugged, hands outstretched. "Guess that's what makes me a prince of a fellow. And you don't have to take my word on it. Everybody says so."

"God, you're impossible," Jennifer said, suppressing a smile. "Not to change the subject, but I had a wire from Mother. She's coming home tomorrow."

"Wonder what happened in Santa Fe. She lit out of here like her skirts were on fire."

"I haven't the vaguest idea. Of course, she thrives on all that political skulduggery. I think she'd really like to be governor."

"No, you're wrong," Morg said, a grin plastered on his face. "She'd rather pull the strings and watch everybody dance. She's got the knack for it, too."

"Perhaps," Jennifer said in a musing tone. "But it's a shame women don't have the vote. She could be elected to any office she wanted."

Full of himself, Morg laughed. "Speaking of women and babies . . . when are you gonna get married?"

"None of your business," Jennifer said airily. "I rarely give it a thought."

"Who're you kidding?" Morg joked. "Even lady doctors get the hankering now and then. You're still human."

Jennifer enjoyed the bantering. She was reminded that Morg was her closest friend as well as her brother. While she was away at medical school, she'd feared all that might change. Yet, upon returning, she found that Morg harbored no resentment about her education. He admired her accomplishment, but he had no desire himself to attend college. He valued instead the lessons won from experience. What he called "the school of hard knocks."

When Jennifer looked at him, she often saw a younger version of her father. A man of limited education, her father had possessed a steel-trap mind and the courage to dare greatly. He was the product of an era when bold men challenged a raw frontier with gritty determination. Before his death, he had achieved the aura of legend, one of the rough-hewn pioneer visionaries. She saw those same characteristics in Morg, coupled with fierce ambition. She thought their father would have been proud.

A tingling sensation swept over her. While she'd never considered it in just that light, she saw it now as a full-blown revelation. Her mother was the most powerful woman in New Mexico, commanding the respect

of friends and enemies alike. Her brother was a bur-
geoning timber baron, smart and resourceful, capable
of one day assuming the mantle of Spur. And she
herself was the first, not to mention the only woman
doctor in the whole of the territory. So her father's
legacy had been borne out just as he'd intended. Nobody in the Brannock family rested on his laurels.

"Here they come!"

Morg whooped and turned toward the door. From
the window, Jennifer watched as he hurried up the
street. She saw a gang of tough-looking men climb out
of the stagecoach and gather before the express office.
Then Morg burst into their midst, shaking hands and
talking a mile a minute. His face was split in a nut-
cracker grin.

She thought the timber business would never again
be the same.

The Capitan Mountains towered against the skyline.
Sierra Blanca rose twelve thousand feet in the air, the
summit still capped with snow. A westering sun limned
the craggy battlements in a coppery glow.

By midafternoon the wagons were approaching timber country. Morg rode out front on his bay gelding,
blazing a trail where no roads existed. The campsite
he'd selected was on the southern slope of a forested
mountain. A stream, cascading over jumbled rocks,
swept past a natural clearing. With water for men and
animals, it seemed made to order for a logging camp.

Ponderosa pines, like tall sentinels, marched onward beyond sight. The thousand acres leased by Morg
were strategically located. Abutted on three sides by
public domain, the parcel provided access to a limitless sea of timber. Having done his homework, he was
aware that the federal government placed little value

on remote wilderness lands. There was no watchdog agency to regulate, or hinder, the timber companies.

Loopholes in the Homestead Act permitted timber outfits to harvest millions of acres originally intended for settlement. In mountainous areas, where the land was unsuited for farming, the logging companies became squatters on public domain. The Timber and Stone Act of 1878 provided a loophole of even greater proportions. Under the law, an individual was allowed to buy 160 acres of land "unfit for cultivation" at a price of $2.50 per acre. Land speculators and timber operators hired front men to file on thousands of quarter-sections, and thereby created sprawling domains of virgin forest. Great Lakes timber barons had used the ploy to reap untold millions in profits.

After careful consideration, Morg had added a new wrinkle. The leased parcel gave him a legitimate base, and from there he would expand the operation onto public domain. At some later time, he planned to recruit "dummy" applicants and file on quarter-sections at a cost of only $400 apiece. But for now, unfettered by government restrictions, he was content to harvest public-domain lands. The timber, in effect, was free for the taking.

Halting in the center of the clearing, he left the gelding ground-reined. Chunk Devlin, his new foreman, hopped down from the lead wagon. A burly man, Devlin was heavily built, with a bull neck and a square, thick-jowled face. He was a veteran of the Wisconsin logging camps, and more recently, the timber boss for an outfit supplying roadbed ties to the railroad. He looked like a cross between a pugilist and a circus strongman.

"What do you think?" Morg asked, gesturing around the clearing. "Good spot to set up camp?"

"I've seen worse," Devlin said in a stilled rumble. " 'Course, my boys ain't persnickety. We'll make do."

"How long till we get into operation?"

"Well, as to that, it's first things first. We've gotta build ourselves a bunkhouse and a privy and a corral for the animals. I'd say no more'n a week at the outside."

"Sounds good," Morg said, nodding. "I've got teamsters and wagons ready whenever you are. All we need is timber."

"And timber you'll have!" Devlin said with a wide peg-toothed grin. "All you want and all you can haul."

Some while later Morg rode out of the clearing. At the edge of the treeline, he paused and looked back. Devlin was already barking orders like a Prussian sergeant major. The lumberjacks and the cook jumped every time he yelled.

San Patricio was a small village near the juncture of the Rio Bonito and the Rio Hondo. Deep in the foothills, it was some five miles southeast of Lincoln. The sole industry, supporting fully half the villagers, was lumber.

Tipton's Sawmill was located on the banks of the Rio Hondo. Harry Tipton was lean and weathered, bald as a tonsured monk, with a mouthful of teeth like old yellowed dice. He operated the mill with the benign manner of an indulgent *patrón*. The villagers affectionately called him *ancianito*.

Shortly before sundown Morg dismounted outside the mill. The building was essentially a long open-sided shed, roofed with shingles and ankle-deep in sawdust. Huge circular saws occupied one side and board planers were arrayed along the other. The equipment was operated by *mexicano* workers and powered by a wood-burning steam engine. A cubbyhole office was tacked on to one end of the structure.

At the far end of the building, four men were unloading the last log from a heavy-duty lumber wagon. Morg recognized one of them as his chief competitor, Ralph McQuade. A face appeared at the window of the office; then the door opened and Tipton hurried outside. His face was wreathed in a troubled frown and his manner was curiously edgy. His palm was damp when he shook hands with Morg.

"Hello, Harry," Morg said affably. "Thought I'd stop by and give you the news. I got my men started working on the camp today. Ought to have the first load of timber in a couple of weeks."

"You've come at a bad time," Tipton informed him. "I've just had words with McQuade."

"What's the problem?"

"You," Tipton said simply. "Until now, McQuade's had a lock on the timber business. He's hopping mad."

Morg laughed shortly. "Don't let it worry you, Harry. He'll get used to the idea."

"Maybe, maybe not." Tipton paused, shook his head ruefully. "McQuade's a rough customer. He's liable to cause trouble."

"For you," Morg asked, "or for me?"

"Hard to say one way or the other. I just know I don't trust him."

"Well, let's not jump at shadows. He'll most likely cool down."

"Here he comes!" Tipton hissed. "Watch your step."

Morg turned, thumbs hooked in his belt. He'd heard that McQuade had a reputation as a brawler, and his first impression confirmed the stories. A gnarled, lynx-eyed man, McQuade was beefy through the shoulders and padded with muscle from a lifetime of physical labor. He lumbered to a halt, glowering at Morg.

"You and me need to have a talk."

"All right by me," Morg said lazily. "What's on your mind?"

"You're crowding me," McQuade said, his voice brittle with hostility. "I don't like people horning in on my business."

"Last I heard, it was a free country. Nobody needs permission to cut timber."

"Yeah, you do," McQuade bristled. "Around here, I'm bull-o'-the-woods. I aim to keep it that way."

"Bull-o'-the-woods?" Morg repeated, as though mildly entertained. "What happens when you meet cock-o'-the-walk?"

"You sayin' you're not gonna back off?"

"Sounds that way, don't it?"

"I'm warnin' you," McQuade said churlishly, "don't crowd me no further. You do and you'll wish you hadn't."

Morg laughed in his face. "Whenever you get the urge, wade right in. I enjoy a good scrap, myself."

McQuade's hands hardened into fists. His features mottled with anger and he seemed on the verge of swinging. Morg stared him straight in the eye, challenging him. At last, with an unintelligible oath, the logger wheeled away. Morg let out a slow breath, looked at Tipton.

"Harry, I think you're right. One of these days he's gonna try to haul my ashes."

"Stay away from him," Tipton cautioned. "I've seen him work men over something awful. He fights dirty, no holds barred."

"What the hell," Morg said lightly. "I've been in some knock-down-drag-outs myself. Half the boys on Spur were weaned on tiger spit."

"You just remember what I said. He's loco mean when he comes unwound."

"I'll keep it in mind."

From San Patricio, Morg followed a rutted wagon road along the Rio Hondo. Darkness fell as he crossed onto Spur land and rode toward the headquarters compound. His first day in the timber business had been more eventful than expected. What concerned him most was that McQuade had picked an argument and then backed off. It seemed somehow out of character, and therefore suspicious.

He decided to keep a sharp lookout.

9

Three days before Easter, Clint rode into Santa Fe. On the west side of the plaza, he reined to a halt before the governor's palace and dismounted. He left his horse tethered to the hitch rack.

The U.S. marshal's office was at the south end of the plaza. His gaze fixed on the tall granite monument commemorating the Civil War dead. Erected in the center of the plaza, the monument was a local landmark.

Some six years ago Clint had killed two men at the base of the monument. One was Stephen Benton, the man responsible for his brother's murder. The other was Benton's bodyguard, a hired gun and sometime assassin. In the aftermath of the shootout, a political deal had been struck, and all charges were dropped. The one condition was that Clint get out of New Mexico.

Today, staring at the monument, he smiled with sardonic amusement. One Brannock had been exiled from New Mexico and three had returned. From Indian Territory, he'd crossed the Staked Plains with Lon and Hank. Late yesterday they had parted company at Lamy, a town southeast of Santa Fe. There, the boys had sold their horses and hopped a southbound train. Their destination was Lordsburg.

The choice had been made at Clint's suggestion. Lon wanted fast action and a crack at the high rollers.

Lordsburg, which was one of the richest mining camps in New Mexico, seemed a likely prospect. Apart from that, Clint intended to keep track of them, and a larger camp made the chore easier. At the first opportunity, he planned to contact the Lordsburg town marshal and request a professional courtesy. One way or another, he meant to keep an eye on the boys.

U.S. Marshal Fred Mather was expecting him. While they'd never met, Mather was aware of Clint's long record in law enforcement. Before being exiled from New Mexico, Clint had served for seven years as a special investigator for the army. The intervening years with Judge Parker's court had merely enhanced his reputation as a manhunter. Among peace officers, his name alone commanded respect.

Mather was a ruddy-faced man with a walrus mustache and a quiet voice. Like most U.S. marshals, he was an administrator rather than a seasoned lawman. He reported directly to the governor and had only eight deputy marshals to cover all of New Mexico Territory. His greeting was somewhat taciturn and his manner was decidedly enigmatic. He refused to answer any questions about the transfer until Clint had spoken with Governor Ross. His choice of words indicated he was merely following orders.

Ten minutes later Clint found himself standing in the governor's office. Mather performed the introductions, then unobtrusively slipped out the door. Edmund Ross shook hands with a firm grasp and motioned to one of the leather armchairs before his desk. Clint took a seat and began rolling himself a smoke. All the secrecy seemed to him a bit overdone.

"First off," Ross said in an orotund voice, "let me say I personally requested your transfer. I advised the president that you're the only man for the job."

Clint struck a match, lit up in a cloud of smoke. "What job is that?"

"*Las Gorras Blancas*," Ross replied crisply. "Otherwise known as the White Caps. Have you heard of them?"

"Not that I recollect."

"Well, then, allow me to inform you that they are a threat to the very existence of New Mexico Territory. *Las Gorras Blancas* are nothing less than armed revolutionaries."

"I take it they're *mexicanos*?"

"Precisely," Ross intoned. "A large, well-organized conspiracy composed solely of *mexicanos*. Their leader is a fanatic by the name of Miguel Ortega."

"Never heard of him either," Clint said. "What are they revolting against, just exactly?"

Ross jackknifed to his feet. He paced back and forth behind his desk, his features florid. His voice rose an octave and he punctuated his speech with vigorous gestures. He briefly explained the *mexicanos'* hostility to Anglo business interests in general, and barbed wire in particular. He went on to recount a litany of violence and terror.

Earlier in the year, a San Miguel County grand jury had been convened. After the hearings, indictments were returned against twenty-three *mexicanos* for fence-cutting. That night, sixty masked horsemen brandishing firearms and torches galloped into town. They surrounded first the home of the county prosecutor, and then the courthouse. Their leader spoke of harsh retaliation should the fence-cutters be convicted. Following a quick trial, the jury voted acquittal.

A week later six thousand railroad ties had been destroyed in a mammoth bonfire. Three Anglo teamsters who witnessed the incident testified before a grand jury. When the case came to trial, the teamsters failed to appear, and hadn't been seen since. All charges were dismissed and the accused night riders were allowed to go free. Afterward, a crowd of nearly a thousand *mexicanos* gathered before the courthouse. The celebration was marked by fiery speeches and a fusillade of gunshots.

The sphere of violent outbreaks expanded. The night riders struck throughout Santa Fe County, Bernalillo County, and farther north, Colfax County. Business ground to a standstill, and the tide of homesteaders into New Mexico virtually ceased. *Las Gorras Blancas*, operating in secret, had all but defeated the justice system. Witnesses to the acts were now intimidated, and unwilling to testify. Juries, which were composed largely of *mexicanos*, were sympathetic to the night riders. Conviction, even with strong evidence, was no longer possible.

The governor returned to his chair. Unrest was spreading, he noted, and there was reason to believe the White Caps could forge a movement that would sweep all of New Mexico. President Cleveland was now convinced that the uprisings were part of an organized conspiracy. The goal was to achieve *mexicano* independence by forcing Anglos to flee the territory. *Las Gorras Blancas* would then move to reunite their homeland with Old Mexico.

"We're confronted with war," Ross concluded hotly. "A war we're certain to lose unless we somehow stop Miguel Ortega."

Clint mulled it over a moment. "What makes you think Ortega's that dangerous?"

"We have certain influential friends among the *mexicanos*. They tell us that Ortega patterns himself after Mexico's greatest revolutionary, Benito Juárez. You may recall that Juárez defeated the French emperor Maximilian—and won independence for Mexico."

"Why not call in the military? Sounds like it's a job for the army."

Ross shook his head. "The army's far too cumbersome to catch one man. We need a specialist for this job—someone like you."

Clint's eyes were impersonal. "What do you know about Ortega?"

"Not much," Ross admitted. "I understand he was a farmer before he turned revolutionary. As we've seen, however, he has a natural gift for leadership. His movement has increased a thousandfold in one year."

"Any idea where he might be found?"

"None," Ross confessed. "He's a will-o'-the-wisp, impossible to predict. However, we have reliable information as to his next objective. He plans to organize the White Caps in Lincoln County."

"Is that why you sent for me?"

"Who else knows Lincoln County better? Your family lives there and you've hunted outlaws all throughout that country. I'd say you're eminently qualified."

Clint took a long drag on his cigarette. He blew a perfect smoke ring toward the ceiling, watching it widen. "I'm not a *pistolero*," he said evenly. "I don't kill men on order. Not for you or anybody else."

Ross appraised him through narrowed eyes. "I'm not ordering you to kill Ortega. I want you to track him down and bring him to justice."

"And if he resists arrest?"

"I trust you to use your discretion, Marshal Brannock."

Clint just looked at him.

"One other thing," Ross went on. "Your sister-in-law is opposed to any move against Ortega or the White Caps. Do you have a problem with that?"

"You're saying she doesn't want Ortega killed."

"I believe that represents her main concern."

"Off the record"—Clint hesitated, staring across the desk— "what's your preference?"

"A speedy resolution," Ross said in a measured tone. "Without Ortega, the revolt will wither away. I want it handled in an expeditious manner."

Clint laughed harshly. "I'll do my damndest where Ortega's concerned. As for Elizabeth, I figure she's your problem. I never get involved in politics."

"A commendable attitude."

Ross stood, signaling an end to the interview. They shook hands and Clint walked from the room. Outside he turned downstreet and proceeded to the marshal's office. He found Mather seated behind a battered desk, shuffling papers. There was a moment of stiff silence.

"I passed muster," Clint said dryly. "From the way the governor talks, I've been appointed a one-man fire brigade."

"Quite a compliment," Mather observed neutrally. "Let's hope you can stop it from spreading any further."

Clint flipped a hand back and forth. "What's the latest on these White Caps?"

Mather let his gaze drift out the window. Speaking quietly, he underscored the theory that a revolution was building. The number of *mexicanos* involved in the raids indicated well-planned organization and central command. Within the various counties, no single village could provide the large forces of men engaged in such attacks. The similarity of tactics and targets also pointed to a highly coordinated campaign of terror. All the evidence led to an inescapable conclusion.

"No doubt about it," Mather said, turning from the window. "*Las Gorras Blancas* are actively trying to overthrow the government. Their goal is anarchy—open rebellion."

Clint examined a fingernail. "What was the last report on Ortega?"

"Lincoln County," Mather stated firmly. "We know he's meeting secretly with the *mexicano* leaders. Word's out that he's moving from village to village."

Clint nodded, thoughtful. "The governor stopped just short of ordering me to kill Ortega. How do you feel about it?"

Mather grinned unpleasantly. "I think you'll never take Ortega alive. He's shrewd and he's tough, a real bad hombre. He won't quit without a fight."

Clint accepted the statement at face value. Something told him he'd heard the straight goods, even though no one wanted to say it out loud. A warrant for Miguel Ortega's arrest amounted to a death sentence. A one-way ticket to hell.

And he'd been selected to "expedite" the journey.

On Good Friday the villagers of San Patricio began gathering outside the church. Evening services were scheduled on this holiest of holy days, two nights before Easter Sunday. By ancient custom, the rites were in commemoration of the Crucifixion.

The mood of the villagers was solemn. Congregated out front were the women and children. The men were simply dressed and the women and young girls wore black mantillas draped over their heads. An air of hushed expectancy seemed to permeate the gathering.

Elizabeth stood at the rear of the crowd. She was accompanied by John Taylor and Félix Montoya, the local *jefe político*. At Montoya's insistence, she had finally agreed to attend the services. His reasons were vague, but over the past few days Montoya had persisted in his arguments. There seemed no way to decline without offending him.

The villagers, like almost all *mexicanos*, worshiped

Elizabeth. Her efforts on their behalf, whether in land frauds or the free medical clinic, elevated her to a position approaching sainthood. Even more, her long battle with the *gringo* bosses in Santa Fe was considered a mark of rare courage. Her charitable works throughout the Hondo Valley were equally well known, and she never flaunted her wealth. She was thought to be a true woman of the people.

For all that, Elizabeth still had no idea why she'd been invited to the services. Montoya, who was a short, rotund man with sagging jowls, had deftly evaded her questions. His position as *jefe político*, more than his badgering attitude, had finally persuaded her. A loyal member of her coalition, he had aided her in the past and would do so in future elections. Whatever his reason, he was calling in the debt for services rendered. She felt she had no choice but to accept.

A bell tolled from the church tower. For an instant, a low murmur swept through the crowd. Then the tolling stopped and the villagers abruptly went silent. Dusk turned to darkness, and an inky quiet settled over San Patricio. Off in the distance, the voice of a man, raised in an eerie chant, drifted down from the foothills. In the next instant, a column of fiery torches appeared out of the night. The chant grew louder.

Arrayed in single file, a column of some twenty men descended a rocky path from the westward hills. Half of them were dressed in monks' habits, wooden crucifixes suspended from their necks. The other half wore white cotton trousers and black hoods, their upper bodies bare. An elderly man, carrying a large silver cross, led the procession. Behind him, a cowled monk chanted prayers in a keening voice.

The men dressed in habits carried torches. Of the others, those naked above the waist, eight were soaked with blood. As they trudged into the village, they lashed themselves across the back and chest with short whips fashioned from sharp-thorned cactus spines. Still another man pulled a heavy wooden cart, a coarse horsehair harness strapped around his shoulders. Seated in the cart was a skeleton, cloaked in black, obsidian eyes set deep in the bleached skull. A drawn bow, with the arrow fixed for flight, was wired onto the skeleton's outstretched arms.

The last of the ten half-naked men wore a crown of thorns. He lurched forward, dripping blood, bowed beneath the weight of a cross constructed of hewn timbers. Outside the church he staggered to a halt and dropped to his knees, still supporting the cross on his shoulders. His back was scourged from repeated lashings, latticed with ugly welts and torn flesh. Unable to raise his head, he stared down at the stone steps with a hollow expression.

Elizabeth stood transfixed. Over the years she had heard of a mysterious order of Franciscan monks. Known as the Brotherhood of Penitents, they lived in the remote mountains of New Mexico and southern Colorado. Their order descended from St. Francis of Assisi and their mission was to care for the sick and the dying. Nearly five centuries ago the Roman Catholic Church had outlawed their rites of self-flagellation and scourging. Yet, after all that time, small bands still followed the ancient religious practices.

On Good Friday night, a procession of monks made their way to the church. The *penitentes* were brothers who vowed to flagellate themselves as the Roman soldiers had lashed Jesus. Their whips were yucca cactus, soaked in salt water, and drew blood with every stroke. They were led by the *hermano mayor*, the head brother, and prayers were recited from a religious text passed down from generation to generation.

The cart was called the *carreta del muerto*, and the skeleton represented the figure of Death.

To Elizabeth's knowledge, no Anglo had been permitted to witness the Good Friday ritual. Even Harry Tipton, who owned the sawmill, was instructed to remain indoors. She watched now as the brothers made their way inside the church and stopped before the altar. Prayers were offered and their voices were raised in doleful *alabados*, accompanied by the wail of a flute. At last, the candles were snuffed and the church went dark. The brothers slowly filed out the door.

Once more the *penitentes* began whipping themselves. The brother honored with the role of Jesus again shouldered his cross. Their chant resumed and the procession turned back toward the foothills. The villagers of San Patricio dutifully trailed along behind. Félix Montoya, urging Elizabeth to follow, assisted her on the rocky pathway. Taylor brought up the rear, the last man in line.

A short time later the procession halted on a barren hillside. The villagers fell to their knees, heads bowed, and began muttering prayers. The brothers gathered in a torchlit circle around the man burdened with the cross. Several *penitentes* removed it from his shoulders and laid it flat on the ground. His eyes vacant, the man lowered himself onto the cross, his arms outstretched and his ankles locked together. Other *penitentes* approached with hammers and spikes, and knelt at opposite ends of the crossbeam. Working quickly, they spread his hands wide and positioned spikes over the open palms. Their hammers flashed in the glow of torchlight.

Elizabeth's breath caught in her throat. The night echoed with a metallic ring as the spikes were driven through the man's hands. His mouth opened in a strangled scream and blood spurted with every stroke of the hammers. Elizabeth stared at him with wide-eyed horror and willed herself not to gag. Then the hammers fell silent and the *penitentes* raised the cross for all to see, holding the man aloft. His gaze was fixed, blind with pain, his hands studded to the wooden beam. The head brother led the onlookers in a murmured incantation.

A monk appeared at Elizabeth's side. He spoke her name and she looked around. Then, pushing the cowl off his head, he revealed himself in the torchlight. His features were hawklike, stark and strong, with deep-set onyx eyes and a thick black mustache. He was wiry, somewhat taller than the usual *mexicano*, and his gaze seemed oddly piercing. He nodded, a slight smile at the corners of his mouth.

"Permit me to introduce myself, *señora*. I am Miguel Ortega."

A startled expression crossed Elizabeth's face. She sensed movement as Taylor took a step forward, and motioned him away. "We meet at last," she said, collecting herself. "Was I brought here at your instructions, Señor Ortega?"

"A thousand pardons," Ortega apologized. "Here with the brotherhood seemed the safest place. As you know, I am a hunted man."

"I learned of it only this week. Governor Ross has branded you a revolutionary."

"The governor honors me," Ortega said, smiling broadly. "I am but a humble man working to protect my people. In fact, you and I are much alike, *señora*."

"Yes, perhaps we are," Elizabeth conceded. "Certain men in Santa Fe probably think of me as an *insurrecta*."

"I would not otherwise have arranged this meeting. Your sense of justice is without question."

"What is it you wish of me, Señor Ortega?"

"Your support," Ortega informed her. "Among my people you are known as *La Mariposa de Hierro*. Your name would do much to further our cause."

Elizabeth sounded uncertain. "How would my name benefit you?"

"Lincoln County will be our next battleground. I have come here to organize the people for the fight ahead. Were you to support my efforts, they would rush to join *Las Gorras Blancas*."

"I endorse your cause," Elizabeth temporized, "but I cannot condone your methods. Violence merely breeds more violence, and resolves nothing. I believe your goals will be won at the ballot box—not with guns."

Ortega's expression became immobile and dark. His mouth tightened and his eyes flashed with a formidable glitter. He stared at her with a strange, unsettling look.

"You are wrong, *señora*," he said in a low, intense voice. "For forty years, we tried peaceful means, and where has it gotten us? We are still *peones*, serving under a different master. The time for talk and reason is long past."

Elizabeth felt mesmerized. A messianic quality seemed to emanate from his eyes, and his voice burned with fervor. She understood now why the *mexicanos* were drawn to his cause, spoke his name with reverence. He was like a prophet of olden times, preaching liberty and freedom.

"We will fight," he went on confidently, "and we will win. No longer will we endure the oppression of *ladrones americanos*."

"I must tell you something," Elizabeth said, her voice soft and troubled. "Governor Ross has brought in a new lawman and ordered him to hunt you down. His name is Clint Brannock."

"*Ai, caramba*," Ortega muttered. "Your brother-in-law, *verdad*? I remember the name from long ago. A *pistolero*, very dangerous."

"Yes," Elizabeth said dismally. "Very dangerous and very determined. He won't stop until he finds you."

Ortega laughed. "I am not easily found."

"I am concerned as much for him as for you. He is very dear to me."

"Have no fear, *señora*. I will see to it that we never meet. In the meantime, consider yourself under my protection. *Las Gorras Blancas* will avoid the Hondo Valley. We do not harm our friends."

Elizabeth merely nodded. "I wish you well . . . *buena suerte*."

"*Vaya con Dios*."

With that, Ortega turned away. Elizabeth watched as he skirted the villagers and melted into the darkness. A moment later her attention was drawn to the torchlit circle. She saw the *penitentes* gently lower the crucified monk to the ground. She thought it somehow symbolic, and fearful.

Miguel Ortega might be martyred to yet another cause.

10

Lordsburg lay at the foot of the Pyramid Mountains. Some twenty miles from the Arizona border, the town was located in the southwestern corner of New Mexico. The earth in every direction was a vast repository of copper.

Lon and Hank stepped off the train on Easter Sunday. Their trip had taken them south from the Sangre de Cristo range and along the valley of the upper Rio Grande. After changing trains at Rincon, they had turned westward into a bleak wasteland of rock and sand. The sight of forested mountains brought a welcome end to their long journey.

For Hank, the trip had been a time of wonder. His entire life had been spent on the reservation, far removed from the white man's world. In three short weeks he'd crossed the fabled *Llano Estacado* and traveled through the better part of New Mexico Territory. What seemed the greater marvel, however, was his first train ride. The speeds attained by the locomotive still left him somewhat stupefied.

Even his physical appearance had been altered. At Lamy, the town where they'd parted company with Clint, Lon had introduced him to the wonders of the local tonsorial parlor. First, he'd soaped and scrubbed himself in the steamy waters of a great wooden bathtub. Then the barber trimmed his hair short and slicked

it back with sweet-smelling pomade. The next stop
was a mercantile, where Lon outfitted him from hat to
boots, with extra underdrawers and two extra shirts.
Their last purchase was a used .44-40 Colt, with belt
and holster.

The pistol still seemed strange. Crossing the depot
platform, Hank was all too aware of the weight on his
hip. On the reservation, he'd sometimes practiced shooting with Lon, and he remembered being amazed at his
brother's speed and accuracy. Yet he was uncomfortable carrying a gun, and he had accepted it only at
Lon's insistence. The Colt, like the new clothes and
his scalped haircut, were merely outward signs of
change. On the inside, he was still Bull Calf, a Quahadi
Comanche. And he felt himself an intruder in the land
of the *tahboy-boh*.

From the depot, Lon led the way uptown. Lordsburg
seemed to Hank a carnival in motion, and he could
hardly keep from gawking. The main street was a
hurdy-gurdy assortment of saloons and gaming parlors
and raucous dance halls. A mining camp was open
seven days a week, and Easter Sunday was no exception. The boardwalks were crowded with miners, and
ruby-lipped girls, decked out in spangles, were visible
through the doorways. Despite himself, Hank found
his mouth dropping open every few paces.

Lordsburg was originally a silver camp. In the late
1860s, a discovery lode had drawn prospectors from all
across the West. Over the next decade the town had
prospered in a boom-time atmosphere. Then the silver
began petering out and the emphasis shifted to copper. By 1881, when the Southern Pacific laid tracks
through the mountains, another boom was already
under way. Within a short ride from downtown, there
were eighty-five copper mines.

In large degree, Lordsburg was typical of Western

mining camps. For more than three decades, gold and silver were the mainstays of the mining industry. During the 1880s, however, the age of electricity ushered in an era that made copper a profitable venture. Thomas Edison's remarkable invention—the electric light—was spreading westward across the nation. A growing number of cities and towns were also installing telephones, as well as electric streetlamps and streetcars.

The advent of this new source of energy transformed the mining industry. Copper was previously a metal for which there was no market, and thus it had remained virtually untouched. But the demand mushroomed overnight when it was discovered that copper acted as a conductor for electricity. No less important was the expansion of the railroads into the remote, and sometimes isolated, mountainous camps. The ore could be brought to the surface, freighted to the smelters, and then transported eastward by rail. Exploitation of the West's vast copper deposits began in earnest.

At that point, prospectors and placer miners moved on to other diggings. Large corporations bought up the claims and undertook a search for minerals locked deep within the bowels of the earth. By 1887, copper was king, and Lordsburg was controlled by bankers and financiers. Absentee owners, generally a consortium of wealthy businessmen, pulled the strings from Denver and San Francisco. A thousand or more miners worked the underground shafts, and the monthly payroll exceeded a quarter-million dollars. The town entered still another era of boom-time prosperity.

Technology was the key to the financiers' takeover. A new invention—dynamite—was used to blast through the rock and excavate tunnels. Underground drilling, formerly done by hand, was now accomplished by power drills operating on compressed air. Working in tandem, dynamite and power drills made it possible to

burrow far beneath the earth's surface. Some operations were a thousand feet below the ground and extended through a labyrinth of tunnels.

As the mines probed ever deeper, the danger to
workers multiplied at an alarming rate. Safety measures were virtually nonexistent, and accidents became
commonplace. Men were killed and maimed by cave-
ins, sometimes drowned when subterranean springs
flooded the tunnels, and frequently incinerated when
fire swept through the timbered mine shafts. Yet there
was no shortage of men willing to risk their lives, and
most of the mines worked double shifts. The wages,
compared with other lines of work, were almost mu-
nificent. A cowhand's earnings were generally a third
of those paid to the lowliest miner.

For Lon, it represented an El Dorado. On the Texas
circuit, he'd been lucky to find a five-dollar-limit game.
By comparison, Lordsburg was a town of high rollers,
with table stakes more common than not. The gaming
parlors operated around the clock, and on any given
night a tidy fortune changed hands. He was anxious to
test his skills in a cutthroat check-and-bet game. He
doubted that miners understood poker any better than
Texican cattlemen.

Uptown, Lon paused and surveyed Lordsburg's three
hotels. They were all within a block of one another,
but only one had a veranda. Early on, he'd learned
that a gambling man had a certain reputation to maintain. Word got around, and high rollers preferred to
pit themselves against a gambler who displayed a taste
for the good life. Appearances counted among the
sporting crowd, and nowhere more than within the
gambling fraternity. A solid front invariably attracted
well-heeled players.

The hotel lobby confirmed Lon's judgment. Several
men, chatting and reading newspapers, were seated in

easy chairs and a lone horsehair sofa. The conversation ceased as Lon, trailed closely by Hank, came through the door. The men seemed particularly interested in the youngster, and their appraisal was somehow severe. Lon was aware of their scrutiny, but he chose to ignore it. He moved across the lobby, halting at the registration desk. He nodded to the clerk behind the counter.

"The name's Brannock," he said amiably. "I'd like the best room in the house."

The desk clerk was a gangling man with bony features. He gave Lon a quick once-over; then his gaze shifted to Hank. He subjected the boy to a slow up-and-down inspection, and his expression turned frosty. At length, he looked back at Lon.

"No offense," he said, "but we don't accommodate Indians. Our clientele wouldn't stand for it."

"We'll fix that," Lon said confidently. "Let me talk with the owner."

"I am the owner," the man replied. "You have to understand, there's still a lotta hard feeling in these parts. We lost some good men to the Apache."

"Well, you're in luck," Lon said, motioning to the boy. "Any fool could see he's not Apache."

"Still doesn't change anything. It's a policy of the house—no Indians."

"C'mon, Lon," Hank said, shuffling uneasily. "We'll go somewheres else."

Lon shook his head. He smiled without warmth, staring at the hotel owner. "Here's the story," he said in a faintly ominous tone. "Either I get a room or you better start packin' a gun. I won't be insulted."

"You can't threaten me! I'll have the law down on you."

"Go ahead," Lon told him. "You'll still wind up in the bone orchard. I give you my personal guarantee."

A tense silence settled over the lobby. The hotel owner saw something cold and implacable in Lon's gaze. His Adam's apple bobbed and he swallowed hard. After a moment, he produced a key and slapped it down on the counter. "You're in room two-o-one."

"Much obliged."

Lon grinned, nodding at Hank, then walked to the stairway. In their room, he seemed to dismiss the incident from mind. Unpacking his bag, he laid out a fresh shirt and his shaving gear. At the washstand, he poured water into a porcelain bowl and tested the edge on his straight razor. He glanced up and found Hank watching him in the mirror. He winked and began soaping his face.

"I think I'm gonna like this town, sport. Folks seem real friendly."

"Were you bluffin'," Hank asked, "or would you've shot him?"

"I only bluff at poker," Lon said jovially. "Anything else, I'm as good as my word. You oughta know that by now."

Somewhile later they emerged from the hotel. Lon stopped on the veranda and lit a cheroot. Exhaling smoke, he once again surveyed the string of saloons and gaming parlors. A sign across the street caught his eye and he nodded to himself. He led Hank toward the Tivoli Palace.

The batwing doors opened onto a combination saloon and gaming dive. The backbar was a gaudy clutch of bottles centered around a huge French mirror. On the opposite wall were three faro layouts, a chuck-a-luck game, and a twenty-one spread. Toward the rear, several tables with overhead coal-oil lamps were set aside for poker. There was no piano, no dance floor, and the atmosphere was subdued, almost businesslike.

From all appearances, it was a place devoted to serious gambling.

Lon thought he'd picked a likely spot. What appeared to be a high-stakes game was under way at one of the poker tables. He noted a shotgun guard perched on a tall chair just past the twenty-one spread. Throwing an arm over Hank's shoulders, he walked to the bar. A nearby drinker grumped something under his breath, then turned away. The bartender strolled over, arms folded across his chest.

"Whiskey for me," Lon said, "and a sarsaparilla for my partner."

The barkeep frowned. "You'll have to take your trade elsewhere. Injuns ain't allowed in here."

Lon grunted sharply. "Set 'em up and be damn fast about it. I'm not gonna tell you again."

"And I'm tellin' you to waltz the hell outta here."

A man at the end of the bar hurried forward. His features were coarse and an ugly scar traced a welt along his jawbone. From beneath his jacket the bulge of a short-barreled pistol was visible. He squinted querulously at Lon.

"What's the problem?"

Lon turned from the bar. "Who're you?"

"Ace McMasters. I own the joint."

"Then tell your barkeep to watch his mouth. I ordered a drink and I mean to have it."

"You heard him," McMasters growled. "We don't serve gut-eaters."

Lon gave him a slow go-to-hell smile. "You got a smart mouth yourself."

"Don't push it," McMasters said in a loud, hectoring voice. "Get moving before I bust you upside the head."

"You try it," Lon warned with cold menace, "and I'll make your asshole wink."

McMasters stepped clear, widening the space between them. The shotgun guard rose from his perch, thumbing the hammer on his sawed-off scattergun. All thought suspended, Lon acted on reflex alone. His hand dipped inside his coat and reappeared with a cocked pistol. He leveled the Colt and fired in one fluid motion.

The slug took the guard in the throat. His mouth opened in a breathless whoofing sound and the shotgun dropped from his hands. He teetered on the edge of his chair, then pitched forward and slammed facedown on the floor. A noxious stench filled the room as his bowels voided in death.

Lon wagged his pistol at the bar owner. McMasters froze, his belly-gun halfway out of the holster. A thick silence descended on the room and they stared at each other for a long moment. At last, avoiding any sudden movement, McMasters lowered his arm to his side.

"I call it self-defense," Lon said pointedly. "What do you call it?"

McMasters shrugged. "Guess I shouldn't've sicced him on you."

"Suppose you send for the marshal, Ace. I think he oughta hear you say that."

The bartender went to fetch Lordsburg's town marshal. Lon holstered his pistol, then glanced around, motioning to Hank. They moved past McMasters and walked to the poker table at the rear of the room. There were five players seated at the table and they watched silently as Lon stopped behind an empty chair. He looked from man to man, his mouth curled in a smile.

"Anybody object if I take a seat?"

Nobody objected.

Easter services always drew large crowds. There

were two churches in Lincoln, one Catholic and one
Methodist. *Mexicanos* had traveled long distances to
attend early-morning Mass. The Protestant congregation, comprising only Anglos, began filing into church
shortly before eleven.

Elizabeth was there with the entire family. In all,
they were six, including Brad and Blake Hazlett. Seated
in a front pew, they listened as the pastor delivered a
stirring sermon on the Resurrection. Afterward, the
organ wheezed to life and everyone joined in a final
hymn. Services concluded on the stroke of twelve.

The pastor stationed himself just outside the front
door. As the congregation filed past, he shook hands
with the men and exchanged pleasantries with the
women. Elizabeth, as the matriarch of the town's most
prominent family, was greeted with unusual warmth.
Her generous contributions, which represented fully a
third of the annual budget, made her presence all the
more noteworthy. Had she been a man, the church
elders would have unanimously elected her a deacon.

Following custom, the women were attired in their
Easter Sunday finery. Elizabeth and Jennifer and Louise drew admiring glances as they moved along the
walkway. Blake looked dashing, while Morg and Brad
appeared singularly uncomfortable. Neither of them
was a regular churchgoer, and their serge suits smelled
vaguely of mothballs. Twice a year, Easter and Christmas, they were dragooned into attending services.

A family gathering was planned at Spur. Jennifer
and Blake would follow in a buckboard, while the
others rode in a large phaeton carriage. Elizabeth
believed in celebrating holidays and she always insisted
that the family be together. At her direction, a festive
dinner was even now being prepared back at the ranch.
Like the church services, attendance was considered
mandatory.

Morg assisted Louise into the carriage. He heard a
faint gasp and turned back just as his mother put a
hand to her throat. Elizabeth was staring uptown, her
gaze fixed on a tall rider astride a roan gelding. One
by one the others recognized the horseman, and suddenly everybody started talking at once. They stood
waiting in a tableau of grinning faces.

Clint reined to a halt behind the carriage. When he
swung down from the saddle, Morg and Brad swarmed
him with whooped laughter and arm-pumping handshakes. Jennifer kissed him soundly and performed
the introductions with Blake. Louise waved from her
seat in the carriage, and the church congregation stared
en masse. Those who remembered him agreed it was a
resurrection of sorts for the Brannock family. The
exile to a far land had at last returned.

Clint finally made his way to Elizabeth. Her eyes
shone, glistening with tears, and her face radiated
happiness. She took a tentative step forward, then
moved into his arms and embraced him with a great
hug. He held her close for a moment, and when they
separated, she looked up at him with warm affection.
Her mouth trembled with a smile.

"Welcome home," she said softly. "I've missed you."

"You're a sight for sore eyes yourself."

"Honestly, your timing couldn't have been better.
We're having a family get-together."

Clint laughed. "Sounds mighty good to me. I rode a
long way to get here."

"Oh, I just can't tell you! I'm so happy to see you."

The dinner was transformed into a homecoming celebration. With Clint the guest of honor, the family
gathered around a table loaded with food. They ate
and talked, uncorking three bottles of wine, and peppered him with questions. Clint kept his answers short
and turned the conversation instead to events in their

lives. By the end of the meal, he'd been brought up-to-date on the entire family.

Sated with food, everyone retired to the parlor after dinner. Elizabeth and Clint left the others conversing among themselves and stepped out onto the veranda. There, at last, Elizabeth got him to talk. Seated on the porch swing, he told her of his trip to the reservation, and Little Raven's death. His voice was detached, but she nonetheless saw the hurt in his eyes. Not for the first time, she realized he was a man of deep-felt emotions and intense loyalty. She sensed as well that he would speak of such things to no one but her.

Under her gentle questioning, Clint went on to relate his parting with Lon and Hank. His voice was now troubled, and he seemed somehow at a loss. He held out no great hope that Lon would ever lead a normal life. Yet, however slim, he thought there was still a chance for young Hank. The major obstacle was to separate them, and remove the boy from Lon's influence. Listening to him, Elizabeth understood that he'd now assumed the role of their father. He was talking about his sons.

To the west, the sun dropped lower beyond the mountains. They fell silent, watching the faraway slopes silhouetted against a fiery sky. For Clint, her nearness and the light scent of her perfume suddenly stirred old memories. Even now, after a long year apart, her presence still kindled a starstruck feeling. He knew she was the reason he'd never married, and yet he suppressed the thought. While men sometimes wed their brothers' widows, it would never happen with them. Her affection for him was that of a loving and concerned sister. And he'd always known it wouldn't change.

"I have something to tell you," Elizabeth said in the deepening twilight. "Something you won't like."

Clint looked at her. "Sounds serious."

"Yes, it is," she said with a broken smile. "Two nights ago, Miguel Ortega arranged a meeting with me. He asked me to come out in support of *Las Gorras Blancas*."

"And?"

"I refused," she said, lowering her eyes. "I won't be a party to violence, even for a good cause."

"Glad to hear it," Clint said, still watching her. "Guess you know I've been sent here to run him down."

"Yes, I know."

"Would you consider telling me where this meeting took place?"

"I've already thought it through very thoroughly. I won't help him and I won't help you."

"Hard to stay neutral in a thing like this."

"Be honest," she asked directly. "You intend to kill him, don't you?"

Clint grunted, shook his head. "I've never killed a man who wasn't trying to kill me. Ortega's no different."

"Yes, he is different," she insisted. "He's fighting for a cause, his people! He's not an outlaw."

Clint subscribed to no particular ideology. Nor was he a man of strong political convictions. Yet he held to the belief that no man was above the law. What he saw as his life's work was founded on a single tenet. Those who broke the rules must be made to pay the penalty.

"Ortega's dangerous," he said now. "One way or another, he's got to be stopped. The law don't make exceptions."

"And when you catch him—if he refuses to surrender—what then?"

"I reckon that'll be his choice, not mine."

The statement foreshadowed what Elizabeth feared

most. A cold premonition swept over her and she felt a sudden seesaw of emotions. Somehow she had to ensure that Miguel Ortega was not killed. And that put her at odds with the one man she treasured above all others.

She took Clint's hand and squeezed it tightly. He nodded, merely looking at her, as though reading her mind. Neither of them spoke of it again.

11

The calf bawled in protest. Hair sizzled as Brad pressed down on the red-hot iron, holding it there several seconds. When he pulled it away, the calf's flank was marked with his ⌐Ɒ brand.

Stepping back, he dropped the iron on the ground and shook his lariat free of the calf's neck. Then he moved forward, stooping down, and jerked the piggin' string loose. The hog-tied calf scrambled to its feet and took off at a wobbly lope. Some distance away the mama cow stood watching with flared eyes and lowered head. The calf lumbered into her and immediately began suckling.

Brad kicked dirt onto the small fire he'd built. With the coals smothered, and the branding iron cooled, he walked to his horse. After strapping the iron behind the cantle, he mounted and began recoiling his lariat. His eyes roved out across the land, where his herd of longhorns slowly grazed toward the river. Working by himself, he'd managed to brand three calves within the last hour. By rough count, there were another thirty-one yet to be chased down.

Late that afternoon he had ridden over to the Rio Felix. Sometime next week, barring bad weather, he planned to commence roundup on Spur. Once the gather started, there would be little time left for his own affairs. So he'd decided to get the calves branded rather than put it off until later. But now, with the sun dropping toward the mountains, he was forced to call it quits. He would have to work straight through Sunday to get the job finished.

Unlike other Saturdays, he wouldn't be taking dinner with the Ramírez family tonight. Earlier, upon approaching his cabin, he'd noted smoke coming from the chimney. To his amazement, he found Juanita busily preparing a meal for that evening. She'd already tidied up the cabin, and an earthen vase of wildflowers was centered on the table. She blithely remarked that she was tired of sharing him with her family. She had decided to fix their supper herself.

Something about her manner troubled Brad. Her presence there wasn't peculiar, for she had been to the cabin many times before. But she'd never offered to cook supper, or shown the least interest in cleaning the cabin. She'd even walked the three miles from her father's place, lugging a sackful of food all the way. When he rode out to start the branding, it occurred to him that she was acting strangely like a wife. He wondered if she was in the family way.

Juanita was waiting when he returned. She watched from the door while he unsaddled and turned his horse into the corral. Laughing happily, she kissed him as he entered the cabin and made him wash up before supper. At the table, she heaped his plate with several savory dishes, clearly proud of her cooking. Through the meal she chattered on about inconsequential things, merely picking at her own food. Afterward, when they were finished, she shooed him outside. Humming to herself, she began washing the dishes.

Brad took a seat in the doorway. The night was dark and stars were scattered like flecks of ice through a sky of purest indigo. His gaze roved back and forth, searching the patchwork heavens, as though some immutable truth were to be found in the stars. He found instead the quandary of his own thoughts, and deepening concern. Until tonight, their arrangement had been pleasant and informal, no strings attached. But now he sensed a change, some vague domestic undertone that left him disturbed. He had a hunch he was about to get an earful.

A short time later Juanita joined him in the doorway. She leaned back, her head against his shoulder, pulling his arm tight around her waist. She smelled sweet and alluring, and Brad was all too aware of her rounded hips and high full breasts. She seemed content with the silence and several minutes passed while they stared off into the night. Then, wriggling closer, she arched her head and slowly scanned the sky.

"The old ones," she said softly, "believe the stars foretell the future. Do you think it's true?"

"I dunno," Brad replied. "I've never been much on superstition."

"No, no," she said quickly. "It's not superstition. They believe some things are destined . . . meant to be."

"What do you believe?"

She clamped a hand over her mouth and giggled. "Are you sure you want me to tell you?"

Brad had a feeling he couldn't stop her. "Go ahead," he said. "I'd like to hear it."

"Well—" She laughed her sensuous little laugh. "I believe the stars were meant for lovers. Why else would God put them there?"

"Maybe he just wanted to light up the sky."

"Oh!" she scolded. "Why aren't you more romantic? You never say nice things."

Brad looked at her blankly. "What would you have me say?"

"For one thing," she said with innocent directness,

"you might speak to me of *amor*. Just once, tell me what I mean to you."

"What would you like to mean to me?"

"*Tu corazón*," she murmured, "*tu vida*—everything."

Brad felt a powerful tug of emotion toward her. Yet he was not a man who revealed his innermost thoughts easily. Nor was he all that ready to admit them to himself. His restlessness had grown worse, not better, and he seemed saddled with discontent. He wasn't sure what the hell he wanted.

"Are you talking about marriage?" he asked now. "If you are, let's get it out in the open."

There was something brazen in her eyes. "*Sí*," she said without hesitation. "I have been your woman many months now. I came to you a *virgen* and you knew—I thought you understood."

"Understood what?"

"How it is with my people! A girl does not surrender herself casually. She waits and saves herself . . . for one man."

A moment elapsed while she waited for some response. "I have to know," he said finally. "Are you with child?"

"*No!*"

She recoiled as though slapped. Shoulders squared, she pulled back and held his gaze with a steadfast look. "I am no fool," she informed him. "I watch the moon and I attend to myself. I would never disgrace myself with a *bastardo*."

Brad stared at her, his face very earnest. "Our child would never be born without a name—my name."

"What are you saying?"

An instant of weighing and deliberation slipped past. Brad realized he was about to say the one thing he'd never allowed himself to consider. Still, though he

failed to comprehend the reason, it was what he wanted
to say.

"We will be married," he promised. "But it must
wait until after the fall roundup. I have obligations to
satisfy."

"Are you talking about Señora Brannock?"

"Don't ask me to explain. Just tell me you're willing
to wait."

A vixen look touched her eyes and she moistened
her bottom lip with her tongue. Her voice turned
silky. "I would wait forever, *caro mío.*"

She smiled and her arms encircled his neck. Brad
suddenly stiffened, staring past her with a puzzled
frown. Her arms fell away and she turned, following
the direction of his gaze. Far in the distance, a flare of
light split the darkness.

"What is it?" she asked.

"Fire," Brad said, rising to his feet. "Homer Stockton's place."

"Where are you going?"

"Way it looks, he's bound to need help. Stay here
till I get back."

Brad hurried off to the corral. He quickly saddled
his horse, then opened the gate and swung aboard.
Juanita watched from the doorway as he spurred the
gelding into a lope.

He rode east along the Rio Felix.

The main house was unharmed. Several outbuildings had been doused with coal oil and burned to the
ground. All that remained was a smoky pile of embers.

Homer Stockton stood in the middle of the compound. He looked on without expression as cowhands
carried water buckets from the river and soaked down
the rubble. His eyes were empty, and cold.

Brad dismounted and left his horse ground-reined.

He'd covered the five miles downstream at a steady lope, negotiating the rough terrain by starlight. Along the way, he had spotted tangled knots of fenceposts and barbed wire, and bunches of cattle far off their home range. Someone had methodically stampeded Stockton's herds.

"Hard luck, Homer," Brad said, halting beside the rancher. "Any idea who did it?"

"Who else?" Stockton said in a dead monotone. "*Las Gorras Blancas*."

"How do you know for sure?"

"Last night the sonsabitches snuck in here and tacked a warning on the door. Told me to clear out."

Stockton paused, shook his head dumbly. "Helluva thing, when a man gets posted off his own land. Never figured it'd happen to me."

Brad was silent a moment, thoughtful. Last week, while Clint was at the ranch, they had spoken at length about the White Caps. Clint was confident that *mexicanos* were being organized into bands of night riders. He believed they would strike soon, hitting targets selected as a warning to all Anglos. Upon departing Spur, Clint had taken a room at the hotel in town. From there, he planned to conduct an investigation throughout Lincoln County.

Something else stuck in Brad's mind. After swearing him to secrecy, Clint had told him about Elizabeth's meeting with Miguel Ortega. Apparently she'd taken a neutral stance in the matter, refusing to support or denounce Ortega's movement. And now, Homer Stockton was the first rancher to be hit by *Las Gorras Blancas*. Which raised the question of Stockton's ties to the Brannocks. His daughter was married to Morg, and that made him a relative of sorts. So perhaps the raid was a message meant for Elizabeth. A warning about the prospects of remaining neutral.

Whether coincidence or not, Brad thought the raid was a well-designed object lesson. Stockton was a hard man, and no friend of the *mexicanos*. He'd strung barbed wire across a large stretch of public domain, as well as a chunk of communal pastureland from an old Spanish grant. Worse, he had fenced off parts of the Rio Felix, denying water to nomadic *mexicano* shepherds. All that made him a prime target for *Las Gorras Blancas*. He typified Anglo cattlemen who rode rough-shod over the native people and their customs.

"Guess you ought to know," Brad said now. "Your fences are down between here and my place. From what I saw, your cows are scattered to hell and gone."

Stockton's eyes glazed with rage. "Goddamn greasers! Hit me just before I was fixin' to start roundup. How's that for a kick in the balls?"

"Pretty smart thinkin'," Brad muttered out loud. "Looks like they aimed to put you in a squeeze."

"I'll fight 'em!" Stockton punched a fist into the palm of his hand. "Any peppergut I catch on my land will wish he hadn't been born. Nobody runs me out."

Brad took a deep breath, blew it out heavily. "Only one problem, Homer. Fast as you string fence, they'll tear it down again. You can't patrol your whole spread."

"What's that mean?" Stockton said tightly. "Are you tellin' me I shouldn't string fence?"

"We do all right without it on Spur."

"Hell, yes, you do. Every greaser on the Hondo would kiss Elizabeth Brannock's ass if she'd lift her skirts."

"You watch your mouth where Miz Brannock's concerned. Otherwise you'll have to deal with me."

Stockton eyed him warily. "No need to get your nose out of joint. I didn't mean it personal."

"Just remember what I said, Homer."

Brad walked to his horse. He stepped into the sad-

dle and reined out of the yard. Fording the river, it
occurred to him that he'd never particularly liked Stockton. But then, from the looks of things, he wasn't
alone. Lots of people knew a sonovabitch when they
saw one.

At the head of the line was Miguel Ortega and *Las
Gorras Blancas*.

Weekends were a special time for Jennifer. For
reasons she'd never fathomed, people tended to nurse
their ailments through Saturday night and Sunday.
Whatever the cause, she was thankful for the respite.

After closing her office, her Saturday-night ritual
seldom varied. She took a long luxurious bath, soak-
ing away the week's aches and strains. Then she selected something frilly and feminine from her wardrobe,
and tried to do something special with her hair. The
result, when she finally inspected herself in the mirror,
was always a pleasant surprise. Underneath the doctor
there was a woman of passable good looks.

While she was attending to her toilette, her cook
prepared dinner. A *mexicano* woman, the cook worked
only on weekends, spoiling Jennifer with pastries and
fresh-baked bread and all manner of special dishes. In
part, the cook was also a concession to Jennifer's need
for relaxation and entertainment. One aspect of the
Saturday-night ritual was that she always invited Blake
for supper. He was what the townspeople discreetly
referred to as her "gentleman friend."

Tonight, Jennifer was in an unusually zestful mood.
She'd lost no patients during the past week, and cheating death seemed to her a cause for celebration. At
the dinner table, some of her old vivacity returned,
and she joined with Blake in animated conversation.
He enjoyed telling anecdotes, generally woven around
some courtroom experience, and she found herself

laughing gaily at his dry wit. By the time coffee was served, she felt curiously giddy and carefree.

All that abruptly changed. A loud knock at the front door brought her back to reality. She excused herself with an apologetic smile and hurried through the waiting room. When she opened the door, she recognized Morg's timber foreman, Chunk Devlin. Behind him were four lumberjacks carrying a man on a stretcher rigged from blankets. Devlin's features were shrouded with concern.

'Sorry to bother you, ma'am,'' he said, jerking a thumb over his shoulder. "We've got a man who's hurt bad.''

"Bring him inside.''

Jennifer quickly lighted the lamps in her office. Devlin explained that one of the chains on a logging wagon had snapped. The load shifted, and a log weighing upwards of a thousand pounds rolled onto the man, crushing his leg. A war veteran himself, Devlin had the presence of mind to apply a tourniquet. The accident had occurred at quitting time, just before sundown. Three hours had been required to transport the man into town.

A brief examination confirmed Jennifer's worst fears. After placing the lumberjack on the operating table, she cut away his trouser leg with scissors. His lower leg and foot, still encased in a heavy workboot, had been crushed to a pulp. His upper leg, from a point four inches above the knee, was horribly mangled. The femur bone, broken and jagged, protruded through his lower thigh. The extent of the injuries left Jennifer no alternative. She would have to amputate.

The logger was still conscious. His teeth were gritted against the pain and beads of sweat glistened on his forehead. Jennifer moved to the head of the table and placed a reassuring hand on his shoulder. He licked his parched lips, searching her face.

"I'm sorry," she said gently. "Unless I operate immediately, you'll develop gangrene. I have to remove the leg."

A pinpoint of terror surfaced in his eyes. "Godamight—" his voice cracked. "Ain't there no other way, Doc?"

"Your injuries are too severe. Without an operation, you'll die. We have to do it now."

The logger mustered a feeble smile. "Never thought I'd wind up a pegleg. Guess you just never know."

"Lie back and rest. I'll give you something to ease the pain."

Jennifer dosed him with laudanum, a mild sedative. She then sent Blake to fetch Rosa, her surgical assistant. The cook was hastily drafted to sterilize instruments and prepare bandages. Devlin and his men, under Jennifer's direction, gingerly undressed the lumberjack. When they finished, she ushered them out into the waiting room.

Alone with her patient, Jennifer briskly scrubbed her hands. She used a sterile towel to dry off and then set about cleansing the leg with a carbolic solution. The antiseptic vastly reduced the chances of infection, and death, following surgery. Jennifer was no less thankful for the development of modern-day anesthetics. Before the discovery of ether, surgeons prided themselves on performing amputations in under three minutes. Tonight, mercifully, the logger would be spared such agony.

Within the hour, all the preparations were complete. A sponge soaked with ether had been used to render the lumberjack unconscious. On Jennifer's command, Rosa stretched the skin tight on his pelvis and applied pressure to shut off the femoral artery. Jennifer selected a scalpel from the instrument tray and leaned forward over the man's thigh. Her incision was made through healthy tissue some four inches above the compound fracture. One circular cut of the scalpel opened the leg from the inner thigh to the outer thigh.

Working swiftly, Jennifer separated the tissue and cut through the outer leg muscles. She performed retraction and then incised the deeper muscles attached to the large femur bone. With the scalpel, she carefully separated muscle from bone, to a point three inches above the incision. After applying a linen retractor, she sliced through the tough membrane surrounding the bone. Grasping the leg in one hand, she next sawed through the bone with a small surgical saw. A stroke of the scalpel at last detached the mangled leg.

Jennifer quickly tied off the arteries with thread ligature. She then cut the nerves, allowing them to retract, and sponged the surgical wound with sterilized water. Drying her hands, she delicately quilted the large muscle flaps over the truncated bone. The skin flaps were cut long and sutured loosely, forming a bag to allow for postoperative swelling and drainage. Stepping back, she reviewed the procedure and found nothing left undone. She concluded by wrapping the stump with sterile bandage.

The logger's breathing and pulse were normal. Jennifer instructed Rosa to bundle the severed leg and prepare it for burial. After removing her surgical apron, she moved through the door to the waiting room. Devlin and his men jumped to their feet.

"Everything went fine," Jennifer said. "I prefer to keep him here overnight. We'll move him to the hotel tomorrow."

Devlin nodded somberly. "How long will he be laid up?"

"At least a month, perhaps longer. After that, he'll be able to get around on crutches."

"Tough luck, him gettin' caught that way. Things can sure go haywire fast."

"Actually, he's quite fortunate, Mr. Devlin. Any man who cheats death can afford to lose a leg."

"You're right there, ma'am. Six feet under would've made a poor second choice."

Devlin and his men departed, thanking her profusely. Jennifer dismissed the cook for the night and proceeded toward the rear of the house. She found Blake seated in the parlor, the aroma of his pipe a relief from the smells of the operating room. He poured her a brandy and she dropped wearily into a chair. Surgery always left her depleted but strangely exhilarated. Her face was flushed with excitement.

"Quite a night," Blake commented. "Although not exactly what I'd planned."

"Oh?" Jennifer said, sipping her brandy. "What was that?"

"Maybe you're not up to another surprise so soon."

"You really are terrible. Don't be a tease—tell me!"

"You insist?"

"Yes, for goodness' sake. I insist."

Blake pulled a small box from his jacket pocket. He presented it to her without ceremony or explanation. A slight smile played at the corner of his mouth as he watched her open the lid. Inside, nestled in cotton, was a simple gold wedding band.

Jennifer thought the gesture was so like him. No words of endearment or glowing speeches. Nothing of the impassioned declaration considered to be customary when a man proposed marriage. And his timing, only minutes after she'd finished surgery, was exquisitely unromantic. All in all, it seemed rather informal, almost mundane.

Staring at the ring, Jennifer realized that some hours weigh against a whole lifetime. With Blake, there would be nothing of the great love shared by her mother and father. He was warm and comfortable, infinitely gentle, but he would kindle no fires. Still, he was a professional man, educated and intelligent, at ease with her devotion to medicine. While it was not the stuff of dreams, it was nonetheless a practical match. Nowhere was it written that husband and wife had to be lovers.

She looked up with a melancholy smile. "Am I to assume you're proposing marriage?"

"Nothing less," Blake said with a graveled chuckle. "You'd honor me by becoming my wife."

"Since I'm hardly the coy type—I accept."

Blake set his pipe in an ashtray. He rose, taking her hand, and lifted her from her chair. He tilted her chin and kissed her with considerably more ardor than she expected. His gaze was warm with affection.

"I'll make you a good husband, Jen. You won't regret it."

She merely nodded, somehow touched by his sincerity. Her eyes misted with what she hoped was happiness.

12

On the last day of April, Elizabeth arrived in Santa Fe. She was accompanied by John Taylor, who had long ago learned to interpret the warning signs. Her mood was anything but cordial.

Their train ride north had been spent in glum silence. Elizabeth was carrying a letter from Ira Hecht, and the contents had cast a cloud over her normally sunny disposition. She was upset and angry, and clearly spoiling for a fight. Her eyes blazed with quiet fury.

Apart from Hecht's letter, she was burdened with personal problems. Her concern for Clint's safety had mounted alarmingly over the past three weeks. He was working alone and reportedly scouring the countryside for Miguel Ortega. She feared some harm might befall him in the *mexicano* villages, for Ortega's followers were now everywhere. Fanatics all too often justified unconscionable deeds in the name of a cause. And a lawman, traveling alone, was easily killed.

Ortega, though hardly a personal concern, was nonetheless a constant worry. Never in her wildest dreams could she have imagined how easily he would inflame the *mexicanos*. Starting with the raid on Homer Stockton's ranch, *Las Gorras Blancas* had swept through Lincoln County like a marauding horde. From the Rio Felix in the south, to the Rio Bonito in the north, scarcely a night passed without some act of violence.

A guerrilla campaign, directed at Anglos, recalled the days of the Apache wars.

True to his word, Ortega had not ventured into the Hondo Valley. So far as Elizabeth knew, he'd made no effort to organize the *mexicanos* who lived there. A curious peace, as though centered in the eye of the storm, had settled over the basin. Yet people talked, and there were widespread rumors about her meeting with Ortega. The gossip troubled her, for embattled Anglos were certain to believe the worst. However false, it was being whispered that she had made a pact with the leader of *Las Gorras Blancas*. A secretive deal to spare the ranchlands of Spur from retribution.

Uptown, Elizabeth ordered the hack driver to stop at the hotel. Taylor took their bags into the lobby and left them with the desk clerk. Normally, upon arriving in Santa Fe, Elizabeth insisted on freshening up and changing her clothes. Her departure from routine merely confirmed Taylor's earlier appraisal. She was definitely on the warpath.

From the hotel, they drove directly to Hecht's office. Elizabeth stepped down hardly before the coach rolled to a stop. While Taylor settled with the driver, she marched through the door like a gunnery sergeant on parade. Hecht looked up and seemed to wince as she approached his desk. She pulled his letter from her pocketbook.

"I'd like an explanation of this, Ira."

"Elizabeth, please," Hecht said mildly. "Have a seat and we'll discuss it. There's no need to get yourself exercised."

"No need!" she echoed. "I demand to know what's behind it. And don't you dare try to placate me."

Hecht glanced past her as Taylor entered the office. He lifted his hands in a bemused shrug. "John, would you ask her to calm down? We need our wits about us."

Taylor dropped into a chair. "She's been building up a head of steam ever since we left Lincoln. You might as well let her sound off."

"Stop it!" Elizabeth demanded. "I won't be treated like some dithering female."

Hecht waved a hand. "Then I suggest you get hold of your temper. We'll never get anywhere shouting at one another."

Elizabeth sat down. She tossed the letter on his desk. "Very well," she said, "no more shouting. Now, I'll have an explanation."

"We lost," Hecht said simply. "Our lobbyist ran into a stone wall. The mood in Washington has turned pro-American."

"*Mexicanos* are American. The Treaty of Guadalupe Hidalgo awarded them unconditional citizenship. Any fool knows that!"

"I have to disagree. First off, the *mexicanos* have never considered themselves American. They still look upon Anglos as an occupying army."

"And rightly so," Elizabeth said indignantly. "They've been cheated and hoodwinked for the last thirty years."

"No argument there," Hecht agreed. "But the fact remains, they've refused to assimilate, work within the system. *Las Gorras Blancas* merely underscores their resistance to change."

"Perhaps it reflects the shoddy treatment they've received. By and large, they haven't been made to feel like equals."

"Look at it from the other side. Washington sees them as troublemakers, an obstacle to progress."

"Are you defending that attitude?"

"No," Hecht said quickly. "I'm trying to explain why we lost. A speech President Cleveland made last week was widely reported in the newspapers. He said, and I quote, 'We will not allow anarchists to prevail in New Mexico Territory.' "

"Anarchists?" Elizabeth repeated in a low voice. "Does anyone seriously believe they're trying to overthrow the government?"

"Apparently so," Hecht said in disgust. "The bill has been introduced to establish a land-claims court. Our lobbyist informs me Congress will pass it by an overwhelming margin."

"Legalized larceny," Elizabeth said hotly. "By court order, the *mexicanos* will be robbed of their land."

"Not necessarily," Hecht advised her. "Since I wrote you, I've been doing a lot of thinking. I believe there's a way to stymie the landgrabbers."

"Well, don't just sit there—tell me!"

Hecht proposed a masterful gambit. By law, a settler who homesteaded land was granted valid title after five years. His plan was to petition the federal district court on behalf of the *mexicanos*. The court would be asked to rule that a native New Mexican was entitled to equal protection under the law. He would request that a *mexicano* with ten years' occupancy be awarded clear and unencumbered title to the land. The key to the petition was in doubling the customary five-year time requirement. No court would casually reject such a reasonable request.

"Ira"—Elizabeth laughed aloud—"that's brilliant!"

"Thank you," Hecht said modestly. "I believe it might just work. The court would be under heavy pressure to grant a favorable ruling. To do otherwise would smack of outright prejudice."

Elizabeth stared at him a moment, her expression pensive. When she spoke, her tone was crisp and incisive. "As it happens, I've had my thinking cap on too. I've devised a plan that could—and I stress 'could' —give us control of the legislature."

"Good God," Hecht moaned. "I'm almost afraid to ask. What've you concocted now?"

"I intend to call a convention of all the *mexicano* leaders."

"You're joking."

"I never joke about politics."

Elizabeth went on to explain her idea. She would summon the *ricos*, the *jefes*, and the young *políticos* to a convention on neutral ground. There, with all the warring factions in one room, she would hammer out an accord based on mutual self-interest. The goal would be to win control of the legislature in the upcoming fall elections. By defeating the Santa Fe Ring at the polls, her coalition would then dominate affairs in New Mexico. Central to the success of the plan was the abrasive attitude of Governor Edmund Ross. His hostility toward *Las Gorras Blancas* represented an opportunity to mobilize the *mexicano* vote throughout the territory.

"Sounds good," Hecht said tentatively, "but you'll have a deuce of a time getting them together in one room. Nobody trusts anybody in that bunch."

"Oh, they'll show up," Elizabeth assured him. "Anyone who doesn't would risk being cut out of the arrangement. I guarantee a packed house."

Hecht nodded, reflective a moment. "Assuming you pull it off, I foresee two problems. One has to do with Miguel Ortega."

"What about him?"

"A rumor is circulating, and it's taken on vicious overtones. You're accused of forming an alliance with Ortega to further your own political goals."

"That's a despicable lie!"

"I'm sorry to say, it gets worse."

"How could it possibly get worse?"

Hecht took off his glasses. He wiped them with a handkerchief, avoiding her eyes. "People are whispering that it's more than a political alliance. They say you and Ortega are personally involved—a liaison . . . lovers."

Elizabeth flushed angrily. "How dare anyone say that? I've only met the man one time! I hardly know him."

"I don't have to tell you"—Hecht paused, fixed the spectacles on his nose—"politics is a dirty game. Canby and his crowd started the rumor to smear you and destroy your credibility. A *gringa* involved with a *mexicano* makes for juicy gossip."

"And if I deny it, that merely lends credence to the lie. I can't win either way."

Taylor cleared his throat. "I could always pay a call on Mr. Canby. That'd stop it muy damn pronto."

"No," Hecht said sharply. "We can't afford even a hint of violence. If anything, that would fuel the rumor."

Elizabeth nodded agreement. "You mentioned two problems. What's the other one?"

"A *mexicano* convention," Hecht pointed out, "will play right into Canby's hands. For openers, he'll use it as a fright tactic with Anglos. People will be led to believe it's a show of support for *Las Gorras Blancas*."

"And—?" Elizabeth arched an eyebrow in question. "There's something more, isn't there?"

"I'm afraid so," Hecht said dolefully. "Canby will use the convention to buttress the story about you and Ortega. He'll claim it's proof positive that you've fallen for a *mexicano* revolutionary."

Elizabeth shook her head. "Hold the convention and sully my reputation forever. Is that what you're saying?"

"Something along those lines."

"Or forget the convention and abandon any hope of a true coalition. Isn't that the alternative?"

"Yes, I suppose it is."

"Then the choice is really quite simple. We'll proceed with plans for the convention."

Until today, Elizabeth had kept her personal life separated from politics. But now, forced to confront a harsh truth, she saw that the rules had been altered. Dirty innuendo, and character assassination, were the new order of things.

She vowed Thomas Canby would pay dearly for resorting to gutter tactics.

"Get the lead outta your pants!"

Chunk Devlin glowered fearsomely. The lumberjacks working to fell a tree put more muscle behind their axes. Wood chips flew as the thunk of steel on timber increased to a drumlike tattoo. The sound echoed distantly through the forest.

Morg was a tolerated observer. Twice a week he visited the logging camp, ostensibly to inspect the operation. But there was unspoken agreement between himself and his timber boss. Devlin brooked no interference, and he allowed no one, not even the owner, to tell him his business. He ran the camp with the autocratic manner of a feudal lord.

All things considered, Morg found no reason to object. The logging camp had been in operation exactly one month. In that time, Devlin and his men had already cut a wide swath through the forest of ponderosa pines. The amount of timber delivered to the sawmill far exceeded anything Morg might have expected. He estimated the investment would begin to show a profit by early September, months ahead of schedule. His judgment of Chunk Devlin thus far seemed faultless.

Adding further to the profits was the lumber opera-

tion. Morg had contracted with freighters to haul the
finished lumber from the sawmill. Working through
brokers and lumberyards, he'd arranged to market his
own timber. A swing through Lincoln County had
resulted in steady orders from the mining camps, as
well as the Pecos Valley settlements. By contracting
for the freighting, he had eliminated the investment in
payroll and equipment. The profit was quick and substantial, nearly forty cents on the dollar.

Apart from the financial aspects of the business,
Morg was intrigued by life in a logging camp. He
found the lumberjacks similar in many ways to cowhands. Their home was a crude bunkhouse, with rough
tables, benches, and a potbellied stove. Every morning at five o'clock they were rousted out of their
bunks, and by sunup they were in the woods. Their
workday was sunrise to sundown.

The actual logging seemed to Morg a form of organized chaos. The men who chopped down the trees
were called "fallers." Working in two-man teams, the
fallers first sliced into a towering ponderosa with a long
crosscut saw. Then, using double-bitted axes, they
chopped away at a forty-five-degree angle to create
the undercut. Essentially the undercut weakened a
tree at the base and determined which direction it
would fall. The crosscut saw was then used to cut
through the trunk from the opposite side. Heavy metal
wedges, pounded home with wooden mallets, were
next driven into the back cut. When the tree began to
topple, the cry of "*Timber!*" rang out through the
forest.

Once on the ground, a ponderosa was sawed into
sixteen-foot lengths by the "buckers." A heavy chain,
known as a choker, was then worked under and around
the log, and hooked tight. The next step was to fasten
the choker to steel cables which ran to a donkey

engine. Mounted on a platform, the wood-burning engine was geared to a winchlike drum and created herculean power. Hissing and belching cinders, the donkey engine reeled in the cables and snaked the log out of the woods. At the loading platform, usually situated on a downslope, the logs were rolled onto the bed of a wagon. From there, the teamsters hauled the logs to the sawmill at San Patricio.

The work was grueling and dangerous, hard on men and animals. The lumberjack who had lost his leg was by no means an isolated case. Yet the logging crew willingly accepted the risks, for they were paid double the wages earned by a cowhand. By day's end, when they trudged back to the bunkhouse, scarcely a man among them had escaped without some sort of injury. After supper, they gathered around the stove, smoking and drinking coffee, for stronger stimulants were barred from a logging camp. On the stroke of ten, the lamps were doused and the men crawled into their bunks. At the crack of dawn, the brutal grind started all over again.

Today, standing at the loading platform, Morg watched as the last log was rolled onto a wagon. Heavy chains were cinched around the load, securing the logs for the bone-jarring trip out of the mountains. Devlin approached as the teamster popped the reins and the massive draft horses strained into the traces. He halted beside Morg.

"Well, now," he said in his booming voice. "Are you satisfied with what you've seen?"

"No complaints," Morg said, a pleased look on his face. "You run a tight operation."

Devlin's rumbling laugh sounded like distant artillery. "God's blood!" he said in high good humor. "We're not slackers, me and my timber monkeys. We aim to earn the bonus you promised."

"From the looks of things, that won't be any problem. You're already ahead of schedule."

"And gaining speed," Devlin bragged. "We gonna cost you a pisspot full of money. You mark my word."

Morg smiled, his judgment again reaffirmed. At the outset, he'd allowed Devlin to establish a production quota for the first six months. Then, increasing that figure by half, he had promised foreman and crew a month's extra wages if the new goal were met. The upshot was a gang of lumberjacks who worked like they owned part of the company.

Thinking on it now, he decided to let Devlin gloat on the deal. A pisspot full of money seemed a small price to pay.

Far in the distance, thunderheads roiled over the mountains. Bolts of lightning crackled across the sky, then flashed down to strike the earth. There was a smell of rain in the air.

Morg rode into San Patricio through the gathering dusk. The sawmill was closed for the night and he dismounted outside Harry Tipton's house. Through the window, he saw the movement of shadows against lamplight. He rapped on the door.

Tipton greeted him warmly. "Well, Morg, where'd you drop from? We unloaded your last wagon just before quitting time."

"Yeah, I know," Morg said, moving into the parlor. "I met them on the road headed back to camp."

"Have you had supper? The missus oughta have it on the table any minute now. We'd be proud to have you stay."

"Thanks anyway, Harry. I just stopped by on my way home. You got a minute to talk?"

"Why, sure," Tipton said, motioning him to a chair. "What's on your mind?"

Morg took a seat, his hat hooked over one knee. "Saw Chunk today," he said. "Way it looks, I'll have to put on another wagon. They're dropping timber like there's no tomorrow."

"I'll vouch for that. Your boys keep me hoppin'."

"Guess that's why I'm here. I figure we'll double our output by the end of September. You reckon you'll be able to handle the extra work?"

A sudden frown creased Tipton's brow. "I dunno about that, Morg. Not that I wouldn't like the business, you understand . . ."

His voice trailed off and Morg studied his downcast features. "What's the trouble, Harry?"

"Ralph McQuade," Tipton said in an aggrieved tone. "We had ourselves a few choice words. He wants me to stop milling your timber."

Morg laughed shortly. "I hope you told him where to shove it."

"I didn't tell him yea or nay. McQuade's not the sort of man you wanna cross."

"Hell, he's all wind," Morg said with a bluff air of assurance. "Lots of talk and no action."

Tipton's eyes narrowed. "You don't know him like I do. I told you before, he's got a mean streak."

"If he's so tough, why doesn't he pay me a call? I'm the one taking his business."

" 'Cause he knows I scare easier. And I have to tell you, I'm plenty goddamn worried. He put me on warning."

"What's that supposed to mean?"

"Told me all kinds of accidents could happen around a sawmill. Laughed and called 'em 'manmade' accidents."

"Maybe I ought to have a talk—"

Morg suddenly stopped. He cocked one ear, as though listening, and quieted Tipton with an upraised palm. The thud of hoofbeats swelled until the sound seemed to fill the room. Before either of them could move, a solid wedge of horsemen pounded across the yard and rode toward the sawmill. One of the riders carried a blazing torch.

Tipton bounded from his chair, followed closely by Morg. At the window, they watched as some thirty horsemen reined to a halt before the sawmill. One of the riders rapped out a muffled command and several others rode forward with corked bottles. Arms drawn back, they hurled the bottles at a mountainous stack of timbers and piles of finished lumber. The bottles shattered in a *pop-pop-pop* of glistening liquid.

"Jesus Christ!" Tipton yelped. "That's kerosene in them bottles. They're gonna burn me out."

Morg stepped to the door and jerked it open. He started outside, drawing his pistol as he moved through the doorway. In the flare of torchlight, he dimly registered that all the riders were masked with strips of white cloth. The leader spotted him and barked an order. He realized the man had spoken in Spanish.

Wheeling their horses, several riders opened fire with pistols. Slugs pocked the walls of the house and splintered the doorframe all around Morg. Even as he ducked and spun back inside the house, it crossed his mind that they weren't trying to kill him. The shots had bracketed him instead, warning him off. He kicked the door shut.

The rider with the torch tossed it onto the timbers. A roaring *whoosh* of light illuminated the night with fiery brilliance. The flames spread from the timbers to the piles of lumber and the storage yard was abruptly transformed into a crackling inferno. Spurring his horse, the leader motioned to his men. His voice was raised in a jubilant shout.

"*Vámonos, muchachos! Vámonos!*"

The horsemen formed into a broad phalanx and thundered off into the night. Morg eased the door open as the hoofbeats faded into the distance. Staring at the towering flames, it occurred to him that the raiders hadn't attempted to torch the sawmill itself. Their objective, instead, was the finished lumber and timbers for the mining companies. A blow directed at Anglo business interests rather than Harry Tipton.

Who they were, and what they called themselves, was never in question. Morg silently repeated the name to himself.

Las Gorras Blancas.

13

Las Gorras Blancas struck again the following night. At a ranch east of Lincoln, the raiders destroyed a stretch of barbed-wire fence and stampeded nearly a thousand cows. When they rode off, two men were left dead.

The ranch was located on the Rio Bonito, not far from the juncture with the Rio Hondo. After the fences were cut, and the cattle stampeded, the night raiders swept into the main compound. Their intent, as in previous raids was to burn down the outbuildings. For the first time, they met with armed resistance.

A wakeful cowhand rushed out of the bunkhouse. He opened fire with a saddle carbine just as an equipment shed went up in flames. One of the raiders pitched to the ground and the others instantly returned fire. The cowhand was blown off his feet, riddled with slugs. Before the White Caps could recover their fallen comrade, they came under general fire from the men in the bunkhouse. Their leader ordered retreat rather than fight a pitched battle.

Early next morning, the dead men were brought into Lincoln. The cowhand and the *mexicano* raider were laid out side-by-side in the back of a wagon. A crowd gathered around as the wagon rolled to a halt in front of the courthouse. Summoned from his office, Sheriff Will Grant pulled back the tarpaulin covering the bodies. Several onlookers recognized the *mexicano* and made positive identification. The dead men were then taken to the funeral parlor.

An hour or so later Clint rode into Lincoln. About the same time yesterday, he'd been notified of the raid on Tipton's Sawmill. On the chance he might uncover a lead, he had ridden out to San Patricio. There, after a long talk with Harry Tipton, he had remarked that it was the old story of "same song, second verse." The raiders were masked, and always struck at night, and no one had yet been able to identify a member of *Las Gorras Blancas*. He saw no reason to waste time questioning Morg.

One thing, however, left him intrigued. According to Tipton, the raiders could have easily killed Morg. Instead, they had peppered the doorway with gunfire and driven him back into the house. Clint wondered whether they had known it was Elizabeth Brannock's son. That would have accounted for their actions, for Miguel Ortega had promised her no harm would come to Spur. Still, even if it were true, it raised yet another question. How had they known Morg was inside Tipton's house at the precise moment of the raid? Since Morg had dropped by unannounced, it hardly made sense.

From San Patricio, Clint had attempted to track the raiders. Their trail led west along the Rio Hondo for a distance of some four miles. At that point, the riders had scattered to the winds, hoofprints leading in every direction. On a hunch, Clint had followed the trail of two men headed deeper into the mountains. But then, shortly before dark, the tracks had disappeared along a rocky stretch of terrain. Far from town, he had made camp near the headwaters of the river. He'd spent the night huddled in his rain slicker, waking often to feed a small fire.

The ride back to Lincoln had been a time of sober reflection. Almost four weeks had passed since he'd undertaken the investigation. Searching for a lead, he had visited half a dozen villages, questioning the local *jefes*. To a man, they had proved disinclined to talk about *Las Gorras Blancas*. Whether from fear or loyalty, their answers were politely evasive, revealing nothing. Nor had his luck improved when he'd broadened the search to the scene of the raids. By the time he arrived at the far-flung ranches, the trail was cold and the night riders had vanished into the hills. To date, he hadn't uncovered so much as a trace of Miguel Ortega.

In town, Clint rode directly to the livery stable. Hardly before he'd stepped off his horse, the livery owner began regaling him with the news of last night's raid. His interest quickened when he heard that one of the dead men was a White Cap, a local *mexicano*. He cut short the stable owner's windy report and hurried downstreet toward the courthouse. In his opinion, Will Grant was a poor excuse for a lawman, and practically worthless as an investigator. But the dead *mexicano* gave him a quick lift in spirits. A corpse sometimes told a tale that led elsewhere.

Grant was on his way out the door. "Well, I'll be jiggered," he said, spotting Clint. "I was hopin' you'd show up. Have you heard the news?"

"Just now," Clint replied. "Who's the dead Mexican?"

"A no-account by the name of Bonifacio Pérez. I'm not surprised he got himself killed."

"And you're sure he's a member of *Las Gorras Blancas*?"

"No question a'tall," Grant said jovially. "Sorry bastard got shot right off his horse. Wearin' a white mask, too."

Clint nodded. "What do you know about him?"

"Nothin' special," Grant allowed. "I arrested him a couple of times for drunk-and-disorderly, and once for startin' a knife fight. Him and his family farmed a little plot just outside town."

"Was he married?"

"Nope," Grant said. "Got a brother and sister, though. All of 'em lived with the mother."

"What happened to his father?"

"Passed away a year or so ago."

"Where's their house?" Clint asked. "I'd like to talk with his family."

"Just come on with me," Grant said. "I sent word for 'em to meet me at the undertaker's."

Grant was a tall ferret of a man, loose and rangy. He strode down the street looking rather pleased with himself. Since Clint had arrived in town, he'd been playing second fiddle in the *Las Gorras Blancas* investigation. Today his shoulders were squared and his stride was almost military. He acted like a man who had resumed charge of important matters.

The undertaker greeted them with glum reserve. They were shown into the viewing parlor, where two coffins were arranged on low platforms. The bodies were covered to the chin with blankets, for neither of them had yet been prepared for burial. The cowhand looked somehow surprised, as though he'd met death without sufficient warning. The *mexicano* looked curiously stern, almost angry.

Señora Pérez stood beside the coffin of her son. With her was her daughter, a young girl no more than sixteen. They both wore black *rebozos* over their heads, and the girl's eyes were red from crying. The mother appeared stoic, her features drained of emotion. Her lips moved in silent prayer as she fingered a rosary.

Grant and Clint removed their hats. They exchanged a glance and Clint nodded toward the women. Señora

Pérez continued fingering her beads as the lawmen moved closer. The girl kept her eyes on the floor.

"Excuse the intrusion," Grant said in halting Spanish. "We're here on official business, *señora*. We have to ask you some questions about your son."

The woman's fingers stopped. She clutched the rosary in both hands, her expression resigned. When she made no reply, Grant went on. "Were you aware your son was a member of *Las Gorras Blancas*?"

"*No*," Señora Pérez said without inflection. "Bonifacio kept such matters to himself."

"He never explained where he went?"

"Never."

"How many times was he away at night?"

"Often," Señora Pérez said vaguely. "I did not count the times."

Grant studied her with a calm judicial gaze. "The truth, *señora*. You knew he was attending meetings, didn't you?"

"He told me nothing and I knew nothing."

"Did he mention any names? Other men who were involved?"

Señora Pérez shook her head. "Bonifacio never spoke of his affairs, and I did not ask. I preferred not to know."

With an unpleasant grunt, the sheriff motioned at the coffin. "Your son was killed in a raid on *americanos*. Do you deny any knowledge of the men he rode with?"

"I have already denied it, *señor*. I know nothing."

Clint edged a step closer. His features were sphinxlike, but he spoke with steady authority, iron sureness. "A final question, *señora*," he said. "I believe you have another son, *verdad*?"

"*Sí*."

"What is his name?"

"Florentino."

"Why isn't he here to honor his dead brother? Doesn't that seem strange?"

Señora Pérez fidgeted, suddenly uncomfortable. "I cannot answer for Florentino."

"Where is he today?"

"I do not know."

Clint fixed her with a pale stare. "Was he with his brother last night?"

"*Sí.*"

"And he returned home, told you of Bonifacio's death. Isn't that true?"

Her eyes puddled with tears. Clint waited a moment, then resumed the questioning. "I am an officer of the law, *señora.* You must not lie, even to protect you son. Where is he now?"

Señora Pérez looked down at the rosary in her hands. Her voice dropped to a whisper. "After we talked, he took a few clothes and some food. He rode away."

"Where?" Clint demanded. "He wouldn't leave home without telling you."

There was a beat of oppressive silence. Señora Pérez finally lifted her head, met his gaze. "I have nothing more to say, *señor.* I will not betray my son."

"None of that," Grant blustered. "You speak up or I'll have to arrest you. We're conducting a murder investigation."

"Let it go," Clint said, turning toward the door. "She's told us all we're likely to hear."

Grant sputtered something under his breath. He glowered at the woman, then reluctantly followed Clint through the door. Outside they paused on the street and Grant crammed his hat on his head. He shot Clint a dirty look.

"You shouldn't've cut me off like that. I'm supposed to be the law around here."

Clint ignored the remark. "Any idea where the Pérez boy might've gone?"

"Why, hell, yes!" Grant flung an arm in a wild gesture. "He's off hidin' somewheres with Miguel Ortega. Find one and you'll find the other."

"I don't think so," Clint said slowly. "Ortega wouldn't keep anybody around who's been identified. I figure he sent Pérez packing for parts unknown."

Grant beamed like a trained bear. "By God, you just gimme the answer. I know where he's at!"

"Where?"

"Socorro," Grant said importantly. "One of their cousins moved over there last fall. Heard he went to work in the mines."

"Would he stick his neck out for a wanted man?"

"Jee—rusalem, would he ever! Them boys was always thicker'n fleas."

"What's the cousin's name?"

"Ummm—" Grant concentrated hard, suddenly laughed. "Aguilar. Luis Aguilar!"

Clint quickly assessed the situation. His one solid lead thus far was Florentino Pérez. And through Pérez, he might yet untangle the web of secrecy surrounding Miguel Ortega. The option was to hang around Lincoln and continue to hope for a break. Which seemed to him no option at all. He looked at Grant.

"I'll need descriptions of both men—Pérez and Aguilar."

Grant bobbed his head. "I take it you're headed for Socorro."

"Yeah," Clint said with a clenched smile. "Maybe it'll change my luck."

"What d'you want me to do while you're away?"

"Just what you've been doing, Will."

Grant wasn't sure how to take the remark. Up till now he'd done nothing, and that made it sound like an insult. On the other hand, he had just provided a hot lead to the whereabouts of Florentino Pérez. He decided the latter version made the better story. One he would quietly spread around town.

A sheriff always had to keep one eye trained on the next election.

Socorro was located on the banks of the upper Rio Grande. An established mining town, it was the county seat and a widely renowned hellhole. Local boosters proudly claimed forty-four saloons and a dozen round-the-clock cathouses. The sporting crowd, much like the miners, worked double shifts.

Clint rode into town in the early forenoon. His trip had consumed three days, covering more than a hundred miles. A good part of that time had been spent in crossing the Jornada del Muerto. Aptly named, it was a wasteland of alkaline waterholes and slow death for the unwary traveler. Fording the Rio Grande seemed a deliverance of sorts.

Oscar Packard was the county sheriff. When Clint entered his office, the rawboned lawman jackknifed to his feet. He pumped Clint's arm vigorously, genuinely delighted to see him. In the old days, when Clint was a special agent for the army, they had often worked together. Packard was still sheriff, and that fact alone commanded respect. A lesser man wouldn't have lasted in Socorro's rough, and sometimes deadly, sporting district.

After lighting a cigarette, Clint told his story straight through. He had a warrant for Florentino Pérez; but he first had to find the cousin, Luis Aguilar. Packard listened without interruption or comment, nodding to himself. While the White Caps had not yet organized in Socorro, he kept abreast of their activities elsewhere. He was eager to assist a fellow lawman.

When Clint finished, there was a moment's silence. Packard tilted back in his chair, hands steepled, and tapped his forefingers together. Finally he leaned forward, elbows on the desk.

"Lots of Mexicans in Socorro," he said, "and they stick to themselves. We need somebody who knows his way around."

Clint flicked an ash off his cigarette. "You got someone in mind?"

"Just the man." Packard swiveled toward the door. "Baca! Elfego Baca. C'mon in here."

A *mexicano* appeared from the outer office. He was a stocky, broad-shouldered man with quick eyes and a neatly trimmed mustache. He paused in the doorway, the badge of a deputy sheriff pinned to his shirt. Packard waved him forward and performed introductions. Baca shook Clint's hand with a firm strong grasp.

"An honor," he said, smiling. "Your name is known to all lawmen."

"A pleasure to meet you," Clint said. "I recollect your name's not unknown either."

The offhand compliment was an understatement. In 1884, Baca had arrested a drunken cowhand in a village west of Socorro. Taken before a justice of the peace, the prisoner was fined five dollars and released. When Baca emerged from the courtroom, he was met by a rowdy bunch of cowhands, angered that a *mexicano* had arrested their friend. A shot was fired, and Baca ducked into an alley.

With the crowd on his heels, Baca took refuge in a *jacal* constructed of mud and posts. Led by two ranchers, the mob quickly swelled to eighty armed cowhands. They opened fire and Baca hugged the floor, which was slightly below ground level. He held them off for a day and a half, popping up to return their fire with deadly accuracy. When the siege finally ended, he had killed four men and wounded several others. Since then, Baca's reputation had proved a deterrent in itself. No one cared to tangle with a man who would dare any odds.

"Got a job for you," Packard said now. "Clint's after a member of *Las Gorras Blancas*. The charge is murder."

"Those *bastardos*," Baca cursed. "They dirty the name of all *mexicanos*. I'm at your service, Señor Brannock."

Clint briefly outlined the situation. When he mentioned the men's names, there was no reaction. But then, after remarking that Aguilar worked in the mines, he noted a change in Baca's expression. The *mexicano* deputy looked thoughtful.

"I know that *hombre*," he said. "I've seen him around the *cantinas*. He works the day shift at one of the mines."

"Any idea which one?"

"No," Baca said, then chuckled slyly. "But he has an adobe just outside town. I've heard he's married, three or four children."

Clint considered a moment. "Have you heard anything about Pérez?"

"Nothing."

"Guess we don't have a helluva lot of choice. We'll have to sit on Aguilar's house and hope we get lucky."

Baca laughed, spread his hands. "We wait like the spider, eh? Let him come to us."

"Yeah," Clint said with a hard grin. "Except we have to trap him, not kill him. I want him alive."

"What if he decides to fight?"

"We'll just have to talk him out of it, Elfego. He's no good to me dead."

"*Sangre de Cristo*! I think it will be an interesting night."

A livid moon hung suspended in a black sky. The landscape appeared ghostly, flooded in a bluish, spectral light. Somewhere in the distance an owl hooted faintly.

Clint and Baca were posted on top a hogback ridge. Soon after dark they had left their horses in a gully beyond the reverse slope. For the past hour, seated in the shadow of an outcropping, neither of them had spoken. Their eyes were fixed on an adobe at the bottom of the hill.

The house was located three miles north of Socorro. Cottonwoods lined the banks of the Rio Grande, and a short distance upstream there was a stand of willows. The voices of children carried distinctly in the still night air. From time to time, the voice of a woman, loud and scolding, could be heard. So far, there had been nothing to indicate the presence of a man.

Clint suddenly tensed. He nudged Baca and pointed downstream. A shadowy figure appeared in the wash of moonlight, walking toward the house. As they watched, the figure took the shape of a man dressed in rough workclothes. Words were unnecessary, for they each read the other's thoughts. The man was Luis Aguilar, returning from a day in the mines.

The squeals of laughing children erupted as Aguilar entered the adobe. For a short while the sounds of excited voices carried to the top of the hill. Then the commotion dropped off and things inside the house gradually returned to normal. Some minutes later Aguilar appeared in the doorway. He put his fingers to his mouth and whistled a single sharp blast.

Upstream, a man emerged from the stand of willows. He walked swiftly toward the house, dimly visible in the dappled moonglow. As he approached closer, he was revealed in a shaft of lamplight spilling through the door. His head was bare, but he wore the *vaquero* garb favored by *mexicano* horsemen. Aguilar waved him inside and closed the door.

Clint felt certain there was a horse picketed in the willows. He was equally confident as to the identity of the man. From all appearances, Florentino Pérez hid out along the riverbank during the day. After dark, when his cousin signaled the all-clear, he came out for supper. Whether or not he spent the night in the house seemed a moot point. He was there now.

Quiet as drifting hawks, Clint and Baca made their way down the hill. Cautiously, their guns drawn, they approached a small window at the front of the house. A quick look confirmed that the entire family was seated around the supper table. Clint flattened himself against the wall directly beside the door. He nodded and Baca kicked it open.

There was an instant of dumbstruck silence. The woman sat at the far end of the table, a fork halfway to her mouth. Aguilar was at the head of the table, his back to the door, and Pérez was seated to his immediate right. Abruptly, the woman screamed and the three children shrieked in terror. Pérez bolted to his feet, his eyes glittering with a look of trapped desperation. He fumbled at the gun holstered on his hip, wheeling away from the table.

Clint crossed the room in two quick strides. His arm rose and fell as Pérez cleared leather. The pistol barrel struck Pérez high on the forehead with a mushy whump. His mouth opened in a soundless grunt and the gun fell from his hand. For a moment he stood rigid; then his eyes went blank and his knees buckled. He dropped like a stone.

From the door, Baca covered the room. His sights

were trained on Aguilar, who had risen from his chair. Baca grinned and slowly motioned with his pistol. Aguilar obeyed the unspoken command, resuming his seat. Against the far wall, his wife was huddled with the children, holding them clutched in her arms. Their eyes gleamed dark and wide in the sallow lamplight.

Kneeling down, Clint scooped the gun off the floor and stuck it in his waistband. He then holstered his pistol and pulled a set of manacles from his hip pocket. A moment later he had Pérez's wrists secured, hands locked at the small of the back. He climbed to his feet glancing around at Baca.

"*Gracias*," he said. "You can back my play anytime."

"*De nada*," Baca said casually. "What will you do with him now?"

Clint smiled. "Teach him to sing the right tune."

"*Perdón?*"

"A songbird, *compadre*. Otherwise known as a turncoat."

14

The afternoon stage arrived late. Dusk had fallen over Lincoln as the driver sawed back on the reins. He brought his six-horse hitch to a stop outside the express office.

John Taylor hopped out of the coach. He assisted Elizabeth down and then collected their bags from the luggage boot. The other passengers, most of them bound for Roswell, stepped out to stretch their legs. Upstreet, the sound of laughter drifted from a saloon.

Elizabeth asked Taylor to meet her at the clinic. She knew he wanted a drink and felt reasonably certain he would stop by the saloon. Having fortified himself, he would then retrieve the buckboard and team from the livery stable. She allowed herself at least a half-hour before he would return.

The trip to Santa Fe had been exhaustive. Apart from the travel itself, Elizabeth hadn't rested properly. Her mind was like a whirligig, spinning round and round with too many projects. The *mexicano* convention, in particular, preoccupied her thoughts. Announcements had gone out to the *políticos*, but their response was still an unknown factor. She worried that some of them would refuse to attend.

The clinic was closed for the night. Elizabeth walked along a pathway to the rear, noting that lamps were lighted in the living quarters. Jennifer answered her

knock with a look of surprise and a pleased laugh.
They hugged, kissing each other on the cheek, and
moved into the parlor. When Jennifer offered her
supper, Elizabeth asked instead for a cup of tea. The
jouncing stagecoach had robbed her of her appetite.

Jennifer put a pot of tea to steeping. She returned
from the kitchen and found her mother slumped in an
armchair. Neither of them spoke as she seated herself
on the sofa. Her eyebrows lifted in a slight frown.

"You look tired," she said. "You really should eat
something."

"Oh, I will," Elizabeth said evasively. "I'll have a
bit of something when we get home."

"Why not spend the night here? From the way you
act, you could certainly use the rest."

"I prefer to sleep in my own bed. Besides, I've been
away almost a week. I have things to do at the ranch."

"I might as well tell you myself," Jennifer said after
a moment. "You'll find out when you get home, anyway. There's been a good deal of trouble while you
were gone."

"What kind of trouble?"

Jennifer recounted the raid on Tipton's Sawmill.
She touched briefly on the shooting, commenting that
Las Gorras Blancas had deliberately spared Morg's
life. There seemed no other explanation.

"And Morg's all right?" Elizabeth asked in a concerned voice. "You're not hiding anything from me?"

"No, he's fine," Jennifer said. "Nothing bruised but
his pride."

"I—" Elizabeth hesitated, shook her head. "Apparently Miguel Ortega is a man of his word. He said no
harm would come to anyone on Spur."

"Too bad the truce doesn't extend to everyone.
There was another raid the following night, and more
shooting . . . two men were killed."

Jennifer went on to relate the details. The cowhand and the *mexicano*, Bonifacio Pérez, had been buried on the same day. After securing a murder warrant, Clint had ridden off in search of Pérez's brother. A rumor was circulating that his investigation centered on Socorro.

"Socorro?" Elizabeth repeated. "John and I came through there last night. We caught the morning stage."

Jennifer nodded. "Uncle Clint might have been staying in the same hotel. It's possible you missed him coming and going."

A troubled look settled over Elizabeth's face. "I worry about him more than you know. He's too old to be chasing around after outlaws."

"Well, it certainly doesn't show. He's been here, there, and yon the past month or so."

"That worries me too," Elizabeth said quietly. "Your Uncle Clint won't stop till he catches Miguel Ortega. Nothing good will come of it."

"Tell me, Mother—" Jennifer paused, one eyebrow raised. "Which do you worry about most?"

"Ortega," Elizabeth said with more truth than she intended. "Despite everything, he's a decent man. All he really wants is justice for his people."

"You admire him, don't you?"

"Yes, I do! And I'm not ashamed to admit it. He could have been a great leader . . ."

"But, instead, he's a wanted man," Jennifer finished the thought. "And you're afraid Uncle Clint will kill him."

"How else can it end?" Elizabeth said. "Ortega will never be taken alive. I saw it in his eyes the night we met."

Jennifer could think of nothing reassuring to say. She went to the kitchen and returned with an enameled teapot. Elizabeth accepted a steaming cup and took several quick sips. The hot tea seemed to revive her and she sat straighter in her chair. Her mood suddenly brightened.

"I've had enough depressing talk for one night. What's happening in your life?"

Jennifer shrugged. "Nothing all that extraordinary."

"You know very well I'm talking about Blake. Have you set a date?"

"As a matter of fact, we've decided on June twenty-first."

"Good!" Elizabeth said happily. "I've never believed in long betrothals. Your father and I were married a month after he proposed."

On the verge of replying, Jennifer's features clouded with a shadow of anxiety. Her expression was oddly unsettled, as though pulled back from a distant thought. A thought she couldn't bring herself to confront.

"When you married," she said softly, "were you in love with Father?"

"What a strange question." Elizabeth stared at her over the rim of the teacup. "Yes, I was very much in love. Why do you ask?"

Her reply was so quiet that Elizabeth had to strain to hear. "I don't love Blake," she said. "I respect him, and I'm terribly fond of him. But it isn't the way I always imagined . . ."

"Few things are," Elizabeth said calmly. "Our schoolgirl notions seldom live up to reality. We learn to compromise."

"Was Father a compromise?"

"No, not in the beginning. Quite soon, though, I discovered that marriage fell short of the dream. Hardly a day went by that I didn't compromise in some fashion."

Jennifer smiled wanly. "Perhaps it's easier to compromise when you love someone."

"Are you having second thoughts about marrying Blake?"

"I suppose I am. Wouldn't you, in my position?"

Elizabeth sighed inwardly. "Maybe you ought to call it off. You're still young and there'll be other men. You might even find one you love."

"Do you really believe that?"

"To be perfectly honest, I think you're already married. Your grand love affair is with medicine—not men."

"I know," Jennifer said. "That's why I accepted Blake's proposal."

"What are you saying?"

"Being a doctor will always come first in my life. I think Blake resigned himself to that a long time ago. Not many men could."

"Well then," Elizabeth remarked, "it seems you have a choice between love and an understanding husband. Which do you prefer?"

"Both," Jennifer said with a sudden sad grin. "But as you pointed out, life is a matter of compromise. So I guess I'll marry Blake."

"Why are we talking about it, then? You sound like your mind was made up all along."

"I just needed to hear myself say it out loud. Sometimes it's hard to accept until you actually admit it."

Elizabeth sensed a deeper conflict. Her daughter was a complex woman, and emotional problems were never resolved with oblique reasoning. Still, there was nothing to be gained in pressing beyond certain limits.

She decided to leave well enough alone.

The day began early on Spur. Spring roundup was underway and the hands rode out shortly after sunrise. By seven o'clock the compound was virtually deserted.

Elizabeth slept late. She awoke refreshed, her mind

uncluttered with worries. Simply returning to Spur infused her with energy, for the ranch was her touchstone in life. She somehow drew strength from the land, an inner reservoir of certainty. All things seemed possible on the Hondo.

After fixing her hair, she laid out her clothes for the day. She planned to inspect the roundup and have a talk with Brad. Accordingly she selected a *charro* outfit with a short jacket and split skirt. She'd long ago put aside feminine modesty, as well as her old side saddle, when she mounted a horse. She often marveled that she hadn't done it sooner.

Entering the dining room, she found Morg and Louise still seated at the breakfast table. Morg leapt up, full of restless vitality, and kissed her on the cheek. She then exchanged kisses with Louise, who greeted her with considerably less warmth. Her daughter-in-law resented her, and she'd never been able to establish a comfortable relationship. She supposed it was the natural order of things when two women lived under the same roof. However inequitable, there was only one mistress of the house.

Elizabeth took her seat at the head of the table. A serving girl brought her usual breakfast of coffee, dry toast, and canned fruit. She noted that Morg and Louise had already eaten and appeared to be dawdling over a final cup of coffee. Her intuition told her that something was afoot, something that required her presence. She glanced down the table at Morg.

"Aren't you off to a late start this morning?"

"Figured you'd want a report," Morg said easily. "Lots of things have happened while you were away."

"So I heard," Elizabeth commented. "Jen told me you almost got yourself shot."

"I guess it was a close call. But like they say, close only counts in horseshoes."

"You're being awfully casual about it."

Louise sniffed and Morg darted her a look. When she dropped her eyes, he turned back to Elizabeth. "Got some good news," he said. "We'll turn a profit on the timber company by the end of September."

"That's marvelous," Elizabeth said, clearly impressed. "I never thought you'd do it so quickly."

"Tell you the truth, I'm a little surprised myself. 'Course, now that it's a going concern, we've got ourselves a real opportunity."

"How do you mean?"

"Way I see it," Morg said, "the timber business proves my point. It's time we branched out in a big way."

Elizabeth sipped her coffee. "Are you hinting at another venture of some sort?"

"Nothing else," Morg announced. "I'd like to take a crack at the mining game."

For a moment, Elizabeth was speechless. "Why mining?" she said finally. "Whatever put that idea in your head?"

"Things are booming over at White Oaks. I figure it's the chance of a lifetime."

Morg went on with mounting enthusiasm. His timber business had taken him to the towns of Nogal and White Oaks. Located west of Lincoln, these were the principal mining camps in the distant mountains. Gold had been discovered there in the late 1870s; but the boom had faded as placer mines slowly played out. Technical advances now made it possible to follow the rich veins deep underground.

"The gold's there," Morg concluded, "but hard-rock mining costs money. Tunnels and equipment don't come cheap."

Elizabeth smiled gently. "What do you know about the mining business?"

"Not a whole lot," Morg conceded. " 'Course, I was a greenhorn at the timber business too. It's a matter of finding the right man."

"Are you talking about a foreman?"

"What I had in mind was more on the order of a partner."

Morg quickly outlined his plan. There were many small mine owners around White Oaks who lacked capital. Constantly strapped for funds, they were unable to exploit the true value of their claims. He proposed to search out such an individual and offer to finance the operation. To bind the deal, a corporation would then be formed.

"We'll insist on control," Morg observed. "Divvy the stock fifty-one percent in our favor."

"Even so," Elizabeth said, "how would we know the money was being spent wisely? We've had no experience at mining."

A crafty look came over Morg's face. "Our partner will have to convince me day-by-day, nickel-by-nickel. Otherwise I'll hire an outside mining engineer."

"All that will take time," Elizabeth reminded him. "With the timber company, and the new mining venture, you'll have your hands full. Who's to look after things here at Spur?"

"Brad doesn't need any help. Let him run the ranch and I'll go on to other prospects. That way we've got our bets hedged all the way round."

Elizabeth shook her head wonderingly. She marked again that Morg was hauntingly like his father. As though an echo from the past, she recalled Virgil saying that a man's reach should always exceed his grasp. At length, she let out a deep breath.

"How much money do you need?"

Morg laughed. "Forty thousand ought to turn the trick. Fifty would guarantee it."

For a while longer they talked about the project. Elizabeth finally agreed, on condition that she be kept apprised of the details. After a final cup of coffee, she excused herself, all the more aware of the need to talk with Brad. She left the house and walked toward the stables.

When the front door closed, an uneasy quiet descended on the dining room. Louise suddenly looked wretched, her features pale and drawn. She stared across the table at Morg with an expression of disgust. There was a harried sharpness in her words.

"You were right after all," she said. "Your mother couldn't say no—she never says no!"

Morg was determined not to quibble. "She just knows a good deal when she hears one. Nothin' wrong with that."

"Wrong?" Her voice quivered with anger. "What's wrong is that you're always off tending to business. And this gold mine will just make it worse. I'm sick of it!"

"C'mon, Lou, don't get yourself upset. You knew I wasn't a homebody when we got married."

"I did not! I thought I married a rancher, not a businessman. Why can't you be like everyone else?"

"You always told me I was different from everyone else. I thought that's why you were sweet on me."

"Stop it!" Her eyes flooded with tears. "I won't be fobbed off with your silly jokes. It's not funny."

Morg heard the pain in her voice. He silently wished she'd hurry up and have the baby. But then, on quick reflection, he admitted she had a point. For the last few months his every waking thought had been devoted to business. He knew he hadn't been much of a husband.

On sudden impulse, Morg told her something he'd never told anyone else. His father had believed that nothing extraordinary was ever achieved without the ambition to dare greatly. As a boy, he had watched his father transform a remote valley into a ranch envied by all cattlemen. Spur was his father's legacy, the result of ambition and daring and hard work. He felt honor-bound to build on that legacy, rather than loaf along on what he'd inherited. Otherwise he would be something less than his father's son.

"Don't you see, Lou," he said earnestly, "the ranch was Pa's doing, his dream. I've got to make my mark my own way."

Louise dashed tears from her face with the back of her hand. She knew he had revealed a secret part of himself, something he'd kept locked inside since his father's death. Even more, she realized he had told her out of feeling, a sense of something shared. It was important to him that she understand.

"Yes, I do see," she said in a hushed voice. "In a way, I wish I didn't. It would be easier to stay mad at you."

Morg studied her a moment. "Does that mean you're not mad anymore?"

She smiled an upside-down smile. "What good would it do me? You aren't about to change, are you?"

"Would you want me to change?"

"Yes," she said with a bright little nod. "But I married you for better or worse. I guess I'm stuck."

Morg grinned, rising from his chair. He moved around the table and walked to her side. Tilting her chin, he kissed her full on the mouth and held her close in his arms. When they parted, his hand dropped from her face and playfully rubbed the mound of her stomach. He chuckled softly, his mouth brushing her ear.

"Tell the kid he'd better hurry. His daddy wasn't meant to be a monk."

*   *   *

Four cowhands worked the branding fire. Off in the distance, outriders circled a herd of shorthorns being held on a grassy swale. Bawling calves were lassoed and dragged to the fire, where they were thrown to the ground. The men on foot quickly branded them and castrated the bull calves.

Elizabeth and Brad watched from a nearby knoll. She was mounted on a *grulla* mare and Brad rode a sorrel cowpony. Her inspection of the roundup had brought her to a holding ground not far from the southern foothills. There she'd found Brad checking one of the many branding operations on Spur.

For a time they discussed routine affairs. Brad planned to start the gather for trail herds within the week. Extra men, who drifted from one outfit to another during trailing season, had already been hired. By the end of the month, the first herd would be driven north toward the railhead. From there, the cows would be shipped to eastern slaughterhouses.

Brad foresaw no problems with the trail drives. While attentive to his report, Elizabeth was preoccupied with other thoughts. She'd known for some time that he might quit Spur to build his own outfit on the Rio Felix. Yet now, more than ever, she needed him to stay on as foreman. With Morg distracted by other business interests, she simply couldn't afford to lose Brad. She somehow had to ensure his loyalty to Spur.

"Not to change the subject," she said now, "but I had a talk with Morg this morning. He has his mind set on starting a mining venture."

"Yeah, I know," Brad said, smiling. "He's been bending my ear about it for the past week."

"I've decided to go along with the idea. It sounds promising."

"Well, Morg's got a good head for business. I just suspect he'll pull it off."

Elizabeth tried to keep her voice casual. "With Morg gone so much, that means added responsibility for you. I was thinking we might work out a new arrangement."

"Oh," Brad said without much interest. "What's that?"

"As a matter of fact, I was considering a bonus of some sort. Say ten percent on the increase over last year. How does that strike you?"

"Wouldn't hurt my feelings," Brad said absently. "I could always use the extra money."

"What I'm asking—" Elizabeth hesitated, searching for words. "I need some assurance from you, Brad. I want to know you'll stay on as foreman."

Brad stared stonily ahead, his face blank. "I'll stay on till the end of trailing season. I can't promise anything after that."

Elizabeth looked at him for a long moment. "Would more money change your mind? I'm agreeable to anything within reason."

"It's not the money," Brad said in a faraway voice. "Tell you the truth, I'm sort of betwixt and between. I don't know what I'm gonna do."

"While you're trying to decide, remember that we think of you as family. Spur wouldn't be the same without you."

"I'm not likely to forget."

Elizabeth nodded, all too aware of his quandary. She reined her mare around and rode off. Fording the river, it occurred to her that the conversation had resolved nothing. Yet she couldn't fault Brad anymore than she could take issue with Morg. Nor could she stand in their way.

A young man was entitled to try his wings, wherever it might lead. She wouldn't deny either of them the chance.

15

The passenger coach was crowded. Sante Fe appeared in the distance as the train rounded a curve at the base of a hill. The engineer tooted his whistle with three sharp blasts.

Clint was seated at the rear of the coach. Beside him, hands manacled, was Florentino Pérez. All the other seats were occupied by men whose affairs brought them to the territorial capital. Their curiosity regarding the prisoner was confined to speculative stares. None of them had mustered the nerve to start a conversation.

Early that morning Clint and Pérez had boarded the train at Socorro. The trip to Santa Fe was quicker by rail and Clint had left his horse stalled at a livery stable. Pérez, who was a study in abject resignation, looked somewhat the worse for wear. A large goose egg swelled his forehead where he'd been struck with the pistol barrel.

The long ride from Socorro had passed in silence. Clint hadn't attempted to question his prisoner about the activities of *Las Gorras Blancas*. Instead, he had let Pérez sweat, allowing the tension to build as they neared Santa Fe. He thought a formal interrogation, conducted at the territorial prison, would make a greater impression. The gallows was only a short walk away.

A wire had been sent ahead from Socorro. U.S.

Marshal Fred Mather was waiting at the train station.
Pérez was hustled into an enclosed buggy and they
drove directly to the governor's palace. There the
prisoner was handed over to the jailer and lodged in a
cell at the rear of the building. Clint then made his
report and explained what he had in mind. Mather
agreed it was worth a try.

Vance Traver, the attorney general, was summoned
from his office at the opposite end of the building. A
bloodless man in his early fifties, Traver was stoop-
shouldered with skin the texture of parchment. When
he entered the office, he appeared surprised to see
Clint. After they were seated, Mather briefly outlined
the situation. He ended on a positive note.

"We've got a chance to bust the White Caps wide
open. All we have to do is make Pérez talk."

Traver looked skeptical. "How do you propose to
do that?"

"Offer him a deal," Mather replied. "In exchange
for cooperation, we'll reduce the murder charge to
manslaughter. He'll serve time but he won't hang."

"I see." Traver paused, then glanced around at
Clint. "Was this your idea, marshal?"

"Yessir," Clint said impassively. "Pérez is one of
the small fry in *Las Gorras Blancas*. I'd like to use
him to get Miguel Ortega."

"The governor would certainly endorse that senti-
ment. But you still haven't answered my question.
Why should Pérez talk?"

"I don't take your meaning."

"It was my understanding," Traver said, "that these
people are fanatics. Wouldn't he prefer to hang rather
than betray Ortega?"

Clint's face was dispassionate. "You'd be surprised
what a man will do to avoid the gallows. You follow
my lead and we might just loosen his tongue."

"What is it you want me to do?"

At some length, Clint detailed his plan. Afterward, Florentino Pérez was brought from the lockup, his hands still manacled, and ushered into the office. Traver sat behind the desk, flanked by Clint and Mather. Clint nodded to the prisoner, addressing him in Spanish.

"This man," he said, indicating Traver, "will decide whether you live or die. He is the *jefe* of the courts here and the judges do his bidding. *Comprende*?"

"*Sí*," Pérez said, his eyes cast downward. "I understand."

"You are charged with taking part in a murder. Under the law, you are as guilty as the man who actually pulled the trigger. Is that clear?"

A muscle twitched in Pérez's cheek. "*Sí*."

"Listen closely." Clint's tone was harsh, roughly insistent. "Your life will be spared on one condition. We want information on Miguel Ortega."

Pérez might have been deaf, for all the change in his expression. When he made no reply, Clint went on. "Either you help us or we will have no choice. A court will order your execution by hanging."

"Do what you must, *señor*. I have nothing to say."

Clint interpreted his answer. Traver abruptly stood and fixed the prisoner with a baleful stare. His voice was vindictive and he jabbed a blunt forefinger at Pérez. After he finished speaking, Clint translated into Spanish.

"You have angered the *jefe*. He orders that your mother and sister be taken into custody and brought to Sante Fe. They will be forced to watch you hanged."

All the color drained from Pérez's features. He appeared petrified by the prospect, and his voice sounded parched. "Why would you make them suffer? They have done nothing wrong."

"The choice is yours," Clint said sternly. "Your

mother has already lost one son, and justice requires
that she witness your death. Her grief will be on your
head."

Clint had taken a calculated risk. He waited, allowing silence to exert its own pressure. Family loyalty
now hung in the balance against loyalty to Miguel
Ortega. At last Pérez looked at him with dulled eyes.

"What is it you wish, *señor*?"

"Tell me where I can find Ortega."

"No one can tell you that. Ortega never spends two
nights in the same place."

"Are you saying he doesn't have a hideout?"

"*Sí, señor.* Sometimes he stays overnight with a
mexicano family. Other times he camps somewhere in
the mountains. Even his followers never know."

"When he plans a raid," Clint asked, "how does he
get word to *Las Gorras Blancas*?"

Pérez shrugged. "One man passes the message along
to another and it spreads rapidly. Within a few hours
all the members have been notified."

"Does Ortega travel alone?"

"*No*," Pérez said. "A *pistolero* is always at his side,
night and day. He guards Ortega with his life."

"What is the *pistolero*'s name?"

"I do not know. I have never heard Ortega address
him by name."

"Aside from your brother," Clint said deliberately,
"who are the other members—their names?"

Pérez managed a smile. "All *mexicanos* belong to
Las Gorras Blancas. None would dare to do otherwise."

"Even the *políticos*?"

"As to that, I cannot say. I have never seen a
político at the meetings."

"But they support Ortega, *verdad*?"

"No *mexicano* would oppose Ortega, *señor*. To do
so would be to forfeit your life."

The interrogation continued for a while longer. Yet it was evident to Clint that nothing of immediate value would be uncovered. *Las Gorras Blancas* was operated under a mantle of secrecy designed to protect its leader. However forthcoming, Pérez made only one significant contribution to the investigation. His testimony implicated Miguel Ortega in the death of the Rio Bonito cowhand.

Pérez was finally returned to his cell. Afterward the attorney general complimented Clint on his skill as an interrogator. The threat involving Pérez's mother had proved to be a masterful gambit. Still, Traver expressed disappointment with the outcome. In his view, they were no closer to catching Ortega than before.

Clint strongly disagreed. "Until now," he said, "the only charges we had against Ortega were fence-cutting and destruction of property. As of today, we've got a witness who can put his head in a noose."

"Quite true," Traver conceded. "We'll have no problem obtaining a murder warrant against Ortega. Unless it's served, of course, it's just another piece of paper. You first have to apprehend him."

Clint's mouth set in a hard line. "Ortega doesn't walk on water. Sooner or later he'll make a mistake. When he does, I'll be there."

"Let's hope it's sooner," Mather interjected. "So far, he's made a laughingstock out of the law."

"Way I see it," Clint said, "it's the last laugh that counts. We'll just have to make sure the joke's on Ortega."

Traver nodded solemnly. "Amen to that."

Within the hour a court hearing was convened. The attorney general presented Florentino Pérez as the territory's chief witness. His testimony, backed by Clint's account, proved to be conclusive. The judge rendered an immediate decision.

A murder warrant was issued on Miguel Ortega.

Late that afternoon Clint was called to the governor's office. He found Edmund Ross in a chatty mood, almost jocular. Their handshake was firm and cordial.

When they were seated, Clint rolled himself a cigarette. He lit it and then took a deep drag, exhaling little spurts of smoke. Ross was talking all the while, reviewing the day's events. His manner was at once benign and magnanimous, somehow lordly.

"You're to be congratulated," he remarked. "You've accomplished a great deal under adverse circumstances."

Clint shrugged off the compliment. "We've still got a ways to go. Ortega's plenty slick."

"Don't be modest," Ross admonished. "I knew from the start you were the man for the job. You'll run him down."

"I aim to do my damnedest, governor."

"Bring him to justice and you'll have my everlasting gratitude, Mr. Brannock. Not to mention the esteem of President Cleveland."

Clint looked at him for a long moment. "Governor, I've talked to a lot of Mexicans in the past month or so. Would you like to hear what I found out?"

"Indeed I would."

"Well, just for openers, Ortega's not preachin' revolution. From what I gather, he's never called for an uprising against the government."

"Tommyrot," Ross said crossly. "Everyone knows he wants a realignment with Old Mexico. His goal is to drive all Anglos from the territory."

"Funny thing," Clint said. "The only ones talkin' about revolution are the Anglos. As near as I can pinpoint it, the talk got its start here in Santa Fe."

"What are you driving at, Mr. Brannock?"

"Way it looks to me, Ortega's preachin' reform, not

revolution. He just wants an end to all these land-grabbing schemes."

Ross's voice was clipped, incisive. "Are you saying he's been unjustly branded as a revolutionary?"

"Lots of folks," Clint reminded him, "don't like the sound of reform. Goes against their business interests."

"And you believe they would slander Ortega to further their own interests?"

"Nothing easier, what with him and the White Caps raising so much hell. A murder warrant tends to make it even worse."

"What makes it worse," Ross said shortly, "is your sister-in-law's poor judgment. I understand she's allied herself with Ortega."

"You understand wrong," Clint informed him stiffly. "Ortega asked her to support *Las Gorras Blancas* and she refused. Anybody who says different is a goddamn liar."

"How does that square with her coalition? Not even Elizabeth Brannock would deny that the *mexicanos* support Ortega."

A stony look settled on Clint's face. "Her coalition was around long before Ortega. There wouldn't be any White Caps if she'd got the reforms she wanted."

"Tell me," Ross said heavily, "does your loyalty to Mrs. Brannock affect your attitude as a peace officer? We can't allow anything of a personal nature to influence your investigation."

Clint kept his gaze level and cool. "When I pinned on a badge, I took an oath to uphold the law. Nothing's happened to change that, governor."

Ross studied him a moment, finally nodded. "I want an end written to the matter of Miguel Ortega. Don't disappoint me, Mr. Brannock."

"Anytime you're not satisfied . . ."

Ross dismissed him with a brusque gesture. Clint

stubbed out his cigarette in an ashtray and rose, walking to the door. As he turned the knob, the governor's voice stopped him. "Mr. Brannock."

"Yessir?"

"One last piece of advice. A lawman should never take sides in politics. I suggest you bear that in mind."

"Governor, so far as I'm concerned, the only difference between politics and a bucket of horse apples is the bucket. I wouldn't dirty my hands."

The door opened and closed. Far from being offended, Edmund Ross was amused by the rebuff. A wintry smile lighted his eyes and he slowly nodded to himself. He still thought he'd picked the right man for the job.

Miguel Ortega now had one foot in the grave.

That evening Clint took supper at the hotel. The food was passable, and since he'd engaged a room for the night, he saw no reason to go elsewhere. He ordered the house special, a charred steak and fried potatoes.

After a second cup of coffee, he wandered into the hotel barroom. He planned to be in bed by ten and up by sunrise, in time to catch the morning train. A couple of drinks, on top of a big meal, would ensure a good night's sleep. He seated himself at an empty table opposite the bar.

The first drink went down smoothly. He signaled the barkeep for a refill and began rolling a smoke. As he struck a match, he saw Thomas Canby come through the door. Their eyes met and Canby walked in his direction. He waited without expression.

" 'Evening," Canby said, halting beside the table. "Heard you were in town and thought we might have a talk. Mind if I join you?"

"Suit yourself."

Canby settled into a chair. The barkeep appeared with a bottle and another glass, and poured. When he moved away, neither of the men touched their whiskey. Clint looked across the table.

"What have we got to talk about?"

"Your sister-in-law," Canby said. "I'd be obliged if you would deliver a message."

Clint tapped an ash off his cigarette. "I'm willing to listen."

"Are you aware Mrs. Brannock plans to hold a *mexicano* political convention?"

"I read the papers."

Canby inclined his head. "Then you know she's playing with fire. The only one who will benefit is Miguel Ortega."

"None of my concern," Clint said, meeting his gaze. "Why don't you get to the point?"

"I'll be quite frank," Canby said. "New Mexico is on the verge of a revolution. We want that convention canceled."

"By 'we,' " Clint asked, "do you mean the Santa Fe Ring?"

Canby forced a smile. "I represent men who control the legislature and the territory's major business interests. We're willing to make peace with Mrs. Brannock."

"In exchange for what?"

"We'll wipe the slate clean. An invitation will be extended to Mrs. Brannock, asking her to join with us in forming one political party. In effect, we would then control the destiny of New Mexico."

Clint stared at him. "You still haven't told me the price."

"Let's call it a condition," Canby said. "We would insist that she cancel the convention and sever all ties with the *mexicanos*. We want her coalition disbanded."

"Suppose she met your condition," Clint replied.

"What's to stop Ira Hecht from taking over the coalition?"

Canby's mouth went tight, scornful. "We'll take care of Hecht in our own way. He's no problem."

"Sounds to me like you're running scared."

"I beg your pardon?"

"You're afraid you'll lose the fall elections. You figure Elizabeth's finally gonna unite the Mexican vote. And if she does, your boys will get tossed out of office."

Canby looked at him with a kind of contempt. "I assure you we won't lose, Mr. Brannock. We'll take whatever steps are necessary to ensure a victory."

"Is that meant to be a threat?"

"It's a statement of fact. Forced to the wall, we'll have no choice but to play rough. The stakes are just too big."

Clint's voice was suddenly edged. "Here's another statement of fact. Take care that no harm comes to anybody in my family. One misstep and I'll kill you."

"The governor wouldn't care for that at all. I suspect he'd hang you."

"Wouldn't matter," Clint observed. "You'd still be dead."

Canby appeared unconcerned. "I suggest you deliver my message to Mrs. Brannock. Perhaps she'll accept and save us all some grief."

"Just remember what I said . . . no rough stuff."

Canby got to his feet, his drink untouched. He nodded curtly and walked to the door. Clint took a pull on his cigarette, exhaling a thin streamer of smoke. His expression was stoic, somehow faraway.

He thought he'd got a glimpse of the future. And he didn't like what he saw.

A mealy, weblike darkness cloaked the room. Clint

awoke to a muffled sound and his every sense alerted. He lay perfectly still, feigning sleep.

His room was on the ground floor at the rear of the hotel. While the nights were generally cool in Santa Fe, he always opened a window. Something about the mountain air made him sleep better.

Hardly moving, he slowly turned his head on the pillow. Starlight dimly illuminated the window in a fuzzy glow. He saw a man halfway through the lower portion of the window, one leg in and one leg out. A glint of light reflected off a pistol in the man's hand.

Still frozen, Clint gingerly slid his hand under the pillow. He found the butt of his Colt and hooked his thumb over the hammer. As the intruder stepped through the window, he rolled out of bed and dropped onto the floor. A gunshot limned the room with fiery brilliance, followed instantly by another. The slugs tore ragged furrows in the mattress.

Clint bobbed up at the foot of the bed. He extended the Colt at arm's length, thumbing the hammer. Within the space of a few heartbeats, he touched off five shots, emptying the gun. Across the room, the man stiffened, arms windmilling, driven backward by the impact of the slugs. His head slammed into the upper windowpane and it exploded in a shower of glass. He slumped forward onto the floor.

As the man fell, Clint jerked his gunbelt off a nearby chair. He dropped behind the bed, ejecting spent shells, and reloaded the Colt by feel. Then, alert to any sound, he cautiously rose and circled the bed. At the window, he hugged the wall and took a quick look outside. Satisfied there was no one else, he finally turned to the man on the floor. The body lay crumpled in a welter of blood, visible in the pale starlight. His would-be assassin was *mexicano*.

Some thirty minutes later, Fred Mather walked into the room. Notified of the shooting, he had hurried from his home on the west side of town. He stared down at the dead man, shaking his head from side to side. At last he looked around at Clint.

"Kee-rist," he said. "You cut him to ribbons."

Clint shrugged. "If a man's worth shooting, he's worth killing. I figure he deserved what he got."

"You ever seen him before?"

"Not that I recollect."

Mather massaged his jaw. "Something about it doesn't make sense. Why would Ortega send a man to kill you?"

"Good question," Clint said. "Pérez would've been a more likely candidate. He's the one who talked."

"So where's that leave us?"

"At this point, I haven't got an inkling."

"Anybody else have a reason to kill you?"

Clint was silent for a time. He thought back to his conversation with Tom Canby. He'd threatened the leader of the Santa Fe Ring and that alone might have provoked the attack. Still, something about it didn't ring true. Canby was a meticulous planner, given to details. He wouldn't have sanctioned such a sloppy job. Nor would he have sent just one man.

"You're awful quiet," Mather said. "You know something I don't?"

"Nothing worth repeating."

"Then what the hell are you stewing on so hard?"

Clint smiled. "I reckon it's time I had a talk with Señor Ortega."

"Talk?" Mather echoed. "Don't you have to find him first?"

"I'll find him," Clint said without irony. "It's in the cards."

"Which cards are those?"

"The one's I'm fixin' to deal."

16

White Oaks was located in the foothills of the Jicarilla Mountains. Some thirty miles northwest of Lincoln, the town was rough even by mining-camp standards. In days past, it had been a favorite haunt of Billy the Kid.

On the first Thursday in May, Morg dismounted outside the assayer's office. He was known in White Oaks, for he'd become the principal supplier of timbers to the mines. Today, he meant to capitalize on contacts made in the course of his business affairs. His inside coat pocket was stuffed with hundred-dollar bills.

The town was scattered along a rutted street hardly a half-mile long. Overshadowed by mountains, the frame buildings were wedged side by side, most of them topped with false fronts. Saloons and dance halls were liberally sprinkled among more legitimate forms of enterprise. One of the mainstays of the economy was the girls who worked the whorehouses and back-room cribs. Miners, by nature, were a randy breed.

Morg left his horse tethered at the hitch rail. He crossed the boardwalk and entered a small one-room building. The interior smelled of grit and dust, and bags of ore samples were stacked along the walls. A counter bisected the room, with assayer's scales and other paraphernalia prominently displayed. To the rear

were a lone desk and a workbench crowded with bea-
kers and vials. Beyond that was a huge standing safe,
the massive doors locked tight.

" 'Afternoon, Elmer," Morg said, stopping before
the counter. "How's things?"

"Well, by golly, Morg Brannock."

Elmer Westfall rose from behind his desk. He was a
slender man of medium height, his hairline receding
into a widow's peak. He had a warm smile and an
affable manner, and innocent brown eyes. Those who
knew him well were not deceived by his mild appearance. He was shrewd and quick, a hardnosed businessman.

Morg was scarcely more than an acquaintance. On
occasion, when their paths crossed, he'd bought Westfall
a drink. The assayer was a loquacious man and overly
impressed with his own opinions. What he talked about
most was mining, and Morg had proved to be an attentive audience. Their conversations invariably centered
on prospects around White Oaks.

From these casual meetings, Morg's idea for a mining venture had ultimately taken shape. He knew nothing of Westfall's personal or professional ethics, though
the assayer was widely respected. Still, he'd always
operated on the theory that any man was susceptible
to temptation. In business dealings, he had discovered
early on that money talks loudest. He planned to test
that premise on Westfall.

"You're looking fit," he said now. "Business must
be good."

"Never better," Westfall said in a reedy voice. "I'm
busier than a one-armed paper hanger."

"You and me both. I can't hardly keep the mines
supplied with timbers."

"Doesn't surprise me in the least. Everywhere you
look, somebody's sinking a new shaft."

"Tell you the truth," Morg said in a conspiratorial tone, "that's why I dropped by. Thought we might have ourselves a talk."

Westfall regarded him with a keen sidewise scrutiny. "What's on your mind?"

"I'm interested in making an investment. Figured you're the man to give me some advice."

"Always happy to oblige a friend. How can I help?"

"I've got the gold bug," Morg explained. "Last month or so, I've developed a real itch for the mining game. Finally decided there's no time like the present."

Westfall was not unaware of the Brannock name. He was Morg's senior by some twenty years, but age and experience were relative. What counted most in the world of mining was a man's financial resources. Without adequate funds, the most promising claims were little more than a plot of dirt. The wealth of the Brannock family, he told himself, placed them in the same league as Eastern financiers. His interest suddenly took a sharp upturn.

"Lots of people get the itch," he said amiably. "You could throw a rock in any direction and hit a dozen prospectors. There's no end to them."

"You're right," Morg said with cheery vigor. "And most of them never get within sniffin' distance of the mother lode. That's why I've come to you."

"I'm not sure I understand."

"Way I see it," Morg said cautiously, "nobody knows more about the mining game than an assayer. You get an inside peek before anyone else."

Westfall looked at him questioningly. "You'll have to be a little more specific. What is it you're after?"

"Information," Morg said with a faint smile. "You know who's sitting on a bonanza and who's not. I thought you might steer me in the right direction. All hush-hush, of course."

"Are you aware you're asking me to violate a confidence? After all, I have a professional responsibility to my clients."

"For the right tip, I'd be willing to pay handsomely."

"That sounds vaguely like a bribe."

Morg grinned. "Elmer, a bribe would be beneath a man of your position. Let's call it a finder's fee."

Westfall gave the matter some thought. "Suppose I agree," he said finally. "What kind of fee are we talking about?"

Morg pulled a wad of bills from his inside coat pocket. He fanned them out on the counter, and smiled. "A thousand now for a topnotch recommendation. Another thousand when I actually buy into the property."

There was a prolonged silence. Westfall lightly drummed his fingers on the counter, staring down at the bills. At length he scooped them up and tucked them into his vest pocket. His mouth twisted in a cynical grin.

"You've got a deal," he said. "Now, what sort of property are you after?"

"Something undeveloped," Morg told him. "A claim with good potential but still unworked. I'm looking for an owner who's lean and hungry."

"Do you want to steal it from him or take him on as a partner?"

"Elmer, I've got fifty thousand dollars to invest. For that, I want a partner who knows his stuff, an experienced mining man. I'll have to rely on him to run the operation."

Westfall's eyes narrowed in thought. "The wrong man could rob you blind. What you need is somebody who's honest and got himself a whiz-bang of a claim. Not many of them around."

"Don't forget," Morg added, "he has to be damn

near dead broke. Otherwise he won't need me to develop the property."

Westfall nodded, mulling it over. "Goddurn!" he said abruptly. "I've got just the man. His name's Dave Todd."

"Where's his claim?"

"Couple of miles south of town. He's strictly a one-man outfit, poor as a church mouse. But the way he talks, he's a demon for work. Told me he'd excavated a hundred feet of tunnel all by himself."

"You've had a look at his ore samples?"

"Oh, you betcha," Westfall said. "Assays out to two hundred dollars a ton. He's onto something big."

"In that case," Morg said doubtfully, "how come he's still operating on a shoestring? Why hasn't he found a backer?"

"Because he's snake-bit about outsiders. Anybody who's approached him tried to buy the claim for peanuts. They wanted the whole kit and caboodle, all or nothing."

"So you think he'd be interested in a partner?"

"Only if he trusts you," Westfall cautioned. "Dave's just bullheaded enough that he won't be cheated out of his claim. He figures he's finally struck Eldorado."

Morg deliberated a moment. "Has he got the experience to run a large operation? I'm talking about quartz mining done right."

"Yes, I'd say he does. First time he brought ore samples in, he told me he'd been a foreman at some mine up in Colorado. Way he talks, he's spent half his life underground."

"Elmer, I might just owe you another thousand dollars. He sounds made-to-order."

"Well, make sure you don't mention my name. I've got a reputation to protect."

"Wild horses couldn't drag it out of me. You've got my word on it."

Westfall drew him a map. Morg studied it a moment, satisfying himself as to the mine's location. On the way out the door, he suppressed the urge to laugh out loud. What he'd learned would have been cheap at any price. For a thousand dollars it was a genuine bargain.

He silently gave himself a pat on the back.

South of White Oaks the terrain gradually steepened. Off in the distance the summit of Carrizo Peak towered almost ten thousand feet into the sky. A dusty washboard road snaked through the rocky foothills.

Morg held his horse to a walk. He was embarked on an undertaking of no small proportions, and his mood had turned reflective. He'd already weighed the risk against the potential gain, and the odds favored the project. Yet he readily admitted he was a tyro at the game, and that in itself dictated a certain caution. He mentally cataloged all he knew about hard-rock mining.

Any gold rush began with traces of yellow metal being located in streambeds. In mountainous terrain, erosion due to weather slowly loosened subsurface pockets of ore from rock formations. Seasonal rains then carried the gold from the vein and deposited it somewhere downstream, usually in the form of flakes or fine dust. These runoff deposits were the discoveries originally uncovered by prospectors.

By panning the streams, which was known as placer mining, the prospector was able to work his claim. Before long, however, these surface deposits played out and more elaborate methods were needed to dredge the streams. In the end, when the placers failed altogether, there was no choice but to undertake quartz mining. The first step, and one that defeated most prospectors, was to trace the vein to its origin. Once the lode was located, mine shafts were excavated and the job of transporting the ore to the surface was begun.

Often called hard-rock mining, a quartz operation required freeing the ore from lodes buried deep within the earth. Extracting the gold from a quartz vein was a herculean task that demanded men and machinery, and a heavy investment of capital. The mined ore was first crushed in a stamp mill and then passed over shelves of quicksilver. The process was laborious and time-consuming, but gold in pure form was eventually distilled from the crushed rock. Such an operation required a knowledge of mining techniques and the ability to manage a venture of some magnitude. In short, it was no game for greenhorns.

The thought was foremost in Morg's mind. As he rode into the campsite, he warned himself to take nothing for granted. A crude shack, constructed of rough-sawn lumber, stood on a stretch of open ground. Beyond, on the slope of a hill, he spotted the mouth of the tunnel. No one answered his call as he dismounted in front of the shack. Then, from upslope, he heard a muffled voice. He saw a man emerge from the mine shaft.

"What d'ya want?" the man shouted.

"Are you Dave Todd?"

"Who's askin'?"

"The name's Brannock," Morg called out. "I'd like to talk to you."

"Just stay where you are. I'll be there directly."

Todd started down a trail along the face of the slope. His attitude indicated he was suspicious of strangers. A pistol was strapped to his side, and from his rough tone, he allowed no one near his diggings. Heavy through the shoulders, he was short and muscular and looked to be in his early thirties. His features were hidden behind a full beard.

Halting at the corner of the shack, he subjected Morg to a quick once-over. "You said you wanted to talk."

Morg ignored the abrasive manner. Yet his assessment of the man told him a roundabout approach wouldn't work. He decided to come straight to the point.

"Got a proposition for you," he said. "Hear me out before you get your bowels in an uproar."

"I ain't interested in no proposition."

"Won't cost you nothing to listen."

"Get to it, then," Todd said sourly. "I got no time to lollygag around."

Morg stated his case in brisk, no-nonsense terms. While he mentioned no source, he spoke knowledgeably of Todd's claim. Completely aboveboard, he admitted the mine's potential for uncovering a rich lode. Then, hammering home the point, he declared that potential by itself meant nothing until the ore was brought to the surface. He offered to bankroll the operation to the tune of fifty thousand dollars.

When he paused, Todd eyed him skeptically. "Who told you about my claim?"

"The word's around," Morg said reasonably. "Not many secrets in a mining camp."

"You're not trying to buy me out? You'd actually want me to run the operation?"

"I don't know beans from buckshot about mining. Unless you agree to stay on, I'm not interested."

Todd gave him a long, searching stare. "What d'ya want for your fifty thousand?"

"Fifty-one percent," Morg said flatly, "and it's not

negotiable. I'll give you a free hand running things, but I control the purse strings. It's my money."

Todd examined the notion. "Where'd a young feller like you get such a bankroll?"

"I own a timber company and I'm partners with my family in a cattle spread. Anybody in Lincoln will vouch for the Brannocks."

"Wondered about the name when you mentioned it. You any relation to a gambler name of Lon Brannock?"

Morg looked dumbstruck. "Where the devil do you know Lon from? He's my first cousin."

Todd flashed a yellow-toothed smile. "Him and his half-breed brother drifted into town last week. I seen 'em in the gaming dives."

"White Oaks?" Morg said, astounded. "Last I heard, they were in Lordsburg."

"Well, he's here now. Way I got the story, he killed a man over at Lordsburg. Finally wore out his welcome."

"I'll be damned."

Todd chortled aloud. "Lots of folks don't take to a 'breed livin' in town. 'Course, they keep their traps shut on that score. Your cousin's sorta handy with a gun."

"They're both my cousins," Morg said. "Different mothers but the same father."

"Figured as much," Todd noted. "Maybe you and me can do business after all. Anybody with an honest gambler in the family couldn't be no crook."

"How do you know he's honest?"

" 'Cause a tinhorn wouldn't be travelin' with a 'breed kid. Tends to draw attention to a man's gamblin' habits."

Their conversation turned again to the mining venture. On the basis of a handshake, the deal was struck along the terms outlined by Morg. A formal contract would be drawn, but for now each of them was willing to accept the other's word. As Morg mounted his horse, he was reminded that life sometimes took a strange twist. He'd clinched the deal today because he was related to an honest gambler. It seemed to him a curious recommendation, almost laughable.

He rode back toward White Oaks.

The Lady Gay saloon was packed with miners. A banjo and an upright piano provided the entertainment, and the gaming tables were positioned opposite the bar. Girls with kewpie-doll faces drifted through the crowd.

Shortly after sundown, Lon and Hank emerged from a café across the street. By now they were a familiar sight and no one bothered to stare. From Lordsburg, they had traveled a circuitous route, never stopping long in one place. White Oaks' proximity to the Hondo Valley, and their kinfolk, was a matter of small interest. To them it was simply one more stopover on the gamblers' circuit. When the urge struck them, they would move on to still another mining camp.

Entering the Lady Gay, they started toward the poker tables at the rear of the saloon. One of the barkeeps spotted them and gave Lon the high sign. Followed by Hank, Lon moved to the end of the bar. After waiting on another customer, the barkeep strolled over. He leaned across the counter, lowering his voice.

"A fellow's been askin' about you."

"Who is he?"

"Search me." The barkeep jerked his head toward a table near the front window. "That's him, the one sittin' by hisself. Wandered in about an hour ago."

"Much obliged."

Lon inspected the man at the table. Something about him was familiar, but he couldn't place the face. He noted in passing that the man was about his own age and carried a pistol in a belt holster. He exchanged a glance with Hank, who shrugged. They crossed to the table, halting as the man looked up from a half-empty schooner of beer. Lon gave him an impersonal nod.

"Understand you've been askin' for me. I'm Lon Brannock."

"Hello, cousin," Morg said, grinning broadly. "You don't recognize me, do you?"

"Cousin—?"

"Morg Brannock. Virgil Brannock's boy."

"Well, I'll be a son-of-a-bitch."

Neither of them had seen the other in almost fourteen years. Their last meeting had been in Colorado Springs, where Morg's parents lived at the time. Afterward their paths had diverged, with no mutual contact except their lawman uncle, Clint. But now, caught up in a spirit of reunion, they shook hands warmly. Lon took hold of Hank's elbow and pulled him forward.

"Meet your other cousin," he said to Morg. "This here's my brother, Hank."

"I'm proud to make your acquaintance, Hank. Heard a lot about you."

"Likewise," Hank said, shaking his hand. "Uncle Clint always bragged on you and your family."

"C'mon, sit down." Morg motioned them to take chairs. "We've got a lot of catchin' up to do."

"How's your mom?" Lon asked.

"She's fine," Morg said. "Her and Jen both. They'll expect you to come by for a visit."

Lon made an empty gesture. "Hard to say where we'll light next. We keep on the move."

Morg gave him a quizzical side glance. "You're not worried about Clint, are you?"

"What's he got to do with anything?"

"Way I heard the story, he'd like Hank to move in at Spur. Leastways that's what he told Mom."

"Fat chance," Lon said indifferently. "We thrashed that out once before. Hank stays with me."

Morg laughed. "Then you've got no reason to hold off. Hell, I'm married and about to become a daddy. I want you to meet my wife."

"We'll see," Lon said, deliberately noncommittal. "All depends on how things go."

Morg let it drop there. He turned the conversation to Lon's trade as a gambler and listened with rapt attention. Yet, as they talked, he watched Hank out of the corner of his eye. He saw that the boy idolized his older brother, hanging on his every word. Some inner voice told him that the bond between them was too strong to be broken. A gradual realization came over him, and he recognized it for a sad, but undeniable truth.

Hank Brannock would never set foot on Spur. He was a boy who walked in his brother's shadow, and there he would stay.

17

The convention was held in Albuquerque. Situated on the upper Rio Grande, the town was positioned roughly in the middle of New Mexico. From virtually anywhere in the territory, it was the central location for such a meeting.

All the more important, Albuquerque represented neutral ground. A major railhead, with commerce in timber, farm produce, and livestock, it was fast developing into a city. Because of its rapid growth, the influence of the Sante Fe ring was not a pervasive factor in local issues. Nor were the divisions between Anglo and Mexican so sharply drawn.

In total, Elizabeth had extended invitations to fifty-seven *políticos*. Topping the list were the wealthy *ricos*, who dominated affairs in their districts. Below them were the *jefes*, the men responsible for daily operation of the political apparatus. Lower still were the *jóvenes políticos*, aspiring young politicians who challenged the old order. Of those invited, fifty-one arrived in Albuquerque on May 14.

The convention began the following morning. Elizabeth had rented the banquet hall in a hotel and transformed it into a meeting room. Tables were arranged in rows, five men to a table, with an aisle down the center. There were no seating assignments, which made the affair somewhat more democratic. People sat where they pleased and with whom they pleased. No special consideration was extended to anyone.

An air of animosity and mistrust filled the room. The *ricos* and the *jóvenes políticos* were separated by an ideological chasm. The old order, who thought of themselves as aristocrats, jealously guarded their power. The younger faction, ambitious men from the lower classes, championed reforms for the people. Caught in the middle were the *jefes*, who attempted to appease everyone while offending no one. The overall sense of discord was palpable.

There were only three Anglos in attendance. At the front of the room, Elizabeth and Ira Hecht were seated behind a speaker's table, with a lectern between them. Their principal support was from the *jóvenes políticos* and a handful of *jefes*. On that foundation, their shaky coalition between *mexicanos* and Anglo reformers remained intact. The *ricos*, by and large, viewed the coalition as a menace to the established order. Fearful of losing power, they had given only spotty cooperation in the past.

The third Anglo was John Taylor. Stationed at the rear of the room, he stood beside the wide double doors leading to the hall. He appeared unusually vigilant, not unlike a watchdog alert to danger. Scarcely a week ago, Elizabeth had received a letter from Clint. In it, he'd outlined Thomas Canby's offer of an alliance, as well as the veiled threat should the offer be refused. Without explanation, he went on to state that the governor had ordered him to expand his investigation into San Miguel County. He cautioned Elizabeth to beware at the convention.

Elizabeth found Canby's offer to be revealing. Clearly, he was concerned that the convention would broaden her coalition among the *mexicano* leaders. His concern, quite obviously, was that a groundswell movement would cost him the fall elections. As for the threat, she simply ignored it, evidencing no fear for her own safety. John Taylor, on the other hand, was openly concerned for her welfare. Like Clint, he got deadly serious whenever Elizabeth put herself in harm's way. He'd kept a sharp lookout since their arrival in Albuquerque.

The convention had gotten off to a bad start. Elizabeth was all too aware that the *ricos*, in particular, resented a woman involving herself in men's affairs. They respected the power she wielded, but they were bitterly affronted by the fact that she wore skirts. To allay their resentment, she had limited her remarks to a brief opening statement. Forcefully, she had addressed the need for cohesion and harmony in pursuit of a common goal. Afterward, Ira Hecht had acted as moderator of the meeting.

The squabbling commenced almost immediately. One of the *jóvenes políticos* took the floor to denounce the *ricos* in scathing terms. Outraged, the *ricos*, supported by loyal *jefes*, shouted him down. Time and again, Hecht restored order by pounding his gavel and urging them to seek some common ground. No sooner would the next speaker take the floor than tempers flared anew and the bickering resumed at a hotter pitch. The convention slowly degenerated into a running skirmish between factions.

Watching them fight, Elizabeth despaired of bringing about a truce. Their animosity evolved from one generation attempting to wrest power from another. Her conciliatory remarks at the beginning had done nothing to dampen their antagonism. Hoping to further placate the *ricos*, she'd even worn a tailored suit of navy serge with a high-necked white blouse. Her thought was to remove any hint of feminine influence

and conduct the meeting in a businesslike fashion. She
saw now that her efforts had been largely wasted.

On the verge of speaking out, her attention was
distracted. The door at the rear of the room opened
and three *mexicanos* in white jackets wheeled in a
serving trolley. Looking closer, she noted that the
trolley was loaded with coffee cups and a large coffee
urn. She hadn't ordered refreshments and the appearance of the waiters left her momentarily confused.
Then, jolted into acute awareness, she fixed her gaze
on one of the men. His features were unmistakable.

Miguel Ortega.

John Taylor walked over to the serving trolley. One
of the waiters was whipcord lean, with a face that
looked adzed from hard dark wood. He smiled, pulling a pistol from beneath his jacket, and stuck it in
Taylor's ribs. A moment later Taylor was disarmed
and forced to take a seat at the rearmost table. The
third *mexicano* stepped from behind the trolley and
produced a nickel-plated six-gun. The dark-skinned
man rapped out a sharp order.

"*Silencio!*"

A sudden hush fell over the room. The convention
members turned in their chairs, spotting the men with
drawn pistols. They sat immobilized, as though frozen
in place, a uniform look of astonishment on their
faces. As Miguel Ortega walked down the aisle, they
watched with the spellbound expression normally re-
served for sword-swallowers and magicians. One of
them whispered his name and a buzz of conversation
swept through the crowd.

Ortega moved around the speaker's table. Elizabeth
looked at him, certain now that something momentous
was about to happen. He smiled pleasantly, nodding
to her. "*Con su permiso, señora,*" he said formally.
"With your permission, *señora.*"

Halting behind the lectern, Ortega stared out at the *políticos*. He customarily spoke in quiet commands that others unquestioningly obeyed. Today his voice crackled with authority.

"*Buenos días, caballeros*," he said. "For those of you I have not met personally, I am Miguel Ortega. I bring you greetings from *Las Gorras Blancas*."

The crowd sat mesmerized, reduced to absolute silence. Ortega launched into a fiery speech, gesturing to underscore his points. His tone of voice alternated between sardonic mockery and outright contempt. He railed at the politicians, addressing his remarks directly to the *ricos* and the *jefes*. In harsh terms, he upbraided them for placing greed and self-interest before the welfare of the people. His eyes were alive with a light akin to madness.

Toward the end, he gestured at Elizabeth. He told the crowd she was a woman of goodwill, a friend to all *mexicanos*. He praised her selfless devotion to reform and her long struggle to bring about equality under the law. Then, abruptly, his tone turned ominous and his voice took on a soft, menacing lilt. There was a distant, prophetic look in his eyes, and he seemed to stare at the men one by one. He warned them to settle their differences and join with Señora Brannock in forging a true alliance. To remove any vestige of doubt, he concluded with a bald-faced threat.

"Anyone who withholds his support will be marked as a traitor. And all such men will be dealt with by *Las Gorras Blancas*. Heed my words or we shall meet again."

A turgid silence settled over the crowd. Ortega bowed to Elizabeth, then walked away from the speaker's table. She realized that this was one of those rare moments that alter one's life irrevocably. Her coalition, even she herself, was now linked to the man who

led *Las Gorras Blancas*. On sudden impulse, she rose
and followed him up the aisle.

Ortega's men waited beside the door. The dark-
skinned *pistolero* placed John Taylor's six-gun on the
floor. Taylor started to rise from his chair, but Elizabeth waved him down. The third man opened the
door, motioning the *pistolero* through, and they pre-
ceded Ortega into the hallway. Elizabeth was only a
step behind and she caught up with Ortega outside.
His men moved off to a discreet distance.

"Thank you," Elizabeth said gratefully. "You risked
your life by coming here today."

Ortega smiled with satisfaction. "Perhaps I have
been of some small assistance, *señora*. Those fools
would have argued among themselves and accomplished
nothing."

"I must say you've speeded things along. You're a
very persuasive speaker."

'Some men cannot be dealt with in a reasonable
manner. I felt sterner measures were required."

Elizabeth appeared bemused. "Why is it so important to you that we win the elections? I thought you
had lost faith in the ballot box."

"I have faith in you," Ortega said, then shrugged.
"Besides, a wise man always prepares for the unforeseen. Should anything happen to me, you and your
coalition can continue the fight."

"You once told me you would never be captured.
Has that somehow changed?"

"*No, señora*," Ortega replied. "I will never be
captured."

"Are you—" Elizabeth hesitated, searched his eyes.
"You believe you might be killed, don't you?"

Ortega's mouth lifted in a tight grin. "There are
powerful men who wish me dead. Who knows where it
will lead?"

"Is there no other way?"

"*De seguro*," Ortega said. "No way whatever. God willing, you may yet win at the ballot box. In the meantime, I will fight on."

Elizabeth smiled warmly. "You are a brave and honorable man, and your people need you. I wish you well."

"*Hasta luego, señora.*"

Ortega turned toward his men. As they hurried along the hallway, Elizabeth was struck by yet another realization. A moment ago, in a quicksilver splinter of time, she had seen revealed a new aspect of Miguel Ortega. He was not suffering from messianic delusions. Nor was there any sense of his own immortality.

He saw himself, instead, as the most mortal of men. He believed he would be killed.

Glorieta Pass was at the southern tail of the Sangre de Cristo range. First discovered by the Spaniards in the 1590s, it had been an ancient byway through the mountains. In more recent times it had served as an artery on the Santa Fe Trail.

The pass itself was surrounded by lofty mountains. A quarter of a mile wide, it sliced through rugged heights almost eight thousand feet in elevation. The slopes on either flank were steep and rocky, studded with cedar and stunted pines. At the western end of the pass there was a deep gorge, carved through the aeons by a winding stream.

Some years past, the railroad had spanned the gorge with a bridge. The wooden trestles were like an intricate latticework rising high above the streambed. On the far side of the bridge, the tracks extended through the pass and gradually curved off toward the southwest. At the town of Lamy, a spur line turned northwest into the mountains, terminating at Santa Fe. The

main line descended on a southerly arc into the Rio
Grande valley.

Clint stood at the edge of the gorge, looking westward. Before him, where the bridge had traversed the
deep crevasse, there was now a yawning chasm. Far
below, the streambed was littered with timbers and
charred rubble. Sometime last night, an explosion heard
twenty miles away had blown the bridge to smither-
eens. Staring down at the debris, he idly wondered how
much dynamite had been required for the job. He had
no doubt whatever as to who had lit the fuse.

Not quite two weeks ago a freight train had been
derailed along the Gallinas River. The incident had
occurred the same night he'd shot the *mexicano* in his
hotel room. Early next morning, the governor had
ordered him into San Miguel County, where the sabotage had taken place. While none of the crew had
been killed, railroad officials had apparently put a bee
in the governor's ear. Unless checked, the derailment
of trains could bring commerce to a standstill throughout the territory.

Clint had traveled by rail from Santa Fe. Headed
east through the mountains, he'd toyed with an intrigu-
ing notion. Until now, *Las Gorras Blancas* had been
content to pester the railroad. But derailing trains was
serious business and indicated a high degree of planning. Which raised the possibility that Ortega had
returned to San Miguel County. Nothing was known of
Ortega's lieutenants or their ability to carry out such
an act of sabotage. So the idea hadn't seemed all that
farfetched.

Quickly enough, Clint had been disabused of his
optimism. San Miguel County was where Ortega had
organized the first bands of masked night riders. The
northern *mexicanos*, if anything, were more secretive
than those Clint had encountered in Lincoln County.

He'd spent the last ten days trying to uncover a lead, with nothing to show for his efforts. *Las Gorras Blancas* openly claimed credit for the derailment, but the trail ended there. No one would talk to a *gringo* lawman, particularly an outsider. Any mention of Ortega's name drew blank stares, and silence.

Early that morning, Clint had ridden out to Glorieta Pass. Work crews, supervised by bridge engineers, were already busy assessing the damage. The magnitude of the destruction once again raised the specter of Miguel Ortega. Staring down the gorge, Clint asked himself who else could have planned and executed such a feat. But today, like so many days in the past, he was stumped for an explanation. There were no answers, only tough questions.

A handcar, pumped by two brawny workmen, rolled to a halt a short distance uptrack. Boyce Thompson, sheriff of San Miguel County, hopped down and walked forward. His experience with *Las Gorras Blancas* made him an expert on the subject, though he'd yet to obtain a conviction. He stopped beside Clint, looking out across the gorge.

"Helluva mess," he said. "Somebody shore has a way with dynamite."

Clint made an offhand gesture. "I was thinkin' that same thing myself. You reckon it might've been Ortega?"

"Not unless he's got wings."

"What's that mean?"

"Nothin' you're gonna like," Thompson said with a mirthless laugh. "Wire come in on the telegraph a while ago. Ortega was reported in Albuquerque yesterday mornin'."

"Albuquerque?"

Thompson took a hitch at his pants, cleared his throat. "You know that Mex confab your sister-in-law's holdin'? Word leaked out that Ortega dropped by unannounced. Albuquerque paper reports he made a piss-cutter of a speech."

"Goddamnit," Clint said stolidly. "The bastard's always one jump ahead."

"What d'you aim to do now?"

"Go on back to Lincoln County. I've got a hunch that's where he'll pop up next."

"Why so?"

Clint sidestepped the question. His hunch was part supposition and part fact. Ortega was using Elizabeth and her coalition to his own ends. What stymied Clint was that Elizabeth had nothing to gain. She could only lose by being linked to *Las Gorras Blancas*.

He thought it was time they had another talk.

Homer Stockton rode into Spur three days later. He was accompanied by Aaron Kimble, whose ranch was located on the Rio Bonito. They dismounted outside the main house.

Kimble was a large man, with a broad hard face and close-cropped hair. Scarcely three weeks past he'd buried a cowhand killed during the raid on his ranch. He took small solace from the fact that one of the White Caps had also been killed. A life for a life seemed to him a poor trade.

Elizabeth received them in her office. She had never cared for Stockton, who was a blustering, overbearing man. By virtue of his daughter being her daughter-in-law, she worked hard at maintaining cordial relations. Today, however, there was nothing cordial about either man. Stockton wasted no time on greetings.

"I'll come to the point," he said. "We've been appointed spokesmen for the ranchers on the Rio Bonito and the Rio Felix. We'd like some straight answers."

"Very well," Elizabeth said with icy courtesy. "How can I help you?"

"We're here about that meeting you held over at Albuquerque. Way we got the story, Miguel Ortega showed up and made a speech."

"That's correct," Elizabeth acknowledged. "He urged the *mexicano* leaders to adopt a position of unity in the fall elections."

"Do tell?" Stockton's tone bordered on sarcasm. "I'd say it's a case of one hand washin' the other. Question is, what does Ortega get for helping you whip the greasers into line?"

"I beg your pardon?"

"Let's get down to brass tacks. Folks are sayin' you've thrown your support behind Ortega. There's even talk you let him hide out here."

Elizabeth regarded him evenly. "Whoever says such a thing is a liar. I do not harbor fugitives."

Kimble's face was pinched in an oxlike expression. "If that's so," he demanded roughly, "how come Spur hasn't been raided? Why haven't the White Caps hit you?"

"For one thing," Elizabeth informed him, "I don't believe in barbed wire. For another, the *mexicanos* on the Hondo have always been treated fairly. You would do well to follow the example."

"Bullfeathers!" Kimble said, almost shouting. "We're not talkin' about better treatment for the pepperguts. We're talkin' about you gettin' cozy with Ortega."

"Aaron's right," Stockton said, his face darkening. "We wanna know what kind of game you're playin'. And by God, we mean to have an answer!"

Elizabeth rose from her chair. "Good day, gentlemen," she said with chilly smile. "You're no longer welcome in my home."

"You can't toss us out like that."

"I just have," she corrected him. "Please show your-selves the door."

Stockton and Kimble stormed out of the house. Elizabeth resumed her seat and went back to work. Some while later footsteps sounded in the hallway and Clint appeared in the door. His clothes were covered with trail dust and his face was gaunt with fatigue. On the road, he'd met the two ranchers and heard their side of the story. He asked for an explanation.

Elizabeth was wounded by his abrupt manner. She hadn't seen him in nearly six weeks, and she knew he'd been avoiding Spur. Their last meeting had ended with harsh words about Ortega, and she suspected that was the reason. Even now, as she explained the latest allegations, she realized nothing had changed. She was still on the defensive.

When she finished, Clint just stared at her. "You're dead wrong," he said after a long pause. "You've lost the governor's support and pushed him over into Can-by's camp. And now the other cattlemen have turned against you. Where do you draw the line?"

"I have nothing to apologize for," Elizabeth said patiently. "Miguel Ortega forced his way into the meet-ing at gunpoint. I didn't invite him."

"You didn't ask him to leave, either. Hell, wake up, Beth! You're playing patty-cake with an outlaw—a murderer."

"I've told you before and I'll tell you again: I do not condone his methods. I've told him the same thing."

"So what?" Clint growled, half under his breath. "You're sympathetic to his cause and everybody knows it. Way it looks, you're aiding and abetting."

A veil seemed to drop over Elizabeth's eyes. "Noth-ing outweighs the importance of the fall elections. With Miguel Ortega's backing, I intend to take control of the legislature."

"Christ, it's not worth selling your soul."

"Contrary to what you may think, I've made no pact with the devil."

"Haven't you?" Clint asked sharply. "For your information, Ortega tried to have me killed in Santa Fe. I got his man instead."

"I don't believe that for an instant. He promised me no harm would come to any member of this family— you included."

"One way or another, I aim to see he delivers on the promise."

"By killing him?"

"I'd judge that's his choice, not mine."

Clint declined an invitation to stay the night. When he walked from the office, Elizabeth slumped back in her chair. She felt drained, no longer certain what was right and what was wrong. A bargain with the devil seemed to her an outlandish charge. And yet . . .

She asked herself the question Clint had posed only moments ago. Where should she draw the line?

18

The examining room was awash in sunlight. Jennifer sat at her desk, entering notes on her last patient in a medical journal. She looked around as the door opened.

Rosa, her surgical assistant, motioned a man into the room. His name was Hubert Wallace, which the townspeople had shortened to "Wally." A clerk at the dry-goods store, he was short and chubby with a moonlike face. He appeared to be in considerable pain.

Jennifer finished the entry in her journal. Then, returning the pen to the inkstand, she gestured to a chair beside her desk. Wallace seated himself as Rosa closed the door. He was clutching his left arm tightly against his portly waistline.

"What seems to be the problem, Wally?"

"Goldanged if I know," Wallace said uncertainly. "Got something bad wrong with my wrist."

"Let me have a look."

Wallace reluctantly surrendered his arm. Jennifer laid his hand, palm down, on the edge of the desk. A large bulge was visible on the back of his wrist, just below the cuff on his shirt. She gently touched it with her fingertips.

"Ouch!" Wallace yelped.

"Tender?"

"Sore as a boil, Miss Brannock."

Wallace, like many of the townsmen, still found it difficult to address her as "Doctor." Jennifer ignored the oversight, by now resigned to their unintentional prejudice. She lifted his hand from the desk, holding the forearm straight out. Without warning, she bent his wrist down at a sharp angle.

"Gawdalmightybingo!"

"I take it that hurt?"

"Yes, ma'am," Wallace croaked. "You like to brought me plumb offen this chair."

Jennifer nodded. "Have you noticed any unusual weakness in your wrist?"

"Now that you mention it, I surely have. Last couple of days I can't hardly lift a fork."

From the size of his potbelly, Jennifer doubted he'd missed any meals. She studied his wrist closer and noted that the bulge had popped up, stretching the skin taut with a prominent knot. She examined it a moment longer, satisfying herself of the diagnosis.

"You have a ganglion, Wally."

"Ganglion?" Wallace echoed, his eyes widening. "What the blue blazes is that?"

Jennifer explained it in layman's terms. A lubricated sheath encased every tendon found in the body. While the reason was unknown, a painful bulge sometimes developed in the sheath. The bulge was thought to be a cystic tumor, an abnormal saclike growth filled with fluid. "Ganglion" was the medical term for such growths, most commonly found in the wrist.

The old-fashioned cure for ganglions was a wallop with a heavy book. The blow popped the saclike growth and dispersed the fluid through surrounding tissues. Too often, however, an overenthusiastic walloper also broke the patient's wrist. Advances in medicine now allowed for the reduction of a ganglion through surgery. A quicker method, always tried first, was manual reduction by a physician.

"The procedure's quite simple," Jennifer concluded. "With your help, I can do it right now."

Wallace looked dubious. "Will it hurt much?"

"Not all that badly," Jennifer said. "The alternative is to put you to sleep and operate."

The thought of a scalpel gave Wallace a queasy sensation. "I guess it's okay," he said skittishly. "What d'you want me to do?"

"Take hold of your knuckles with your right hand and keep your wrist bent down over the edge of the desk. And once I start, Wally, you can't move. I want you to remain perfectly still."

"Cripes, I sure hope you know what you're doing."

"Trust me."

Wallace bent his wrist over the desk. Unable to watch, he closed his eyes and turned his head away. Jennifer centered the bulge between her thumbs and firmly squeezed inward. She steadily increased the pressure, her arms straining as the growth was pinched tighter in the viselike action of her thumbs. The ganglion suddenly burst with an almost inaudible popping sound.

Wallace winced and slowly opened one eye. Jennifer grasped his left hand and flexed the wrist up and down. The bulge had disappeared completely, and with it the pain. When she released his hand, Wallace somewhat tentatively rotated his wrist. A relieved grin spread over his face.

"By golly," he said bouyantly, "that's some trick. You're a regular wizard."

"Nothing to it," Jennifer said, smiling. "Especially when you have a cooperative patient."

"Well, I surely do thank you, Miss Brannock. How much do I owe you?"

"Three dollars ought to cover it, Wally."

"I'll bring it around on payday. That okay?"

"Of course."

Jennifer walked him to the door. When she opened it, she heard voices from the waiting room. As Wallace crossed to the outer door, she saw Rosa engaged in conversation with two men. The noon hour was approaching, and except for the men, the waiting room was empty. She nodded to them.

"May I help you?"

"Yes, ma'am," one of them replied. "Leastways if you're the doctor lady."

"Are you ill?"

"Oh, no, ma'am, nothin' like that. We're just lookin' for information."

Jennifer's appraisal was deliberate. The men were tall and rawboned, with hands gnarled from a lifetime of hard work. One appeared to be in his late thirties and the other was perhaps ten years younger. Their clothes, particularly their tall-crowned hats and spurs, identified them as cattlemen. She noted that the younger one wore crossed gunbelts with a brace of holstered pistols.

"Do I know you?" she asked. "I don't recall seeing you around town."

"We're new to the territory, ma'am. We just pulled into town this mornin'."

The older man apparently did all the talking. She caught a drawl in his voice, vaguely reminiscent of Texans she'd met. But the dictates of Western custom prohibited asking where they were from. She smiled pleasantly.

"What sort of information were you looking for?"

"We stopped off at the livery stable jest now. Feller told us you was some relation to Lon Brannock."

Jennifer had the immediate impression he was lying.

She recalled Morg mentioning Lon and Hank, and their chance meeting in White Oaks. Yet, apart from family members, no one was aware of the Brannocks' kinfolk. She knew for a certainty that the livery owner had never heard of Lon.

"I'm Lon's cousin," she said. "Why do you ask?"

"We was hopin' to run acrost him. Heard he'd put down stakes somewhere in New Mexico."

"Are you friends of Lon's?"

The older man laughed. "Yes, ma'am, we're pards from way back. Him and us had some high old times together."

"I suppose that was when Lon lived in Texas?"

The man shuffled uneasily. "I don't know as you could say he lived there. His home was mostly up in the Injun Nations."

"Then you must know his brother."

"Uh—" The man faltered, clearly taken aback. "I do recollect him mentionin' it. 'Course, he never talked much about his kin."

"Oh?" Jennifer said innocently. "But you knew he had family here?"

"Well, that there's a different story altogether. He used to brag a heap on you folks. Told us you got a big ranch hereabouts."

Jennifer knew he was lying now. Everyone in the family was aware that Lon considered himself a Brannock in name only. To think that he would brag on them was patently absurd. "Quite honestly, I've never concerned myself with Lon's affairs. Have you inquired at the ranch?"

"C'mon, Bob," the younger man cut in gruffly. "She don't know nothin'."

"Do try at the ranch," Jennifer said helpfully. "Perhaps my mother could tell you something."

"Yes, ma'am," the older man said, bobbing his

head. "We'll ride out first chance we get. Obliged for your time."

Jennifer realized the men hadn't volunteered their names. As they went out the door, she was struck by their similarity in build and features. The thought suddenly occurred that they were quite probably brothers. She turned back into her office.

From the corner window she watched them amble up the street. The younger one was talking now, gesturing angrily with his hands. Some dark premonition told her that they were hunting Lon, meant him harm. She waited until they were out of sight.

After removing her medical apron, she ordered Rosa to close the clinic. She then walked uptown to the hotel and asked for Clint. The desk clerk informed her the marshal had ridden out of town early that morning. She stood there a moment, indecisive as to her next move. Abruptly, she decided to ask Blake's advice.

Outside she angled across the street. Blake's law office was in a small frame building beside the courthouse. As she entered the door, she saw the two men leading their horses from the livery stable. She quickly stepped inside, closing the door, and watched from the window. The men halted before a saloon a short distance upstreet.

"What's so interesting?"

She turned at the sound of Blake's voice. He was seated behind a broad desk strewn with papers and open lawbooks. His expression was quizzical, and she hurriedly motioned him forward. He gave her an indulgent look, then rose from his chair and circled the desk. He stopped beside her at the window.

"I don't get it," he said. "What's the big mystery?"

"See those men?"

Blake followed the direction of her gaze. He saw two men, dressed in range clothes, hitching their horses outside the saloon. The bartender and owner, Dutch Fredericks, was sweeping the boardwalk with a straw broom. The older of the two men greeted him and Fredericks paused, leaning on the broomstick. They began talking.

"You mean the cowhands?" Blake asked. "What about them?"

Jennifer frowned. "Do you think they could be peace officers?"

Blake took a closer look. "From their appearance, I'd have to say no. They're a little too scruffy for lawmen. Why do you ask?"

"They're looking for Lon," she said. "A few minutes ago, they came by the clinic. They tried to pass themselves off as Lon's friends."

"What makes you think they're not?"

"Because every other word was a lie."

Jennifer quickly recounted the conversation. She stressed the older man's uneasy manner and the implausible story he'd told. Proud of herself, she explained how she'd tripped him up with leading questions.

"I have a bad feeling," she said at length. "Something about them just doesn't seem right."

Blake considered a moment. "On the face of it, I suspect you have a point. No one lies without a reason."

"Well, anyway, Lon's in no immediate danger. They'd never think to look for him in White Oaks."

"On the contrary, I have an idea that's their next stop."

"What—?"

"See for yourself."

Jennifer stared out the window. She saw the older man and the saloonkeeper with their heads together. As she watched, they turned and disappeared into the saloon, followed by the younger man. She glanced back at Blake.

"I don't understand what that has to do with Lon."

"Dutch Fredericks is the town gadfly. He's sure to let the cat out of the bag."

"Will you please make sense?"

"Jen, I just assumed you'd heard it too. Word's around that a gambler relative of the Brannocks has set up shop in White Oaks. No one has mentioned him by name, but those men—"

"Will worm it out of Dutch Fredericks."

"—and put two and two together."

"Omigod!" Jennifer cried. "We have to get to the ranch!"

"What good will that do?"

"Uncle Clint might be there. Or if he's not, Mother will think of something. Hurry up, go get your buckboard!"

Blake obediently got his hat and rushed out the door. Jennifer stood at the window, fidgeting nervously as he walked toward the livery stable. Her eyes strayed to the saloon and her mouth compressed in a tight line.

She suddenly wished Dutch Fredericks would be struck dumb.

A midafternoon sun heeled over toward the mountains. Blake hauled back on the reins and brought his sweat-lathered team to a halt. Jennifer jumped down and ran inside the house.

She found her mother and Morg seated in the office. Only a step behind, Blake followed her down the hallway. Louise emerged from her bedroom, startled by the commotion, and gave him a strange look. She joined him in the doorway.

Jennifer began talking the instant she entered the office. Elizabeth appeared disconcerted, and then, as the story unfolded her expression turned to open concern. Morg listened impassively, trying to follow his sister's scrambled account of the morning's events. She finally paused to catch her breath.

"Way it sounds," Morg said lightly, "you're jumping at shadows. Maybe those fellows have got personal business with Lon."

"Very personal," Elizabeth said in a troubled voice. "Unless I'm mistaken, they are the last of the Jarrott brothers. They've come here to kill Lon."

Jennifer stared at her, aghast. "Why would they want to kill him?"

Until now, none of the family had been told of Lon's past. Elizabeth knew the details, for Clint had kept her informed over the years. But he had sworn her to secrecy and she'd never betrayed his trust. Today there seemed no way around an explanation.

Elizabeth briefly sketched a tale of violence and death. As a youngster, Lon had killed a cowhand in a barroom argument. Later, the dead man's four brothers crossed over from Texas onto the Comanche reservation. Their family name was Jarrott, and their purpose was retribution. They wanted an eye for an eye.

Warned by his Comanche friends, Lon ambushed the Texans on a mountain trail. He killed two and sent the other two scurrying back across the Red River. Yet the last of the Jarrott brothers had never relented, vowing to avenge the deaths of their kinsmen. For years, they had tracked Lon unsuccessfully when he worked the gambling circuit in Texas. And now, still intent on vengeance, they had tracked him to New Mexico.

"We have to warn Lon," Elizabeth said at last. "The Jarrotts are certain to find him this time."

"I'll do it," Morg volunteered. "There's a back trail through the mountains to White Oaks. I can be there before dark."

Elizabeth nodded in approval. "Clint has to be alerted as well. It's possible he might somehow stop the Jarrotts."

"Leave that to me," Blake said briskly. "One way or another, I'll locate him. Someone's bound to know where he's gone."

"Thank you, Blake," Elizabeth said graciously. "When you find him, send him directly to White Oaks. In the meantime, Morg will have advised Lon of the situation."

"No!" Louise said in a shrill voice. "Why should Morgan risk getting himself killed? He won't just warn Lon—he'll try to help!"

"For Chrissake," Morg grumbled. "Would you button your lip for once? We'll talk about it later."

Louise started to protest, but Morg brushed past her and went through the doorway. A moment later Jennifer and Blake followed him along the hall. The front door slammed and a sudden stillness fell over the house. Louise burst into tears.

Elizabeth went to her. The girl tried to pull away, but Elizabeth firmly sat her down in one of the chairs before the desk. She then seated herself in the other chair and waited for the tears to subside. Louise slowly got control of herself and pulled a hanky from her sleeve. She blew her nose loudly.

"We need to have a talk," Elizabeth said. "I think it's time you became part of the family."

Louise stared daggers at her. "You kicked my father out of this house and you'd like to be rid of me too. Don't you think I know that?"

"Whatever differences I have with your father, it doesn't affect how I feel about you. I've always hoped we could be friends."

Louise tossed her head. "You've resented me from

the day I walked into this house. You never wanted me to marry Morg."

"You're so very wrong," Elizabeth said with some dignity. "What you haven't realized is that you didn't marry Morg alone. You married the entire Brannock family."

Surprise washed over the girl's face. "I don't understand what you're talking about."

"Yes, I know," Elizabeth said. "When I married into the family, it all seemed very strange to me too. I couldn't understand why my husband loved his brothers at least as much as he loved me."

"Are you serious?" Louise asked with a confused little laugh. "You really felt that way?"

"Oh, yes, indeed," Elizabeth observed. "And that's how I know what you're going through right now."

"No, you don't," Louise said in an injured voice. "Your husband didn't go running off when you were pregnant and leave you to wonder if he'll come back alive. I'll never forgive Morg!"

"When I was twenty-one," Elizabeth said quietly, "I was pregnant with Jennifer. Virgil, my husband, walked out of the house with his brothers on a cold October morning. An hour later they killed four men who were trying to kill them."

"How could you let him go?"

"How could I stop him? He had a responsibility to his brothers which overshadowed all my tears and agonizing. Morg feels that same responsibility toward Lon."

"Yes, but that was different. Lon's just a cousin—not a brother."

"Family is family," Elizabeth said, an observant look on her face. "You have to understand how it is with the Brannocks. We stand by one another, whatever the cost to us personally. We simply couldn't do less."

Louise's voice was thoughtful. "You're saying I have to feel that way too. Or else I'll never be a Brannock."

"You are a Brannock," Elizabeth said firmly. "To every member of the family, you're not just Morg's wife. You are one of us, one of our own."

"I . . . ." Louise stopped, her eyes suddenly misty. "I'm just so scared. So terrified I'll lose him."

"Before he was your husband, he was my son. I know exactly how you feel."

"But you let him go anyway."

"And so must you."

Louise looked down at her hands. She sat there for a long moment, twisting the handkerchief between her fingers. Then she straightened, wiping her eyes, and forced herself to smile. She tried to sound strong.

"It's not easy, being a Brannock."

"I'll help you. I've spent a lifetime learning how."

Elizabeth extended her hands, clasping the girl's in her own. Neither of them spoke, but some silent communion passed between them. What they shared was what all the Brannock women somehow came to know.

The family, however cruel the adversity, would endure.

19

In the lowering dusk Bob and Charley Jarrott rode into White Oaks. Nightfall was fast approaching and the town's streetlamps were already lighted. They reined to a halt outside a saloon.

Dutch Fredericks, the Lincoln saloonkeeper, had proved to be a repository of information. At Bob Jarrott's prompting, he'd revealed every scrap of gossip, past and present, about the Brannocks. One item, related with a sly wink, had to do with the latest rumor.

The Brannocks, according to Dutch Fredericks, had a "family skeleton." For all their high-and-mighty airs, it appeared that one of their relatives ran with the sporting crowd. The man in question was a gambler and he'd been reported in White Oaks. His game was poker, and word had it that he was something of a cardsharp.

Bob Jarrott had done all the talking. His younger brother, Charley, was surly and short-tempered and hadn't joined in the conversation. After a final drink they'd parted with Fredericks, who took them to be saddle tramps in search of work. Their ride from Lincoln to White Oaks had consumed the balance of the afternoon.

Neither of the Jarrotts had ever seen a mining camp. But they had driven herds up the Western Trail to

Dodge City, largest of the Kansas cowtowns. Their
first impression of White Oaks was favorable, for like
the cowtowns, it was wide open and populated by
rough men. They began their search with a tour of the
saloons and gaming dives.

The Jarrotts didn't know Lon on sight. Yet, over
the years, they had put together a fairly accurate physical description. Tonight, as they'd done on the gamblers' circuit in Texas, they engaged bartenders in
conversation. After inquiring about the hottest poker
game in town, they turned the talk to gamblers. One
way or another, they managed to raise the name of
Lon Brannock.

The Jarrotts were a stubborn lot, and proud. Though
largely uneducated, they practiced a rigid code of honor.
Any man who wronged a member of their family
wronged them as well. And it made no difference that
Lon had killed their brothers in defense of his own
life. For six years, whenever they could spare the time
from their ranch, they had resumed the hunt. Never
before had they been so close, so confident it would
end. White Oaks seemed to them the last stop on a
long and tortuous trail.

After hitting three saloons, they wandered into the
Lady Gay. One of the barkeeps, in response to Bob
Jarrott's question, jerked his thumb toward the rear of
the room. He indicated a poker table and identified
one of the players as the gambler named Brannock.
The other players included two businessmen, attired in
conservative suits, and three rough-clad miners. The
barkeep remarked that it was a table-stakes game.

Bob Jarrott nodded to his brother. They moved
through the crowd, skirting the faro layouts on the
opposite side of the room. At the rear of the saloon,
beyond the three poker tables, there was a lone pool
table. They idly noted a half-breed kid and a grungy

miner with cue sticks, playing a game of eight ball. Their attention centered on the poker table positioned near the left-hand wall. Lon Brannock was seated on the far side of the table, facing them.

The Jarrotts separated. Charley moved off to the left and Bob halted to the right of the table. Even in a personal dispute, the law demanded that a certain code be observed. A man could be called out and killed so long as he was given an even break. To shoot a man in coldblood was considered unsporting, and inevitably resulted in a murder trial. Or worse, since they were strangers in town, they might find themselves lynched from the nearest tree. For appearances' sake, they somehow had to provoke their man.

Bob Jarrott took the lead. He stood a pace away from the table, staring directly at Lon. "I'm lookin' for a sorry sonovabitch name of Brannock. Somebody told me you was him."

The challenge froze the other players in a stilled tableau. Except for a startled glance, none of them moved, and they kept their hands on top the table. Lon looked up from his cards, assessing the man who had spoken. His gaze shifted to the younger man, noting the crossed gunbelts and the tense stance. Some instinct told him the younger man was faster and therefore more dangerous. He directed his attention to the older one.

"I'm Lon Brannock," he said. "What's that to you?"

"Name's Jarrott," Bob Jarrott grated out. "You put three of my brothers in their graves. Ambushed two of them and gunned 'em down without warnin'."

An ironic smile touched the corner of Lon's mouth. He understood that the speech was for the benefit of the onlookers. Jarrott was laying the groundwork for what later might be ruled justifiable homicide. It was a smart move, well thought out.

"Tell the whole story," Lon said in a flat voice. "You and your brothers were out to nail my hide. Four to one wasn't exactly a fair fight."

"We was within our rights! You'd already killed one of my brothers."

"Mister, you've got things catty-wampus. I seem to recollect your brother drew first."

A brittle silence had now settled over the other poker tables. Toward the rear, Hank stood behind the pool table, listening intently. While he'd never seen the Jarrotts, he was aware of their past efforts at killing Lon. His eyes moved from one brother to the next, studying them carefully. He thought Lon would take the younger one first.

Hank suddenly stiffened. He saw Morg rush through the front door and look wildly around the saloon. It flashed through his mind that Morg's unexpected appearance was somehow tied to the Jarrotts. Then, spotting Lon at the poker table, Morg bulled a path through the crowd. From his expression, he hadn't yet grasped the situation. There was nothing to indicate he'd recognized the Jarrott brothers.

"You gonna fight?" Bob Jarrott flared, glowering at Lon. "Or you gonna show your yellow streak?"

A cold tinsel glitter surfaced in Lon's eyes. "You've got me at a disadvantage, Jarrott. Two to one and I'm still in my chair."

"Then get on your gawddamn feet."

"Lon—!" Morg called out, hurrying forward.

The Jarrotts were momentarily distracted. They half-turned toward the sound of the voice, then recovered. In that instant, Lon kicked back his chair and stood erect. The other players hit the floor as his Colt appeared from the crossdraw holster. His arm leveled at the exact moment Charley Jarrott pulled both guns.

Lon fired across the table. Charley Jarrott stood

perfectly still, a great splotch of red covering his breast-
bone. He fired his right-hand gun into the floor, dropping the other one, and then he wilted at the middle.
As he toppled forward, Bob Jarrott got off a hurried
snapshot. The bullet ripped through Lon's left thigh
and his leg went dead. He collapsed sideways onto the
floor.

Jarrott started around the table. He raised his gun,
intent on finishing the job with a second shot. From
the rear of the room, Hank extended his pistol at arm's
length. He fired over the pool table, triggering two
rounds a split-second apart. The slugs jolted Bob Jarrott
back a step at a time, splattering his shirtfront with
blood. He went down like a puppet with its strings
gone haywire.

A dense cloud of gunsmoke hung over the poker
table. For a long moment everyone in the saloon stared
at the three men on the floor. The Jarrotts lay motionless, their eyes fixed blankly on nothing. Lon slowly
raised himself up on one elbow, his features waxen,
teeth gritted against the pain. His pants leg was soaked
with blood.

Morg abruptly broke the spell. He circled the poker
table and dropped to one knee beside Lon. A quick
inspection revealed that the bullet had struck Lon in
the upper thigh. After ripping the pants leg apart,
Morg saw that the wound was still pumping blood. He
jerked a kerchief from his pocket and began fashion-
ing a tourniquet. The men around him watched with
morbid curiosity.

Hank walked forward from the pool table. He appeared shaken and studiously avoided looking at the
man he'd shot. The pistol was still clutched tightly in
his hand, as though he had forgotten to holster it. He
seemed unaware of the poker players and other nearby
onlookers, who were watching him strangely. At the
table, he knelt down as Morg tied off the tourniquet.

Lon's forehead was beaded with sweat. He took hold of Morg's arm, pulled him closer. "Get me out of town," he said. "I'll never get a fair shake here."

"Sure, you will," Morg said earnestly. "Hell, they're the ones that started the fight. You just defended yourself."

"Won't matter," Lon told him. "Hank and me aren't liked around here. Nobody'll take my side."

Hank nodded agreement. "Lon's right," he said in a low voice. "Folks tagged him an Injun lover 'cause of me. They'd like to make trouble for him."

"So what?" Morg said, turning back to Lon. "You're liable to bleed to death if we don't get you to a doctor. You're wounded bad."

Lon shook his head. "I'm likely to get my neck stretched before I bleed to death. Take a look around."

Morg glanced up at the men gathered nearby. Their faces were cold and implacable, somehow unfriendly. He recalled the resentment against Lon for forcing the town to accept a half-breed. Until now, fearful of offending Lon, no one had dared to speak out. But a wounded man no longer posed a threat.

A sudden murmur swept through the crowd. George Watson, the town marshal, eased past the front rank of onlookers. As he approached the poker table, he quickly surveyed the carnage, taking note of Lon's bloody leg. He stooped down, checking both the Jarrotts in turn for a pulsebeat. Satisfied they were dead, he looked across at Lon.

"What happened here, Brannock?"

"Old business," Lon said, grimacing against the throb in his leg. "They trailed me into town . . . picked a fight."

Watson stared at him. "You kill both of them?"

"Hell, no!" one of the crowd yelled. "He pulled first and got the younger one. The 'breed potshot the older fellow from over at the pool table."

"That right?" Watson asked, still looking at Lon. "You draw first?"

"I beat 'em to it," Lon said in a weak voice. "They were fixin' to throw down on me."

Watson grunted something unintelligible. His gaze flicked to Hank, spotted the pistol in the boy's hand. "How about it?" he said roughly. "You shoot the older one before he saw you?"

"I didn't do nothin' till after he'd shot Lon."

"Guess that's for a coroner's jury to decide. I'm placing you both under arrest."

"What for?" Hank protested. "You got no right."

'None of your lip." Watson advanced another step, extended his hand. "I'll take that gun."

Hank reacted on impulse. He raised the pistol, thumbing the hammer, and pointed it at the lawman. "Just stay back."

Lon struggled to push himself erect. His strength failed him, and he grabbed Morg's arm. "Don't let 'em take us," he said. "They'll lynch Hank, too."

An instant of leaden silence slipped past. Morg looked at the marshal, then scanned the faces of the crowd. He saw it in their eyes and the feral set to their mouths. They wouldn't hesitate to hang a 'breed kid.

Morg climbed to his feet. He drew his pistol from the holster, glancing at Hank. "We'll need a buckboard or a wagon. Lon wouldn't last any time on a horse. Go see what you can round up on the street."

Hank moved through the crowd, waving his pistol. A path opened before him and he hurried out the door. Morg nodded to the lawman. "Don't get brave, marshal. We're not looking for trouble."

Watson glowered at him. "You think I don't know you? Your name's Morgan Brannock."

"What of it?"

"You're supposed to be a respectable businessman.

Why get yourself involved in a sucker's game? You'll never get away with it."

"I'm gonna make a damn good try."

Hank returned within minutes. He'd commandeered a wagon and team and had it waiting on the street. With his assistance, Lon was able to hobble outside on his good leg. Morg followed close behind, brandishing the pistol as he backed away. At the door he paused, looking at the crowd.

"Everybody stay put till we're long gone. Anybody pokes his head outside will wish he hadn't."

The door swung open and Morg stepped into the night. Hank popped the reins as he scrambled aboard the wagon. They drove south out of White Oaks.

No one attempted to follow them in the darkness.

Jennifer was awakened shortly after midnight. She threw on a housecoat and hurried from her bedroom through the clinic. The pounding at the front door grew louder.

After lighting a lamp in the waiting room, she opened the door. Her breath caught in her throat and she quickly moved aside. Morg and Hank edged through the door, carrying Lon in their arms. His left pants leg was dark with blood.

Holding the lamp for them, Jennifer lighted the way into her office. She ordered Lon placed on the operating table and then lit the overhead reflector lamp. As she turned to the instrument cabinet, Morg told her that he had periodically loosened the tourniquet. She deftly snipped open the trouser leg with medical scissors.

While she worked, Morg explained what had transpired in White Oaks. She let him talk, but her attention was focused on Lon. His breathing was shallow, and though he'd lost a great deal of blood, his pulse rate was still strong. She satisfied herself that he was

unconscious before turning to the wound itself. The
flesh around the entry hole was puffy and bruised,
caked with dried blood. From all outward appearances, the femoral artery had not been severed.

With Morg's help, she got Lon undressed. Hank
stood by, gathering the blood-soaked clothing as it was
tossed aside. Jennifer next examined the backside of
the leg, determining that the slug had not exited. She
felt reasonably confident that the thigh bone hadn't
been shattered, but the track of the bullet remained a
mystery. She wouldn't know for certain until she
operated.

Jennifer scrubbed her hands with strong soap and
cold water. As she finished, she caught Hank watching
her with an awestruck expression. It occurred to her
that she and her Comanche cousin had never met until
tonight. Nor had she seen Lon since she was a small
girl, some fourteen years ago. Wondering on it, she
suddenly realized she'd never before operated on one
of her relatives. She quickly pushed the thought aside.

There was always a chance that Lon would regain
consciousness. She accordingly instructed Morg on the
proper method of administering ether. While she talked,
she put together a tray of surgical dressings and sterilized instruments. She then cleansed the wound with a
carbolic solution and prepared to operate. Morg took
his place at the head of the table, ready with a sponge
and a small can of ether.

The operation proceeded without complications. Jennifer located the bullet with a probe and gingerly
extracted it from the wound channel. There was no
excess bleeding and she found no evidence of foreign
matter in the wound. In the process, she reaffirmed
her belief that the femur bone had not been damaged.
She completed the procedure by applying a loose bandage to permit drainage. Stepping back, she told her-

self Lon had drawn heavily on his gambler's luck. The bullet had missed the femoral artery by only a few centimeters.

The front door banged open. A moment later Clint appeared in the entrance to the operating room. He looked from one to the other and his gaze finally came to rest on Lon. His expression darkened.

"What the hell's going on here?"

"Where have you been?" Jennifer demanded. "Blake's out trying to find you."

"I just got back from Fort Stanton. I saw a light on and thought I'd better check."

"You missed the party," Morg said, moving away from the operating table. "Lon and Hank bagged the last of the Jarrott brothers. Killed 'em stone dead."

"The Jarrotts?" Clint repeated hollowly. "Where'd they come from?"

"Showed up out of the blue. Started asking questions here and finally tracked Lon down at White Oaks."

"Looks like Lon caught one himself."

Jennifer held up the bullet. "So far as I can tell, there's no permanent damage. He should recover nicely."

Clint nodded. "How'd it come to a shooting?"

Morg started at the beginning and told the story straight through. His one reservation was that he'd arrived too late to warn Lon. He credited Hank with quick thinking and quick shooting, which was all that had saved Lon's life. When he finished, there was a moment of profound silence. Clint's features congealed into a tight scowl.

"Jesus Christ," he said slowly. "You actually put a gun on George Watson?"

"No choice," Morg countered. "It was that or a lynching bee. Watson couldn't have stopped that crowd."

"What's the difference?" Clint grumbled. "Lon and Hank both will be charged with murder. In case you forgot, that's a hanging offense."

"Yeah, but they have to be caught first. We'll hide 'em someplace on Spur."

"Don't be a fool," Clint said, annoyed. "Watson's probably putting a posse together right now. You think you're gonna fight him off with your cowhands?"

Morg waved his hand, as though dusting away the problem. "There's always the ranch in the Outlet. Nobody would look for them there."

"What about yourself?" Clint persisted. "You'll be charged with obstructing the law and harboring fugitives. You figure to ride the owlhoot too?"

Morg smiled uneasily. "I never thought of that."

Clint pondered it a moment, and then, almost as though he was thinking out loud, he glanced at Jennifer. "How long before Lon can be moved?"

"In an emergency," she said, "he could be moved now. Of course, it would have to be done carefully. We can't risk reopening his wound."

"Here's what I want," Clint said, nodding to Morg. "Load Lon in that wagon and take him out to Spur. Your mother's a pretty fair nurse. She'll tend to him proper."

Morg appeared puzzled. "You sound like you've got something up your sleeve."

"Let's just hope it works. I'm gonna try to talk turkey with George Watson."

"You mean, get him to drop the charges?"

Clint shrugged, then turned away. His gaze fell on Hank and his features softened. "Don't blame yourself for what happened. Anybody worth his salt would've done the same thing. Your brother's lucky you were there."

The boy gave him a hangdog look. "I wish't them Jarrotts hadn't never showed up."

"Some men are bound to get themselves killed. You couldn't have stopped it."

Clint patted the youngster on the shoulder. Then, looking around at Morg, he made a short, emphatic nod. "Get Lon out of town before daylight. I'll see you at the ranch."

Without waiting for a reply, he walked from the room. The front door opened and closed and there was a moment's silence. At length, Morg turned to the boy. His expression was bemused.

"I've been wonderin'," he said. "Where'd you learn to shoot like that?"

Hank smiled sheepishly. "Lon and me practice just about every mornin'. I got to where I generally hit the mark."

"By God, you hit it dead center tonight! Lon oughta thank his lucky stars he taught you so good."

Jennifer couldn't bear to listen. By rough calculation she placed Hank's age at fifteen. She thought him far too young to have killed his first man. But then, on quick reflection, she realized there was no good age for such things. In the end, whether young or old, killing left its mark.

She wondered how it would end for Hank.

20

A faint blush of dawn lighted the sky. Clint slowed his horse to a walk as he rode into White Oaks. Upstreet, his gaze was drawn to a knot of men outside the marshal's office.

George Watson stood on the boardwalk. Before him was grouped a motley collection of miners and townspeople. The men were grim-eyed, their features cold and hard in the sallow overcast.

The posse was composed of volunteers. Their love of a good fight, rather than civic pride, had enabled Watson to recruit them from the town's saloons. The greater incentive, however, was the likelihood that they would hang the 'breed kid along with his smartass brother. No one believed the fugitives would be brought back alive.

All the men were armed and leading horses. Watson had delayed pursuit until first light, though he had no intention of tracking his quarry. He felt reasonably confident that they would have taken refuge at Spur, with a brief stopover in Lincoln for medical attention. His plan was to arrive at the ranch in force and demand their surrender from Elizabeth Brannock. He doubted she would let it come to a fight.

Watson was still counting heads. Fourteen men had volunteered, but so far only ten had shown up. He was debating whether to roust them out of bed when he

spotted Clint. The posse members caught his startled
expression and craned for a better look. They saw a
tall, broad-shouldered rider with a badge pinned to his
shirt. None of them knew him, but the shape of the
badge was distinctive. The murmured words "U.S.
marshal" swept through their ranks.

Clint dismounted at the hitch rack. He looped the
reins around the crossbar and moved to the boardwalk.

" 'Mornin', George," he said. "I'd like a word with
you."

Before Watson could reply, Clint brushed past him
and entered the office. The men were staring at him
curiously and Watson tried to put the best face on it.
"Don't you boys wander off," he ordered. "I'll be
with you in a jiffy."

Turning away, he hurried inside the office. Clint
stood beside a wood-burning stove, pouring himself a
mug of coffee from a smoke-blackened galvanized pot.
He replaced the pot and took a long swig from the
steaming mug.

"Tastes damn good," he said. "I've been on the
road all night."

Watson smiled without humor. "You could've saved
yourself a trip. I was just about to head over your
way."

"Yeah, I know," Clint said pointedly. "I saw the
boys at my niece's place. You'll recollect she's the lady
doctor."

"Figured as much when you rode up. Guess they
must've told you about the fracas last night."

"That's what I wanted to talk to you about."

"Won't do no good," Watson said in a raspy voice.
"Nobody pulls a gun on me and gets away with it. Not
even your kinfolk."

Clint's features were impassive. "Let's understand

one another. Are you saying they're charged with
evading arrest . . . nothing else?"

"Hell, no." Watson paused, regarding him with a
dour look. "Way the witnesses tell it, Lon drew first.
That makes it murder."

"You ever play suppose, George?"

"I dunno what you mean."

"Well, just for example, let's suppose Hank wasn't
a half-breed. Then we'll suppose Lon never forced
everybody to tread light around his Injun brother.
Supposin' all that, you reckon anybody would give a
goddamn that they killed the Jarrotts?"

"Suppose whatever you want," Watson said bale-
fully. "How's that change anything?"

Clint's eyes were pale and very direct. "You're gonna
drop all the charges, George. Otherwise, you'll end up
with egg on your face."

"Maybe you'd like to spell that out."

"Glad to."

Clint stuck to the salient details. He recounted the
Jarrott brothers' six-year vendetta against Lon. In passing, he observed that the Jarrotts had ridden all the
way from Texas for the sole purpose of revenge. Lon,
on the other hand, had sought to avoid trouble at
every turn.

"You force me to it," he concluded, "and I'll bring
'em before the judge at Lincoln. How do you think
he'd rule?"

"So what?" Watson muttered lamely. "They still
resisted arrest and took off in a stolen wagon."

"That's what I meant about egg on your face. You
could have prevented all that just by listening to their
side of the story. Instead, you took the word of a
bunch of rumdum barflies."

Watson let out his breath in a low whistle. "Thunderation, Clint, I can't just call it off. I've got a posse waitin' out there! I'd look like the town idiot."

Clint shrugged. "You press charges and you'll come off like a real dimdot. C'mon, admit it, you've got no case."

"Goddamnit, they stuck a gun in my face! How'd it look if I just let that drop? I've got to uphold the law in this town."

"All right," Clint allowed. "We'll have the judge stick 'em with a stiff fine for resisting arrest. Will that get you off the hook?"

"What about the wagon and team they stole?"

"I'll have it returned with a hundred dollars for the owner's trouble. That ought to satisfy everybody."

"Still not enough," Watson grouched. "I want 'em posted out of White Oaks—permanent."

Clint was silent a moment, thoughtful. "Where Lon and the boy are concerned, that's no problem. Morg's an altogether different matter. He's got business affairs over here."

"Have it your way," Watson conceded glumly. "But you tell them other two to stay the hell outta my town. I've had a bellyful."

"George, I'll tend to it personal. You've got my word on it."

Watson appeared somewhat mollified. They shook hands and Clint placed his coffee mug on a table beside the stove. Then, as they turned toward the door, Watson abruptly stopped. He gave Clint a sidelong look.

"Your kinfolk got me so pissed-off I almost forgot I'm a lawman. I come damn close to not tellin' you what I stumbled across."

"What's that?"

"Well, like I said," Watson remarked, "this here's my town. I keep my ear to the ground."

"So?"

"So we've got a fair number of greasers that live hereabouts. I got wind somebody's been recruitin' for *Las Gorras Blancas*."

"Miguel Ortega?" Clint asked.

Watson shook his head. "Nobody mentioned any names. What I heard was, they're plannin' another raid on the Rio Bonito."

"Any idea which rancher they aim to hit?"

"Nope," Watson said, then shrugged. "I only heard it night before last. For all I know, it's so much hot air."

"Who's your source?" Clint said, looking at him. "You wouldn't get something like that on the grapevine."

Watson ducked his head. "I see a little Mex gal now and then. We was workin' on a bottle of tequila and—" He hesitated, lifted his hands. "What with one thing and another, she let it slip."

"What makes you believe her?"

"Hell, she was drunker'n a hoot owl! Had no notion what she was sayin'."

Clint considered briefly. "You think she might talk to me?"

"Not sober," Watson said, chuckling. "Let me work on her my own way. Anything turns up, I'll send you word."

"I'd be obliged, George."

Outside the office, Clint walked directly to the hitch rack. He mounted, reining the gelding around, and rode off at a trot. Behind, as Watson ordered the posse disbanded, he heard catcalls and heated curses from the men. He smiled to himself, amused by their anger.

In a manner of speaking, George Watson had just spoiled their fun. Nobody would be hanged today.

*   *   *

Shortly after sunrise, the wagon lumbered to a halt outside the main house. Morg wrapped the reins around the brake lever and jumped down to the ground. He waved to several hands walking toward the corral.

Lon was stretched out in the back of the wagon. A pallet of blankets had cushioned him on the bumpy road from town. Hank sat beside him, ready with a bottle of laudanum provided by Jennifer. So far, Lon had refused to take any of the sedative. He was alert and thoroughly irritated.

Halfway from Lincoln, Lon had finally regained consciousness. When informed he was being taken to Spur, he'd flatly rejected the idea. Between them, Morg and Hank had finally convinced him that there was no choice. For the moment, the ranch was the one place where he could recuperate while being looked after properly. With grudging reluctance, he had at last agreed. Yet he was still in a grumpy mood.

Elizabeth appeared on the veranda. A moment later Brad approached the wagon, followed by several cowhands. Lon was unloaded, with the pallet of blankets serving as a stretcher, and they carried him into the house. Leading the way, Elizabeth showed them to one of the spare bedrooms at the end of the hall. There Lon was transferred from the blankets to a wide brass-knobbed bed.

After the hands trooped out of the house, Elizabeth demanded an explanation. Morg wearily recounted the story, ending with Clint's decision to ride to White Oaks. At that point, Louise appeared in the doorway, rubbing sleep from her eyes, a housecoat thrown on over her nightgown. She shrieked with a mixture of happiness and relief and rushed into Morg's arms. He looked oddly embarrassed by her teary welcome.

Elizabeth finally shooed everyone out of the room.

Louise led Morg away, peppering him with questions. Brad volunteered to get Hank some breakfast and they walked toward the kitchen. When Elizabeth closed the door, she found Lon watching her from the bed. His expression was unreadable, although she suspected he was in considerable pain. She moved to the side of the bed, mustering her warmest smile.

"Are you comfortable?" she asked. "Anything I can get you?"

"No, I'm fine," Lon said. "Don't go to any trouble on my account."

"It's no trouble," Elizabeth assured him. "We're really very pleased to have you here. I just wish it could have been under happier circumstances."

"Well, I'll try not to be a bother. Soon's I can ride, Hank and me will be on our way."

"Nonsense," Elizabeth said cheerily. "You're both welcome as long as you care to stay. I want you to think of this as your home."

Lon just stared at her. When he didn't reply, Elizabeth turned back the sheet and bent to examine his wound. He wore only his undershorts and he looked vaguely uncomfortable at her attentions. The bandage on his thigh was lightly spotted with blood but otherwise unsoiled. She lifted the edge, checking for drainage, and nodded to herself. He appeared visibly relieved when she draped the sheet back over his chest.

"Aren't you fortunate?" she said, smiling. "Not everyone has a doctor in the family. Jennifer took care of you very nicely."

"Funny thing," Lon said slowly. "I never even saw her. I was passed out the whole time she was workin' on me."

"I shouldn't wonder," Elizabeth commented. "You lost a good deal of blood. Anyone would pass out."

"Except for Hank, I would've lost a lot more blood. He saved my bacon just in the nick of time."

"How does Hank feel about that? I mean—apart from saving you—does he regret having killed a man?"

Lon looked faintly amused. "Why would he regret killin' a no-account like Jarrott? I'd say he deserves a medal."

A thought tugged at the corner of Elizabeth's mind. Because of Lon, young Hank had been subjected to a harrowing experience. Yet Lon seemed impervious to even the simplest emotion. On the face of it, he had no concept that the boy might suffer some lingering aftereffect. Thinking about it, a strange sadness came over her. She actually felt sorry for Lon.

"I don't know about medals," she said, trying to treat it lightly, "but you must be in some pain. Would you like a spoonful of laudanum?"

Lon's smile was cryptic. "I'd sooner keep my wits about me. I'm not hurtin' all that bad."

"Are you hungry, then? I could ask the cook to fix you something special."

"Whatever you got will suit me just fine. I'm not hard to please."

Elizabeth excused herself. When she went out the door, Lon slumped back against his pillow. He stared up at the ceiling and silently cursed whatever fate had brought him to Spur. He'd sworn never to set foot on the place or to get himself involved with the family. He felt somehow like a charity case. Or worse, a poor relation.

Some while later there was a knock at the door. John Taylor stepped into the room, balancing a serving tray on one hand. After closing the door, he crossed to the bed, nodding to Lon. His smile was inquisitive.

"How you feelin'?" he said. "I brought you some eats."

"No complaints," Lon said evenly. "Who're you?"

"John Taylor. I work for Miz Brannock."

Lon pushed himself to a sitting position. His leg throbbed with the effort, and he winced, swearing softly. Taylor watched without comment, then placed the tray across his lap. On it was a bowl of beef broth and a pot of tea.

"What's this?" Lon asked. "You'd think I was an invalid."

Taylor chuckled. "Miz Brannock figured you oughta stick to liquids. Go ahead, it'll do you good."

Lon spooned the broth, slurping loudly. He glanced up at Taylor. "I heard about you from my uncle. Aren't you the one from Texas?"

"I'm the one," Taylor said with a wry smile. "Some folks used to call me a hired gun. 'Course, I'm retired now."

"Why's that?" Lon said. "Way I heard it, you're still pretty fast."

"Well, there's always somebody a little faster. You might say it's a temporary occupation."

"Temporary?"

A ghost of a grin touched Taylor's mouth. "I've never yet seen a man that couldn't be beat. That includes yours truly."

Lon took a sip of tea. "So you just quit?"

"Anybody with a lick of sense knows when to fold his cards. I reckon that goes for gunhands the same way it does gamblers."

Lon gave him a quick, guarded glance. "Why do I get the feelin' you're trying to tell me something?"

"What's to tell?" Taylor said equably. "You win some and you lose some. 'Course, when you lose with a gun, it's a mite different than cards. You cash out for good."

There was the merest beat of hesitation. "When the time comes," Lon scoffed, "maybe I'll fold my cards too. Just now, I'm still playin' into luck."

Taylor walked to the door. He turned, looking back with a sardonic smile. "You should've kept that slug your cousin dug outta you. You'll never see the one that kills you."

The door opened and closed before Lon could frame a reply. He told himself he'd been sandbagged, and by his aunt no less. She wanted a message delivered, but she knew he wouldn't listen to a woman. So she hadn't returned with the tray herself.

She'd sent John Taylor instead.

Clint arrived late that afternoon. He hadn't slept in thirty-six hours and his eyes felt lead-weighted. Outside the corral he dismounted and turned his horse over to a wrangler. As he walked toward the house, his boot heels seemed to drag the ground.

Elizabeth was relieved to see him. She listened attentively to the account of his meeting with George Watson. Her relief was all the more evident when he told her Morg would not be posted from White Oaks. After talking awhile, he left her and moved down the hallway to Lon's room. He knew he wouldn't rest until he'd spoken his piece.

Lon was propped up in bed. His leg was hurting, but he steadfastly refused to be dosed with laudanum. He expressed neither surprise nor gratitude when informed that the charges had been dropped. Yet his anger flared when Clint told him he was no longer welcome in White Oaks. His tone was hotly indignant.

"I go where I please," he said. "Damned if I'll be posted out of town when I've done nothin' wrong. Hell, I've got my rights!"

Clint gave him a straight hard look. "I made the deal and you'll stick by it. I don't want any argument."

"Some deal!" Lon bridled. "Christ, it was the Jarrotts that come hunting me. You talk like it was the other way round."

"Lemme tell you something," Clint said with a lightning frown. "Trouble hunts those who look for it, and you've got a chip on your shoulder. You're too goddamned cocky for your own good."

Lon eyed him with a steady, uncompromising gaze. "What's got your nose out of joint? You're not that mad over the Jarrotts, are you?"

A vein pulsed in Clint's forehead. "I don't know any way to say it except straight-out. You've made a killer of Hank."

"Jesus, that's rich!" Lon laughed harshly. "Where do you come off lecturing me? You're not exactly a shining example yourself."

"I never encouraged a kid to pack a gun. You ought to be real proud of what you've done for your brother."

"Tough titty makes strong baby. Hank's a half-breed in a white man's world. He's gotta learn how to hold his own."

Clint fixed him with a terrible look. "All your life you've had a crosswise attitude about things. I won't have Hank infected with your brand of poison."

"Won't you?" Lon said sullenly. "You might recollect what happened the last time we had this discussion. Hank decided to tag along with me."

"Maybe shooting somebody has brought him to his senses."

"Nobody's stoppin' you from asking him."

"I damn sure don't need your permission, Lon. I never did."

Clint turned and walked from the room. Outside he

found Elizabeth waiting in the hallway. Her features were clouded with concern.

"What happened?" she said. "Your voices carried throughout the house."

"Beth, he's just no goddamn good. I've got to separate him and Hank somehow."

"I'm afraid that's easier said than done. Like it or not, you're just an uncle. Lon is his brother."

"Where's Hank now?"

"Out with Brad," Elizabeth replied. "I thought he'd like to see the ranch."

Clint's jawline tightened. "When he gets back, we'll have ourselves a talk. I aim to settle this once and for all."

"Would you listen to a suggestion?"

"Try me."

"You'll accomplish nothing by putting Hank in the middle. Until now, he's been forced to choose between you and Lon. Why not allow him to choose a different way of life?"

"I don't follow you."

"Time is on your side," Elizabeth said. "Lon won't be able to ride for at least a week, perhaps longer. While he's recuperating, let Hank see what we have here on Spur." She paused, nodding wisely. "He might just decide it's the life for him."

Clint looked impressed. "You've gotten shifty with age, Beth. That's not a half-bad idea."

"I'll even enlist Brad's help. He and Hank seem to have hit it off."

"By God, I like it! I like it a lot."

"Good," Elizabeth said, taking his arm. "Because that's the end of the conversation. I'm going to insist that you get some sleep."

"I think maybe you're right. I'm plumb tuckered out."

Elizabeth walked him to one of the spare bedrooms. At the door, she kissed him on the cheek and gently shoved him inside. As she turned back up the hallway, it occurred to her that they hadn't once spoken of Miguel Ortega. Instead, family matters had again brought them together, perhaps healed the wound. She wanted desperately to believe that all the bad times were past.

One silver lining in a world of storms seemed little enough to ask.

21

Early the next morning the compound was a flurry of activity. Various crews, bossed by *segundos*, were assigned the day's work. They rode out shortly after sunrise.

Brad's routine seldom varied. He met with the *segundos* following breakfast and reviewed their instructions for the day. Some were assigned to work roundup, while others were responsible for putting together trail herds. A select few were permanently assigned to the horse-breeding operation.

The balance of Brad's day was spent in the saddle. He relied on the *segundos* to carry out his orders and complete their separate tasks. His job was to inspect the various operations and ensure that everything went according to plan. He generally managed to check out four or five work crews in the course of a day.

Usually, Brad rode alone. Overnight, however, he'd had a long discussion with Elizabeth. Their talk had centered on Hank, and how the youngster might be encouraged to stay on at Spur. The first step, Elizabeth stressed, was to intrigue the boy with life on a ranch. Only then could they contend with the influence of his older brother.

Brad readily volunteered his services. Yesterday he had shown the boy around the compound, as well as visiting one of the roundup camps. He'd found Hank to be an intelligent youngster, filled with curiosity. He also sensed that the boy felt somewhat out of place, an interloper of sorts. Hank seemed overly sensitive about the fact that he was a half-breed.

Today, the boy eagerly accepted Brad's invitation. Their first stop was at the eastern end of the valley, where the next trail herd was being gathered. Hank was fascinated by every aspect of the operation, asking an endless stream of questions. Apart from his time in the mining camps, he knew virtually nothing of the white man's world. He evidenced a willingness to learn that belied his youth.

From the cow camp, they turned northwest. By midmorning they arrived at the breaking corrals, known among the hands as the "riding academy." There they watched broncbusters in the initial stages of working raw range stock. The horses were green four-year-olds, tough and fiery-tempered. Within the month, they would be converted into well-schooled cowponies.

Encouraged by Hank's questions, Brad explained the operation in some detail. Virgil Brannock, the founder of Spur, had begun a crossbreeding program in the late 1870s. At first, mustang brood mares were topped by a thoroughbred stallion imported from Kentucky. By culling the mares, and continually breeding up, the offspring soon possessed the best traits of both strains.

Colts sired by the original stallion further extended the bloodline. The horses were now known for their stamina and catlike agility, and their blazing speed over the short stretch. In recent times, the term "quarter-mile horse" had been coined, denoting an animal capable of bursting speed from a standing start. A decade of selective crossbreeding had resulted in the ultimate cowpony.

Within the cattle industry, these barrel-chested

quarter-mile horses were highly prized for cutting and roping. Throughout the summer, horse buyers from across the West traveled to Spur to look over the stock. At peak season, the herds totaled more than a thousand head, and annual sales exceeded $250,000. Livestock dealers who traded in blooded saddle mounts provided still another market.

Hank was visibly impressed. His ancestors, the Comanche, had been the most superb horsemen of all the Plains tribes. No less a personage than General Phil Sheridan had dubbed them "the finest light cavalry in the world." Their herds numbered in the thousands, and their ancient term for the horse was the "god-dog." Even on the reservation, a man's wealth was still measured in horses.

"My people bred horses too," Hank said now, watching a broncbuster fork a snorty cowpony. "Long ago, the Comanche stole pure-blood stock from Mexican *rancheros*. They were then mixed with our own herds."

Brad eyed him in silence for a moment. "You ever think of raisin' horses yourself?"

"Sure," Hank said with a gee-whiz grin. "What Comanche wouldn't?"

"Lookit here," Brad said. "You mind if I ask you a personal question?"

"No—I guess not."

"Well, you're just as much white as you are Indian. So why do you keep callin' yourself a Comanche?"

Hank looked at him with some surprise. "A half-breed don't have much choice. Way most folks figure, the white part don't count."

"On Spur," Brad ventured, "we're pretty much color-blind. Around here, you're just another Brannock."

"You tryin' to tell me nobody thinks of me as a 'breed?"

"I'm sayin' everybody looks on you as one of the family. The fact that you're half Comanche doesn't change a thing."

Hank beamed happily. "I'd sure like to believe that. You reckon the others think the same way?"

"Hell, yes," Brad said reasonably. "Your Aunt Elizabeth heads the list. Her and Morg talked it over last night."

"Talked what over?"

"How they'd like you to stay on at Spur. There's more dangblasted work than we can handle. We need another Brannock to help run things."

"No kiddin'?" Hank said with soft wonder. "They actually told you that?"

"Like I said, you're family. We tend to stick together."

Hank thought for a moment. "I haven't heard you mention Lon. How do they feel about him?"

"No different," Brad said with a vague wave of his hand. "You and Lon both are welcome to make your home here. Your Uncle Clint figures it's where you belong, anyhow."

"Yeah, I know," Hank said, his face serious. "Trouble is, Lon's got other ideas. He's dead set against it."

"How about your ownself? Would you like to stay on?"

"I dunno," Hank said slowly. "What would I do on a ranch?"

"For openers, you could lend a hand with the horse-breeding operation. You said yourself a Comanche has an eye for blooded horseflesh."

"I gotta admit it sounds good."

"Why not try it?" Brad asked carefully. "You could do lots worse."

"All depends on what Lon says. I don't wanna get on the outs with him."

"Maybe you ought to have a talk with him. Unless I'm wide of the mark, you're not too keen on a gambler's life."

"You won't get no argument there. I just tagged along because of Lon."

"So talk to him," Brad persisted. "You're old enough to know your own mind."

Hank smiled manfully, nodded. "I suppose it wouldn't hurt nothin'. All he could do is blow his cork."

Brad regarded him somberly. "Lemme ask you something straight out. You got any particular itch to kill people?"

"I'd sooner raise horses."

"Then cut the knot with Lon before it's too late. You stick with him and you're bound to kill somebody else. He draws trouble like a lightning rod."

Hank shrugged. "He's still my brother."

"That don't make him your keeper. Or vice versa, either."

There was an awkward silence. After a time they reined away from the breaking corral and rode south. Brad sensed that his last remark had struck a nerve. He could almost hear the boy thinking out loud. And loyalty was no longer the issue.

Hank was considering instead the *price* of loyalty.

Late-afternoon shadows played across the bedroom wall. Lon lay with his hands locked behind his head, staring at the ceiling. His mood was testy.

Earlier, Clint had dropped by to check on him. For Lon, their conversation had all the overtones of an old sermon. He'd listened with one ear, indifferent to the admonition that he mend his ways. The good news was that Clint was leaving for Lincoln, presumably on law business. Lon was happy to see him go.

Shortly before suppertime the door opened. Hank

stepped into the room, smiling tentatively, and crossed to the bed. Lon perked up noticeably, pushing himself upright against the pillows. So far as he was concerned, the youngster's was the first friendly face he'd seen all day. He felt trapped in a household of people intent on converting the family heathen.

"How you feeling?" Hank asked. "Your leg still hurtin'?"

"Only when I smile," Lon replied, deadpan. "Which ain't too often around here."

"What happened now?"

"The usual," Lon said. "Old stick-in-the-mud popped in to give me another lecture."

"Uncle Clint?"

"Nobody else."

"What'd he have to say?"

"Nothin' worth repeating," Lon observed. "Lucky for me, he was on his way into town. I got off light."

"Guess you can't blame him too much. He just figures he knows what's best."

The boy's reply was overdrawn, a little too guileless. Lon was silent a moment, watching him intently. Never before had the youngster defended their uncle, and that bothered Lon. Finally, he decided to let the remark pass.

"How was the grand tour?" he said. "Brad show you around the place?"

Hank smiled broadly. "I never seen nothin' like it. All them stories Uncle Clint told us . . ."

"Yeah?"

"Well, he wasn't fibbin'," Hank went on. "They've got more goldurn horses and cows than you could shake a stick at. Lots bigger'n I expected."

Lon frowned. "Sounds like you had yourself quite a looksee."

"Brad says we only just got started. He's gonna show me the rest of it tomorrow."

"What else did he have to say?"

"I don't follow you."

Lon squinted at him. "They're not givin' you the royal treatment without a reason. You must've got a clue of some sort."

The boy squirmed under Lon's ugly stare. "No need to lie about it," he said with a lame grin. "Brad offered me a job workin' horses. Him and the family want me to stay on."

" 'Course, they do!" Lon said, his face pale and furious. "The whole connivin' bunch aims to split us up. They're tryin' to drive a wedge between you and me."

"No such thing," Hank protested. "Brad says the family wants you to stay on too. He says we could make ourselves a good home here."

"Quit tellin' me what Brad says! He's just a polly-parrot for Clint and the rest of 'em. You think I'm not wise to their game?"

Hank shook his head vigorously. "We're family and they're tryin' to look out for us. What's wrong with that?"

"Plenty," Lon said, his voice tight with rage. "Jesus Christ, you wanna be a shitkicker the rest of your life—a hired hand?"

"Brad's done all right for himself."

Lon's laugh was scratchy, abrasive. "A foreman takes orders too. Family or not, he's still workin' for wages."

"Mebbe so," Hank said, averting his eyes, "but leastways it's honest work."

Lon gave him a dirty look. "You sayin' there's something crooked about gambling?"

"I'm sayin' we could make a place for ourselves here. Hard work never hurt nobody."

"Suit yourself," Lon said with chilly finality. "I'm leavin' as soon as I can ride a horse. You mark my word on it."

A moment elapsed while they stared at one another. Hank stood as though nailed to the floor, his expression faintly stricken. At length, he flushed and bobbed his head.

"Guess you're right," he said. "We ought to stick together."

"Now you're talkin' sense."

Lon permitted himself a thin smile. Yet he seethed with bitter anger toward all the Brannocks. After today, he knew they would stop at nothing to separate him from the boy. He vowed to himself that it would never happen.

One way or another, he and Hank would leave Spur together. The sooner the better for all concerned.

Clint took supper that night with Jennifer and Blake. The meal was simple fare, served at the small dining table in Jennifer's living quarters. Their conversation centered principally on family matters.

Late that afternoon Clint had stopped by the sheriff's office. Without revealing his source, he'd informed Will Grant that *Las Gorras Blancas* were planning another raid. The tip seemed to him reliable and some hunch told him it would happen fairly soon. He asked to be contacted the minute the attack was reported.

Tonight, however, he made no mention of the White Caps. Whenever possible, he kept his law duties separate from private affairs. The talk turned instead on Lon and Hank, and the deal he'd struck on their behalf. Apart from being posted out of White Oaks, he explained, they would be fined for resisting arrest. All other charges would be dropped.

"Way it worked out," he concluded, "they'll just

get a rap on the knuckles. I doubt the judge will fine 'em more than fifty dollars apiece.''

Blake speared a bite of steak with his fork. He popped it into his mouth and chewed thoughtfully. ''I wonder if they know how lucky they are. Except for your intervention, they could have been in serious trouble.''

''Hank knows,'' Clint said solemnly. ''Lon wouldn't admit it come hell or high water. He don't like to be in my debt.''

''Why is that?'' Jennifer asked. ''You're practically the only father he's ever known.''

''Maybe that's the problem,'' Clint replied. ''Lon always resented me trying to keep him on the straight and narrow. He's bound to go his own way.''

''It's an unfortunate situation,'' Jennifer said rather sadly. ''All the more so because of his influence over Hank. I hate to think what might happen.''

''Yeah, me too.'' Clint suddenly laughed, spread his hands. ''Let's talk about something a little more pleasant. How's your wedding plans comin' along?''

''Quite well,'' Jennifer said, smiling brightly. ''We'll be married on a Sunday and back to work on Monday. We've both agreed a honeymoon will have to wait.''

''Never thought to ask,'' Clint said, ''but maybe you just answered the question. You aim to keep on practicin' medicine?''

''Of course,'' Jennifer said, lifting her chin slightly. ''A woman is no less entitled to a career than a man.''

Blake grunted, smothering a laugh. ''Given a choice, I'd keep her barefoot and pregnant. But she's too much the suffragist to play housewife.'' He paused, gave Jennifer an affectionate look. ''I'm afraid we're stuck with a doctor in the family.''

Jennifer wrinkled her nose. "You wouldn't have it any other way. Admit it."

"I certainly will not," Blake said with great relish. "Every woman a pot-walloper, that's my motto."

"Good Lord," Jennifer said, rolling her eyes. "You really are impossible."

Clint watched their byplay with a bemused expression. Age had made him more tolerant, but some ideas died hard. He often thought the suffragists would benefit by the old "barefoot-and-pregnant" theory. The notion of a petticoat politician and a lady doctor in the same family still seemed to him an oddity of nature. He sometimes wondered if he'd outlived his time.

After coffee and dessert, he decided to call it a night. Jennifer walked him to the door and kissed him good night on the cheek. Outside, he turned uptown and strolled off in a thoughtful mood. Beyond the hotel, the lights of a saloon beckoned, casting a tallowed glow onto the street. He stepped inside for a drink.

Several men stood at the bar. Clint moved past them, nodding, and took a seat at an empty table. The barmaid drifted over with his usual nightcap, a tumbler of rye whiskey. Her name was Molly O'Day and she was a rarity in Lincoln. She hustled drinks but she never sold herself. Her favors were dispensed only to a select few.

" 'Evening, marshal," she said, placing his drink on the table. "How goes the battle?"

Clint looked up at her. "So far, it's just another day. How're things with you?"

"Why complain?" she said, laughing softly. "God has a tin ear when it comes to whiners."

"You talk to God, do you?"

Molly O'Day caught his bantering tone. She was an impressive woman, short and buxom, with dark auburn hair. Her green eyes held a certain bawdy wisdom and her voice was low and throaty. She gave him a slow once-over.

"When I was younger," she said, "I used to talk with God all the time. Then I found out he's just like other men."

"How so?"

"All promises," she said lightly. "He never answers a girl's prayers."

"Are you praying for something special?"

A vixen look touched her eyes. She moistened her lips with the tip of her tongue and her voice turned silky. "Why don't we talk about it when I get off work?"

Clint smiled. "What makes you think I'll answer your prayers?"

"Well . . ." She paused, batted her eyes. "You didn't do so bad last time."

"You still get off at twelve?"

She nodded, her laughter somehow musical. As she walked away, Clint watched the wig-wag of her hips with an appreciative look. Over the past month she had invited him into her bed at least once a week. She made no secret of the fact that she saw other men, and he'd never raised the subject. Their arrangement was casual, no strings attached, and he was content to keep it that way. He wanted no ties.

All his life Clint had avoided entanglements. He preferred romping women of zest and laughter who made no demands on him. Such women were easily forgotten, for there was no emotional attachment, no lasting bond. While he seldom reflected on it, he was aware he purposely sought out women like Molly O'Day. With them, when the good times faded, there were no regrets, no reason for hard feelings. They invariably parted friends, no one the worse for the experience.

As he sipped his whiskey, Clint's mind suddenly leapfrogged. For no discernible reason, his thoughts jumped to Elizabeth. He pondered what her life had been like since Virgil's death. To all appearances, she was not involved with a man, preferring the privacy of her memories. Yet she was a good-looking woman and far too young for the self-imposed abstinence of a nun. It occurred to him that he'd never allowed himself to think of her in that way. Instead, treating her like an icon of sorts, he had always suppressed such thoughts.

The realization jarred him. He wondered how she would react if, after all these years, he were to make his feelings known. For a moment, he turned the idea this way and that, studying it like a multifaceted prism. Then, on sudden impulse, he ruthlessly suppressed the notion. What mattered most was how she felt, and he already knew the answer to that. She saw him as a brother and a friend, an old and trusted confidant. The odds on her ever feeling more were too dismal to calculate. No better, certainly, than a snowball in hell.

Clint downed his drink. He turned, about to signal Molly for a refill, when the front door slammed open. Will Grant rushed into the saloon, looking around wildly. Upon spotting Clint, he waved and hurried toward the table. His features were grim.

"Word just come in," he said, halting beside the table. "The White Caps hit Joe Hobson tonight."

"Hobson?" Clint repeated in a remote voice. "I recollect his place is west of here."

"Yep," Grant affirmed. "On the Rio Bonito, maybe ten miles out."

"That gives us plenty of time. We can't start trackin' till dawn anyway."

"We?" Grant repeated. "You want me to go along?"

"You and your deputies," Clint told him. "Any objections?"

"No, I don't suppose so."

"Then you'd better get a move on. We'll meet at your office in an hour."

Grant nodded, turning back toward the door. Clint rose from his chair and crossed to the far end of the bar. He stopped beside Molly.

"Something's come up," he said. "We'll have to make it another night."

"Trouble?" she asked.

"Nothing out of the ordinary."

"Look after yourself, anyhow. I figure you owe me one."

Clint chuckled. "I always square accounts with a lady."

Molly O'Day watched him out the door. She'd always thought him a curious man, prodded by strange devils. But of all her gentlemen friends, he was the most considerate of the lot. Which made him stranger still.

No one expected kindness of a man who traded in sudden death.

22

A dingy haze lighted the sky at false dawn. The riders were like warm ghosts, caught in that moment when night turns to day. None of them spoke as they forded the Rio Bonito.

Clint rode in the lead. Strung out behind him were Will Grant and three deputies. Since leaving Lincoln, they had followed the stage road on a westerly track. But now, where the river made a dogleg to the north, they dropped off the road and crossed at a shallow ford. Farther on, the mountains rose in dim silhouette against a gray horizon.

Signs of the raid were immediately evident. Where a fence line had once intersected the stream, there was now a great tangle of barbed wire and splintered posts. From all appearances, horsemen had roped the posts and rolled sections of fence into spiked masses of wire. The process had been repeated at intervals, leaving the rangeland dotted with balls of downed fence. None of it looked salvageable.

A short while later Clint and the lawmen spotted the ranch compound. Smoke drifted lazily from the embers of a large barn that had burned to the ground. The main house and several nearby outbuildings appeared undamaged. Outside the bunkhouse a group of cowhands stood bunched in a tight knot. Their clothes were singed and their faces streaked from having vainly fought the barn fire. They looked like soot-blackened scarecrows.

The door of the main house banged open. A stocky man with a nose the color of rotten plums stalked outside and halted in the yard. His eyes were bloodshot and his eyebrows were singed off, clearly lost in battling the fire. He planted himself, waiting as the lawmen reined to a halt. He glared angrily at Will Grant.

"By Christ!" he said dourly. "You took your own sweet time. I sent a man to fetch you last night."

"C'mon now, Joe," Grant said with a pained expression. "Wasn't nothin' we could've done last night. You know that."

"I don't know no such thing."

Hobson glowered at them. Clint and the sheriff dismounted and left their horses ground-reined. As they moved forward, Clint dug out the makings and began rolling himself a smoke. He nodded to the rancher.

"Don't blame Will," he said. "I'm the one that decided to wait for first light. You can't track anybody in the dark."

Hobson snorted. "Way I hear it, you can't track anybody a'tall—night or day."

Clint popped a match on his thumbnail. He lit his cigarette, then dropped the match and ground it underfoot. He glanced up, exhaling a streamer of smoke. "You heard wrong."

"Says you." Hobson flipped a hand in scorn. "We've never met, but folks talk. I know all about you."

"Yeah?" Clint said levelly. "Such as?"

"You're no closer to catchin' Ortega than you was the day you hit town. There's them that says you don't wanna catch him . . . never did."

"Any of these big talkers got a name?"

"Damn right!" Hobson said in a voice webby with

phlegm. "How about Homer Stockton? That ring any bells?"

Clint shrugged. "His daughter married my nephew. What's that got to do with me?"

"Way Stockton tells it, you've got personal reasons for not catchin' Ortega."

"What personal reasons?"

"Elizabeth Brannock," Hobson said flatly. "Everybody knows her and Ortega are thick as thieves. Only makes sense you'd try to protect your sister-in-law."

"Homer Stockton said that?"

"Him and lots of others. If you don't believe me, ask the sheriff."

Clint glanced sideways at Grant. "I'd like a straight answer, Will. Any truth to it?"

Grant avoided his eyes. "Hell, talk's cheap, Clint. Why bother you with it?"

"You should've let me decide that."

"I figured you'd just as soon not hear it."

Clint took a drag on his cigarette. He let out a thread of smoke and his gaze shifted back to Hobson. "Next time I see Stockton," he said in a flinty voice, "I'll tell him what I'm gonna tell you now. He's a goddamn liar, plain and simple."

Hobson's face twisted in a prunelike mask of skepticism. "Why should I take your word over Stockton's?"

"Would you believe Miguel Ortega instead?"

"Come again?"

"Ortega tried to have me killed," Clint said. "Check with the U.S. marshal in Santa Fe. He'll verify the story."

Hobson gave him a short look. "I don't get it. Unless you were breathin' down his neck, why would Ortega want you dead?"

Clint smiled with hard irony. "I think you just answered your own question."

"I'll be damned," Hobson muttered. "How come nobody ever heard about it?"

"The man Ortega sent after me wasn't able to testify. He got himself killed."

"All the same," Grant interjected, "you should've told me. I thought we was workin' together on this thing."

"Slipped my mind," Clint noted dryly. "Next time you'll be the first to know."

When Grant mumbled an inaudible reply, Clint turned back to the rancher. "I'd like the particulars on what happened last night. How many men were in the raiding party?"

"Three, maybe four," Hobson said uncertainly. "Nobody suspicioned anything till they'd already fired the barn. After that, they skedaddled pretty quick."

"So they just went after the barn? None of the other buildings?"

"Yeah, now that you mention it, that's right. They could've fired every building on the place before we woke up."

"Any shooting?" Clint asked.

"Not a helluva lot," Hobson replied. "One of my boys got off a couple of shots, but it was wasted lead. They were hightailin' it by then."

"And they didn't fire back?"

"Like I said, they were lookin' to be long gone."

"Which way were they headed?"

"Off to the southwest," Hobson said, motioning with his arm. "That would've put 'em on a direct line with the river."

Clint took a final pull on his cigarette. He hesitated a moment, as though considering a matter of weighty importance. At length, after grinding the cigarette underfoot, he nodded to Hobson.

"Guess that ought to do it," he said. "We'll pick up their trail and see where it leads."

"You want some help?" Hobson offered. "I could send along four or five of my boys."

"We'll manage," Clint assured him. "From the looks of your fences, you'll need all your hands anyway. I'd wager your cows are scattered to hell and gone by now."

"Sonsabitches!" Hobson cursed savagely. "I'd like to be there when you catch Ortega and his greasers."

"We'll let you know how it works out."

Clint turned away, followed closely by the sheriff. On foot, they led their horses past the ruins of the barn. The three deputies, still mounted, tagged along behind. Some distance from the house, Grant finally looked around at Clint. His brow puckered in a frown.

"I'm curious," he said. "Why'd you ask Hobson all them questions about the raid?"

"Just satisfying myself," Clint informed him. "There's a pattern to the way the White Caps operate. I wanted to see if they stuck with it."

"What d'you mean—pattern?"

"Well, first off, they never set fire to a building with people in it. Everything they've torched has been a shed or a barn, some sort of outbuilding."

Grant looked puzzled. "What's that tell you?"

"By itself, nothing," Clint said. "But there's more to it. You'll recall they never shoot at anybody. Leastways not till they're fired on first."

"Judas Priest," Grant groaned. "Are you sayin' they're not out to kill anybody?"

"That's how it tallies in my book."

"How about that cowhand they killed east of town?"

"Proves my point," Clint said. "He dropped one of their men before they opened fire on him."

"Even so, it don't make a nickel's worth of difference. The law still calls it murder."

"No argument there, Will."

"What about yourself?" Grant demanded. "You said Ortega tried to have you killed. Don't that blow your theory all to hell?"

Clint cracked a smile. "Señor Ortega made an exception in my case. He probably figures lawdogs are fair game."

"Especially when you're hot on his trail."

"Speakin' of which, look what we've got here."

Their position was perhaps fifty yards past the smoldering barn. Clint motioned for Grant and the others to remain where they were. He walked forward a step at a time, slowly scanning the ground. Every three or four paces, his gaze swept an arc off to either side.

For an old cavalry scout, the sign was readily apparent. Hoofprints indicated that four riders had converged together some distance from the compound. Studying on it, Clint saw that they had spread out upon riding away from the barn. The tactic made them less likely targets while they were still visible in the blazing firelight. After gaining the safety of darkness, they had joined up in a rough formation. Their direction was almost due southwest.

Clint noted that the horses had been driven at a hard gallop. His assessment was quick but certain, based on the length of the stride and the depth of the tracks. He thought it quite probable that neither the men nor their mounts had been wounded by gunfire. There were no traces of blood and the hoofprints were hammered into the ground at an unbroken pace. From all indications, the night riders had escaped in good order.

Turning back, Clint walked toward the waiting lawmen. He was reminded of the old days, when a cavalry patrol waited for him to scout the trail ahead. At various times, before the horseback tribes were defeated, he'd campaigned against the Comanche as well as the Apache. Tracking *Las Gorras Blancas* seemed to him little different from pursuing bands of hostiles. In the end, it was a game of hide-and-seek with a deadly twist. The loser, more often than not, got killed.

Will Grant was already mounted. Clint stepped aboard his horse, gesturing off into the distance. "Four men," he said. "I'd judge they were on a beeline for the river. Not wastin' any time, either."

"Four here," Grant said carefully, "means there were probably twice that many tearin' down fence and scattering cattle. All told, we're talkin' about twelve men, maybe more."

Clint nodded agreement. "I've got an idea they planned a rendezvous somewhere along the river. From what I've seen before, Ortega likes to regroup after a raid."

"What makes you think he led it himself?"

"Ortega's still building an organization in Lincoln County. Takes time to train farmers and teach 'em tactics. I doubt he's found himself a lieutenant just yet."

Grant raised an uncertain eyebrow. "Way it looks, we're outnumbered better'n two to one. Ortega leadin' them only makes it worse."

"What's your point, Will?"

"Maybe we ought to accept Hobson's offer. Four or five of his boys would sorta balance the odds."

"No." Clint's voice was hard and determined. "A bunch of trigger-happy cowhands wouldn't solve anything. We'll tend to it ourselves."

"Lemme ask you something." Grant hesitated, gave him an odd look. "Up till now, you've always played a lone hand. Why'd you bring us along this time?"

Clint was aware of the three deputies watching him intently. He returned Grant's stare with a cryptic expression. "So far," he said, "Ortega has stuck to that pattern I mentioned. I've got a hunch we can make it work to our advantage."

Grant appeared confused. Before he could frame a reply, Clint rode off at a sharp trot. The sheriff glanced back at his men, then motioned them onward. The trail they followed led once more toward the Rio Bonito.

The river was molten with sunlight. Overhead a hawk floated past on smothered wings, scanning for prey. Nothing moved along a shoreline studded with cottonwoods.

To the west, the mountains rose against a backdrop of limitless sky. The Rio Bonito curved in a graceful, southwesterly bend toward its headwaters in the high country. The rushing waters tumbled beneath a bridge on the stage road, which sliced east to west through the mountainous terrain. Far in the distance, the majestic spire of Sierra Blanca was rimmed with cottony clouds.

Clint called a halt just north of the stage road. He shaded his eyes against the noonday sun and stared at the bridge for a long moment. Then he dismounted, leaving his horse with Grant and the deputies, and walked along the riverbank. Upstream he angled off to the right and stopped beneath a copse of trees. After a time, he slowly quartered the shoreline, his gaze fastened to the ground. He paused where the treeline ended, staring again at the bridge.

The expression on Clint's face was abstracted. He hauled out the makings, his movements somehow mechanical, and rolled himself a cigarette. He cupped his hands around the flare of a match and lit up in a wreath of smoke. For what seemed an interminable time, he stood puffing on the cigarette, apparently lost in thought. Finally, he turned back downstream.

Grant and the deputies waited where he'd left them. Clint flipped the cigarette into the river, then swung aboard his horse. He jerked his chin toward the copse of trees.

"That's where they met," he said. "The four we were trailin' joined up with the rest of the bunch. By their tracks, I put the count at eleven."

"Eleven," Grant repeated without inflection. "Any idea where they headed?"

"You'll recollect I talked about a pattern."

"Yeah?"

"Well, nothing's changed," Clint observed. "They regrouped, then they scattered like jackstraws. Five took off crosscountry toward White Oaks. Four more headed in the direction of Lincoln. The last two turned upstream."

"Damned odd," Grant said, staring past the bridge. "Up that way, the river skirts around Fort Stanton. You'd think they'd steer clear of the military."

"Maybe not," Clint said thoughtfully. "For anybody with the nerve, it'd make a fine hideout. Lots of rough country up there."

Grant studied him quizzically. "Are you talkin' about Ortega?"

"Not much question he's nervy enough to give it a try."

"How long have you suspected?"

"A week or so," Clint replied. "I paid a call on the post commander just a couple of days ago. Asked him to have the troops keep a sharp lookout. So far, I haven't heard anything."

Grant was silent a moment. "Let's assume it was

Ortega that went upstream. Who would he have ridin'
with him?"

"His *pistolero*," Clint said. "I've been told he always travels with a bodyguard. Appears I got the
straight goods."

"What're we waitin' for, then? We oughta be sniffin'
out his trail."

Clint smiled. "No offense, but it's like you said back
at Hobson's ranch. I prefer to work alone."

"Jesus H. Christ!" Grant fumed. "You mean to say
you're cuttin' us out of it?"

"What I had in mind was splittin' up."

Clint quickly sketched the plan. Grant and one of
his deputies would follow the White Caps in the direction of Lincoln. The other two deputies would take
the trail leading toward White Oaks. By splitting forces,
the odds of capturing at least one raider were greatly
increased.

"Hell's bells," Grant retorted. "Somewhere down
the line they're gonna scatter to the winds. We'll end
up with trails headed ever' whichaway."

Clint shrugged. "Stick with the one that looks the
most promising. You might get lucky."

"And meantime, you're takin' Ortega for yourself!"

Grant was still grumbling when they parted at the
bridge. With one of his deputies, the sheriff rode
eastward on the stage road. The other deputies followed the tracks angling off toward the northwest.
Clint watched until the four lawmen were out of sight.
He then turned upstream along the Rio Bonito.

A brooding loneliness hung over the mountains.
Somewhere in the distance a squirrel chattered, and a
bluejay, sounding a scolding cry, took flight. Within
moments, an empty silence once again settled across
the timbered slopes.

By late afternoon Clint was some eight miles upstream. The terrain was rugged and steep, ascending
steadily into the high country. Weathered boulders
and rocky outcroppings jutted from a ridge overlooking the river. A game trail, beaten into the hard earth
by deer, bordered the streambed.

Fresh hoofprints covered the deer tracks. The game
trail had begun a short way past Fort Stanton, where
the Rio Bonito skirted the garrison. At that point,
Clint had lost any lingering doubt about the men he
trailed. The riders had swung sharply east, detouring
around the army post. A mile farther on their tracks
had merged once again with the river.

Halting now, Clint studied the trail ahead. The stream
curved westward, dropping below a craggy bluff. There
was nothing out of the ordinary, but suddenly, for no
apparent reason, his scalp tingled. Years of living on
the razor edge of death had honed in him a sixth sense
for danger. He'd learned to trust his instincts, and he
sat for a moment staring at the jagged outcropping.
His hand moved to the butt of the rifle in his saddle
scabbard.

A flicker of sunlight on metal caught Clint's eye. He
vaulted out of the saddle, grabbing the pump-action
repeater as he kicked free of the stirrups. The report
of a carbine reverberated through the mountains and a
slug sizzled past his head. He hit the ground and
rolled, heaving himself over the edge of the riverbank.
His horse spooked and bolted back down the trail.

The carbine barked twice in rapid succession. Dirt
showered him as the shots plowed furrows across the
top of the bank. From high on the outcropping, he
spotted puffs of smoke beside a stunted juniper.
Quickly, acting almost on reflex, he removed his hat
and flung it into the air. Then, crouching lower still,

he scuttled several yards upstream. He paused to catch his breath, slowly counted to ten.

The carbine remained silent. Clint waited a moment longer, reasonably confident his assailant had been distracted by the hat. He got to his knees, the pump-action rifle at the ready, and cautiously peeked over the riverbank. High above, he saw a man rise from behind the juniper, gripping a saddle carbine. As he watched, the man edged forward, straining for a better look into the streambed.

Clint jammed the butt of the rifle into his shoulder. The big .50-95 boomed and he instantly jacked another shell into the chamber, triggering a second shot. The man on the bluff jerked upright, his mouth open in a strangled scream. His hands splayed, dropping the carbine, and he clawed at empty air. He pitched forward and tumbled end-over-end down the face of the outcropping. His body slammed to a halt on the game trail.

Still watchful, Clint held his position for several minutes. He carefully inspected the bluff, alert to any sign of movement. At last, he scrambled over the riverbank and walked forward. The dead man was a *mexicano*, sprawled on his back with blood plastered across his chest. A Remington revolver was cinched around his waist and cartridge bandoliers were criss-crossed over his shoulders. Staring down at him, Clint felt any vestige of doubt drain away. He'd just killed Miguel Ortega's *pistolero*.

Some three hours later Clint located the campsite. High in the mountains, near the headwaters of the Rio Bonito, the hideout was situated in a grove of trees. Supplies and assorted gear were piled beneath a lean-to, but the clearing itself was deserted. There were no signs of recent activity and ashes in the campfire were at least two days old. A picket line for horses showed no fresh droppings.

Standing there, Clint felt a keen sense of disappointment. Yet, even though he'd come up short, he was moved to a grudging admiration. For the first time, he understood fully the hold that Ortega exerted over the *mexicanos*. The *pistolero*, far from a hired gun, was a martyr to a cause. Thinking back, Clint saw now that the man had sacrificed his own life so that his leader might escape. No greater act of loyalty could be asked, or rendered.

Still, where Clint was personally concerned, it was an altogether different matter. Twice now, Miguel Ortega had tried to have him killed. He resolved to end it before there was a third time.

23

"How are we doing, now?"

"Terrible," Louise said. "My backbone feels like it's going to snap."

"Unfortunately, you'll have to grin and bear it. That's all part of having a baby."

Elizabeth pulled the bedsheet aside. She placed her hand on the girl's rounded abdomen and waited for the next contraction. Louise turned her head into the pillow, still embarrassed at being examined by her mother-in-law. The fact that Elizabeth was an experienced midwife hardly relieved her discomfort.

Early that morning Louise had gone into labor. An initial examination convinced Elizabeth that it would be a slow birth. Years ago, when she'd been active at the clinic, she had assisted in dozens of deliveries. On her own she had acted as midwife for countless *mexicano* women throughout the Hondo Valley. She recalled that first babies were often difficult, and seldom born quickly.

Fearful of complications, she had sent John Taylor to fetch Jennifer. By modern standards, the old midwifery methods were hopelessly outdated. She wanted a doctor in attendance, and Louise's condition allowed some leeway in time. The round trip into town would consume the better part of the day; but she wasn't worried. At the latest, she expected Jennifer to arrive well before nightfall.

Louise moaned softly when the contraction hit. By silent count, Elizabeth determined that the spasms were now occurring some three minutes apart. She lifted the girl's nightgown and saw a light spotting of blood on the bottom sheet. Her concern suddenly mounted, for she realized the birthing time was fast approaching. A quick glance out the window alarmed her even more; sundown was slowly fading to dusk. She stepped back, draping the top sheet over Louise.

"Everything's fine," she said. "You're progressing right on schedule."

"How much longer?" Louise asked. "It seems like it's taking forever."

Elizabeth forced herself to smile. "No complaints, young lady. You're actually having an easy time of it. I've seen women in labor for two days, sometimes longer."

Louise groaned. "I'll never have another one. Not after this."

"You'll change your mind," Elizabeth said lightly. "One baby just never seems enough. They're so sweet and cuddly, you always want more."

"Was that how you felt?"

"I remember it just like yesterday. After I had Jennifer, I couldn't wait to get pregnant again. Morgan was born scarcely a year later."

"I hope it's a boy," Louise said dreamily. "Morg wants a son so much."

"All men say that," Elizabeth remarked. "But you needn't worry yourself about it. He'll be perfectly satisfied with a daughter."

"Are you sure?"

"Positive," Elizabeth said with conviction. "Morgan is very much like his father, more than he realizes.

And Virgil was too proud for words when Jennifer was born."

Louise suddenly appeared pensive. "Do you think Jen will get here in time?"

"Why, of course," Elizabeth assured her. "After all, she's about to become an aunt. She wouldn't miss that for anything."

"I hope not," Louise said, averting her eyes. "To tell you the truth, I'm a little scared."

"Why don't I send Morg in to keep you company. I'm sure Jennifer will be here any moment now."

Elizabeth smiled confidently, patting her hand. Turning from the bed, she crossed to the door and stepped into the hallway. Morg was waiting outside.

"How's Louise?" he said anxiously. "Everything all right?"

"She's fine," Elizabeth noted. "I want you to stay with her for a while. And smile for heaven's sake—act cheerful!"

Morg appeared troubled rather than nervous. Like many first-time fathers, he'd thought having a baby was a routine affair. He was clearly concerned that it was taking so long.

"What'll I say to her?" he wondered aloud. "Last time I was in there, she seemed pretty upset."

"She has more spunk than you give her credit for. Hold her hand and tell her you love her—and smile!"

Elizabeth waited until he entered the bedroom. She then walked to the vestibule and opened the front door. A moment passed while she searched the quickening darkness, straining for any sign of the buckboard. She finally turned and proceeded to the dining room.

Supper was being served. Brad sat on one side of the long table, and seated opposite him were Lon and Hank. Elizabeth greeted them quietly, taking her place at the head of the table. She wasn't particularly hungry, and when Brad offered a platter of beefsteak, she declined. She had a cup of coffee instead.

Brad inquired about Louise. Sparing the details, Elizabeth commented that her condition was unchanged. The talk then turned general, with Brad and Hank carrying the conversation. Lon ate in silence, like a man performing a necessary, if somewhat tedious, chore. Sipping her coffee, Elizabeth watched them with a thoughtful look.

She found little hope for Lon. His leg wound was mending and he'd recently begun hobbling around on a crutch. He wasn't yet strong enough to leave the house, but he now took his meals at the table. Still, his recovery was slow and his mood was one of sullen impatience. He was clearly champing to be gone from Spur.

Hank was an entirely different matter. On occasion, Elizabeth thought he showed signs of wavering. He spent his days working with the horse herd and he seemed drawn to life on a ranch. All the more important, he'd been influenced by the strong sense of unity among the family. He was by no means distanced from Lon, but something about him had changed. He appeared in no rush to leave the Hondo.

Any reflection on the boy inevitably led to Clint. Yet Elizabeth was far less sanguine where her old friend was concerned. Some two weeks had passed since the gunfight in the mountains and Miguel Ortega's narrow escape. A few days afterward, Clint had stopped overnight at the ranch. He was headed south, following a lead that Ortega was recruiting in the Seven Rivers district. From his attitude, the manhunt had now become a personal matter.

Elizabeth worried about him constantly. Seven Rivers was a remote stretch of backcountry located some

ninety miles southeast of Lincoln. Far removed from
the county seat, it was isolated and lawless, a stronghold of hard-bitten Anglo ranchers. An outbreak of
violence by *Las Gorras Blancas* would almost certainly
result in reprisals against the local *mexicanos*. Whether
or not Clint could maintain order in such a climate was
an arguable point. He might easily find himself caught
in the middle.

The passage of time merely aggravated Elizabeth's
concern. The date was June 2 and she'd heard nothing
from Clint in almost ten days. She still found it hard to
believe that Miguel Ortega had tried to take his life.
Yet the evidence seemed insurmountable, particularly
after the ambush in the mountains. Even worse, in the
remote Seven Rivers country a man could be bush-
whacked and never heard from again. She'd always
thought Clint invincible, like the proverbial cat with
nine lives. And yet there were limits beyond which . . .

Jennifer suddenly appeared in the doorway. John
Taylor was only a step behind, carrying her medical
bag. She advanced into the dining room, nodding to
her mother. "Sorry I'm so late," she said. "I was in
the middle of an operation when John arrived. I had
to finish."

"You're here now," Elizabeth said, pushing back
her chair. "That's all that matters."

"Louise hasn't had the baby?"

"I think you've come just in time. She's very close."

Jennifer ordered hot water brought to the bedroom.
Morg was ushered into the hallway and told to wait
outside. In separate washbasins, Jennifer and her mother
both scrubbed their hands. Then while Elizabeth laid
out instruments and sterile gauze, Jennifer took a stethoscope from her medical bag. She approached the bed,
smiling at Louise.

"Well, now, suppose we have a look."

Louise smiled bravely. "The way I feel, you'd better make it quick."

After turning back the sheet, Jennifer placed the stethoscope on her swollen abdomen. The fetal heartbeat was loud and rapid, gratifyingly strong. Laying the stethoscope aside, Jennifer then timed the contractions. She found them occurring regularly, one after another, hardly a minute apart.

With Elizabeth assisting, Jennifer helped the girl slip out of her nightgown. She next spread Louise's legs and performed an internal examination. The cervix was dilated sufficiently to allow the insertion of three fingers. She withdrew her hand, smiling brightly.

"Louise, you're about to become a mother. Take deep breaths and do exactly what I tell you."

The contractions abruptly quickened. Louise uttered a stifled shriek, her forehead dotted with perspiration. She gulped a shuddering breath as the pain mounted in intensity. Elizabeth moved behind her, standing between the wall and the head of the bed. She leaned forward, grasping Louise beneath the knees with her hands. When she pulled back, the girl's straining buttocks were lifted slightly off the mattress.

Jennifer positioned herself at the foot of the bed. She crouched on her knees and began massaging the girl's widened vulva. She kneaded the flesh, drawing it outward, gently forcing it to stretch without tearing. She commanded Louise to bear down, and the girl puffed, gasping air, and strained harder. The baby's forehead appeared and Jennifer stretched the folds of the vulva wider still. Then, with a sudden rush, the head emerged cradled in Jennifer's hand. She gingerly worked the shoulders free and a moment later lifted the newborn infant from the bed.

"It's a boy," she said, laughing. "A perfect baby boy."

Louise strained for a better look, tears flooding her eyes. Unable to speak, she slumped back on the bed, utterly exhausted. Jennifer slapped the baby on the rump and he squawled a loud cry of outrage. She then cut the umbilical cord, deftly tying it off, and turned the baby over to Elizabeth. When the afterbirth emerged, she wrapped it in a cloth and set it aside. Finally, with gauze and warm water, she began cleaning Louise.

A short time later Jennifer stepped into the hall. Her eyes were bright with happiness and she nodded to Morg. "Congratulations," she said. "You have a son."

"A son." Morg beamed. "I'll be damned."

"And I'm happy to report, mother and child are both doing fine."

"I'll be double damned."

Jennifer smiled. "You may be triple damned before you get him away from Mama. So far, she refuses to let go of her grandson."

Morg threw back his head and roared laughter.

Louise slept the night through. Her energy was spent from the long hours of labor and the ordeal of birthing. She awoke only to nurse the baby.

At dawn, Jennifer entered the bedroom. She aroused Louise only long enough to perform a final examination. All the bleeding had stopped the evening before and there was nothing to indicate unforeseen complications. The baby was in perfect health, strong and lusty, with bright blue eyes. Jennifer thought the only danger he faced was in being spoiled by a doting grandmother.

The household was already stirring with activity. Elizabeth walked Jennifer to the door, embracing her with a warm hug. Outside, Taylor waited with a buckboard and team, prepared to drive Jennifer back to town. She had no qualms about leaving Louise and the baby in her mother's care. Elizabeth was like a dowager empress at last assured that the bloodline would be extended. A male child ensured still another generation of Brannocks.

Shortly before sunrise Morg slipped into the bedroom. Following the delivery, he and Louise had talked briefly. While she was lucid, she kept dropping off to sleep and he'd finally let her rest. To afford her some degree of privacy, he had bunked last night with Brad. Today, he returned hoping to find her restored. There were things he felt compelled to say.

The baby was asleep, swaddled in a crib beside the bed. Morg stood there, looking down at the tiny, peaceful face, his throat dry with emotion. He was suffused with pride, the almost overwhelming realization that he'd fathered a son. His ears buzzed and he felt curiously light-headed. A dopy, moonlike grin wreathed his features.

"Do you like him?"

Her voice startled Morg. Louise was sleepy-eyed but awake, radiant with happiness. She held out her hand and he took it, seating himself on the edge of the bed. He suddenly seemed at a loss for words.

"I had a speech all prepared," he said, "but now I've forgot it. I'm just so damn proud I can't hardly stand myself."

"I'm glad," she said softly. "I prayed it would be a boy."

"Well, somebody up there must've been listenin'. We've got ourselves a son, Lou."

"Have you given any thought to a name?"

"Yeah, I have," Morg acknowledged. "Unless you're dead set against it, I'd like to call him Lucas."

"Lucas." She repeated it to herself. "Lucas Brannock. I think it's a fine name."

"Took it after my great-great-grandfather. He's the one that founded the family way back when."

"Then it's settled," she said. "And we'll call him Luke, for short."

Morg squeezed her hand. "Glad you approve, Mrs. Brannock. Now, you lay back and get yourself some rest. I'll see you later."

"Where are you going?"

"San Patricio," Morg replied. "But don't get yourself upset. I'll be back tonight."

She frowned prettily. "Promise?"

"On my oath. You and Luke look for me about dark."

"We'll be waiting."

Morg kissed her gently on the mouth. He walked to the door, still grinning, then waved and stepped into the hall. When the door closed, Louise leaned over the bed and looked into the crib. She touched the baby's face, her fingers like the caress of a snowflake. Her eyes misted and she tenderly spoke his name. Lucas Brannock.

She thought it was a good name, a proud name. A fitting name for her son. *Luke.*

A brassy sun stood high in the sky. Summer had come at last to the Hondo, and the foothills west of the valley were splotched with wildflowers. Borne on gentle winds, the scent of their fragrance was like a heady nectar.

As Morg approached San Patricio, his spirits still soared. He was intoxicated with himself and his world, drunk with the wonder of the day. The birth of his son somehow expanded his horizons and all things seemed possible. Nothing was beyond his reach.

Nor was it simply a matter of cockeyed optimism. His business ventures had prospered far beyond what he'd originally anticipated. Dave Todd, his mining partner, had proved to be an engineering marvel. In less than a month, Todd had organized an operation to rival anything in White Oaks. A stamping mill was under construction, and raw ore, rich in gold, would start pouring through within the week. On the mountainside, another crew of workers had extended the mine shaft almost a quarter-mile. The vein was wider than even Todd had suspected, with no end in sight. By late fall, perhaps sooner, the operation would begin to show a profit.

Expectations for the logging company were even brighter. Under Chunk Devlin's able management, production had doubled over the original estimates. To keep pace, Morg had expanded his sales efforts throughout the mountains and across the Pecos Valley. Earlier in the week he'd been awarded a lumber contract for proposed construction at Fort Stanton. Devlin was after him to increase the size of the timber crew and thereby double production again. The idea was sound and Morg had decided to go along. Given time, he might very well corner the timber market.

The prospect of expansion had prompted his trip to San Patricio. The capacity of the lumber mill was a critical factor in his plans, and he wanted to talk with Harry Tipton. Devlin was scheduled to deliver a load of timber today and the timing would never be better. The three of them could hash it out in detail and determine a course of action for the future. If pressed, Morg was willing to invest a sizable sum for part-ownership of the mill. One way or another, he meant to ensure that his timber got converted into lumber.

When he arrived at the mill, Devlin and the timber crew were already there. Every Saturday, when the last delivery was made, the loggers accompanied the teamsters and helped with the off-loading. Afterward, with a week's wages in their pockets, they backtracked to Lincoln for a night on the town. By the next morning, most of them were broke and they were all suffering gargantuan hangovers. The return trip to camp was inevitably an agonizing experience.

Morg dismounted outside the mill office. Devlin jumped down from one of the wagons as Harry Tipton appeared in the office doorway. After a round of handshakes, they stood talking for a moment. A sudden commotion from the road attracted their attention and they turned in unison. Three timber wagons, loaded with Ralph McQuade's logging crew, rolled into the yard. McQuade stepped down from the lead wagon.

"I was gonna warn you," Tipton whispered to Morg. "He's spoiling for trouble. Watch yourself."

McQuade halted a pace away. "Brannock, I wanna talk with you."

"Nothin' stopping you," Morg said equably. "What's on your mind?"

"You undercut me on that Fort Stanton job. Everywhere I go anymore, it turns out you're the low bidder. I'm not gonna stand for it."

"Way it looks to me, you haven't got a lot of choice. It's a matter of like it or lump it."

"In a pig's ass!" McQuade snarled. "I'll be gawddamned if I'll let you drive me into the poorhouse."

"Try lowering your prices," Morg told him. "There's contracts enough to go around."

"I got a better idea."

"What's that?"

McQuade glowered at him. "You're gonna get the hell outta the timber business. 'Cause if you don't, I'm fixin' to haul your ashes."

"You're sure you won't have it any other way?"

"I just finished tellin' you—get out or get whipped."

Morg hit him. The blow caught McQuade flush between the eyes, staggered him backward. A roar went
up as McQuade's timber crew jumped off the wagons
and advanced in a burly wedge. Several of them carried lengths of logging chain and their eyes glinted
with cold ferocity. From the opposite end of the mill,
Devlin's men hurried forward to join the fray. Harry
Tipton darted into his office and slammed the door.

McQuade somehow recovered his balance. Uncom-
monly agile for his size, he feinted with his left and
threw a murderous roundhouse right. Morg slipped
inside the blow and exploded two splintering punches
on the other man's jaw. Knocked off his feet, McQuade
went down like a wet sack of oats, out cold. Devlin
waded in at the forefront, almost shoulder to shoulder
with Morg. Together, their fists flying, they clubbed
and hammered in a blurred flurry.

The men on both sides battered their way into the
center of the action, hurling themselves at one another. Their struggle quickly became a contest of brute
strength. Over the grunts and curses, men fell in increasing numbers, trampled and crushed underfoot.
The momentum of the battle slowly shifted as Devlin's
loggers surged forward, arms flailing, and forced the
other side to give ground. McQuade's men gradually
broke ranks before the onslaught, and then, with abrupt
suddenness, those still on their feet scattered across
the yard. The melee ended as they retreated toward
their wagons.

Blood oozed down over Morg's cheekbone and an
ugly cut split his lower lip. Beside him, Chunk Devlin
stood with his shirt ripped loose at the shoulder and
his scalp laid open along the hairline. Their men were
grouped around them, bloodied and mauled, breathing hard. On Morg's signal, they backed away and

allowed the other crew to load their fallen comrades onto the wagons. The last man to be lifted aboard was Ralph McQuade, his jaw broken and three teeth missing. A moment later the wagons turned away from the mill and rumbled onto the road.

Not far behind were the wagons of Devlin's loggers. Early that afternoon they roared into Lincoln like a band of conquering warriors. Laughing and shouting, they invaded one of the saloons and took it over. Morg, flush with victory, ordered the bartender to keep the drinks coming.

He arrived home late that night, drunk as a lord.

24

The *mexicano* was a wizened man with a face like a
walnut. He wore a tattered *jorongo*, a sort of sleeve-
less jacket, and white cotton pants now faded with
grime. A floppy sombrero covered his head and his
feet were encased in bullhide sandals. His name was
Jesús Mantanzas.

Outside the house Mantanzas dismounted from a
prancing coal-black stallion. The horse seemed at odds
with a man who looked the part of a humble *peón*.
Had anyone asked, he would have denied ownership
of the fiery-eyed stud. Yet, even on threat of death,
he would have admitted nothing more. The *hombre*
who owned the horse had sworn him to silence.

At the door, he asked for Señora Brannock. The
serving girl, herself a *mexicana*, gave him a distasteful
look. She left him standing on the veranda and disappeared into the house. Several moments elapsed while
he waited, shifting from one foot to the other. Then
the door swung open and Elizabeth paused in the
entryway. She smiled pleasantly.

"*Buenos días,*" she said. "You wished to see me?"

Jesús Mantanzas doffed his sombrero. "*Buenos días,
señora.* I have been sent by a friend."

"Does your friend have a name?"

"*No,*" Mantanzas said quickly. "He told me you

would know him by what I say now. He last saw you with the *políticos,* in Albuquerque."

A sudden foreboding crept over Elizabeth. She asked herself why Miguel Ortega would contact her in such an oblique manner. She was almost afraid to ask.

"What does your friend want of me?"

Mantanzas' voice dropped. "He needs your assistance, *señora.* He is *muy enfermo.*"

"Sick?" Elizabeth said, taken aback. "What's wrong?"

"We do not know, *señora.* My woman has tended him, but nothing helps. He grows worse."

"Tell me of his condition. How is he sick?"

Mantanzas patted his belly. "He has a terrible hurt here. He cannot hold his food and he is hot to the touch."

"*Fiebre?*" Elizabeth asked. "You're certain he has fever?"

"*Sí, señora.* My woman has given him herbs and bathed him with cold water. And still he burns with sickness."

"Why has he sent you to me?"

"*La doctora,*" Mantanzas said. "He asks that you bring your daughter, *señora.*"

"You could have asked her yourself. Why come to me?"

"Our friend does not know your daughter, *señora.* He trusts you to do this thing in secret—*sin hablar.*"

"In other words," Elizabeth said, "he believes I will not inform the law. *Verdad?*"

Mantanzas bobbed his head. "Unless you help, he will not live, *señora.* Even now, *muerte* is written on his face."

Elizabeth took an instant to collect herself. She appeared calm, but inwardly she was torn with mixed emotions. How could she help Ortega without betraying Clint? Yet, even as she asked herself the question, she

knew she couldn't refuse. Miguel Ortega would never
have sent for her unless his situation was desperate.

Whatever happened, she realized she had no choice.
An outlaw, no less than other men, could not be
denied medical attention. The decision made, her
thoughts quickly turned to Louise and her grandson.
The baby was only three days old and she was reluctant to leave the ranch. Still, mother and child were in
perfect health and she saw no reason for concern.
Should anything serious develop . . .

She looked at Mantanzas. "Where is your friend
now? How far away?"

"Not too far, *señora*. I have a small flock of sheep
on the Rio Bonito, outside Lincoln. He took refuge in
my home."

"When was this?"

"Yesterday, before dark," Mantanzas said uneasily.
"When he stopped, I thought he wanted only a meal.
But he was too sick to ride on and we made room for
him. I gave him my own bed."

"Was he alone?"

"I saw no one else."

"Wait for me here," Elizabeth told him. "We will
leave in a few minutes."

"*Sí, señora.*"

Inside the house, Elizabeth proceeded to the office.
Morg was seated at a small worktable opposite her
desk. He glanced up from an accounting ledger as she
moved through the door. His gaze was mildly interested.

"What was that all about?"

"Someone's sick," Elizabeth said. "I have to go
out."

"Anyone I know?"

Elizabeth sidestepped the question. "I may be gone
overnight. If Louise or the baby needs any help, I
want you to send for Rosa."

"Rosa?" Morg repeated. "Jennifer's assistant?"

"Yes."

"Why wouldn't I send for Jen?"

"She's going with me."

"With you?" Morg said, faintly mystified. "What's the big emergency?"

"I told you," Elizabeth said vaguely. "Someone needs medical attention."

"C'mon now, Mom, you haven't told me anything. Who's this *someone*?"

"Oh, honestly, stop asking so many questions."

Morg stared at her, baffled. "I don't like the idea of you and Jen traipsing off somewhere. Who's the man at the door?"

"You needn't worry," Elizabeth said. "John will drive me in the buckboard. I'll be perfectly fine."

"And you won't tell me where you're going?"

Elizabeth gave him an enigmatic look. "I'll tell you when I get back. Let's not discuss it any further."

A short while later the buckboard pulled out of the yard. John Taylor held the reins and Elizabeth sat beside him, staring straight ahead. Jesús Mantanzas, mounted on the stallion, brought up the rear.

Morg stood on the veranda watching them. He felt oddly disturbed by his mother's evasive manner. Even more, he was troubled by the *mexicano* on the barrel-chested stud. The horse looked far too grand for the man.

For no apparent reason a name came into his mind. And he somehow knew he'd guessed right. His mother was on her way to Miguel Ortega.

A midafternoon sun blazed down on Lincoln. The buckboard rolled to a halt in a swirl of dust. Elizabeth stepped down before Taylor could move to assist her. She hurried toward the clinic.

Jesús Mantanzas had parted with them east of town. He thought it unwise to draw attention to himself, or the stallion, by parading through Lincoln. Instead, he'd arranged to meet them on the stage road, a mile or so to the west. From there, he would lead them to his adobe.

Entering the door, Elizabeth was surprised to find the waiting room empty. Then she remembered that it was a Monday, not one of the regular clinic days. She crossed to the open door of the inner office and stepped inside. Jennifer looked up from her desk.

"Mother!" she said happily. "What a surprise."

"I wish it weren't," Elizabeth remarked. "Would it be possible for you to close the office?"

"Is anything wrong with Louise or the baby?"

"No, they're fine," Elizabeth said promptly. "It's someone else."

"Who?"

"Miguel Ortega."

Jennifer stared at her with shocked round eyes. "You're not serious," she said slowly. "You want me to treat Miguel Ortega?"

"Does your physician's oath exclude wanted men?"

"I was thinking of you. After all, people are already talking about your involvement with *Las Gorras Blancas*. Why compromise yourself further?"

"I've no choice," Elizabeth said resolutely. "Without Ortega's help, my coalition would have fallen apart. I won't refuse him now."

Jennifer looked at her curiously. "Are you thinking of bringing him here?"

Elizabeth quickly explained the situation. She outlined everything she'd been told by Jesús Mantanzas. He was waiting now, she noted, to act as their guide.

"From what he said," she concluded, "Ortega can't be moved. We have to go there."

Jennifer was thoughtful a moment. "The symptoms he described could be any number of things. How can I be certain until I examine Ortega?"

"Prepare for the worst," Elizabeth said, her voice low and urgent. "Take everything you might need."

Working swiftly, Jennifer began gathering items from the medical cabinet. She included ether and surgical instruments as well as a portable stomach pump and various pharmaceutical powders. Elizabeth helped her pack the equipment in an oversize leather storage case. Her normal paraphernalia was carried in her black medical bag.

Jennifer advised Rosa that the office would be closed for the remainder of the day. She and her mother then hurried outside and secured the bags in the back of the buckboard. When they were seated, Taylor popped the reins and drove off upstreet. As they approached the courthouse, Blake Hazlett came down the stairs. He hailed them with a wave.

Taylor reined the team to a halt. Blake smiled, tipping his hat to Elizabeth, then looked at Jennifer. "What's wrong?" he asked. "Someone ill?"

"Yes," Jennifer said hesitantly. "A *mexicano* family sent word to Mother."

"Why would they . . . ?"

Blake paused, glancing at Elizabeth. Her expression was unreadable, and his gaze shifted back to Jennifer. "What's going on here?" he demanded. "You're not telling me something."

"I—" Jennifer faltered, reluctant to lie. "There's no reason to concern yourself. We'll talk about it later."

"I'd prefer to talk about it now."

"We haven't time. You'll just have to trust me."

"Trust you?" Blake echoed. "Look here—"

"I'm sorry," Jennifer cut him off. "We have to go."

Taylor snapped the reins. The team lurched into a

startled trot and the buckboard pulled away. Blake
was left standing in the middle of the road staring after
them. His features dissolved into a bewildered frown.

Somehow he felt patronized, even belittled. He promised himself it wouldn't end there. A man deserved
more from the woman he intended to marry.

And a lady doctor was no exception.

Something over an hour later the buckboard forded
the Rio Bonito. Jesús Mantanzas led them northwest,
toward a line of sawtoothed foothills. The trail they
followed was narrow and rutted, hardly more than a
wilderness trace.

A mile or so from the river they pulled into a
clearing. From the rough countryside the Mantanzas
family had hacked and hoed a small plot of land.
Beyond the house was a well-tended garden, and a
flock of some thirty sheep grazed on sparse grasses. A
belled milk goat, udders swaying, ran with the sheep.

The adobe was stoutly built, situated near a shallow
mountain stream. Three young children, two boys and
a girl, were weeding the garden. Off in the distance,
an older boy stood watch over the sheep. A woman,
aged before her time, waited in the doorway. Her
features were expressionless as the buckboard rolled
to a halt.

Mantanzas greeted his wife with a somber nod. She
stepped aside as he led Jennifer and Elizabeth into the
house. Taylor unloaded the case of medical gear and
followed them inside. The interior was crude, with a
dirt floor and a few pieces of rough furniture. A bee-
hive fireplace provided heat for cooking and warmth.

Ortega lay on a rickety bed. He was stripped to his
undershorts, motionless on a mattress of coarse ticking
stuffed with straw. His features were pallid and his
eyes seemed clouded with pain. His forehead glistened

with perspiration and he had the blotchy coloring of a seriously ill man. He smiled weakly, focusing on Elizabeth.

"Gracias, señora," he said in a parched voice. "I knew you would not fail me."

Elizabeth forced herself to smile. "We came as soon as we could. I'm sorry it took so long."

"Do not apologize, *señora*. It is I who am in your debt."

"This is my daughter," Elizabeth said, indicating Jennifer. "She is the one you asked for, the physician. You can have faith in her power to heal."

Ortega coughed raggedly. "I am in need of healing. A *bruja* tears at my insides."

Jennifer moved to the side of the bed. "Señor Ortega, I want you to forget I'm a woman. A doctor cannot afford modesty. Show me where you hurt."

Ortega placed a shaky hand on his abdomen. "All across here. I have never known such pain."

"Are you queasy, sick to your stomach?"

"Sí."

"Have you experienced vomiting, loose bowels?"

Ortega appeared embarrassed by the question. He nodded his head with a clenched smile. Jennifer sat down on the edge of the bed, opened her medical bag. She took out a thermometer and popped it into his mouth. While she waited, she gripped his wrist, her forefinger on the artery. His pulsebeat was abnormally rapid, hammering against her fingertip.

After a short time, she removed the thermometer and held it to the light of a nearby window. The reading was dangerously high, confirming a raging fever. Her expression betrayed nothing as she returned the thermometer to its wooden case. She smiled in apology and lowered his undershorts down over his groin. Gingerly, her hands centered on his belly, she palpated the stomach wall. Ortega's face twisted in a grimace.

Jennifer noted that the stomach wall was rigid. She lightly touched a spot between his bellybutton and his right side. "Does it hurt most here or somewhere else?"

"There," Ortega rasped. "Your finger is like a nail driven through my soul."

"Tell me how this sickness came on you. Was the pain gradual or did it start all at once?"

Ortega described a punishing ordeal. A week past, he'd been in the Seven Rivers district. At first, his stomach had been only slightly tender to the touch. He had experienced nausea and diarrhea; but he attributed it to some digestive disorder. Then, as he rode north toward Lincoln, the pain had intensified, centering to the right of his navel. By the time he happened upon Mantanzas' home, he could barely sit a horse. Since yesterday, he'd been unable to hold down food.

Jennifer nodded. "Your symptoms lead to only one diagnosis. You have appendicitis."

Ortega looked at her blankly. "I do not know that word."

"The appendix," Jennifer explained, "is an outgrowth off the large intestine. Yours is inflamed and badly swollen. I can feel it through your stomach."

"What is the cure?"

"We must remove it."

"You intend to cut me open?"

"There's no alternative," Jennifer said. "Should your appendix rupture and burst, your insides would be flooded with poison. The medical term for it is peritonitis."

"And then?" Ortega asked. "What would happen?"

"I wouldn't be able to save you. Death would occur within a matter of hours."

"So I have no choice but the knife?"

"I'm afraid not."

"Suerte del cielo baja," Ortega said with a faint smile. "Fortune comes from above. God will guide your hand."

"Then I suggest we proceed, Señor Ortega. We haven't a moment to lose."

Jennifer asked Señora Mantanzas to boil a pot of water. With the help of Taylor and Jesús Mantanzas, she then moved Ortega to the rough-hewn dining table. When the water boiled, Elizabeth joined her at a stone basin beside the fireplace. They began scrubbing for the operation.

"Be honest," Elizabeth whispered. "How dangerous is it?"

"God only knows," Jennifer said gravely. "It's a surgical procedure of last resort. In medical school, I saw it performed just once."

The concern in her voice was justified. The first recorded appendectomy had been performed in 1736 at St. George's Hospital in London. The physician was Claudius Amyand, surgeon to the royal family, and thereafter a name known to medical students around the world. Over the next century, however, the procedure had remained largely ignored. Considered risky, it had been relegated to a position of obscurity in surgical textbooks.

Still another fifty years passed before an appendectomy was performed in the United States. In early 1886, a surgeon at New York's Roosevelt Hospital had successfully undertaken the operation. Only then was the procedure introduced into the classrooms of medical institutions; not one doctor in ten had ever seen it performed. An exception to the rule, Jennifer had observed an appendectomy during her last week in medical school.

Yet she was hardly an expert on the subject. Standing beside the improvised operating table, she waited while her mother administered ether to Ortega. In those final moments, she mentally reviewed the steps in the procedure. Her one small comfort was in the statement she'd made earlier. Without the operation Miguel Ortega would never see another sunrise.

Jennifer took a scalpel in hand. She made a vertical incision three inches long over the right side. Her next cut separated the deeper muscles and exposed the pouch of the large intestine. Slipping her fingers into the wound, she followed one of the longitudinal bands downward to the base of the appendix. Where the appendix was attached to the bowel, she tied it off to preclude bleeding from arteries. She then severed the appendix from the bowel.

Thus far there were no complications. Jennifer paused a moment to catalog the remaining steps, each one crucial to the survival of her patient. Working to a large extent by feel, she isolated the base of the appendix and wound it tightly with catgut. At last, the scalpel once more in hand, she cut the appendix loose from the large intestine. After removing it, she laid the scalpel aside and slipped the stump of the appendix beneath the intestinal pouch. Finally, with a surgical needle, she stitched the membrane lining of the pouch over the invaginated stump.

The procedure ended in reverse order. Working outward, she sutured first the abdominal muscles and then closed the surface incision. When she stepped back, she felt reasonably confident that the operation had been performed without mishap. Her gaze was drawn to the severed appendix, where she'd dropped it on the table. Shaped like a lumpy grubworm, it was swollen to twice normal size. Another hour, she told herself, and it would have ruptured. So perhaps Miguel Ortega had been right after all.

Suerte del cielo baja.

The sun sank lower, smothering in a bed of copper beyond the mountains. Elizabeth and Jennifer stood outside the adobe, talking quietly. Across the yard, Taylor waited beside the buckboard.

Ortega was still sedated. Following the operation, he'd been lifted from the table and moved back to bed. There was nothing more to be done, and now, with nightfall approaching, Jennifer was preparing to leave. Taylor was reluctant to chance the winding trail in the dark.

Tomorrow was clinic day and Jennifer felt obligated to return to town. Elizabeth had elected to stay the night, concerned that Ortega was not yet out of danger. Apart from infection, which was always a threat, Jennifer foresaw no complications. She thought all the signs pointed to a full recovery.

"Unless I hear from you," she said now, "I'll be back late tomorrow afternoon. We'll know by then whether or not there's any infection."

"Except for you," Elizabeth said, smiling warmly, "he would never have pulled through. I want you to know I'm very proud of you."

Jennifer laughed. "Modesty aside, I'm rather proud of myself. Not many sawbones could have snipped an appendix."

Elizabeth enfolded her in an affectionate hug. When they parted, Jennifer walked to the buckboard, turning back to wave. A moment later Taylor snapped the reins and they drove out of the yard. Not far down the trail they disappeared from sight.

For a time Elizabeth stood motionless in the waning

light. Somewhat reflective, her thoughts went back to a comment made earlier by Ortega. Before the operation, he'd mentioned his torturous ride from Seven Rivers. She wondered now whether or not Clint was on his backtrail. All the more, she felt a sudden rush of guilt.

Clint would never understand what she'd done today. She wasn't sure she understood it herself.

25

The sky was sprinkled with stars. A crescent moon, tilted at an angle, advanced slowly across the eastern foothills. From the mountains, a cool evening breeze rustled through the treetops.

Clint was seated on the veranda of the hotel. Upstreet the sound of male laughter racketed from a saloon. He felt no urge for a drink and the idea of other men's company appealed to him even less. His mood was withdrawn, oddly embittered.

Fireflies darted though the dusky night. He watched them without interest, slouched back in a cane-bottomed rocker. His cigarette glowed as he took a long drag, exhaling smoke. After supper in the hotel dining room he had retired to the veranda. For the past hour he'd sat there brooding, mired in disgust.

Late that afternoon Clint had ridden into Lincoln. His journey to the Seven Rivers country had proved to be a washout. He'd found the ranchers cooperative but wary, mistrustful of outside lawmen. Their attitude toward *Las Gorras Blancas* was one of low contempt. Any raids, they told him, would bring harsh reprisals against all *mexicanos*. They prided themselves on keeping the greasers in line.

Quickly enough, Clint discovered that their bragging contained an element of truth. There were rumors that Miguel Ortega had been sighted in the Seven

Rivers district. Yet his efforts to incite violence had come to nothing. The *mexicanos* wanted no part of an uprising against Anglo cattlemen. Nor were they moved by Oretega's exhortations about land fraud and the spread of barbed wire. Life was unjust, but they feared retribution by the *gringos* even more. They refused to join *Las Gorras Blancas*.

In Clint's mind, the decisive factor was dread. Seven Rivers was remote and sparsely populated, a land where might made right. Over the years the ranchers had intimidated and terrorized the *mexicanos*. However brutal, the force of Anglo rule was a fact of life. So the call to revolution, unlike in other parts of New Mexico, had fallen on deaf ears. Peace at any price was preferable to the wrath of the cattlemen. Where horse thieves were routinely hanged, no man would risk the fate of a night rider.

For all that, Clint had been unable to turn up a lead. He'd covered lots of ground, but he always seemed to be a day behind. Not quite a week ago, word began circulating that Ortega had quit the Seven Rivers country. Logic dictated that the White Cap leader would turn north, toward Lincoln. Having failed at Seven Rivers, Ortega would almost certainly resume raiding elsewhere. A quick show of force was needed to counter the Seven Rivers setback and embolden partisan *mexicanos*. Lincoln seemed the most likely spot.

To Clint, it was like starting over again. The man-hunt was now entering its third month, and he'd been euchred at every turn. Yet, while he was disgruntled, he was no less determined. A wily fugitive somehow chaffed his stubborn streak, made him bow his neck. In the past, he had prevailed, running down wanted men, through sheer tenacity. Ortega was a smooth article, devilishly clever; but Clint operated on the theory that every dog had his day. All he needed was a fresh lead.

Along those lines, his mind turned to Elizabeth. On his way into town he had stopped by at Spur. To his surprise, he discovered he'd become a great-uncle. Morg and Louise proudly displayed the baby, and he had made all the obligatory remarks. But later, when he inquired after Elizabeth, he'd got a strange story. According to Morg, she had gone off with a *mexicano* on some unexplained mission of mercy. Though Morg hadn't stated it outright, he had dropped several broad hints. The sick man might well be Miguel Ortega.

Clint's first stop upon arriving in town had been the clinic. When he found it closed, he had then paid a call on Blake Hazlett. The story he got tended to support everything he'd heard from Morg. Elizabeth and Jennifer, accompanied by John Taylor, had driven westward out of Lincoln. Blake knew nothing of the *mexicano* horseman, and that in itself made Clint all the more suspicious. A Mexican riding a blooded stallion would have drawn a crowd outside the clinic. Clearly, all those involved were reluctant to attract attention to themselves. Which meant they had something to hide.

On reflection, Clint thought it all dovetailed. Elizabeth and Jennifer were by nature the most forthright of women. Their secretive manner today was uncharacteristic of either of them, and led to a troubling conclusion. The *mexicano* was known in Lincoln, probably lived somewhere nearby. Whether he was a member of *Las Gorras Blancas* was a moot point. The fact remained that he was a go-between as well as a guide. And while the destination was unknown, Elizabeth and Jennifer had gone along willingly. There seemed little question that they had been summoned by Miguel Ortega.

The belief served to darken Clint's mood. That Elizabeth would act as an angel of mercy for Ortega left

him hurt and stunned. She knew beyond doubt that
Ortega had twice tried to have him killed. Yet she'd
still rushed off to provide aid for the man. He felt
betrayed, somehow double-crossed, for she was family. Even more, she was the one woman who had won
his trust and his lifelong devotion. His world suddenly
seemed smaller, strangely empty.

A buckboard passed by the hotel. Clint stiffened,
straining for a better look. In the pale moonlight, he
saw Taylor at the reins and Jennifer's unmistakable
profile. He searched for some sign of Elizabeth, baffled that she wasn't with them. Then, as though struck
a hard blow, it hit him. She was still with Ortega.

Clint slammed out of the rocker. He stepped off the
veranda and hurried downstreet. Ahead, he saw the
buckboard roll to a halt before the clinic. Taylor jumped
down, then assisted Jennifer from her seat. She stood
waiting while he unloaded what seemed to be a box of
some sort. Neither of them was aware of Clint until he
rounded the tail of the buckboard.

"Uncle Clint!" Jennifer gasped. "What are you doing
here?"

"Waiting for you," Clint said, frowning heavily.
"Where's your mother?"

"Why?" Jennifer stalled. "Are you looking for her?"

Clint's voice was reproachful. "Suppose we quit beat-
ing around the bush. I'd like a straight answer to my
question. Where is she?"

"You needn't be so gruff. What gave you the idea
she was with me?"

"Stop trying my patience, missy. You drove out of
town with her and you've come back without her. So
I'll have an answer—right now."

"I'm sorry," Jennifer said softly. "I can't tell you."

"You mean you won't tell me."

"Either way, it amounts to the same thing."

"Then I'll tell you," Clint said angrily. "She's with Ortega, isn't she?"

A smile froze on Jennifer's face. "I really couldn't say."

There was a moment of deadened silence. Clint's features took on a sudden hard cast. "All right, let's forget family. I'm talking to you as a law officer now." He paused, glaring at her. "Ortega's a killer and I have a warrant for his arrest. Where is he?"

Jennifer's lingering smile faded. "I save lives," she said. "Enforcing the law isn't my concern."

"You're gonna leave it like that?"

"Yes, I am."

Clint eyed her, considering. "I reckon there's other ways. For instance"—his gaze shifted to Taylor—"I'll just trail along behind you."

Taylor shrugged indifferently. "What makes you think I'm headed anywhere?"

"Because I know you," Clint announced. "You wouldn't leave Beth alone with Ortega overnight. You're fixin' to turn right around, aren't you?"

"Whatever I do," Taylor said casually, "it's not gonna change anything. You still won't find her."

"Why the hell not?"

"You're right when you said I wouldn't leave her alone. But I won't let you follow me, either."

Clint squinted at him. "How do you propose to stop me?"

Taylor met his gaze levelly. "I'm still pretty handy with a gun. You try to follow me and I'll use it."

"You're not that good," Clint said tightly. "You never were. You'd just get yourself killed."

"Yeah, probably so," Taylor agreed. " 'Course, that wouldn't help you none. You still wouldn't find her."

Clint shook his head. "I never took you for a damn fool. Maybe I was wrong."

Taylor spread his open-palmed hands. "Miz Brannock kept me on the payroll all these years and I never once had to earn my keep. Let's just say I owe her."

Clint accepted the statement for what it was, a blunt truth. John Taylor had signed on as a hired gun some seven years past. In that time, he'd lived an easy life and never been forced to draw his gun. He felt an obligation, a certain debt of honor. He wouldn't back off now.

"Tell you the truth," Clint said finally, "Ortega's not worth it. I won't have your blood on my hands."

Taylor stared at him for a moment. "Have I got your word you won't follow me?"

"On one condition," Clint muttered. "You make goddamn sure Beth doesn't come to any harm. Savvy?"

"Don't give it another thought. I'll get her back safe and sound."

Taylor climbed into the buckboard. He hauled on the reins and brought the team around in the road. Jennifer and Clint watched as he drove west out of town. At length, Clint hefted the medical case and turned up the walkway. Jennifer hurried along to open the door.

Inside the waiting room, Clint lowered the case onto the floor. Jennifer placed her medical bag on a chair, then lighted a lamp. When she turned around, Clint was standing at the door staring out into the night. He didn't look at her.

"Sorry I got rough," he said. "It's got nothing to do with you."

"I know," Jennifer said quietly. "You're worried about Mother."

Clint was silent so long she wasn't sure he would respond. At last, he turned from the door. "What's wrong with Ortega?"

"Appendicitis," Jennifer replied. "One of his internal organs became poisoned. I had to operate and remove it."

"Will he recover?"

"Yes, I believe so."

"Good." Clint's voice hardened. "Wouldn't want him to miss his date with the hangman."

Jennifer was pensive a moment. "I hope you don't blame Mother too much. She felt she had to stay with him, at least for tonight."

"Why?" Clint asked sharply. "What's Ortega to her?"

"I'm afraid you wouldn't like my answer."

"Try me and see."

"Well—" Jennifer paused, searching for words. "To be perfectly honest, I think she's attracted to him. And I suspect she doesn't even know it."

Clint looked at her with disbelief. "How in Christ's name could she be attracted to somebody like him?"

"Have you ever met him?"

"No."

"Until today, I hadn't either. I have to admit it was something of a shock."

"I don't follow you."

Jennifer smiled. "Speaking as a woman, I found him very handsome. But that's only part of it." She hesitated, uncertain what she wanted to say. "There's a mystery about him, something almost indefinable. He's a compelling man . . . forceful . . ."

"He's a man with a price on his head—an outlaw!"

"Aren't you really saying something else?"

"Such as?"

"He's a *mexicano*," Jennifer remarked. "And no white woman—especially Mother—should be attracted to a Mexican. Isn't that it?"

"You're putting words in my mouth."

"Am I?"

"For your mother's sake," Clint said, ignoring the question, "let's hope she isn't attracted to him. Señor Ortega's not long for this world."

"How ironic," Jennifer observed. "I save him and you hang him. Somehow it doesn't seem fair."

"Maybe not," Clint said, "but it's a damnsight more than he deserves. Lots of people are dead on his account."

Blake stepped through the door. "I saw a light," he said, nodding to Jennifer. "Have you been here long?"

"Only a few minutes."

"Where's your mother?"

Clint cleared his throat. "I think I'll call it a night. Let me know if you hear anything."

Before Jennifer could reply, he turned and walked from the clinic. When the door closed, Blake looked at her strangely. His expression was at once critical and concerned.

"I take it you and Clint had words?"

"Yes, we did," Jennifer acknowledged. "He's upset because Mother stayed behind . . ."

"With Ortega," Blake finished it for her. "Is that what you were going to say?"

"I see you already know."

Blake shrugged. "Clint and I figured it out for ourselves this afternoon."

Jennifer laughed without humor. "Apparently it wasn't much of a secret."

"No, not much," Blake said in a carefully measured voice. "Why did you feel it was necessary to lie to me?"

"I didn't lie to you."

"On the contrary," Blake corrected her, "you lied by omission. You let me believe something that wasn't true."

Jennifer looked down at the floor. "I merely honored Mother's request. She thought it was better that way."

"Then I'm doubly disappointed. I expected a little more in the way of trust."

"Oh, for God's sake, Blake! Don't be such a stuffed shirt."

Blake shook his head in stern disapproval. "There's nothing stuffed-shirt about honesty. I have every right to be offended."

"Do you?" Jennifer said crossly. "Well, don't expect an apology. You won't get one from me."

"What I expect," Blake informed her, "is that it won't happen again. I have no secrets from you and I demand the same in return. I won't settle for less."

"And I won't be dictated to!"

"Listen closely," Blake said in a solemn tone. "I'm stating an unalterable condition for our marriage. The matter isn't open to debate, now or in the future."

A cone of silence enveloped them. Jennifer saw an aspect of him she'd never seen before. Beneath the gentleness, there was a deliberate and very forceful man. He would indulge her in many things, but he would not be deceived. She suddenly realized her next words would decide their marriage.

"One mistake doesn't affect a lifetime, does it?"

"So far as I'm concerned," Blake allowed, "we can forget it right now."

"Then let's kiss and make up . . . agreed?"

Blake took her in his arms. He kissed her soundly on the mouth and squeezed her so tight she came up on tiptoe. She seemed to melt within his embrace, and for the first time she didn't want it to end. His kiss was ardent and curiously demanding.

She thought making up might be fun.

Elizabeth awoke at dawn. She had slept fitfully,

seated beside the bed with her back to the wall. She was wrapped in a tattered blanket that smelled faintly of woodsmoke.

The Mantanzas family was still asleep. John Taylor, with a blanket pulled around him, was snoring lightly. He lay curled on the floor near the fireplace, one arm tucked under his head. No one stirred as Elizabeth got stiffly to her feet.

She felt brittle and unrested. During the night she had awakened periodically to check on Ortega. His fever had abated and his pulse rate was steady. From all indications, there was no sign of postoperative infection. A single dose of laudanum had kept him quiet throughout the night.

In the chilly dawn, Elizabeth almost wished she'd taken a dose herself. Taylor had returned from town shortly before midnight. His recounting of the encounter with Clint had left her shaken. She was relieved that Clint hadn't attempted to follow the buckboard. But she was now all the more concerned that he felt betrayed, and deeply hurt. She worried that the breach between them might be irreparable.

She worried as well that the truce was only temporary. Clint was personally affronted, and the greater part of his anger would be directed toward Ortega. Once the search resumed, his efforts would be redoubled, with the ugly overtones of a vendetta. The surgery, performed to prolong life, was in reality a fleeting reprieve. Ortega, more than at any time in the past, was now doomed. Given the slightest excuse, Clint would kill him.

"Buenos días, señora."

Startled, Elizabeth turned toward the bed. She found Ortega awake and alert, watching her. "How do you feel?" she asked. "Are you in pain?"

Ortega smiled. "I am much better now, *gracias.* You are a good nurse."

"Thank my daughter," Elizabeth said. "Her skill is what saved you."

Ortega nodded, silent a moment. "You seem troubled, *señora*. Am I still in danger?"

"No, I don't believe so."

"Then why do I see concern in your eyes?"

Elizabeth hesitated, choosing her words carefully. She told him of Clint's return to Lincoln, and the shaky agreement with Taylor. She expressed the belief that it wouldn't last.

"I'll have to leave today," she said. "Once I'm gone, Clint won't delay much longer. His search will begin again."

"I expect no less," Ortega said matter-of-factly. "But do not alarm yourself, *señora*. Nothing will stop me from completing my work."

"We both know that isn't true. Your only hope is to take refuge in Mexico. Otherwise he will find you . . . and kill you."

"I cannot desert my people when they need me most. There is no one to take my place."

"Would your death serve them any better?"

Ortega scrutinized her closely. "Why do you fear for my life, *señora*? What importance does it have for you?"

Elizabeth's heart suddenly pounded. His eyes were darkly intense and she saw mirrored there her own confusion. She felt drawn to him in ways that disturbed her, almost an emotional attachment. Yet she'd fought it from the outset, and all the more so because of Clint. In the end, she'd somehow known it would come down to this moment. A choice between one or the other, with no turning back. Which made it no choice at all.

She took a deep breath to steady herself. "I must ask you something," she said. "Is it true you tried to have Clint killed?"

"Sí," Ortega readily admitted. "But it has nothing to do with you, *señora.* One of us must kill the other." He paused, staring at her. "You cannot change what will be."

Elizabeth was quiet for a long moment. When she spoke, there was an echoing sadness in her voice. "Without your help, the reform coalition would have fallen apart. You rendered a great service and I will always be thankful. But now, I feel I have repaid the debt."

"You and your daughter saved my life, *señora.* It is I who am in your debt."

"Then I release you," Elizabeth said quickly. "Neither of us owes the other anything. As of today, we are even."

"I understand," Ortega said in wistful agreement. "It will be as though we had never met. *Verdad?*"

"Yes."

Elizabeth let it end there. She checked his temperature and his pulse and found his condition stable. By then the others were awake and she instructed Señora Mantanzas on the care he would need. Sometime that afternoon, she advised, Jennifer would return to examine him. Ortega merely listened, his expression stoic.

Their parting was formal, a brief handshake. As the sun crested the horizon, Elizabeth and Taylor drove out of the yard. She suppressed the urge to look back, and instead stared straight ahead. Her eyes glistened in the brilliant flare of sunrise.

She told herself it could have ended no other way. She suddenly hated the sound of the truth.

26

Lon stepped onto the veranda. His leg was still bothersome, but he was walking now with a cane. He moved to a rocker and seated himself.

A midmorning sun blazed down on the valley. The Rio Hondo meandered off in the distance like a silvery ribbon. The day was already sweltering, and shimmering heat waves obscured the western foothills. Along the river a listless breeze rippled through the treetops.

From his shirt pocket Lon removed a slim black cheroot. He struck a match and lit up in a lazy cloud of smoke. Settling back, he puffed on the cheroot, his cane hooked over the arm of the rocker. His gaze wandered out across the compound, settling on the corral. He stared at the horses with a faraway look.

To his great disgust, Lon found himself involved in a petty subterfuge. He mentally calculated the date as June 12, marking his third week at Spur. His leg was stiff, still somewhat weak, but the bullet wound was completely healed. In the secrecy of his room, he'd tested his leg without the cane, experiencing little difficulty. He walked with only a slight limp.

In effect, the cane was a stage prop. As he puffed the cheroot, his gaze remained fixed on the corral. He knew he could saddle one of the horses and ride away anytime it suited his purpose. Yet he continued the pretense of favoring his leg, hobbling about on the

cane. His reason for acting the invalid centered on a
nagging uncertainty about Hank. He was no longer
confident of his hold over the boy.

The nub of the problem was Brad. As foreman of
the ranch, he struck a bold figure. On a daily basis he
commanded the respect of a crew of roughshod cowhands and their *segundos*. All the more significant, he
was responsible for thousands of head of livestock,
both cattle and horses. To an impressionable youngster like Hank, it was heady stuff. He hung on Brad's
every word, eager as a puppy. His awe was apparent
even to the casual observer.

For Lon, it was a source of festering hostility. With
each passing day he saw Brad's influence growing
stronger. He was all too aware that he'd lost ground in
the fight for Hank. The boy was starstruck by the
ranch and increasingly drawn to the life of a stockgrower.
His greater interest was in the horse herds and the
breeding program. But he listened like an acolyte when
Brad talked of Durham cows and blooded bulls. He
was slowly being won over.

Today, as he sat brooding on it, Lon had a sense of
time slipping away. He still felt reasonably certain of
Hank's loyalty, for the bond between brothers exerted
a strong pull. But he was reluctant to put it to the test,
force a showdown between himself and Brad. Instead,
he continued to hobble around on the cane and delay
any mention of leaving Spur. He wasn't at all sure the
boy would follow him when he rode out.

The one bright spot was that he no longer had to
worry about Clint. From what he gathered, Clint and
Elizabeth were at loggerheads over the *mexicano* troublemaker Miguel Ortega. Clint hadn't visited the ranch
in more than a week, and so far as Lon was concerned
it was good riddance. In fact, he hoped the squabble
might last indefinitely, or at least until he'd resolved

his more immediate problem. With Clint out of his hair, he had only to contend with Brad, and he meant to somehow force the issue. He'd already let it go too long.

Off in the distance he spotted two riders approaching from the south. As they forded the river, he saw that one was Brad and the other was Hank. He took a thoughtful pull on his cheroot, considering how he might turn the moment to advantage. It crossed his mind that he had nothing to gain by acting in a roundabout manner. He decided to call a spade a spade.

Brad and Hank dismounted at the corral. They left their horses hitched to the fence and walked toward the house. Lon rose from his chair as they stepped onto the veranda. He stuck the cheroot in his mouth and limped forward, leaning on the cane. Hank grinned, veering off in his direction. Brad merely nodded and started into the house.

"Hold on, Brad," Lon called out. "You and me need to have a talk."

Brad turned at the door. "I've got to see Mrs. Brannock. Will it wait?"

"Hell, no," Lon said with a corrosive glare. "We're way past overdue."

For a moment they stared at one another in silent assessment. Hank appeared confused, uncertain which way to turn. At length, Brad crossed the veranda.

"Awright," he said. "What's so important it won't keep?"

Lon's voice was edged. "I don't like people trying to put one over on me. You think you've got me hoodwinked, but you don't."

"Hoodwinked about what?"

"You know damn well I'm talkin' about Hank."

A look of puzzlement crossed Brad's face. "You just lost me."

"C'mon," Lon taunted, "why act so innocent? I know what you've been sayin' behind my back."

"Wait a minute," Hank broke in quickly. "Nobody's been talkin' behind your back."

"Stay out of it," Lon ordered. "This here's between me and Brad."

"Whatever it is," Brad told him, "you're gonna have to give me a clue. I still haven't got your drift."

Lon let go a mocking humorless laugh. "Hell's bells and little fishes," he said loudly, "you're tryin' to turn Hank against me. Any fool could see that."

"You're way off the mark, Lon. I never tried any such thing."

"Are you callin' me a liar?"

"Nope," Brad said carefully. "I'm just sayin' you're wrong."

"Am I now?" Lon muttered with a cold smile. "I suppose you haven't been workin' on Hank to keep him here at the ranch? Go ahead, let's hear you deny it."

"Nothin' to deny," Brad said. "I've told him he's welcome to stay on."

"Sure you have," Lon said sarcastically. "And you told him nobody'd think the worse because he's a half-breed. Just one big family, wasn't that how you put it?"

"What of it?"

"You're full of hot air, that's what! He'd spend his life workin' for wages . . . the same as you."

Brad's face went chalky. "I haven't done so bad."

"Yeah?" Lon needled him. "Then how come you're runnin' cows over on the Rio Felix? Way it looks, you're fixin' to quit the Brannocks yourself."

"Lay off," Hank interrupted, stealing a glance at Brad. "You got no call to put him on the spot like that. What's between him and the family is his business."

"Family, my ass!" Lon crowed. "Why do you think he's all set to quit Spur? Christ, he's not family, no more'n you would be. He's a hired hand."

Brad shook his head. "I never said nothin' about leaving Spur."

Lon's smile grew broader. "Well, now's your chance to set the record straight. Are you movin' on or not?"

Too late Brad saw the trap. Whatever he said, it would sound as though he'd misled Hank. How could he recommend Spur to the boy when he was thinking of leaving himself? No reasonable answer occurred to him.

"Whatever I do," he said finally, "I've got no complaints about the family. They've treated me square from the day I rode onto Spur."

Lon knew when to keep silent. He had planted a seed of doubt in the youngster's mind, and Brad's lame reply merely reinforced his argument. He lightly punched Hank on the shoulder.

"C'mon, sport," he said, grinning. "Let's have ourselves a little target practice. Never pays to let yourself get rusty."

"I dunno," Hank said hesitantly. "We were gonna talk to Miz Brannock about some colts. I saw one that sorta took my fancy."

"I'll sound her out," Brad assured him. "You go ahead and enjoy yourself. I'll catch up with you later."

An evil light began to dance in Lon's eyes. "What the hell," he said to Brad, "the more the merrier. You're welcome to come along."

"Not today," Brad replied. "I've got other business with Mrs. Brannock."

"Sure, you go on," Lon said with an offhand gesture. "It'll save you some embarrassment, anyway. Never yet saw a cowhand worth his salt with a gun."

The words were a direct challenge. Brad saw no way to refuse and still retain Hank's respect. Even now, he sensed the youngster watching him closely. He motioned casually to Lon.

"Tell you what," he drawled, "a dollar says I don't miss. You interested?"

Lon feigned indifference. "Low stakes don't make much of a game. How about a dollar a shot?"

"You've got yourself a bet."

Hank collected an armload of airtights from the trash heap behind the cookhouse. They walked down to the river and Brad indicated a spot upstream where the bank rose sharply from the river. The empty tin cans were arranged in a line, with the riverbank serving as a backstop. They stepped off ten paces.

The toss of a coin decided who went first. Lon won and he turned to face the riverbank, leaning slightly on the cane. His arm moved in a shadowy blur and the Colt appeared in his hand. The shots blended into a staccato roar and four cans leapt into the air. On the fifth shot, a spurt of sand kicked up beside a tomato can.

"Damn!" he swore under his breath. "I singed the label on that sonovabitch."

Brad smiled. "Close don't count when there's money on the line."

"Four outta five's nothin' to sneeze at. Let's see you beat it."

Brad squared off against the riverbank. His draw was deliberate, without waste motion, and he brought the Peacemaker to shoulder level. He concentrated on the front sight, feathering the trigger and thumbing the hammer with practiced ease. While he was a shade slower than Lon, he emptied the pistol in a matter of seconds. Every shot sent a can flying.

"Hello, down there."

A man's voice brought them around. John Taylor appeared downstream, drawn by the sound of gunfire. He walked toward them, looking from one to the other. His expression was inquisitive.

"What's all the shootin' about?"

"Just poppin' some cans," Brad said. "Had a wager of a dollar a shot."

"Who won?"

"Not me," Lon grouched. "I touched one off a mite too quick."

Taylor sensed the antagonism between them. He'd been a distant observer of their struggle for Hank's loyalty. The shooting match, he decided now, was all part of the same contest. Still, it worried him, for he had an instinctive mistrust of Lon. Shooting cans was only a step away from shooting people.

"Wanna try your hand?" Lon inquired. "I've heard you're pretty fair with a gun."

"I'll pass," Taylor said pleasantly. "You boys are too good for me."

"Go ahead," Brad urged him. "We could both use a lesson in fast and fancy."

"Yeah, why not?" Lon added with a go-to-hell smile. "Old dogs are supposed to know all the tricks."

Taylor ignored the gibe. He directed Hank to stack five tin cans one atop the other. The boy looked puzzled, but obediently followed instructions. When the airtights were arranged in a wobbly stack, he rejoined the men.

Facing the riverbank, Taylor pulled and fired, too quick for the eye. The bottom can jumped backward and the other four came tumbling down. There was scarcely a pulsebeat between shots as Taylor blasted the cans while they were still in midair. The last one went spinning crazily an instant before it touched the ground.

Without a word, Taylor shucked the empty shells and began reloading. The others watched him in silence, like an audience witnessing a magician perform some staggering sleight-of-hand. At last, Hank let out a low whistle between his teeth.

"Goddurn," he said huskily. "I never seen nuthin' like that."

Taylor smiled. "Your Uncle Clint showed me that stunt. 'Course, he does it a hair faster'n me."

"Faster?" Hank repeated. "You mean he could beat you?"

"Six days a week and all day on Sunday. I'm plumb slow up beside him."

Lon laughed out loud. "All that trick shootin' don't mean a hill of beans. Tin cans don't shoot back."

Taylor fixed him with an austere look. "What's your point?"

"I'm just sayin' Clint's past his prime. A younger man could take him easy."

"Well, as for that," Taylor said in a dry cold manner, "there's been a few young squirts that tried it. He put 'em all in the bone orchard."

Lon snorted. "You talk like he's got you buffaloed."

Taylor's eyes narrowed, and a smile appeared at the corner of his mouth. "When the Lord was handin' out nerves, Clint didn't take none. I'd sooner tangle with a grizzly bear."

"Well, I still say he's round the bend. Hell, he can't even catch that asshole greaser—Ortega."

Taylor wagged his head. "Sonny, if I was you, I wouldn't say that to Clint's face. He's liable to box your ears."

Lon appeared on the verge of saying something

more. But then he evidently thought it over and changed his mind. Taylor waited, studying him with a look of amused contempt. After a marked silence, the older man holstered his gun and walked away.

Brad followed him up the riverbank. Neither Lon nor Hank said anything for a long while. Yet the boy easily read his brother's thoughts. A choice to go or stay would have to be made soon.

Lon was the odd man out at Spur.

The sound of footsteps echoed through the hallway. Elizabeth looked up from her desk as Brad appeared in the door of the office. She beckoned him inside.

"I heard shooting," she said. "What's going on?"

Brad dropped into a chair. "That was Lon and me havin' a little target practice. He's pretty handy with a gun."

"Too much so," Elizabeth said in a firm voice. "I take it he's feeling better. Or doesn't a cane inhibit his shooting?"

"Not so's you'd notice."

"Well, anyway, I'm glad you're here. I wanted to ask you about the next trail herd."

"Everything looks good," Brad said. "I figure to get 'em headed out by the first of the week."

"Just in time," Elizabeth sighed. "We're running short on operating funds."

"Anything wrong?"

"Nothing besides Morg. I've authorized more money to expand his business ventures. Not that it won't return a profit, of course. It just takes time."

"Where's he at now?" Brad asked. "I hardly ever see him anymore."

"Roswell," Elizabeth said uncertainly. "Or maybe it's White Oaks. I lose track myself."

"Well, there's no two ways about it. He's a whiz-bang once he gets started."

"Which reminds me," Elizabeth commented. "Have you given any thought to our last discussion? I'm afraid we've lost Morg to the ranch entirely."

Brad had thought of little else. Whether or not to stay on at Spur preoccupied his mind. All the more so since Juanita was pressing him to get married. He seemed bogged down in indecision.

"Wish I had an answer," he said. "I'm just not sure what's best."

Elizabeth saw the troubled look in his eyes. "You'll recall I offered you a bonus. What if we increased it another two or three percent? Would that influence your thinking?"

Brad leaned forward, elbows resting on his knees. He stared down at the floor. "I'm not holdin' out for more money. Tell you the God's honest truth, I'm not even sure I want my own ranch." He paused, his expression bemused. "Things just don't seem so cut-and-dried anymore."

"I understand," Elizabeth said gently. "At one time or another, we all go through a period of soul-searching. Such things are never easy."

"Trouble is, I've got no idea what I'm searchin' for. It's like I want to be movin' on, start fresh some-wheres. Only I don't know where."

"Whatever you decide, you'll always be a part of the family. Nothing could change that."

"I'm obliged," Brad said, uncoiling from his chair. "I'll try not to let you down."

"I know you too well to worry about that."

"One other thing . . ."

"Yes?"

An indirection came into Brad's eyes. "I heard you're on the outs with Ortega. Any truth to it?"

Elizabeth smiled stiffly. "Apparently there are no secrets on Spur."

"One of the serving girls heard you and Morg talkin'. Word got around."

"I see," Elizabeth said, looking at him. "What interest do you have in Miguel Ortega?"

Brad shrugged noncommittally. "Just wondered whether I'd heard the straight goods."

"In a word—yes."

"Sorry if it sounds like I'm pryin' into your business. Never meant it that way."

"I'm sure you didn't. Anything else?"

"No," Brad said. "I'll get on back to work."

Elizabeth watched him out the door. His curiosity about Ortega reminded her of deeper concerns. She hadn't seen Clint since the operation on the *mexicano* leader. She'd sent him a note, trying to explain, but there had been no response. By now, it was apparent he was avoiding her, punishing her with his silence. She felt miserable about the whole affair.

For the first time in memory, her life seemed weighted down with problems. Aside from Clint, there was Morg's increasing involvement in other businesses. Someone needed to visit the Cherokee Outlet ranch; but Morg was too busy, and with the uncertainty about Brad, she was reluctant to absent herself from Spur. Then too, there were the upcoming fall elections and the never-ending burden of holding her coalition together. Sometimes it all seemed too much.

John Taylor rapped on the door of the office. She blinked, jarred from her reverie, and quickly regained her composure. As he halted before the desk, she began shuffling through a stack of correspondence.

"Yes, John," she said busily. "What is it?"

"Something you oughta know," Taylor commenced

in a sandy voice. " 'Course, it's not rightly any of my affair. So if you figure I'm out of line . . ."

Elizabeth smiled. "That's never stopped you before."

"Well, howsomever," Taylor said, suddenly flustered, "it's about Lon. He's fixin' to make trouble."

"Why do you say that?"

Taylor recounted his part in the shooting match. He went on to relate his general impression of Lon's attitude. Finally, he told how he'd walked back from the river with Brad. In that short time, he had learned of the earlier argument between Brad and Lon.

"Way it looks to me," he concluded, "Lon's not gonna let it drop. Chances are he'll try to goad Brad into a fight."

"Over Hank?" Elizabeth asked, somewhat surprised. "Do you really think the boy means that much to him?"

"Miz Brannock," Taylor said seriously, "that kid's all the family Lon's got. Leastways, that's how he sees it."

"Well, something has to be done right away. We can't have Lon and Brad fighting."

"No, ma'am, you can't," Taylor agreed. "Specially since Lon would pull a gun. He's mean as a snake."

"I'll have a talk with him," Elizabeth said. "If he wants to blame someone, he can blame me. It was my idea that Hank stay on here."

"If it was me," Taylor said with studied calm, "I'd run him off the place today. You gimme the go-ahead and I'll do it for you."

Elizabeth seemed to look at him and past him at the same time. Lon was intractable and abrasive, probably immune to reason. But she felt compelled to give it one last try. He was, after all, family.

"Thank you, John," she said at length. "I really

prefer to settle it without any ill will. Of course, should
that fail . . ."

"All you gotta do is say the word, Miz Brannock."

"I'll keep that in mind."

Taylor turned back into the hallway. Elizabeth heaved
a sigh that would have blown out a candle. The one
thing she didn't need was still another problem. Yet it
was there and she could hardly shunt it aside. Nor
could she allow reason to fail.

The alternative was John Taylor.

27

A vagrant breeze stirred the window curtain. Clint lay with his hands locked behind his head, staring at the ceiling. His gunbelt was hooked over the bedpost.

The room was sparsely furnished. A washstand, with a faded mirror dangling from the wall, was positioned opposite the bed. Wedged into the corner near the window was a battered dresser, and beside it, a johnny pot. Apart from a small bedside table, the remaining furniture consisted of a single straight-back chair.

Clint was only vaguely aware of his surroundings. A good part of his life had been spent in hotel rooms or monastic quarters assigned to him on army posts. One was like another, impersonal and utilitarian, with little to mark a man's passage. He never thought of them as home or associated them in any way with comfort. It was a place where he slept.

Tonight, he was in a reflective mood. After supper, he had returned to the room and lit the bedside lamp. The desk clerk had given him a day-old Santa Fe newspaper and he'd scanned that with no great interest. Then, stretching out on the bed, he had smoked several cigarettes, dropping the butts into a glass of water on the table. The room was so quiet he could hear the tick of his pocket watch.

What preoccupied him most was Miguel Ortega. For all intents and purposes, the man had vanished from the face of the earth. No one had reported sighting him and there was little or no talk about him among the *mexicanos*. Nor was there any activity on the part of *Las Gorras Blancas*, either in the form of raids or clandestine meetings. Over the past fortnight it was as though Ortega had ceased to exist.

At first, Clint thought he might have died. Any operation, even one performed by Jennifer, was a risky proposition. But the death of Miguel Ortega would have been widely reported. He was a heroic figure to *mexicanos* and word of his passing would have surfaced almost instantly. So the odds dictated that he was alive and well. His whereabouts was another question entirely.

Though tempted, Clint hadn't spoken with Jennifer. He knew she had visited Ortega the evening following the operation. Yet he had honored his word and made no effort at trailing her. Since then, insofar as he could determine, she'd had no contact with her patient. His reason for not interrogating her was of a personal nature. Any conversation would inevitably lead to talk of Elizabeth. And he wasn't ready to broach the matter.

Elizabeth's note hadn't swayed him. In it, she had attempted to justify her actions with respect to Ortega. Her arguments were filled with compassion for the sick, and the belief that anyone, even an outlaw, should not be denied medical attention. She assured Clint that she hadn't meant to betray his trust, or to choose sides. Nor was there any intent to hamper his investigation. She asked for understanding and faith in her sincerity. She wanted nothing to come between them.

Clint felt stung by her tone. However persuasive her arguments, the facts were undeniable. She had given aid to a man who tried to kill him. Worse, she excused her actions on humane grounds rather than offering an apology. Her choice of words, at least in Clint's reading, somehow made it seem he was at fault. She expected understanding and faith, but ignored what was really at issue. By assisting Ortega, she herself had broken faith.

From Clint's viewpoint there was still another factor involved. The day after the operation he'd waited for Elizabeth to contact him. He fully expected her to come forward, volunteer to lead him to Ortega. In good conscience, having saved the *mexicano*'s life, she could have assisted in his capture. Instead, she had passed through town without stopping and returned to the ranch. She had deliberately chosen to shield Ortega from the law.

Her note, delivered by a cowhand, had arrived the following day. Upon reading it, Clint's worst doubts had been confirmed. She had stepped over the line and she meant to stay there. By her continued silence, she was protecting a fugitive, thwarting his apprehension. Jennifer, by virtue of her physician's oath, avoided any charge of culpability. Elizabeth, on the other hand, had no plausible excuse for her actions. She had simply elected to stand with Ortega.

For Clint, the law itself was a matter of secondary importance. His anger stemmed from what he saw as a breach of trust, a personal slap in the face. Tonight, as he had for the past week, he tried to fathom Elizabeth's behavior. His mind kept returning to Jennifer's remark, that her mother was somehow attracted to Ortega. If true, then it seemed to Clint the cruelest blow of all. Everything he felt for Elizabeth was now tinged by the thought. He searched for another reason, wanting not to believe. And yet . . .

A knock at the door brought him bolt upright out of bed. He pulled the Colt from its holster and moved quietly to the door. It passed through his mind that he was being overly cautious. Still, Ortega had tried once before in a hotel room and he saw no reason to take chances. He flattened himself against the wall.

"Who is it?"

"Brad," a voice replied.

Clint turned the key. When he opened the door, Brad saw the pistol and gave him a strange look. Stepping aside, Clint motioned him into the room.

"Expecting company?" Brad asked. "Or do you always answer the door with a gun?"

"Old habits are hard to break. Where'd you spring from?"

"Wanted to have a word with you. Figured I'd take a chance on catching you in town."

Clint twisted the key in the lock. He turned from the door, his eyes questioning. "Anything wrong at the ranch?"

"No, not a thing," Brad said. "Everybody's fine."

"Have a seat."

Brad took the straight-back chair. Clint holstered his pistol and sat down on the edge of the bed. He began rolling himself a smoke.

"Long ride into town," he said. "What's so important?"

"Well, first off," Brad replied, "I wanted to tell you I'm leavin' Spur. I decided this afternoon."

Clint lit his cigarette. He snuffed the match, nodding. "Elizabeth told me about it sometime ago. She hoped you'd agree to stay on."

"I had a talk with her this mornin'. Guess that's what finally decided me. Just wasn't fair to drag it out any longer."

"You think they can manage without you?"

"A good foreman won't be hard to find. Lots of men will jump at the job."

"How about you?" Clint said, exhaling smoke. "Got any plans?"

"For openers," Brad said, grinning, "I'm gonna get married. Decided that this afternoon too."

"The girl over on the Rio Felix?"

Brad's grin faded. "Some folks think white and Mexican shouldn't mix. Way I see it, that's nobody's business but my own."

"No argument there," Clint agreed. "A man can't let other people run his life."

" 'Course, there's them that might try. All the more so if a man was lookin' for work."

"I thought you'd started your own cattle spread."

"Yeah, in a half-assed way," Brad said hollowly. "Trouble is, I'm wore out with raisin' cows. I finally admitted it to myself today."

Clint stared at him in puzzlement. "Sounds like you've been doing some serious thinking."

"Guess that's one of the reasons I wanted to talk to you. I'd like your advice on something."

"What sort of advice?"

"You know me about as well as anybody. How do you think I'd stack up as a law officer?"

"Law officer?" Clint said, taken aback. "Where'd you get a notion like that?"

"Watchin' you," Brad said with a vague gesture. "Looks to be a line of work where a man wouldn't get bored. I've got an idea it'd be just the ticket."

"Maybe so, except you're plannin' on getting married. How would your woman feel about you wearing a badge? It's not the safest occupation in the world."

"Juanita's not the worryin' type. Besides, I don't aim to make her a young widow. I figure to live a long time."

"Way you talk, you've already made up your mind."

"In a manner of speaking," Brad said, "I've taken the first step. That's the other reason I'm here."

"How so?"

"I've got information on Miguel Ortega."

Clint looked at him quick, fully alert. "What sort of information?"

Brad wormed around in his chair. "Before we get into that, I have to explain something. I wouldn't want you to think I'd sold out Mrs. Brannock."

"I don't take your meaning."

"When I talked to her this mornin', she said her and Ortega are quits. She's washed her hands of him."

Clint studied him thoughtfully. "She told you that?"

"In so many words," Brad noted. "Otherwise I wouldn't be here now. She's been too good to me."

Clint's expression revealed nothing. Yet he felt an overwhelming sense of relief. Elizabeth's break with Ortega eliminated his greatest personal concern. Something told him that her decision had been prompted by the attempts on his life. Her loyalty, in the end, had remained constant.

"One thing bothers me," he said now, looking at Brad. "Elizabeth knew how I felt about her and Ortega. Why wouldn't she tell me they're quits?"

"No mystery there," Brad remarked. "She's too proud to admit she was wrong. You and her are a lot alike."

Clint reviewed her note in his mind. It occurred to him that she had tried to say something without actually saying it. He thought Brad's point was well taken. Pride ran strong in the Brannocks.

"Let's get back to Ortega," he said. "What've you got?"

"A rumor," Brad informed him. "But I'd lay money it's more'n idle talk. Juanita told me about it herself."

"Why would she spill the beans on Ortega?"

"Her and her folks don't support him. I convinced 'em he'll do *mexicanos* more harm than good."

Clint appeared satisfied. "What's the rumor?"

"Ortega's in Roswell," Brad said. "Word's out he's gonna hold a meeting tomorrow night. He aims to recruit new members for *Las Gorras Blancas*."

"Any idea where the meeting will be held?"

"All Juanita heard was somewhere outside Roswell. Details were pretty sketchy by the time the news drifted over to the Rio Felix."

Clint accepted the statement. From Brad's place on the Rio Felix to Roswell was a distance of some twenty-five miles. Few *mexicanos* would travel that far to attend a meeting. On the other hand, it made sense that Ortega would attempt to organize *Las Gorras Blancas* along the upper Pecos. The area around Roswell was fast being overrun by Anglos.

"No question, though?" Clint said. "You're sure the meeting's set for tomorrow night?"

"That's the word."

Clint doused his cigarette. He rose from the bed and motioned Brad to his feet. "Raise your right hand."

Brad looked startled. "What's the idea?"

"You said you wanted to be a lawman, didn't you?"

"Yeah . . ."

"Then we'll make it official. Repeat after me."

Clint issued the oath and swore him in as a deputy. Afterward, as though thinking out loud, Clint debated whether to notify Sheriff Grant. He finally rejected the thought of a force so large it would draw unwanted attention. He and Brad would handle the matter themselves.

They decided to leave at first light.

Roswell was situated near the juncture of the Pecos and the Rio Hondo. The land was relatively flat, a valley stretching north and south along the Pecos. *Llano Estacado,* the fabled Staked Plains, wandered off northeast into a vast emptiness.

Formerly a crossroads trading post, Roswell had been a supply point for cattle drives. The Goodnight-Loving Trail, which began in Texas, had passed through on its way to the High Plains of Wyoming. At one time, the valley had been the private domain of John "Jinglebob" Chisum, largest of all the Western cattle barons.

Following Chisum's death, homesteaders flooded into the valley. The water from rivers, and natural artesian springs, eventually led to irrigation and widespread farming. Yet the upper Pecos remained a stronghold of Anglo cattlemen. While the farmers were irrigating, the ranchers were stringing barbed wire.

The town itself doubled and redoubled in size. As the population swelled, the business district expanded and residential areas sprang up in every direction. A progressive atmosphere, bustling with commerce, centered on what was once a wayside trading post. The sound of hammers on fresh-sawed lumber rang out across the valley.

Morg emerged from the office of Goddard's Lumber Yard. He halted on the boardwalk as a late-afternoon sun slowly retreated westward. Thumbs hooked in his vest, he congratulated himself on a nifty piece of business. After some minor haggling, he had just clinched a deal with Alex Goddard. Starting immediately, the lumber yard's weekly orders would be increased by half.

For Morg, the deal was a harbinger of the future. In the growth of Roswell he saw an affirmation of everything he'd originally envisioned. The Pecos Valley, like other parts of Lincoln County, was entering an era of unimaginable prosperity. He intended to share in those boom times, expanding from timber and mining into other businesses. These days he often reminded himself of his father's favorite axiom: A man's reach should always exceed his grasp.

Still, for all Morg's confidence, there were obstacles
to progress. Chief among them was *Las Gorras Blancas,*
and the spread of unrest among *mexicanos.* He thought
it timely that his mother had broken with Miguel Ortega. By whatever means, the budding revolt would
have to be crushed, and Ortega brought to justice.
Otherwise an era of growth and prosperity might be
transformed into anarchy, a racial bloodletting. Something he'd heard today added a note of urgency to his
concern.

"Look who we got here! The prodigal son himself."

Brad's voice jarred him from his woolgathering.
Somewhat dumbstruck, he saw Brad and Clint rein to
a halt at the hitch rack. They stepped down from the
saddle before he could collect his wits. Brad inspected
him with a wry grin.

"What's the matter, cat got your tongue?"

"Damn near it," Morg confessed. "Where'd you
two come from?"

"Lincoln," Brad said. "We've been on the trail since
sunup."

"What brings you all the way over here?"

Clint edged forward. "Keep it under your hat," he
said in a low voice. "We got word Ortega's holding a
meeting hereabouts. I deputized Brad to lend a hand."

"I'll be dipped," Morg said, astounded. "Alex Goddard just told me the same thing."

"How'd Goddard find out?"

"One of the Mexicans that works for him let it slip."

Clint fixed him with a speculative look. "Goddard
say anything about where the meeting's taking place?"

"Nooo," Morg said slowly. "But I'll bet the Mexican knows. Why don't we ask him?"

"Tell you what," Clint said. "You just introduce me
to Goddard and I'll take it from there. I don't want
you involved."

"What the devil's that supposed to mean?"

Clint's genial face toughened. "It means I want you to go on about your business. Leave Ortega to me."

"Nosiree," Morg declared. "You deputized Brad and you can deputize me. You're liable to need an extra gun, anyway."

"Save your breath," Clint said flatly. "You're out of it and that's that. Savvy?"

"Savvy what?" Morg persisted. "Why don't you want me along?"

Clint hesitated, considering. "I'll give it to you straight. Your mother would scald me good if anything happened to you. I won't have you on my conscience."

Morg burst out laughing. "You're not gonna brush me off that easy. Like it or not, I'm going along."

"Goddamnit," Clint said stolidly, "you'll do what you're told to do. I don't want any more argument about it."

"Won't wash," Morg said with a devil-may-care grin. "Whether you deputize me or not, I plan to tag along. There's no way you can stop me."

Clint smiled in spite of himself. "I could toss your butt in the local pokey. How's that sound?"

Morg squared himself up. "It'll take you and Brad both to do it. Why not save your fight for Ortega?"

"How the hell'd you get so pigheaded?"

"Guess it runs in the family."

"You're sure you won't listen to reason?"

Morg's grin widened. "We could jawbone all day and it wouldn't change nothin'. You've got yourself a volunteer."

"Lucky me," Clint growled, half under his breath. "All right, we've wasted enough time. Let's go talk to that Mexican."

Brad and Morg exchanged a quick smile. Clint moved around the hitch rack and started across the board-

walk. Sober as three judges, they went through the
lumber-yard door. A few minutes later, in the privacy
of Alex Goddard's office, they began grilling the
Mexican.

He told them everything they wanted to know.

A copse of trees stood in dark silhouette against a
starswept sky. Beneath the cottonwoods, the deepening indigo of nightfall was broken by torches jammed
into the ground. The shadowed figures of men, appari-
tions in the flickering light, were visible in a small
clearing.

The grove was some four miles north of Roswell.
Situated on the west bank of the Pecos, the clearing
overlooked a lazy bend in the river. A short distance
downstream Clint lay hidden in the shelterbelt of the
woods. Beside him were Brad and Morg, bellied down
on the ground. Their attention was fixed on Miguel
Ortega.

Ortega's voice rang out across the clearing. He stood
with his back to the riverbank, limned in the flare of
torchlight. For the past hour, he had spoken with
impassioned eloquence. A mesmerizing figure, he addressed the injustice of land frauds and the evil of
those who governed in Santa Fe. When he spoke of
gringo cattlemen, his eyes became black pinpoints of
hate. He called for war without quarter on any
americano who defiled the land with barbed wire.

A gathering of perhaps thirty *mexicanos* listened in
spellbound silence. Some of them nodded, their faces
mirroring bitterness and anger. Others appeared stoic,
torn between caution and a simmering urge for vengeance. At last, when Ortega sounded a final call to
action, their voices were raised in a sharp unleashing
of rage. They crowded forward, a clotted mass of
men, pledging themselves to *Las Gorras Blancas*. Then,

one by one, they moved past Ortega, their sombreros clutched in their hands. To a man, they vowed to ride with him in the days ahead.

From downstream, Clint watched as the meeting drew to a close. He thought the *mexicanos* here tonight were unlike those he'd met in the Seven Rivers district. These men were being pressed on all sides by an invasion of Anglos, and they would fight to protect their land. Which was all the more reason to remain hidden and await developments. Until the crowd thinned out, any attempt to arrest Ortega would be nothing less than suicide. Yet, even as he cautioned himself to patience, he was gripped by a sense of newfound respect. After what he'd just witnessed, he finally understood why men were drawn to *Las Gorras Blancas*. Ortega was like a prophet of old, preaching deliverance from bondage. A stark figure seemingly ordained for greatness.

The *mexicanos* slowly scattered into the night. Within a short time only three men were left with Ortega. One of them carried a rifle cradled in his arms and the other two wore holstered pistols. They stood huddled together, listening intently while Ortega spoke of future raids. To all appearances, they had been selected as his lieutenants on the upper Pecos.

Clint motioned to Brad and Morg. Quietly, careful of betraying their presence, they got to their feet. Fanning out, their guns drawn, they ghosted through the woods. As they stepped into the circle of torchlight, Ortega suddenly stopped talking. The other *mexicanos* turned in the direction of his gaze and Ortega hissed a warning out of the side of his mouth. An eerie stillness settled over the clearing.

"Don't move," Clint commanded. "I'll shoot the first man that tries anything."

Ortega flicked a glance at Brad and Morg, assessing

the situation. His gaze shifted back to Clint. *"Buenas noches, hombre,"* he said coolly. "We meet at last."

"No funny business," Clint said evenly. "I have a warrant for your arrest."

Ortega laughed. "Are you asking me to surrender?"

"That's about the size of it."

"And then you will put me on trial and hang me. *Verdad*?"

"You'll get your day in court. After that, it's up to a judge and jury."

"No, my friend," Ortega said, shaking his head. "I have no taste for hanging. I prefer to settle it here."

Clint's jawline tightened. "You force me to it and I'll kill you. Why do it the hard way?"

"Why not?" Ortega said with wintry malice. "You would prefer it that way yourself. We will oblige one another, agreed?"

"What about your men?" Clint asked. "Will they stay out of it?"

Ortega spoke to the *mexicanos*. They hesitated, reluctant to accept the order, then moved aside. When they were safely out of the way, he looked back at Clint. "Have no fear, *hombre*. They will honor my request."

Clint holstered his pistol. "Brad," he said, still staring at Ortega, "you and Morg watch yourselves. Anybody so much as blinks, start shooting."

"Hold on, now," Brad demanded. "What if he beats you?"

"Not likely," Clint said with a faint smile. "But if he does, he's a free man. Understood?"

"You're sure that's the way you want it?"

"I'm sure."

A peculiar glitter surfaced in Clint's eyes. He nodded to Ortega. "Whenever you're ready."

For a sliver of eternity they stared at each other.

Ortega's mouth curled an instant before his hand moved. The telltale giveaway was all the edge Clint needed. He pulled and fired just as Ortega cleared leather. A starburst of blood darkened Ortega's chest and a surprised look came over his face. His gun roared, kicking up dirt at his feet. Then he sagged at the knees and slumped limply to the ground. One leg kicked in a spastic jerk of afterdeath.

Clint stared at the body only a moment. Without a flicker of emotion, his gaze swung to Ortega's men. *"Vaynase,"* he ordered. "Tell your people it's over. Miguel Ortega *está muerto.*"

The *mexicanos* slowly backed out of the clearing. At the edge of the treeline, they mounted their horses and vanished into the darkness. Clint stood listening until the hoofbeats faded off into the distance. At last he turned to Brad and Morg. His features were grim in the sallow torchlight.

"Helluva note," he said. "I've got a hunch Ortega had the last laugh."

"What d'you mean?" Morg blurted. "He's dead."

"Some dead men live a long time. Ortega's liable to live forever."

There was a sobering truth to the statement. Clint saw now that it wasn't a matter of cheating the hangman. Ortega had chosen to die with honor, a *guerrero* to the end. The story would be told and retold, the stuff of legend.

Las Gorras Blancas would stand as testament to the man and the legend. Miguel Ortega in death would emerge larger than life.

28

A funeral Mass was held three days later. People began filing into the Catholic church in Lincoln shortly after sunrise. By ten o'clock that morning the crowd spilled out into the street.

An open casket rested on a bier garlanded with mounds of wildflowers. The body of Miguel Ortega was laid out with an amethyst rosary draped over his hands. He was dressed in peasant clothes, with his mustache trimmed and his hair neatly combed. He looked like he might awaken at any moment.

The mourners gathered there were principally *mexicano*. They had traveled from San Patricio and White Oaks and remote villages scattered across the county. Drawn by the news of Ortega's death, they had come to witness his burial. Their presence honored his passage and memorialized him in the minds of their children. In life, he had been the champion of their cause, their defender. He was now a figure of reverence.

The front pews were occupied by prominent *políticos*. Félix Montoya, the *jefe* of San Patricio, was there with his family. Across the aisle were Roberto Díaz from Lincoln, and Juan Herrera from White Oaks. In the pew directly behind them, Elizabeth was seated with Ira Hecht, who had traveled all the way from Santa Fe. The story of Elizabeth's alliance with Ortega was by now part of the growing legend. The people spoke of her not by name but as *La Mariposa de Hierro*—the Iron Butterfly.

Following the Mass, Father Narváez, the local priest, delivered a stirring eulogy. He praised Miguel Ortega as a man of the people, one of *los pobres*. In a solemn voice, he spoke of the deceased as a paladin of liberty, a martyr to the cause of justice. He declared that *Las Gorras Blancas* would stand as the dead man's epitaph, a symbol of sacrifice and valor. The fight would go forward, he prophesied, until *mexicanos* enjoyed the rights of all free men. Miguel Ortega, even in death, would continue to lead his people.

A low murmur swept through the church as the priest finished his eulogy. The *jefes políticos* nodded their heads, and those in the packed congregation muttered approval. Watching them, Elizabeth knew that the priest's words would spread from village to village, gathering force as the message was repeated by *los pobres* throughout New Mexico. She doubted that a man of Ortega's stature would emerge to lead the fight. Yet she was certain that the struggle had only just begun. No *mexicano* would ever again stand alone in the face of injustice.

From the church, a funeral cortege formed on the street. Six stout men hefted the casket onto their shoulders, and the mourners, some three hundred strong, fell in behind. The procession, led by Father Narváez, slowly made its way to the Mexican cemetery on the outskirts of town. There, over a freshly dug grave, the priest delivered a final prayer. The pallbearers, holding the casket suspended on ropes, then lowered Miguel Ortega into the ground. A granite headstone would later be set into place.

When the graveside service ended, the *jefes políticos* made a point of paying homage to Elizabeth. Their deference left no question that she would continue to command their allegiance. To the throng of *mexicanos* it was obvious that her coalition would not suffer by Ortega's death. No one spoke of her brother-in-law, the *bárbaro americano* who hunted men. Instead, they whispered of how she and her daughter, the lady doctor, had once saved Ortega's life. As she walked from the cemetery, the men doffed their sombreros and the women bowed their heads. She smiled, holding firmly to Ira Hecht's arm, trying not to betray her discomfort. She felt deeply humbled by their adulation.

Uptown, Elizabeth and Hecht stopped outside the express office. There were pressing matters in Santa Fe and he planned to catch the noon stage. Last night, upon arriving in town, he had presented Elizabeth with a letter from Thomas Canby. In it, the leader of the Santa Fe Ring outlined a sweeping proposal. He offered to support her fight for land reform, as well as an end to corruption in the territorial legislature. From her, he asked only the assurance that certain business legislation would not be opposed. He guaranteed cooperation with respect to her struggle on behalf of the *mexicanos*.

Because the funeral was scheduled for midmorning, Elizabeth had spent the night with Jennifer. But she'd gotten little sleep, for Canby's letter left her with great misgivings. She roamed the clinic like a distracted ghost, weighing all the possible ramifications. At breakfast, she hadn't mentioned the letter and Hecht had tactfully avoided the subject. However, he could scarcely fail to notice that her features were drawn and tired. She looked somehow burdened.

Outside the express office, they stood wrapped in silence. Hecht thought she was preoccupied with the funeral and he had no wish to intrude. Still, there were affairs to be discussed, and the stage was due shortly. He decided on an oblique approach.

"Quite a turnout," he said. "Were you surprised by the number of people who showed up?"

"No, not at all," Elizabeth commented. "For them, Miguel Ortega was like a saint on horseback. He restored their faith in themselves."

"Speaking of faith," Hecht observed, "you're not doing so badly yourself. The *jefes* were at some pains to exhibit their respect. I got the feeling they're anxious to climb aboard the bandwagon."

Elizabeth nodded, then smiled a little. "I suppose it's only natural. We're almost certain to carry the fall elections, and they know it. Everyone loves a winner."

"Everyone including Tom Canby. He's convinced we'll win by a landslide."

"Yes, his letter indicates as much."

Hecht looked at her. "Have you given his proposal any thought?"

"Before I answer," Elizabeth said, "I'd prefer to hear your assessment. How do you see it?"

"Essentially, Canby's trying to cut his losses. His crystal ball tells him we'll wind up with a majority in the legislature. He thinks it's time to strike a deal."

"What about the business legislation he mentions? Should we just look the other way?"

"Well, let's evaluate it," Hecht suggested. "He's talking about legislation that affects banks and railroads and various tariffs. He and his cronies want to protect their financial base."

Elizabeth's face was troubled. "In other words, an under-the-table tradeoff. He supports land reform and we pretend to overlook the vested interests. Is that it?"

"Quid pro quo," Hecht temporized. "One hand washes the other. Nothing unusual about that."

"Except for the fact that we've associated ourselves

with a gang of thieves. Doesn't that dirty us in the process?"

"At some point, I suppose pragmatism becomes unavoidable. Government operates on the principle of give-and-take. No one ever gets it all his own way."

Elizabeth couldn't dispute the argument. Compromise, in the end, was the lifeblood of politics. The system was by no means perfect, but it was the way things worked. Nothing of consequence was achieved without some form of quid pro quo.

"So then?" she said. "Are you advising me to accept his offer?"

Hecht's gaze did not waver. "A majority doesn't necessarily mean we *control* the legislature. Tom Canby could still buy the votes to deadlock us on reform. I believe the wiser course would be to accept."

"Magnanimous in victory, is that it?"

"Something along those lines."

A note of concern came into Elizabeth's voice. "What guarantees do we have that Canby will honor his word? You've said yourself he's totally without scruples."

"Our motto," Hecht quipped, "will be eternal vigilance. We'll have to watch him like a hawk."

"I prefer something a bit more concrete. Suppose we attach a condition to the arrangement."

"What sort of condition?"

Elizabeth smiled. "Your appointment as attorney general should do it rather nicely. Don't you agree?"

Behind his wire-rimmed glasses, Hecht's eyes did a slow roll. "We certainly wouldn't have to worry about any shenanigans. Canby's only road would be the straight and narrow."

"Exactly," Elizabeth said with calm assurance. "And if he strays, we won't be quite so magnanimous. I think Tom Canby would look rather dapper in a prison uniform."

Hecht chuckled softly. "You've learned to play a rough game."

"On the contrary, I simply play to win. And win we will, Ira. I won't settle for less."

"The Mexicans got it right when they nicknamed you the Iron Butterfly. You're a true-blue original."

"Why, thank you, Mr. Attorney General."

"God save us." Hecht beamed. "Wait till Canby hears that!"

A short while later Hecht boarded the west-bound stage. He took a seat by the window and gave Elizabeth an offhand salute. She waved as the driver popped his whip and the six-horse hitch pulled away. She watched until the stagecoach was out of sight.

Elizabeth started toward the clinic. John Taylor was waiting for her there and she still had to talk with Jennifer. The wedding was Sunday and all the arrangements weren't yet complete. She made a mental note to have a word with the preacher.

One thought prompted another. Elizabeth was suddenly struck by the incongruity of life. Today she had attended a funeral and on Sunday her daughter would be married. She recalled a line she'd read somewhere: a season of endings and beginnings. She felt it was perfect to the moment, worth remembering. Whatever the circumstances, life went on in the midst of death.

As she turned downstreet, her gaze was drawn to the courthouse. She saw Clint and Will Grant emerge from the sheriff's office. For almost three weeks, she hadn't spoken with Clint. At first, he had avoided her because he felt betrayed. He was avoiding her now because he'd killed Miguel Ortega. Alive or dead, the *mexicano* leader seemed to stand between them.

Clint spotted her outside the express office. She looked straight at him, her head high, and waited. After a moment, he said something to Grant, who turned back into the courthouse. She experienced a tremulous sensation as he came down the steps and started across the street. She was all too aware that there would never be another chance. Unless their differences were reconciled now, there was no hope for the future.

"Hello, Beth," Clint said, halting in front of her. "How're things with you?"

"Fine," Elizabeth said agreeably. "I just saw Ira Hecht off on the stage. He asked me to give you his regards."

"Yeah, I heard he was in town. Guess you had a lot of political matters to talk over?"

"Well, that wasn't the real reason for his trip. He actually came down for the funeral."

"Ortega was a popular fellow," Clint said uneasily. "I suppose some folks felt obliged to pay their respects."

"I was one of them," Elizabeth said in a low voice. "Do you hold that against me?"

Clint shook his head. "Brad gave me the lowdown on how you busted off with Ortega. I stopped being sore the minute he told me."

"Then why haven't you come by the ranch?"

"Figured I wasn't welcome."

"Not welcome?" Elizabeth echoed. "Whatever gave you that idea?"

"Beth . . ." Clint hesitated, his eyes dwelling on her. "Whether you believe it or not, I tried my damnedest to take Ortega alive. He all but forced me to kill him."

"Yes, I know," Elizabeth acknowledged. "Morg told me everything."

Clint studied her. "Are you sayin' you don't fault me for what happened?"

"How could I? You gave him every chance."

"In that case, what's been holdin' you back? How come I haven't got an invite out to the ranch?"

"Stubborn pride," Elizabeth said honestly. "We're alike in that respect."

"I reckon we are," Clint admitted. "Even Brad's of the same opinion. He told me so straight out."

Elizabeth smiled warmly. "Perhaps we're too stubborn for our own good."

A slow grin tugged at the corner of Clint's mouth. "Tell you the truth, I was thinkin' the same thing. What say we just forget the whole mess?"

"Oh, we have to! Otherwise Jennifer would disown us both."

"Jennifer?"

"Of course." Elizabeth's eyes suddenly shone, and she laughed. "Had you forgotten she's being married Sunday? She expects you to give her away."

Clint's grin broadened. "Tell her I'd count it an honor."

"I have a better idea." Elizabeth took his arm. "Let's both tell her."

Arm in arm, they walked off toward the clinic. As though by mutual accord, neither of them again made reference to the past. They spoke instead of the future.

The marriage of a Brannock was considered the social event of the year. By half-past twelve on Sunday, the street outside the Methodist Church was clogged with buckboards and wagons. The ceremony was scheduled for one o'clock, and shortly before the hour the steeple bell began to peal.

Every pew in the church was packed. Elizabeth and the family, which included John Taylor, occupied the entire front row. Juanita Ramírez, with a black mantilla covering her head, was seated beside Brad. The congregation, both townspeople and ranchers, had stayed over after the regular Sunday-morning services. No one wanted to miss the most talked about wedding in recent memory.

A few latecomers hurried through the vestibule. Off to one side, Jennifer stood with her hand tucked in Clint's arm. She was a vision in white, her wedding gown molded to her like the curves in melting ivory. Her hair was upswept, with curls fluffed high on her forehead, and the train of her veil brushing the floor. Her cheeks were flushed with color and her eyes sparkled with excitement. She looked radiantly beautiful.

Clint was attired in a black broadcloth coat and striped trousers. A pearl stickpin gleamed from the cravat cinched around his stiff winged collar. The outfit was spanking new, bought especially for the occasion. On his left side, the coat bulged where he'd jammed his pistol in the waistband. Over all protests, he had refused to come without it. Even his niece's wedding was no reason to go unarmed.

As the last of the guests filed through the doorway, he patted Jennifer's hand. "I never told you before," he said, "but I'm mighty proud of you. Just thought I'd mention it."

"Thank you, Uncle Clint." She gave his arm an affectionate squeeze. "You being here makes today extra special."

"My sentiments exactly."

The organ rumbled to life. As the strains of the wedding march filled the church, Clint led her down the aisle. The congregation turned in their seats, craning for a better view of the bride. Elizabeth, who wore a dress of teal-blue cambric, looked marvelously elegant. Watching Jennifer, she thought her heart would burst. She dabbed at her eyes with a lace hanky.

Blake waited at the altar. His gaze fixed on Jennifer and their eyes remained locked the entire time she moved down the aisle. Clint paused, placing her hand in Blake's, as the organ mounted to a crescendo. Then he turned, stepping back from the altar, and took his seat beside Elizabeth. She managed a teary smile.

The preacher moved forward with an open Bible. He wore a hammertail coat and his hair looked buttered to his head. Smiling down at the bride and groom, he let the last strains of the organ fade away. At last, with the church gone silent, he stared out over the congregation.

"Dearly beloved," he intoned, "we are gathered together in the sight of God to join this man and this woman in holy wedlock."

The ceremony lasted not quite ten minutes. When they were pronounced man and wife, Blake lifted Jennifer's veil and kissed her gently on the mouth. Her eyes glistened with happiness as the organ once again wheezed to life. They turned up the aisle and slowly made their way from the church. Outside, a crowd of well-wishers pelted them with rice and shouted congratulations. A buggy festooned with colored streamers was waiting on the street.

Jennifer had finally relented and agreed to a brief honeymoon. She and Blake would spend two days in Roswell, the nearest town of any size. But now, under a downpour of rice, they retreated to the clinic and changed into traveling clothes. When they emerged, Jennifer exchanged a teary-eyed hug with her mother before stepping into the buggy. At the last instant, she took deliberate aim and tossed her bridal bouquet to Juanita. Blake snapped the reins and they took off in a fresh barrage of rice.

The crowd began departing by the time the buggy was out of sight. Some of the ranchers and a few of the more prominent townspeople stopped off to pay their respects to Elizabeth. Within minutes, the last hand had been shaken and the immediate family was left by themselves outside the clinic. Clint excused himself and walked toward the hitch rack, where Lon and Hank stood with their horses. They appeared anxious to be on their way.

Clint had resigned himself to the inevitable. Hank was determined to follow his brother, rather than remain on at Spur. In the end, loyalty had decided the matter, and there was no way to force the youngster against his will. While Clint was concerned, he saw nothing to be gained by further argument. Some things, however grudgingly, could only be accepted.

"All set?" he asked, halting beside the hitch rail. "Got everything you need?"

Lon shrugged lazily. "We're fixed just fine."

"Whereabouts are you headed?"

"Anywhere they play poker," Lon said. "One of the mining camps most likely."

Clint nodded, glancing at Hank. "I'll expect a letter every now and then. That was our deal."

Hank bobbed his head. "Don't worry, we're gonna be all right. I'll keep you posted."

"And you," Clint said, frowning at Lon, "make damn sure you take care of your brother. Otherwise you'll answer to me."

Lon grinned crookedly. "I'll teach him everything I know."

"Yeah, that's what worries me."

After a round of handshakes, the brothers climbed aboard their horses. Lon tugged his hat low and Hank waved as they reined about from the hitch rack. Clint watched them ride off, a leaden feeling in his chest. He finally turned away when they disappeared along the westward road.

Brad and Juanita waited nearby. As Clint approached

them, the girl smiled shyly and Brad extended his hand. "Wanted to thank you," he said, pumping Clint's arm. "Your talk with Will Grant turned the trick. I'll sign on as a deputy right after fall roundup."

"Save your thanks till later," Clint advised. "You're liable to change your mind about wearin' a badge."

"Not much chance of that."

Clint looked at the girl. "I understand you're getting married. How do you feel about a lawman for a husband?"

Juanita laughed. "A woman follows where her man leads, *señor*. I trust him to know what is best."

"Well, I wish you both all the luck. I'll try to get back for your wedding."

Brad shook hands again, then walked with Juanita to their buckboard. Morg and Louise, along with John Taylor, were standing beside the phaeton carriage. Elizabeth, as though biding her time, waited on the clinic pathway. Clint joined her, his features suddenly sober. She smiled, nodding to the younger couples.

"All these Brannocks," she said. "We've done well, haven't we?"

"Yeah, we have," Clint agreed. "Some of us tend to scatter out, but that doesn't change anything. Family's still family."

There was a look of deep sadness in Elizabeth's features. "Won't you reconsider?" she asked. "You could retire with honor and leave the law to younger men. You've earned it."

"Not just yet," Clint said, avoiding her gaze. "Got a wire from the governor ordering me back to Santa Fe. Guess there's always plenty of work for men like me."

"There's work here," Elizabeth said, her voice husky. "You could stay on and help me run Spur. You know that's what I want . . . don't you?"

A mad jumble of images and recollections flashed through Clint's mind. He'd often lain awake brooding on the road not taken, the words not spoken. Years ago he might have told her what he felt, what she meant to him. How she would have reacted was something he would never know. The time for asking had long since passed and would never return. Neither of them could recapture what they were, or what might have been. It was too late.

"One of these days—" He paused, cleared his throat of a sudden tightness. "Well, you never know, I might just take you up on your offer. There's worse places than the Rio Hondo."

Elizabeth's eyes filled with emotion. She cupped his face in her hands and brushed his mouth with a soft kiss. "I'll miss you terribly," she said, her voice curiously vibrant. "Don't stay away too long."

"I won't," Clint promised. "That's one thing you can always count on."

Elizabeth smiled, unable to speak. She whirled quickly away and walked to the carriage. John Taylor assisted her into the front seat while Morg and Louise seated themselves in the rear. A moment later they drove off toward the Hondo Valley.

Clint waited even though he knew she wouldn't look back. Their partings were always bittersweet and neither of them prolonged it beyond certain limits. At last, when the carriage passed the outskirts of town, he turned upstreet. Hands jammed in his pockets, he ambled off in the direction of the hotel.

Somewhile later Clint led his horse from the livery stable. He'd changed from the suit to range clothes, and the Colt was once again strapped around his waist. He stepped into the saddle and reined the gelding onto the road. His thoughts were no longer inward, but rather somewhere ahead. He too refused to look back.

Outside town, he heeled the gelding into a smooth, ground-eating trot. He squinted against the late-afternoon sun, content once more to be on the trail. One day he would return to the Hondo, and the Brannocks. But for now his gaze was faraway, fixed on a distant land. A land that still called him on beyond.

He rode west toward the mountains.

About the Author

Matt Braun is the author of twenty-seven novels, and the winner of the Golden Spur Award from the Western Writers of America for his novel *The Kincaids*. A true Westerner, he was born in Oklahoma and descends from a long line of ranchers. He writes with a pas-sion for historical accuracy and detail that has earned him a reputation as the most authentic portrayer of the American West. Matt Braun's other Signet novels include *The Brannocks*, *Windward West*, and *Rio Hondo*.